PAUL JENKINS

LEILA LEIZ

ALTERS

VOLUME
2

THE STORY OF NO-DAMN-NAME:
A LOVING MOTHER

LEONARDO PACIAROTTI

RYANE HILL

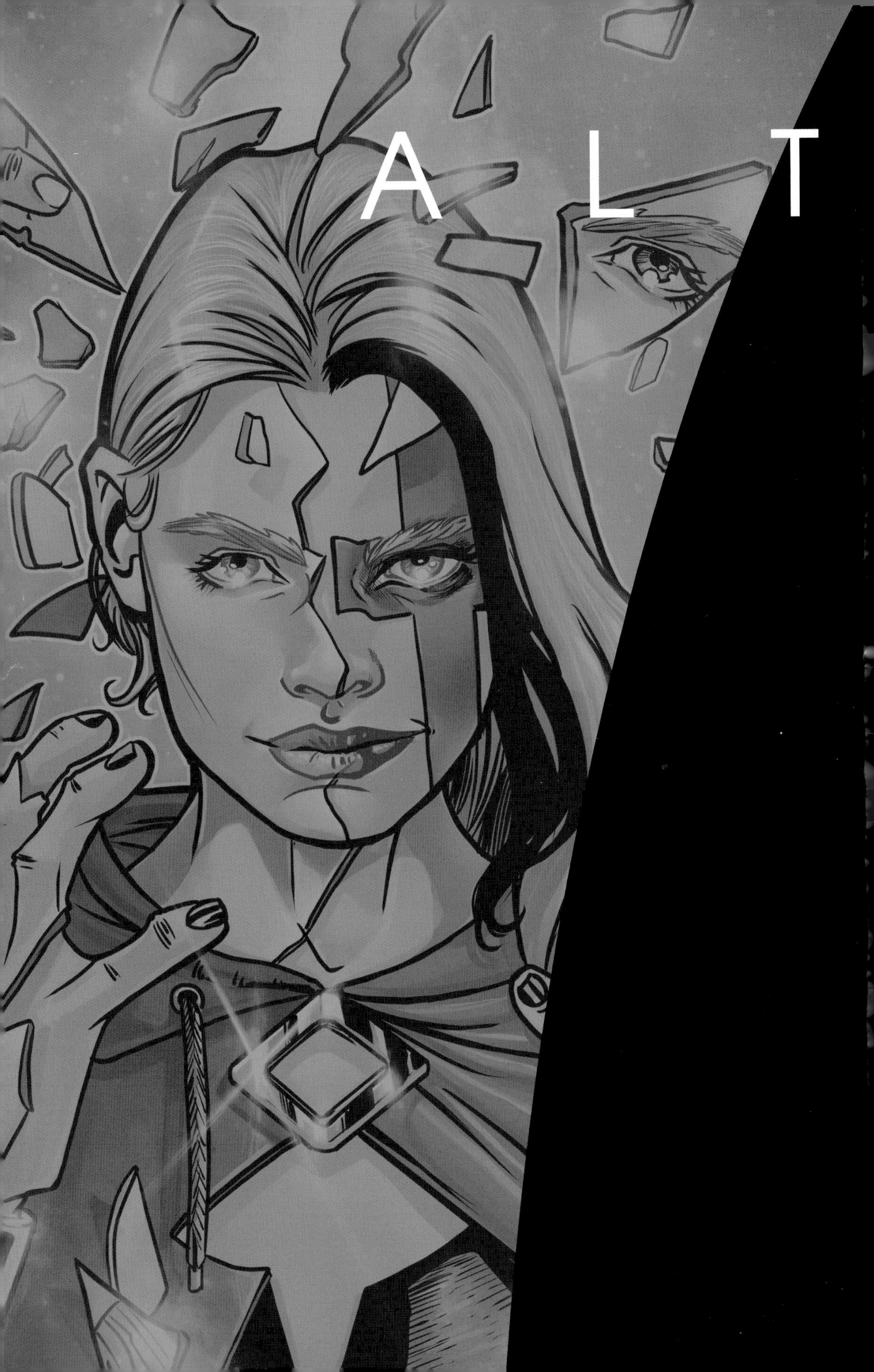
A L T

E R S
V O L U M E 2
THE STORY OF NO-DAMN-NAME: A LOVING MOTHER

PAUL JENKINS creator & writer

LEILA LEIZ artist

LEONARDO PACIAROTTI colorist

RYANE HILL letterer

LEILA LEIZ w/ **LEONARDO PACIAROTTI** front & orginal covers

JOHN J. HILL logo designer

COREY BREEN book designer

MIKE MARTS editor

LIZ LUU creative character consultant

MAEVE BARUK special thanks

AFTERSHOCK

MIKE MARTS - Editor-in-Chief • JOE PRUETT - Publisher/ Chief Creative Officer • LEE KRAMER - President
JON KRAMER - Chief Executive Officer • MIKE ZAGARI - SVP, Brand • LISA Y. WU - Retailer/Fan Relations Manager
CHRISTINA HARRINGTON - Managing Editor • JAY BEHLING - Chief Financial Officer • JAWAD QURESHI - SVP, Investor Relations
AARON MARION - Publicist • CHRIS LA TORRE - Sales Associate • KIM PAGNOTTA - Sales Associate • LISA MOODY - Finance
CHARLES PRITCHETT - Comics Production • COREY BREEN - Collections Production • TEDDY LEO - Editorial Assistant
SIMON WHITE - Proofreader

AfterShock Trade Dress and Interior Design by JOHN J. HILL • AfterShock Logo Design by COMICRAFT
Publicity: contact AARON MARION (aaron@publichausagency.com) & RYAN CROY (ryan@publichausagency.com) at PUBLICHAUS
Special thanks to: IRA KURGEN, STEPHAN NILSON and JULIE PIFHER

ALTERS VOLUME 2: THE STORY OF NO-DAMN-NAME: A LOVING MOTHER Published by AfterShock Comics, LLC, 15300 Ventura Boulevard Suite 507, Sherman Oaks, CA 91403. Originally published as ALTERS #6-10. PRINTED IN KOREA.
First Printing: June 2018. 10 9 8 7 6 5 4 3 2 1

AFTERSHOCKCOMICS.COM Follow us on social media

INTRODUCTION

I was in the swing of writing a short story based upon a dysphoria fueled re-occurring dream, when ALTERS first blipped on my radar late August of 2016. A friend linked me to an article about it with the message, *"Have you seen this yet?"* They knew it'd tickle my curiosity since one of the main characters is a trans woman just starting her transition and grappling with the intense question a lot of us ask ourselves, "What happens from here?" They also knew that the premise of the comic's juxtaposition of having super powers while having to also deal with a strong disadvantage would appeal to my taste for comics where the super hero is more human than they are an idealized abstract .

Initially, my skepticism prickled a bit at the idea of a cis author writing a trans character, as this frequently leads to a less than stellar outcome. When I finally saw the teaser pages for the 1st issue, I hunted down Paul to discuss the comic. I saw what he was striving for with the character of Chalice, as well as the potential for her as she came into her own right both transition wise and with taking up the mantle of a super hero. I was delighted that Paul was quite open to discussing Chalice and the comic. He has an honest eagerness to not just listen when trans people talk, but to also learn about the variety of experiences we go through.

In consulting on scripts for ALTERS, I have gone back and forth with Paul about dialogue and suggested how to tune some scenes for a stronger effect. In these discussions, we also shared personal stories, comparing notes on ones that paralleled each other's, and sharing ones that were distinctly ours. Such as when I told him about the pain and sadness of coming to terms with hard truths about my biological parents. Then to Paul sharing with me about the times he was homeless (which is the seed for the 2nd ALTERS story arc).

As Paul put it, *"Writers tend to be a curious bunch—our primary function, I believe, is to examine the human condition."* The super heroes of ALTERS may possess great powers, but the fulcrum upon which it moves is the real world situations the characters face. In spite of their powers, they are ordinary people like many of us, dealing with the problems society and life saddle us.

MAEVE BARUK
Fantasy & comics writer
Trans rights advocate
Twitter: @WitchyWriterMae

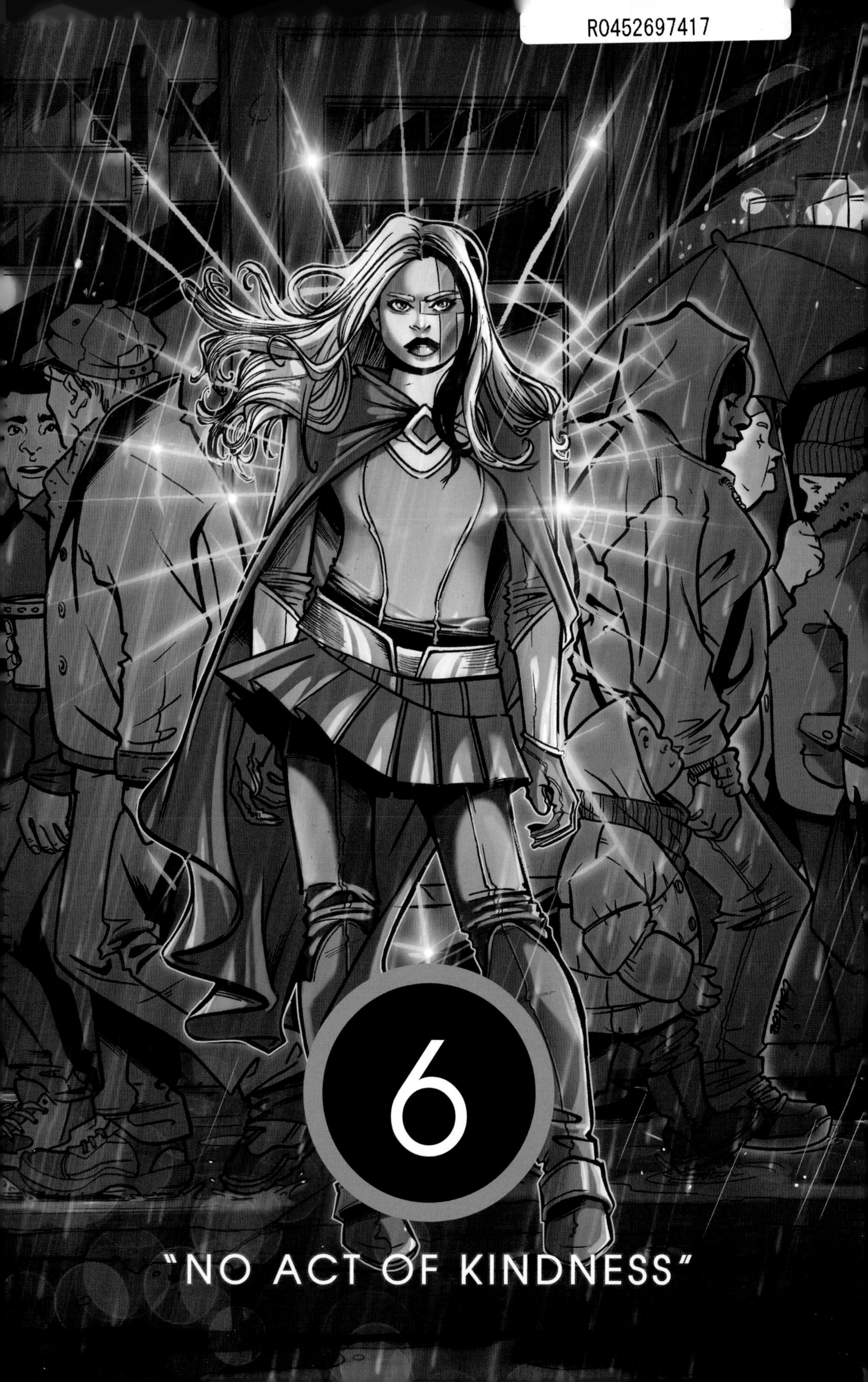
6
"NO ACT OF KINDNESS"

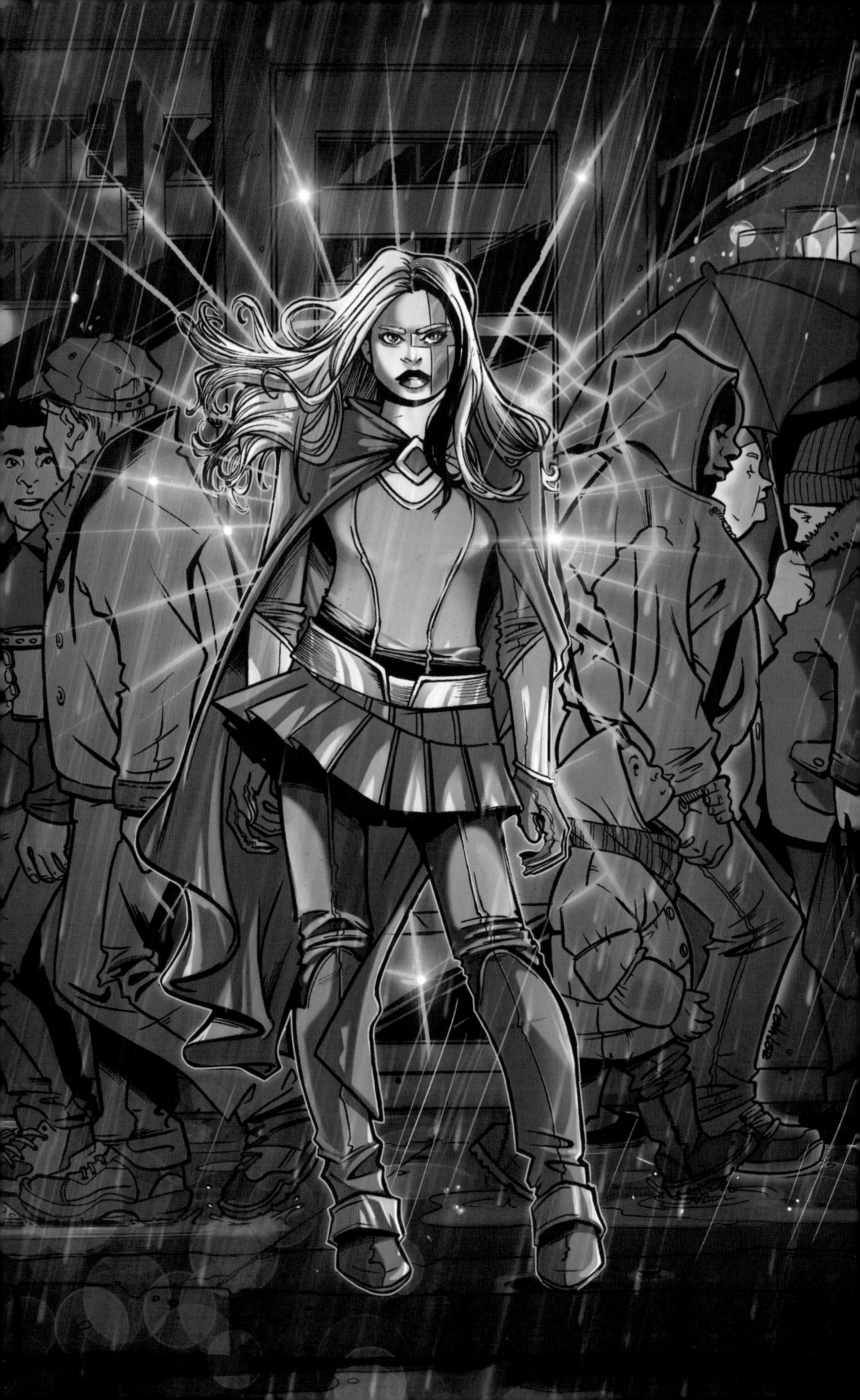

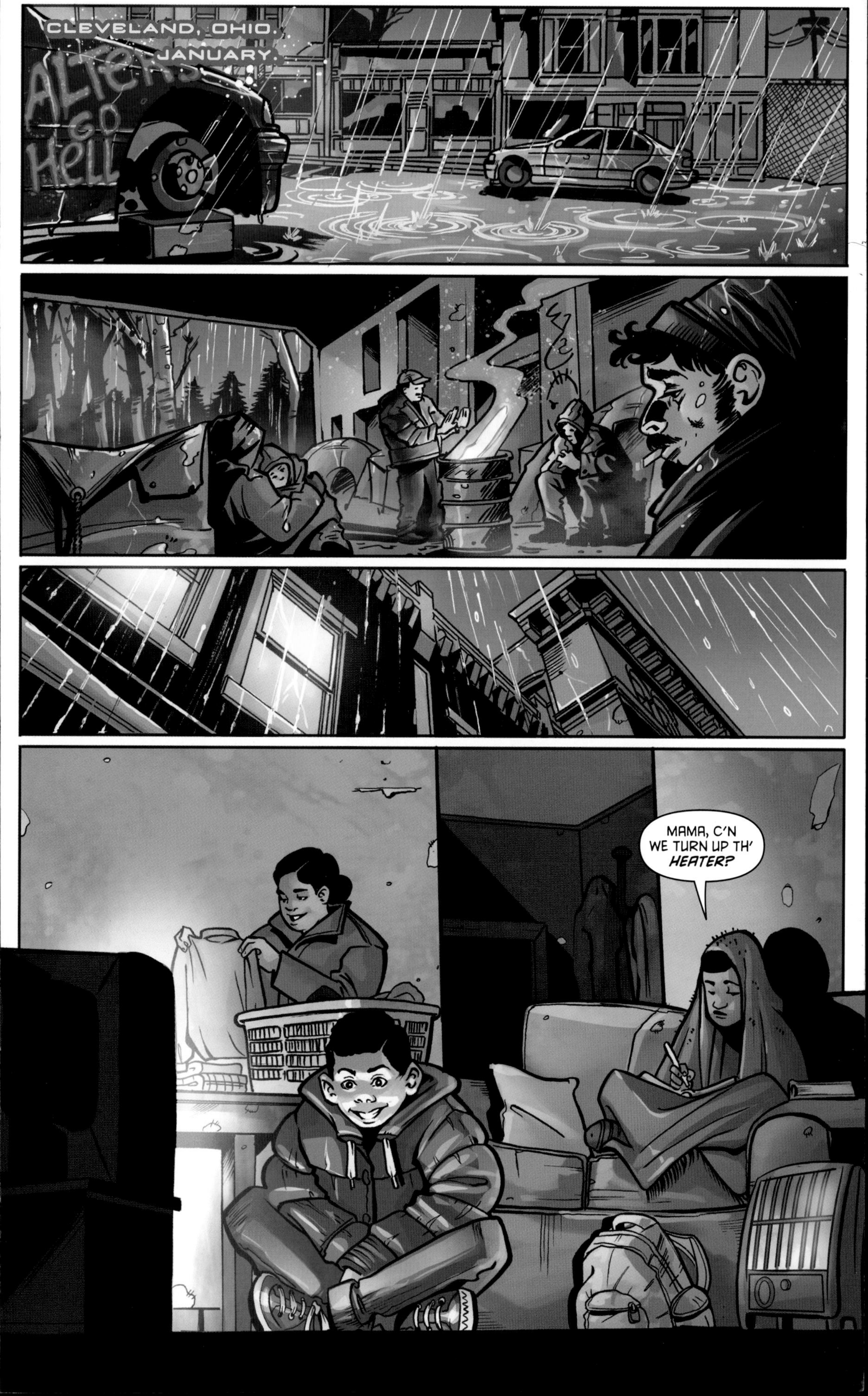
CLEVELAND, OHIO.
JANUARY.
ALTERS GO HELL
MAMA, C'N WE TURN UP TH' *HEATER?*

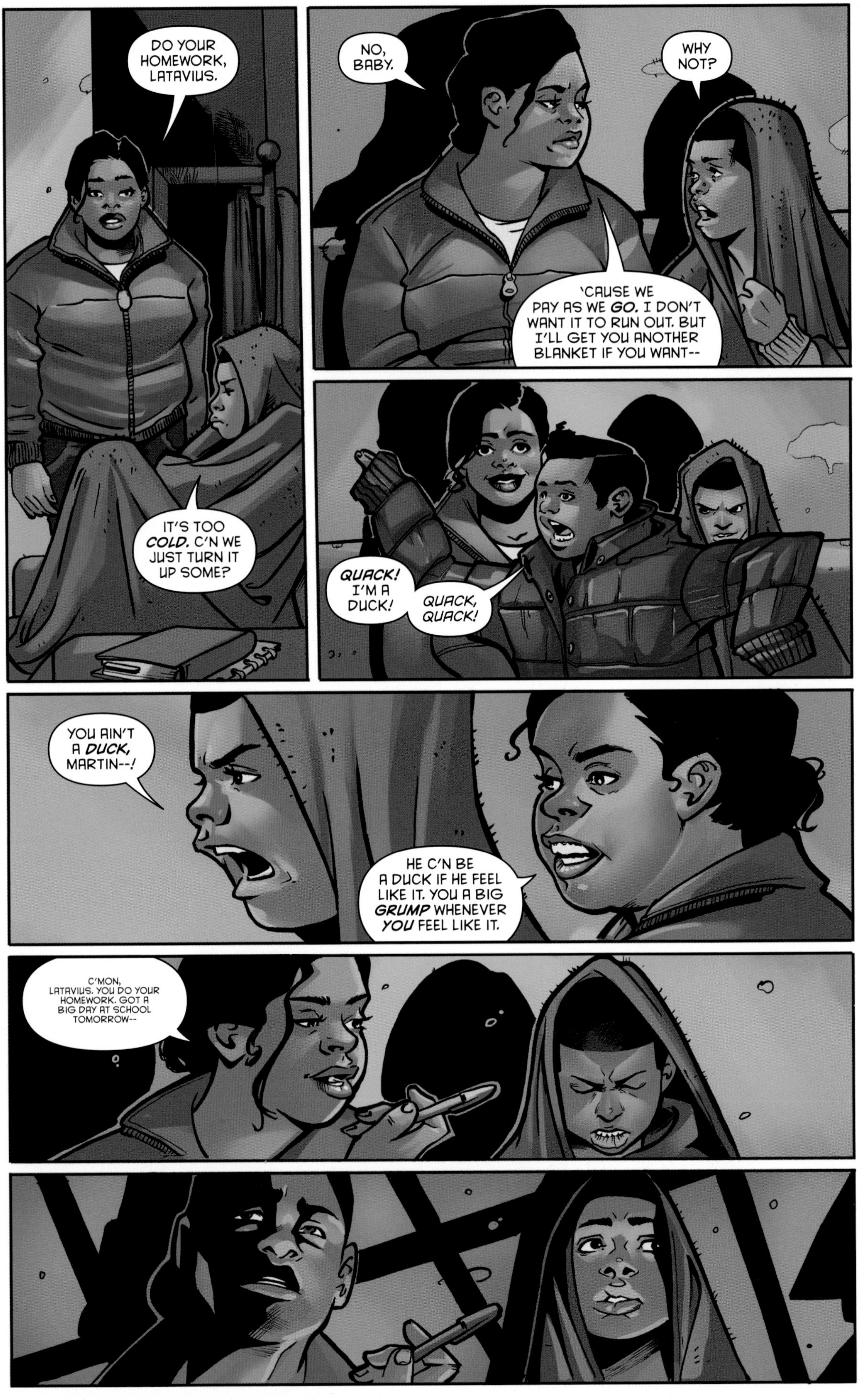
DO YOUR HOMEWORK, LATAVIUS.
IT'S TOO COLD. C'N WE JUST TURN IT UP SOME?
NO, BABY.
WHY NOT?
'CAUSE WE PAY AS WE GO. I DON'T WANT IT TO RUN OUT. BUT I'LL GET YOU ANOTHER BLANKET IF YOU WANT--
QUACK! I'M A DUCK!
QUACK, QUACK!
YOU AIN'T A DUCK, MARTIN--!
HE C'N BE A DUCK IF HE FEEL LIKE IT. YOU A BIG GRUMP WHENEVER YOU FEEL LIKE IT.
C'MON, LATAVIUS. YOU DO YOUR HOMEWORK. GOT A BIG DAY AT SCHOOL TOMORROW--

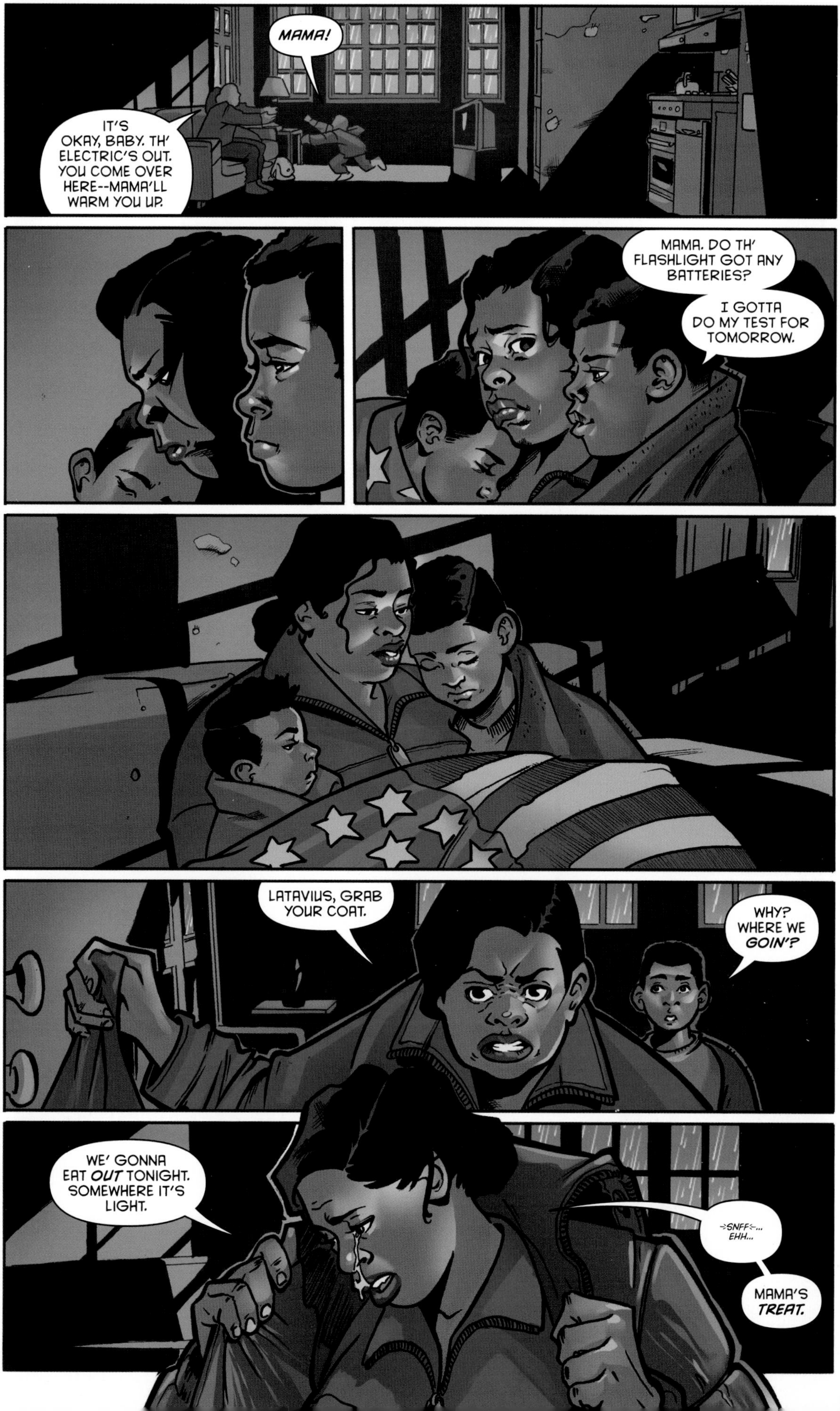
MAMA!
IT'S OKAY, BABY. TH' ELECTRIC'S OUT. YOU COME OVER HERE--MAMA'LL WARM YOU UP.
MAMA. DO TH' FLASHLIGHT GOT ANY BATTERIES?
I GOTTA DO MY TEST FOR TOMORROW.
LATAVIUS, GRAB YOUR COAT.
WHY? WHERE WE GOIN'?
WE' GONNA EAT OUT TONIGHT. SOMEWHERE IT'S LIGHT.
SNFF... EHH...
MAMA'S TREAT.

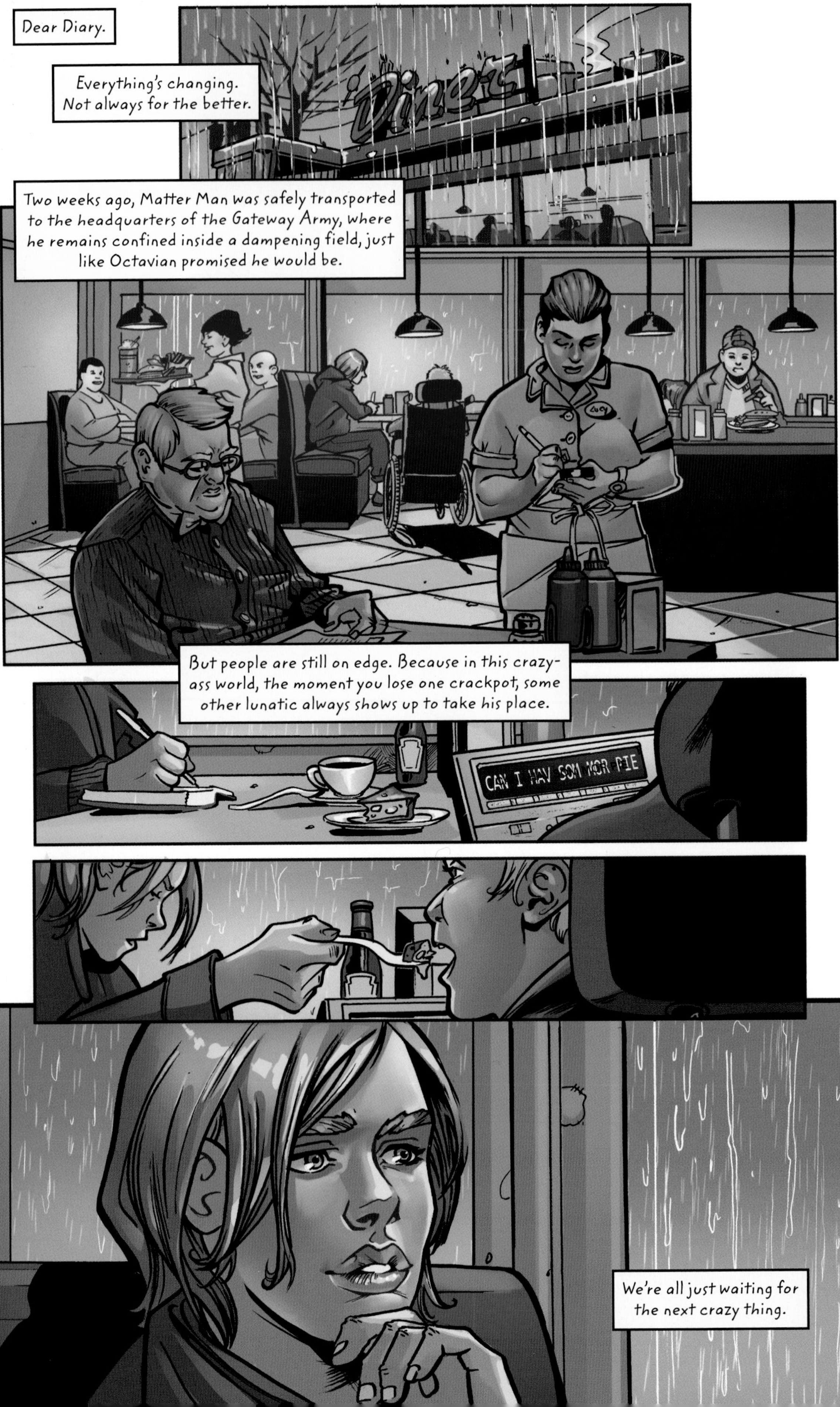
Dear Diary.
Everything's changing. Not always for the better.
Diner
Two weeks ago, Matter Man was safely transported to the headquarters of the Gateway Army, where he remains confined inside a dampening field, just like Octavian promised he would be.
Lucy
But people are still on edge. Because in this crazy-ass world, the moment you lose one crackpot, some other lunatic always shows up to take his place.
CAN I HAV SOM MOR PIE
We're all just waiting for the next crazy thing.

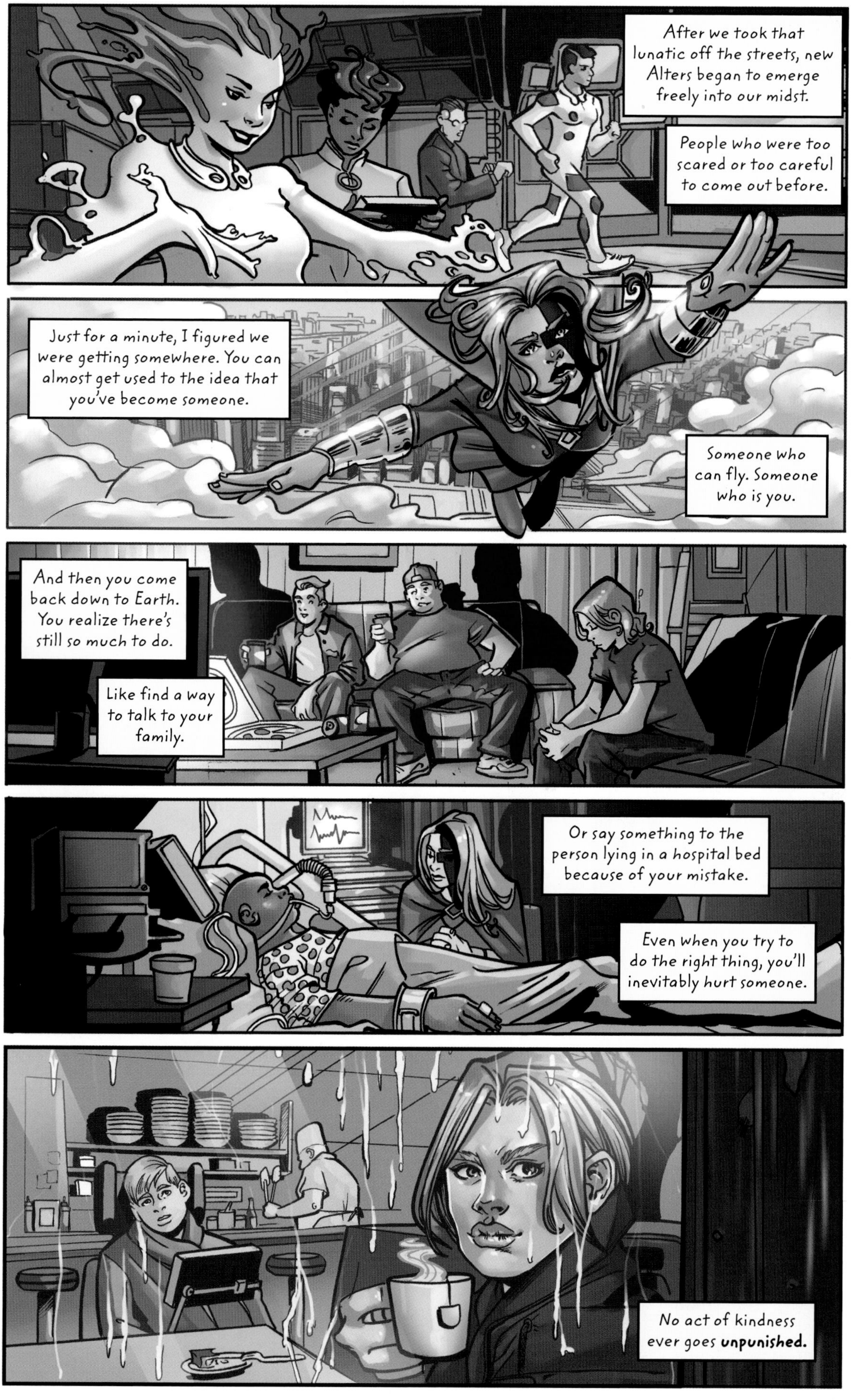
After we took that lunatic off the streets, new Alters began to emerge freely into our midst.
People who were too scared or too careful to come out before.
Just for a minute, I figured we were getting somewhere. You can almost get used to the idea that you've become someone.
Someone who can fly. Someone who is you.
And then you come back down to Earth. You realize there's still so much to do.
Like find a way to talk to your family.
Or say something to the person lying in a hospital bed because of your mistake.
Even when you try to do the right thing, you'll inevitably hurt someone.
No act of kindness ever goes **unpunished.**

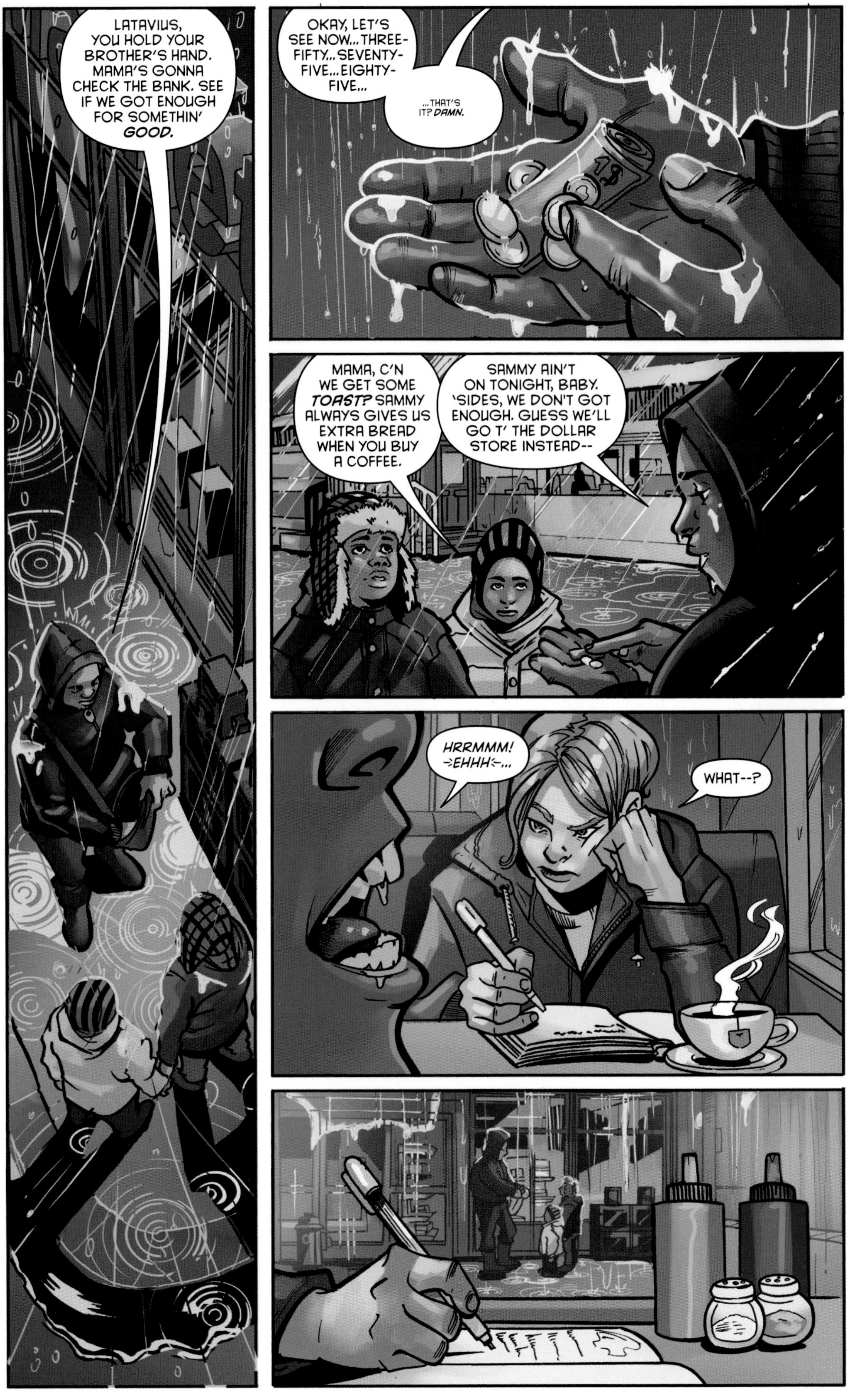
LATAVIUS, YOU HOLD YOUR BROTHER'S HAND. MAMA'S GONNA CHECK THE BANK. SEE IF WE GOT ENOUGH FOR SOMETHIN' *GOOD.*
OKAY, LET'S SEE NOW... THREE-FIFTY... SEVENTY-FIVE... EIGHTY-FIVE...
...THAT'S IT? *DAMN.*
MAMA, C'N WE GET SOME *TOAST?* SAMMY ALWAYS GIVES US EXTRA BREAD WHEN YOU BUY A COFFEE.
SAMMY AIN'T ON TONIGHT, BABY. 'SIDES, WE DON'T GOT ENOUGH. GUESS WE'LL GO T' THE DOLLAR STORE INSTEAD--
HRRMMM! *EHHH*...
WHAT--?

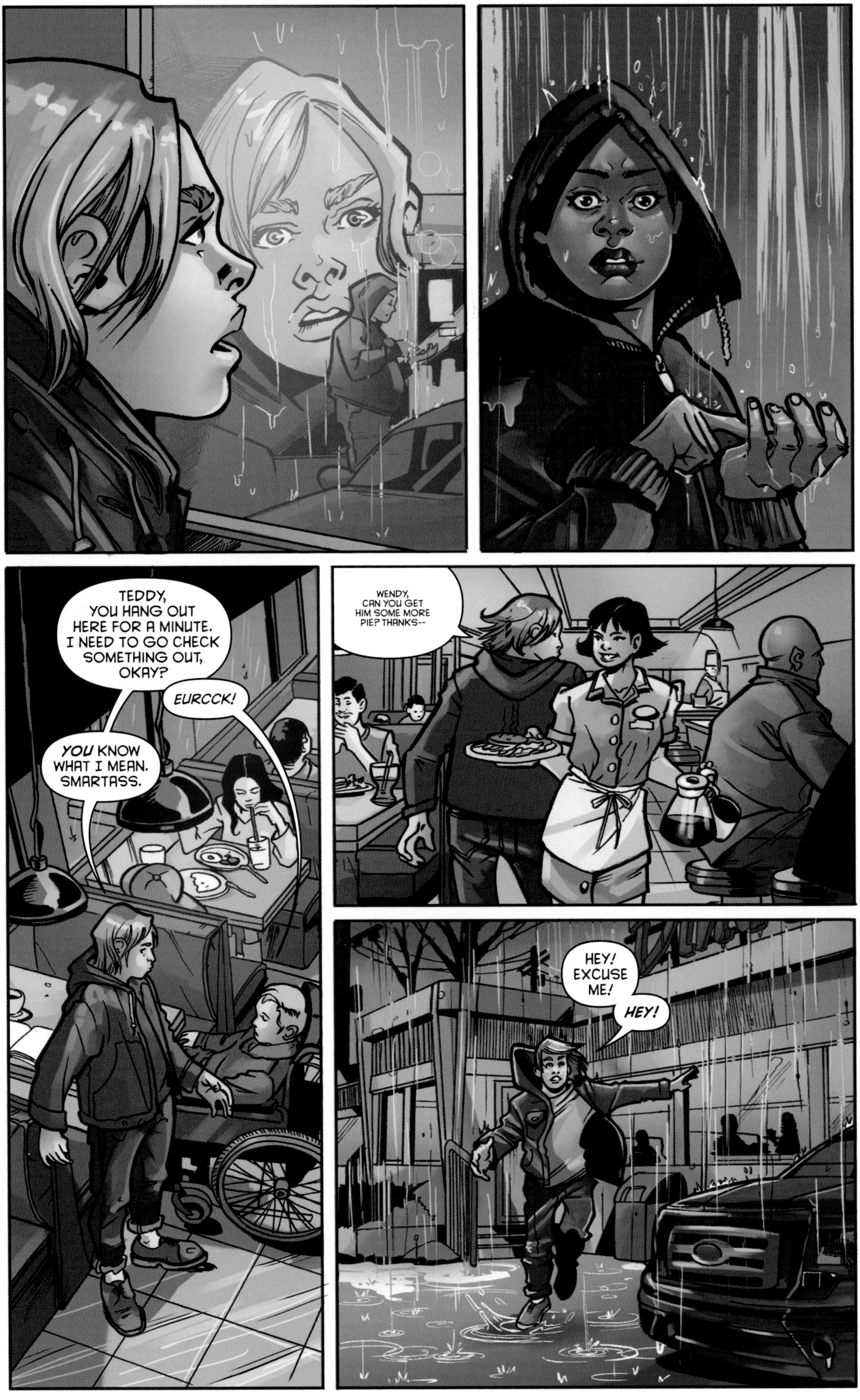
TEDDY, YOU HANG OUT HERE FOR A MINUTE. I NEED TO GO CHECK SOMETHING OUT, OKAY?
EURCCK!
YOU KNOW WHAT I MEAN. SMARTASS.
WENDY, CAN YOU GET HIM SOME MORE PIE? THANKS--
HEY! EXCUSE ME!
HEY!

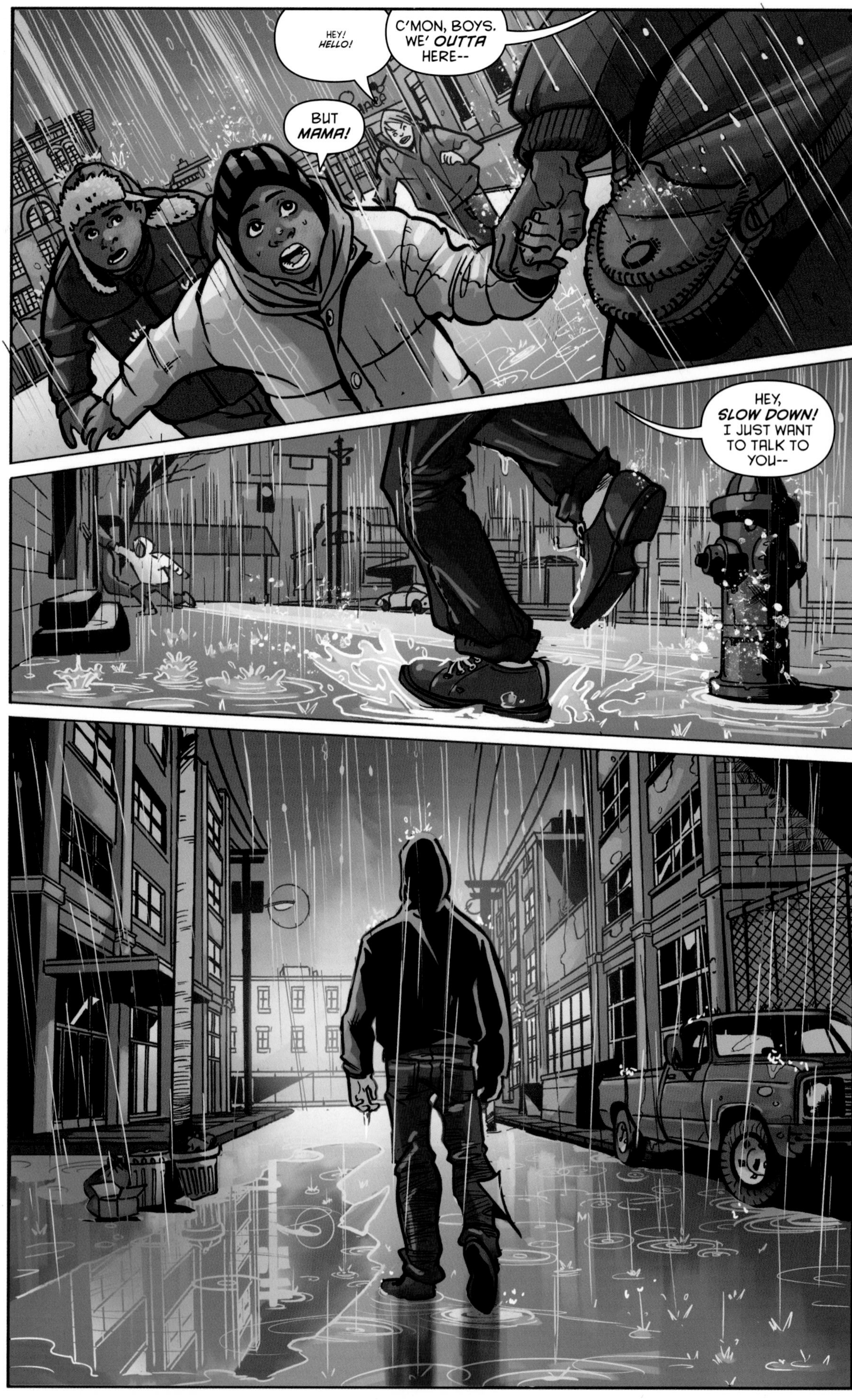
HEY! HELLO!
C'MON, BOYS. WE' OUTTA HERE--
BUT MAMA!
HEY, SLOW DOWN! I JUST WANT TO TALK TO YOU--

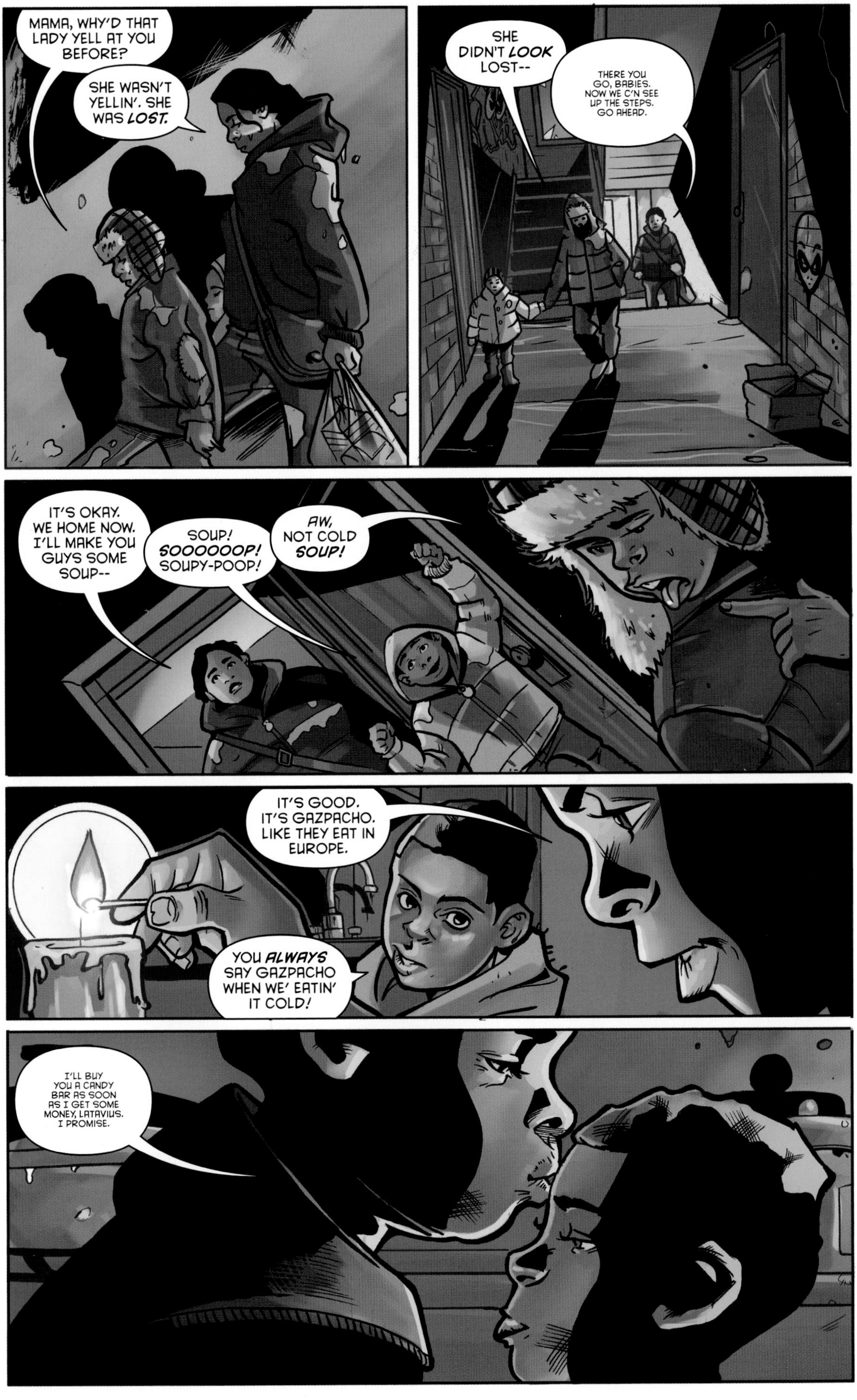
MAMA, WHY'D THAT LADY YELL AT YOU BEFORE?
SHE WASN'T YELLIN'. SHE WAS *LOST.*
SHE DIDN'T *LOOK* LOST--
THERE YOU GO, BABIES. NOW WE C'N SEE UP THE STEPS. GO AHEAD.
IT'S OKAY. WE HOME NOW. I'LL MAKE YOU GUYS SOME SOUP--
SOUP! *SOOOOOOP!* SOUPY-POOP!
AW, NOT COLD *SOUP!*
IT'S GOOD. IT'S GAZPACHO. LIKE THEY EAT IN EUROPE.
YOU *ALWAYS* SAY GAZPACHO WHEN WE' EATIN' IT COLD!
I'LL BUY YOU A CANDY BAR AS SOON AS I GET SOME MONEY, LATAVIUS. I PROMISE.

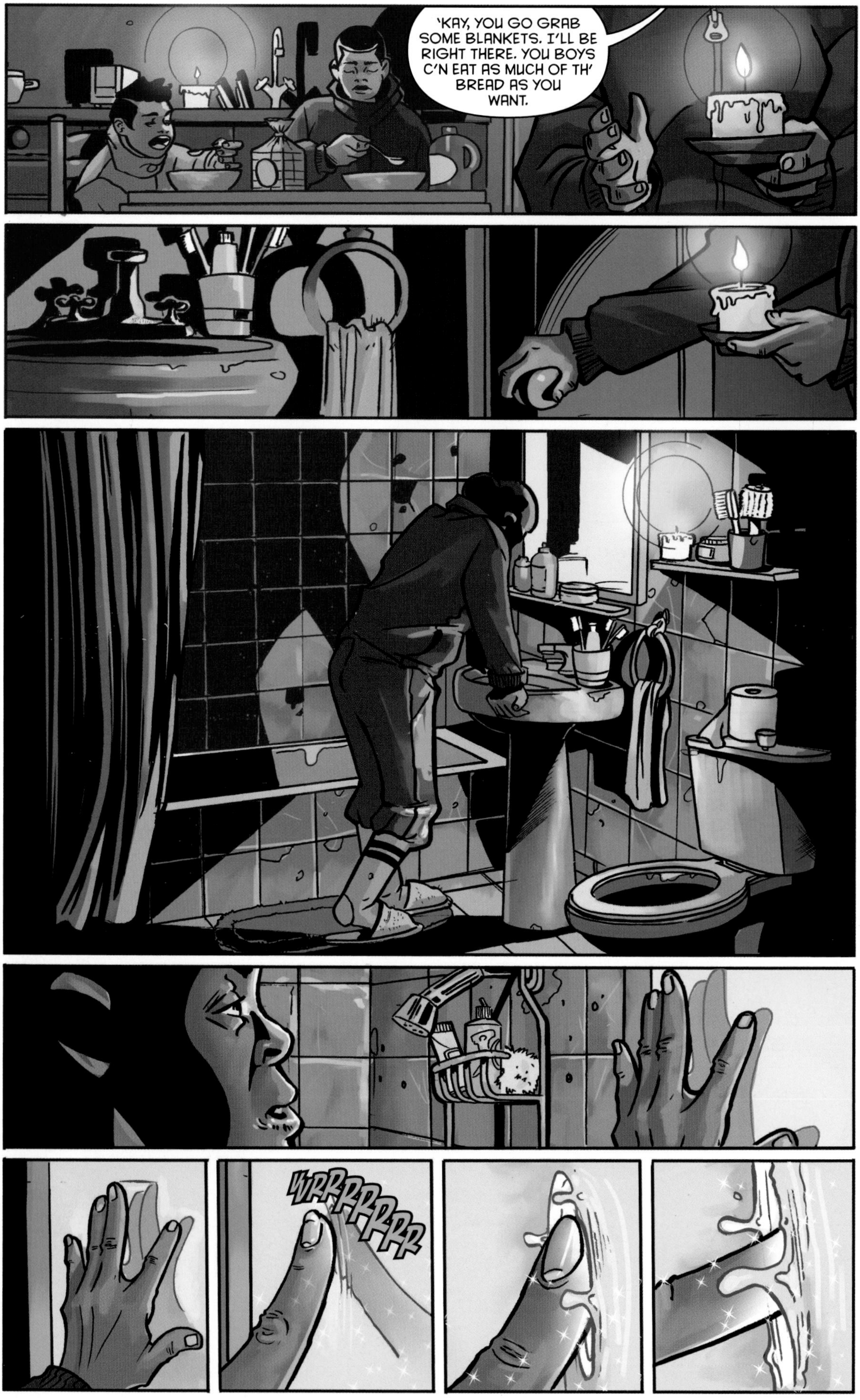
'KAY, YOU GO GRAB SOME BLANKETS. I'LL BE RIGHT THERE. YOU BOYS C'N EAT AS MUCH OF TH' BREAD AS YOU WANT.
WRRRRRRRR

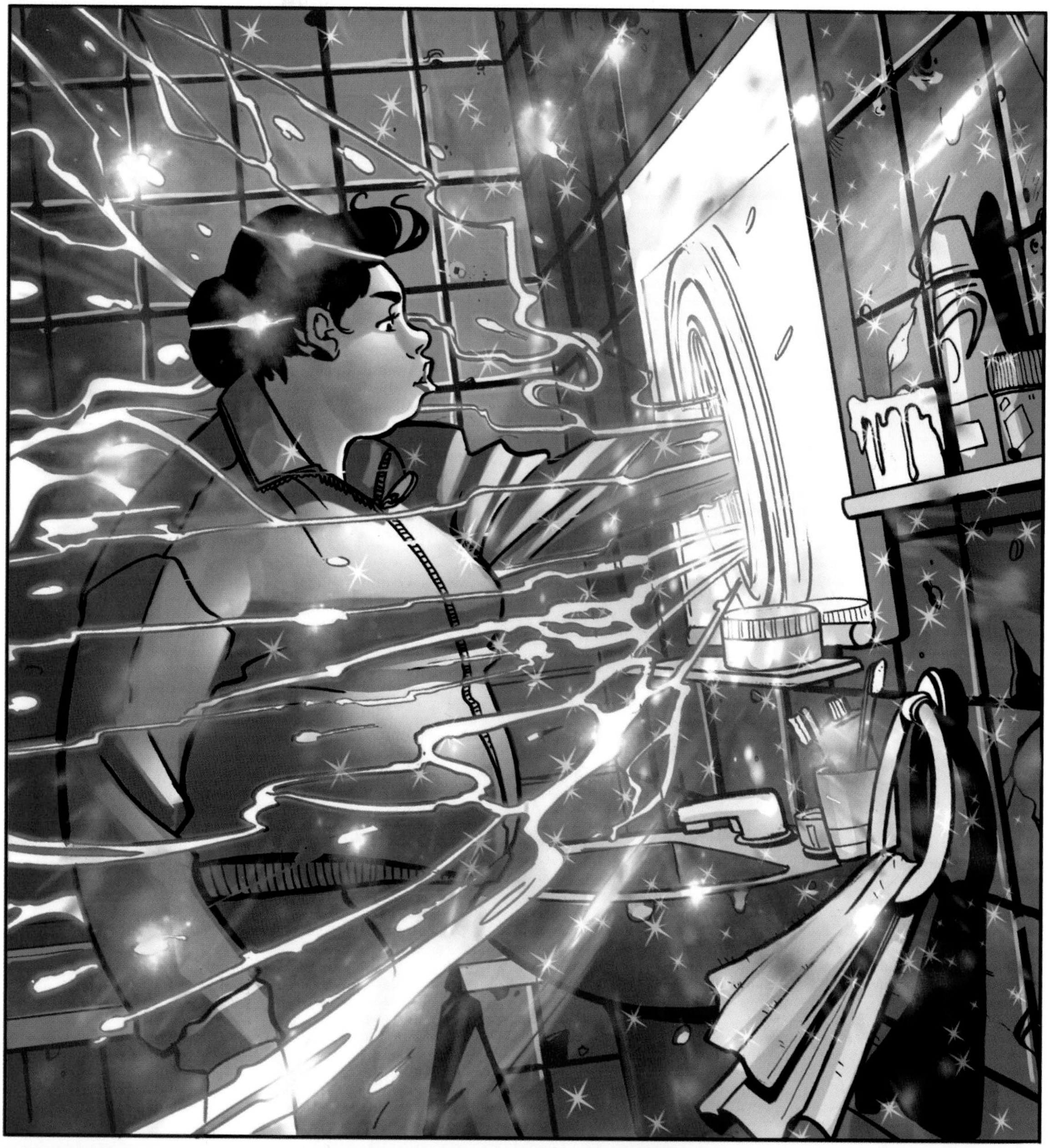

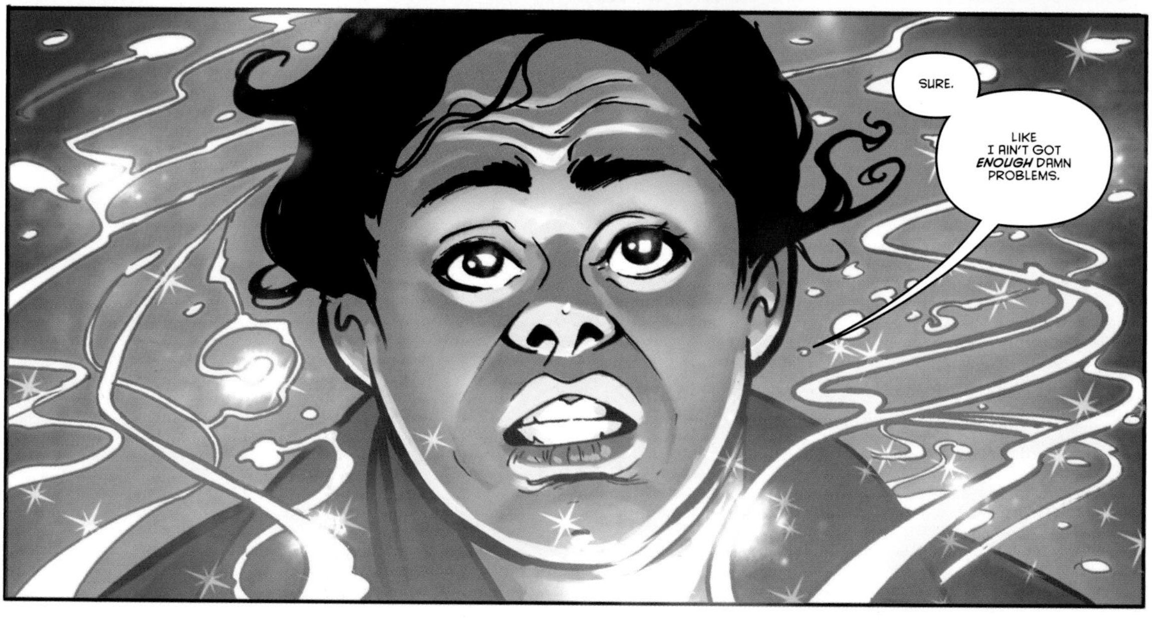
SURE.
LIKE I AIN'T GOT *ENOUGH* DAMN PROBLEMS.

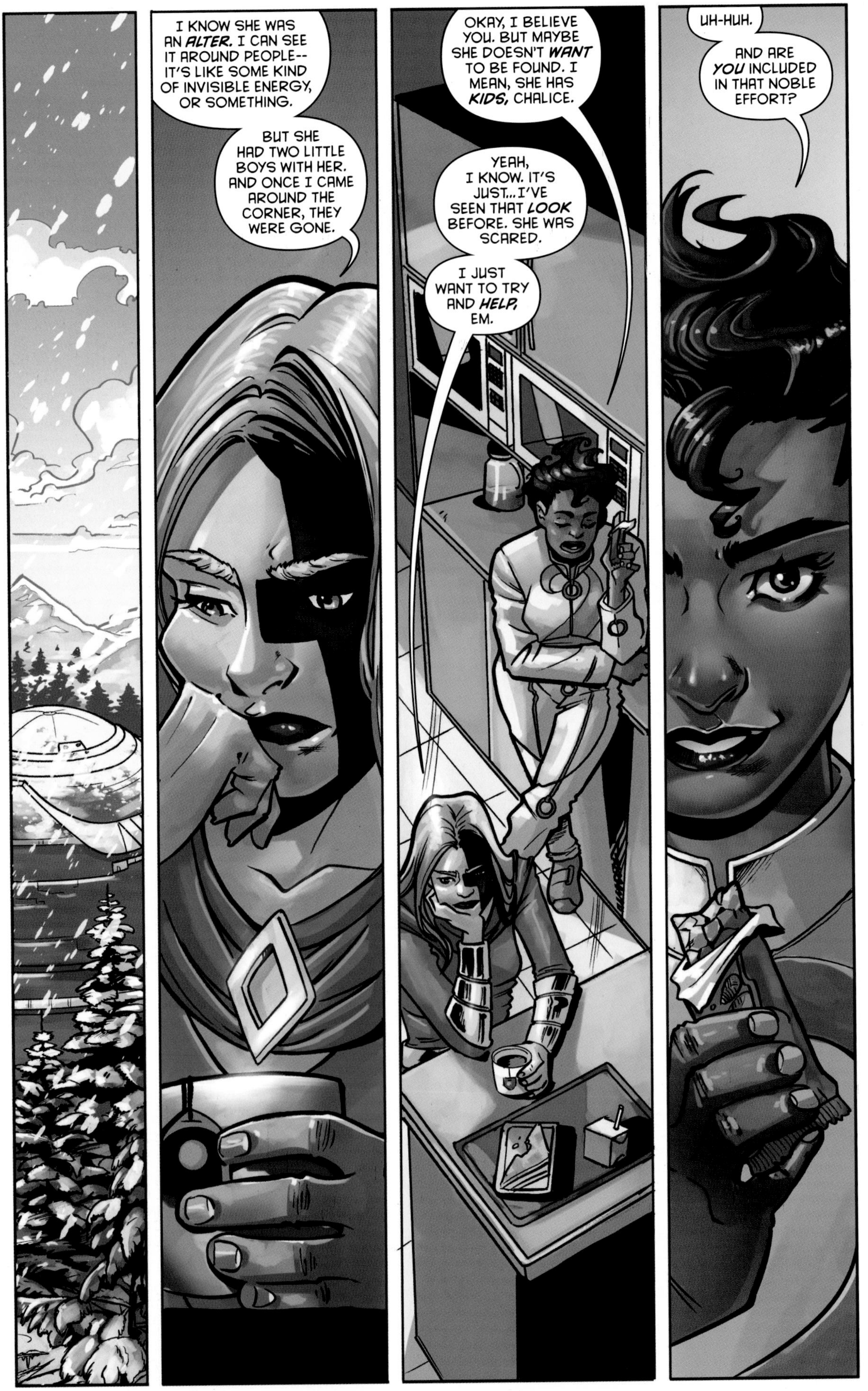
I KNOW SHE WAS AN ALTER. I CAN SEE IT AROUND PEOPLE-- IT'S LIKE SOME KIND OF INVISIBLE ENERGY, OR SOMETHING.
BUT SHE HAD TWO LITTLE BOYS WITH HER. AND ONCE I CAME AROUND THE CORNER, THEY WERE GONE.
OKAY, I BELIEVE YOU. BUT MAYBE SHE DOESN'T WANT TO BE FOUND. I MEAN, SHE HAS KIDS, CHALICE.
YEAH, I KNOW. IT'S JUST...I'VE SEEN THAT LOOK BEFORE. SHE WAS SCARED.
I JUST WANT TO TRY AND HELP, EM.
UH-HUH.
AND ARE YOU INCLUDED IN THAT NOBLE EFFORT?

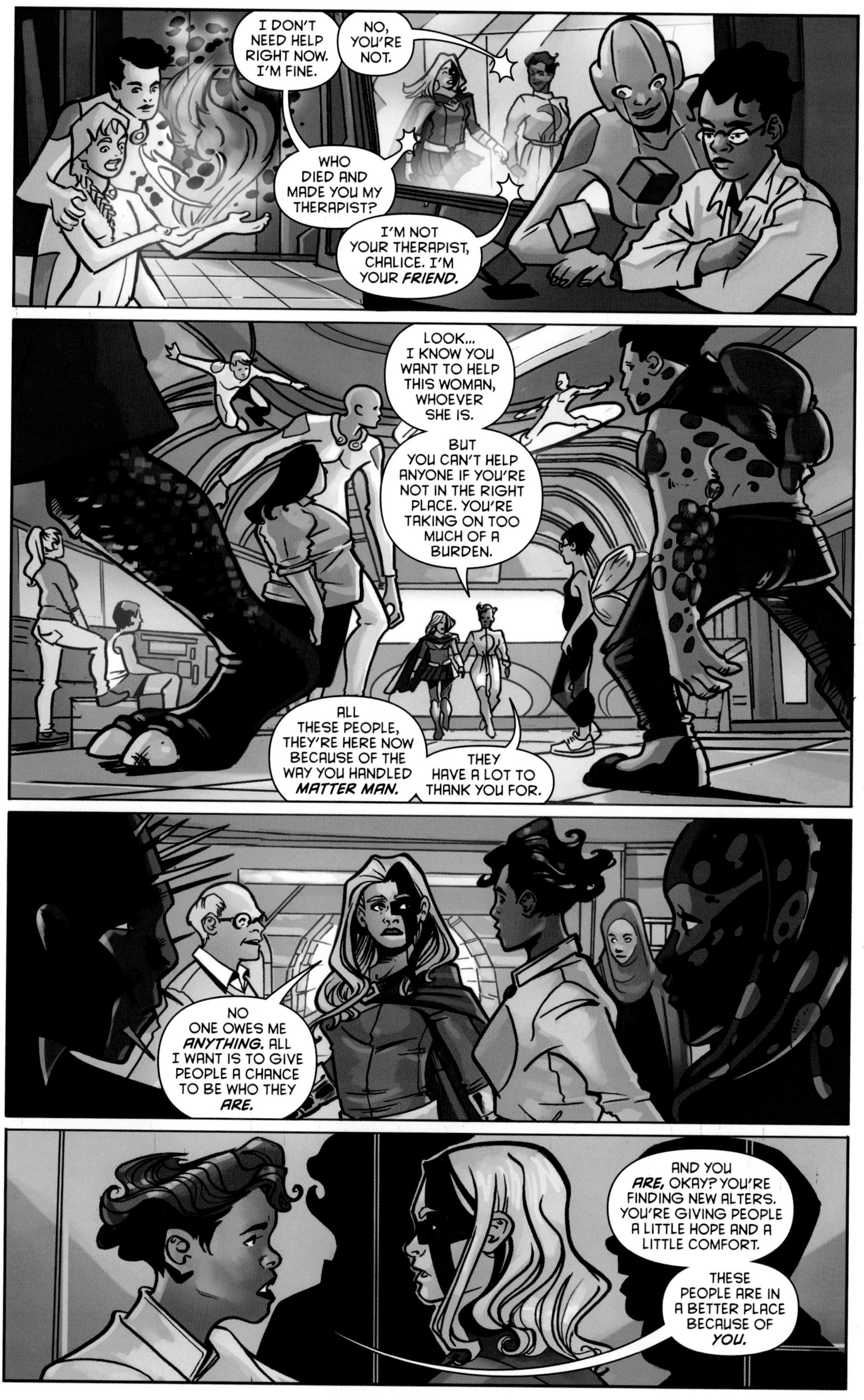
I DON'T NEED HELP RIGHT NOW. I'M FINE.
NO, YOU'RE NOT.
WHO DIED AND MADE YOU MY THERAPIST?
I'M NOT YOUR THERAPIST, CHALICE. I'M YOUR *FRIEND.*
LOOK... I KNOW YOU WANT TO HELP THIS WOMAN, WHOEVER SHE IS.
BUT YOU CAN'T HELP ANYONE IF YOU'RE NOT IN THE RIGHT PLACE. YOU'RE TAKING ON TOO MUCH OF A BURDEN.
ALL THESE PEOPLE, THEY'RE HERE NOW BECAUSE OF THE WAY YOU HANDLED *MATTER MAN.*
THEY HAVE A LOT TO THANK YOU FOR.
NO ONE OWES ME *ANYTHING.* ALL I WANT IS TO GIVE PEOPLE A CHANCE TO BE WHO THEY *ARE.*
AND YOU *ARE,* OKAY? YOU'RE FINDING NEW ALTERS. YOU'RE GIVING PEOPLE A LITTLE HOPE AND A LITTLE COMFORT.
THESE PEOPLE ARE IN A BETTER PLACE BECAUSE OF *YOU.*

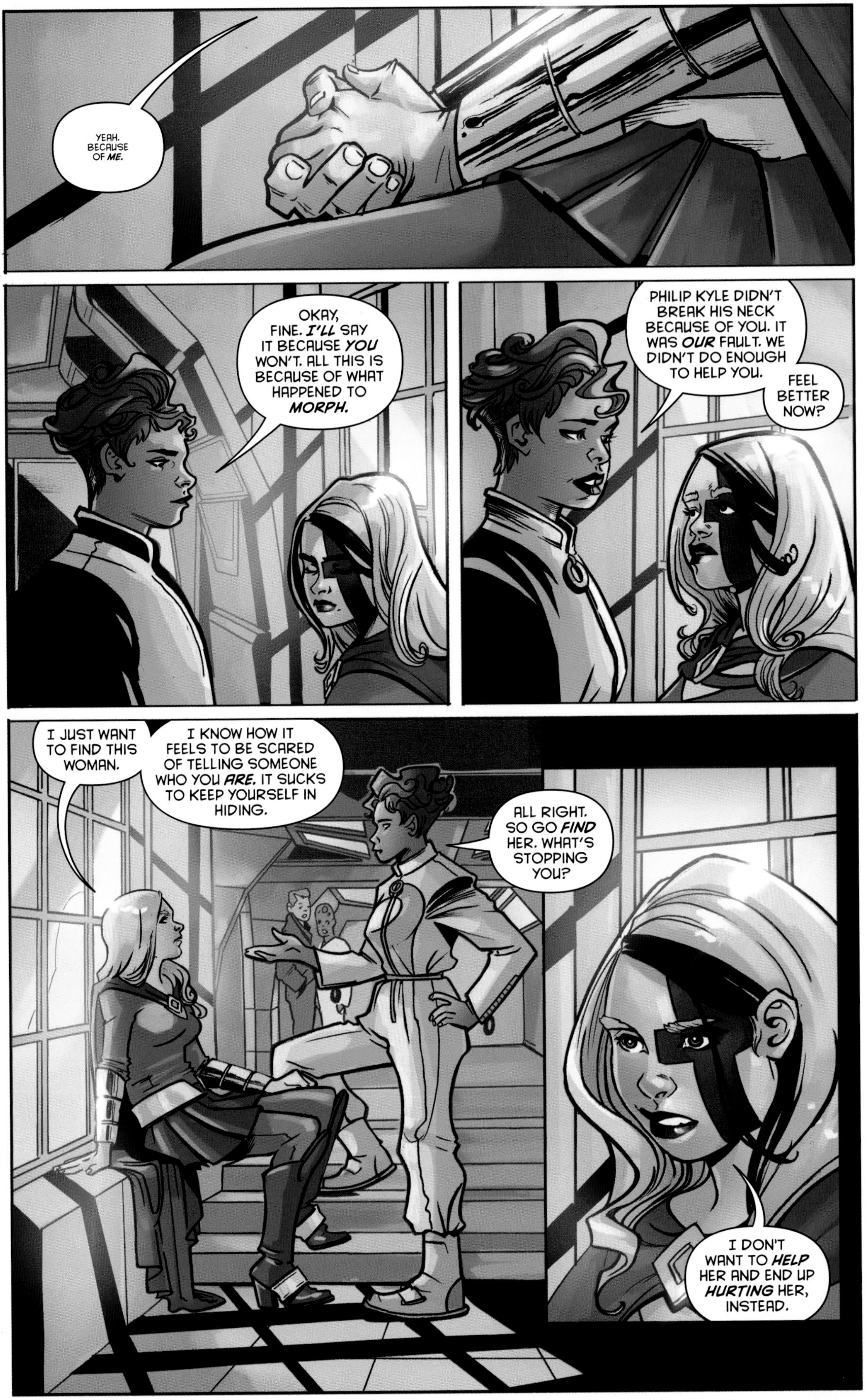
YEAH. BECAUSE OF ME.
OKAY, FINE. I'LL SAY IT BECAUSE YOU WON'T. ALL THIS IS BECAUSE OF WHAT HAPPENED TO MORPH.
PHILIP KYLE DIDN'T BREAK HIS NECK BECAUSE OF YOU. IT WAS OUR FAULT. WE DIDN'T DO ENOUGH TO HELP YOU.
FEEL BETTER NOW?
I JUST WANT TO FIND THIS WOMAN.
I KNOW HOW IT FEELS TO BE SCARED OF TELLING SOMEONE WHO YOU ARE. IT SUCKS TO KEEP YOURSELF IN HIDING.
ALL RIGHT. SO GO FIND HER. WHAT'S STOPPING YOU?
I DON'T WANT TO HELP HER AND END UP HURTING HER, INSTEAD.

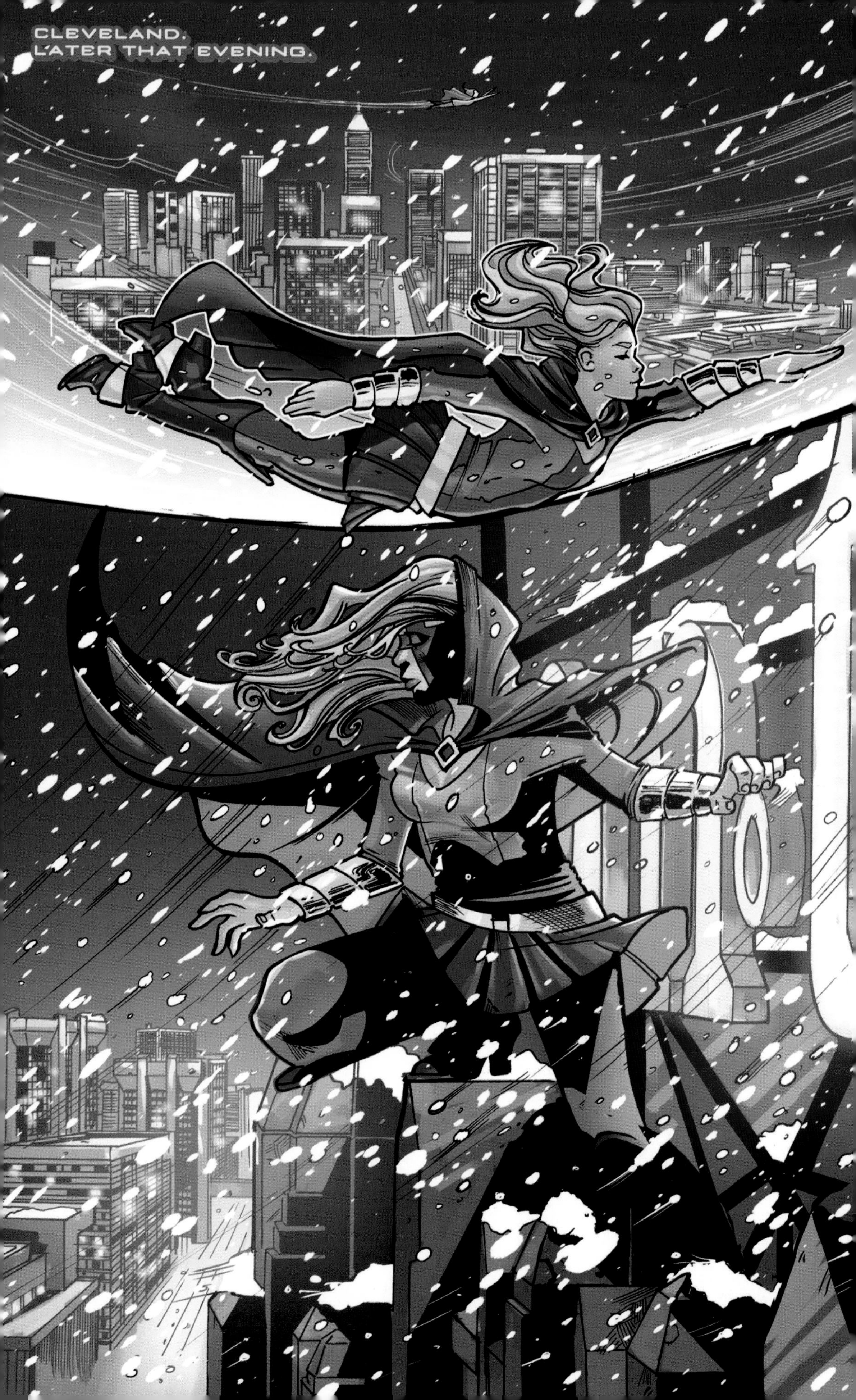
CLEVELAND.
LATER THAT EVENING.

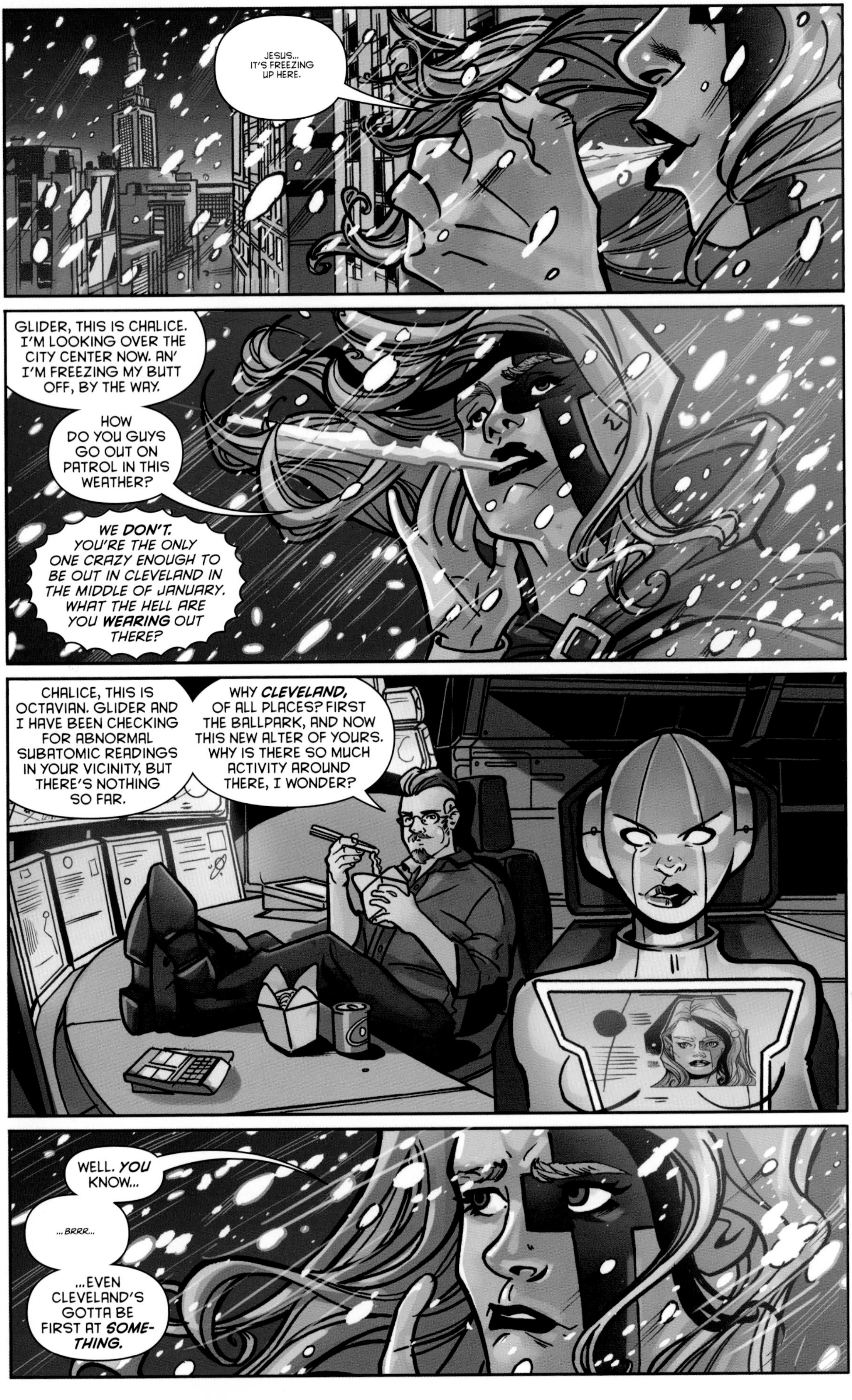

JESUS... IT'S FREEZING UP HERE.
GLIDER, THIS IS CHALICE. I'M LOOKING OVER THE CITY CENTER NOW. AN' I'M FREEZING MY BUTT OFF, BY THE WAY.
HOW DO YOU GUYS GO OUT ON PATROL IN THIS WEATHER?
WE DON'T. YOU'RE THE ONLY ONE CRAZY ENOUGH TO BE OUT IN CLEVELAND IN THE MIDDLE OF JANUARY. WHAT THE HELL ARE YOU WEARING OUT THERE?
CHALICE, THIS IS OCTAVIAN. GLIDER AND I HAVE BEEN CHECKING FOR ABNORMAL SUBATOMIC READINGS IN YOUR VICINITY, BUT THERE'S NOTHING SO FAR.
WHY CLEVELAND, OF ALL PLACES? FIRST THE BALLPARK, AND NOW THIS NEW ALTER OF YOURS. WHY IS THERE SO MUCH ACTIVITY AROUND THERE, I WONDER?
WELL. YOU KNOW...
...BRRR...
...EVEN CLEVELAND'S GOTTA BE FIRST AT SOME-THING.

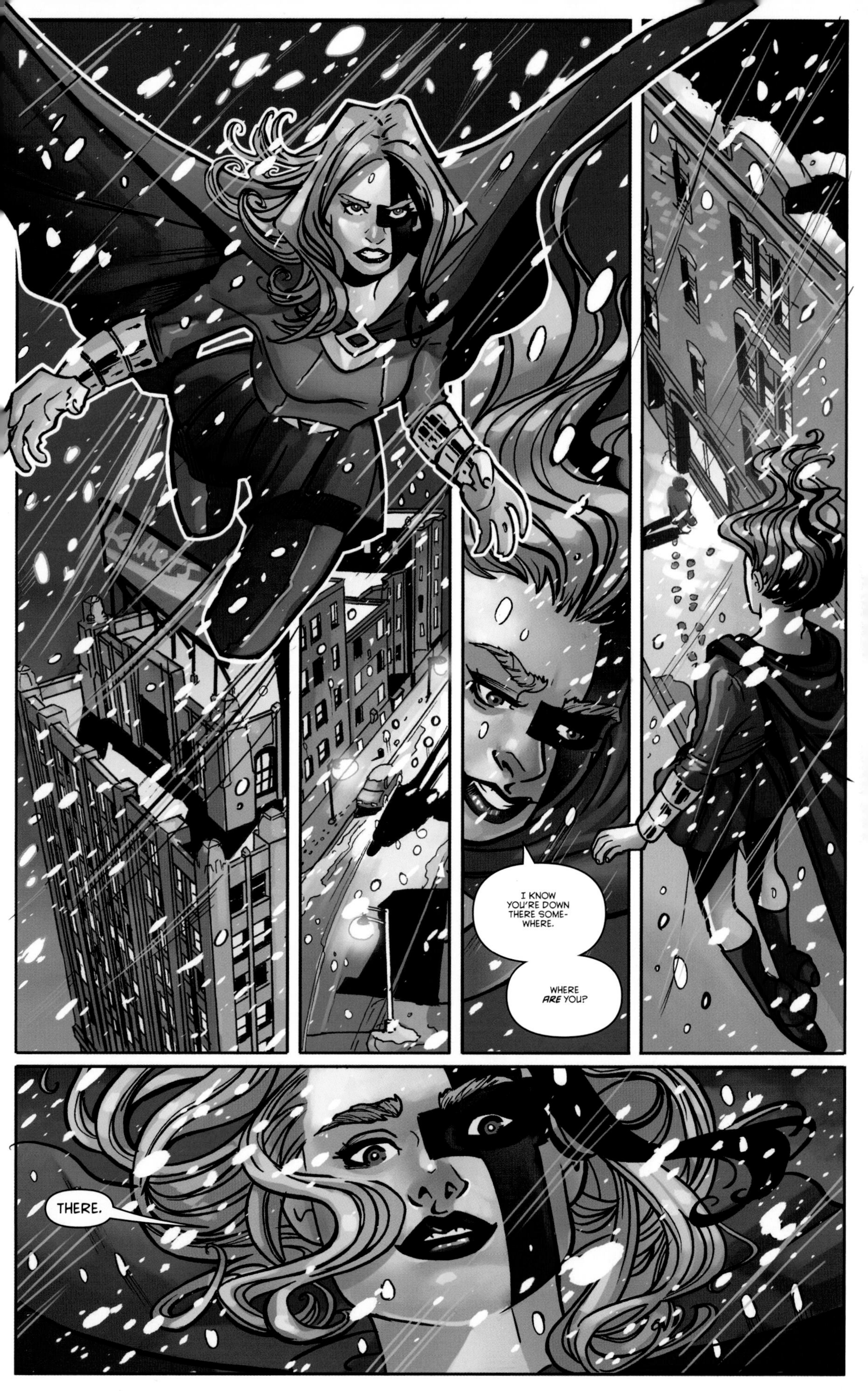
I KNOW YOU'RE DOWN THERE SOME-WHERE.
WHERE *ARE* YOU?
THERE.

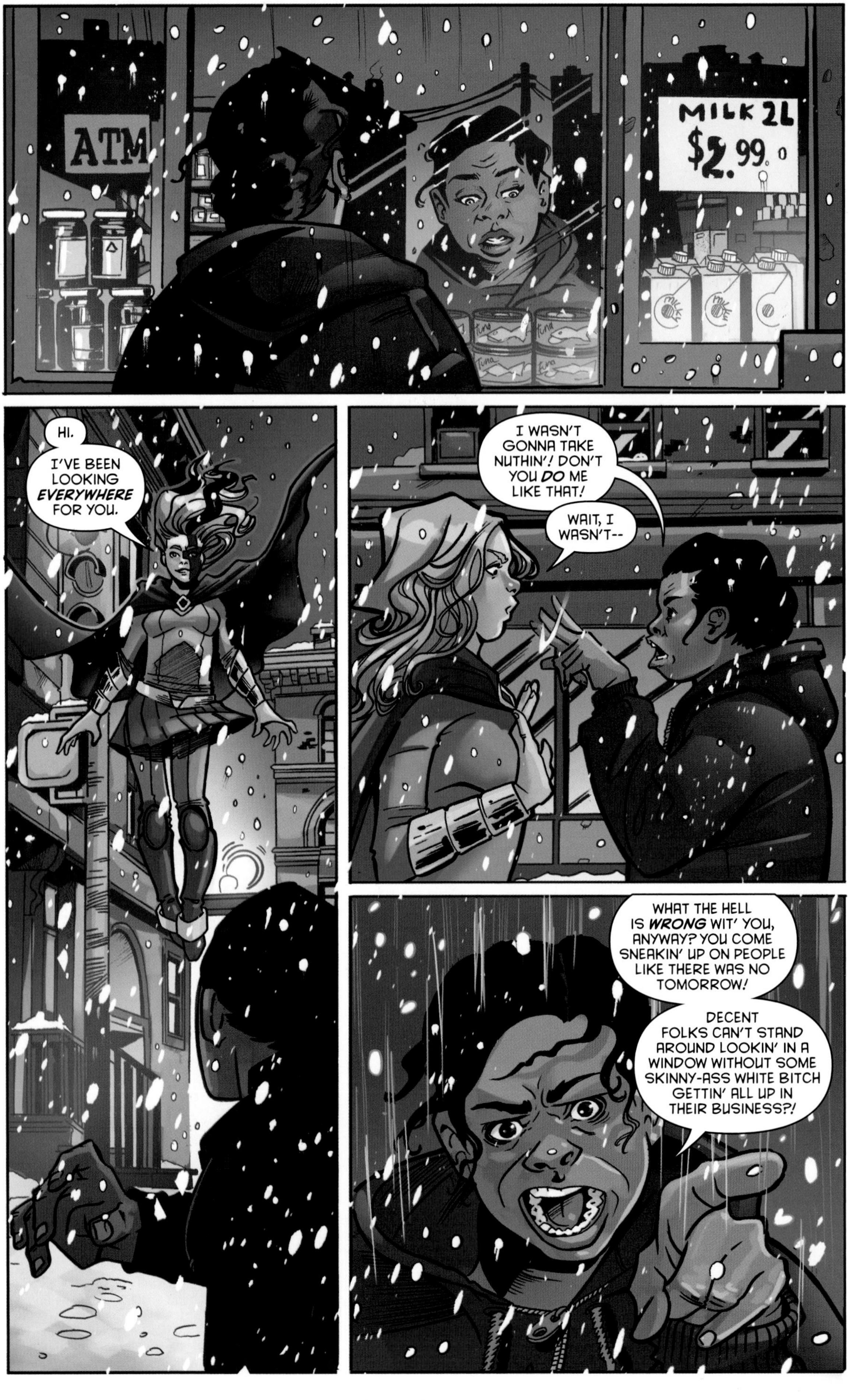
ATM
MILK 2L
$2.99
HI.
I'VE BEEN LOOKING EVERYWHERE FOR YOU.
I WASN'T GONNA TAKE NUTHIN'! DON'T YOU DO ME LIKE THAT!
WAIT, I WASN'T--
WHAT THE HELL IS WRONG WIT' YOU, ANYWAY? YOU COME SNEAKIN' UP ON PEOPLE LIKE THERE WAS NO TOMORROW!
DECENT FOLKS CAN'T STAND AROUND LOOKIN' IN A WINDOW WITHOUT SOME SKINNY-ASS WHITE BITCH GETTIN' ALL UP IN THEIR BUSINESS?!

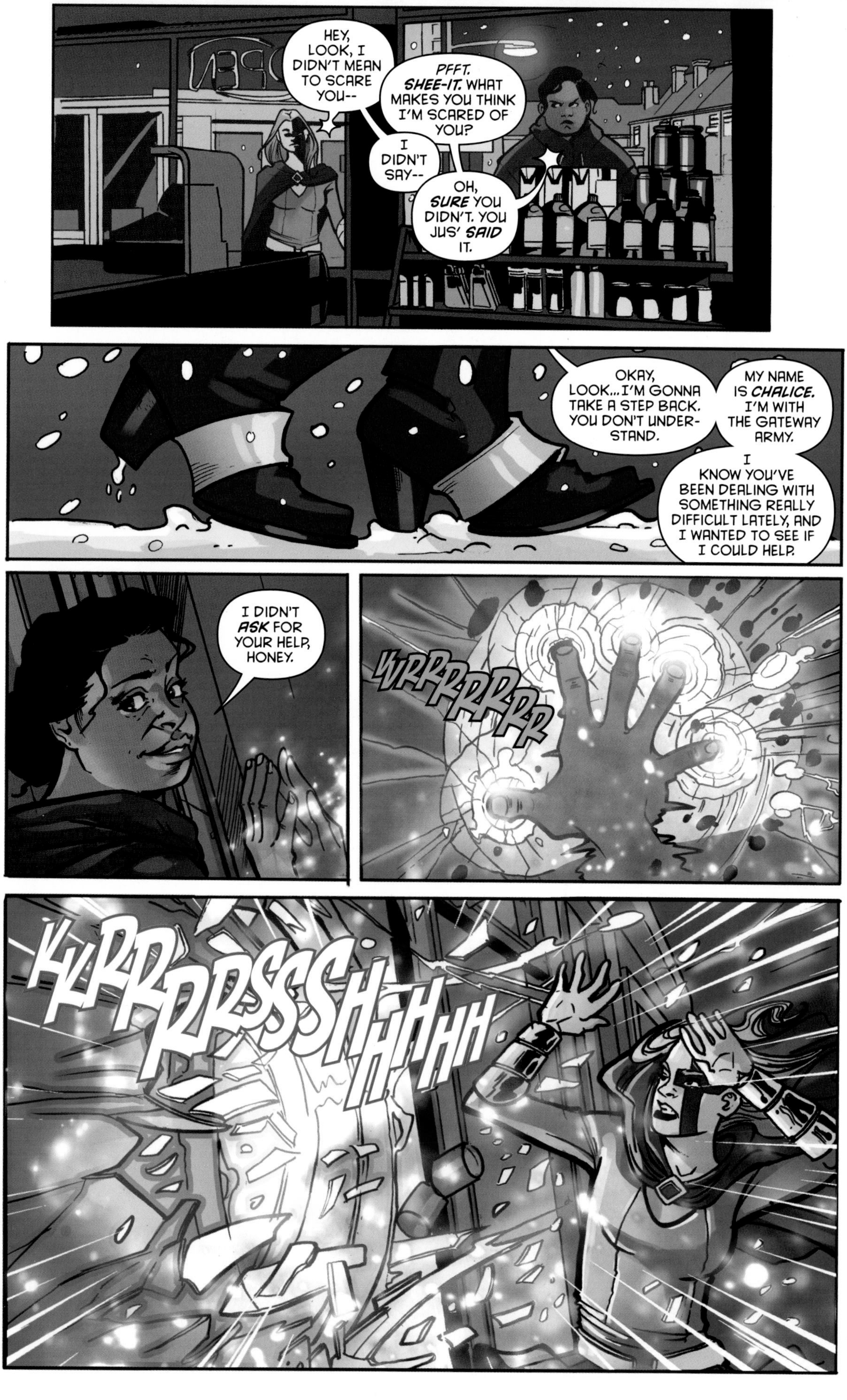
HEY, LOOK, I DIDN'T MEAN TO SCARE YOU--
PFFT. SHEE-IT. WHAT MAKES YOU THINK I'M SCARED OF YOU?
I DIDN'T SAY--
OH, SURE YOU DIDN'T. YOU JUS' SAID IT.
OKAY, LOOK... I'M GONNA TAKE A STEP BACK. YOU DON'T UNDER-STAND.
MY NAME IS CHALICE. I'M WITH THE GATEWAY ARMY.
I KNOW YOU'VE BEEN DEALING WITH SOMETHING REALLY DIFFICULT LATELY, AND I WANTED TO SEE IF I COULD HELP.
I DIDN'T ASK FOR YOUR HELP, HONEY.
VRRRRRRRRR
KKRRRRSSSSHHHHHH

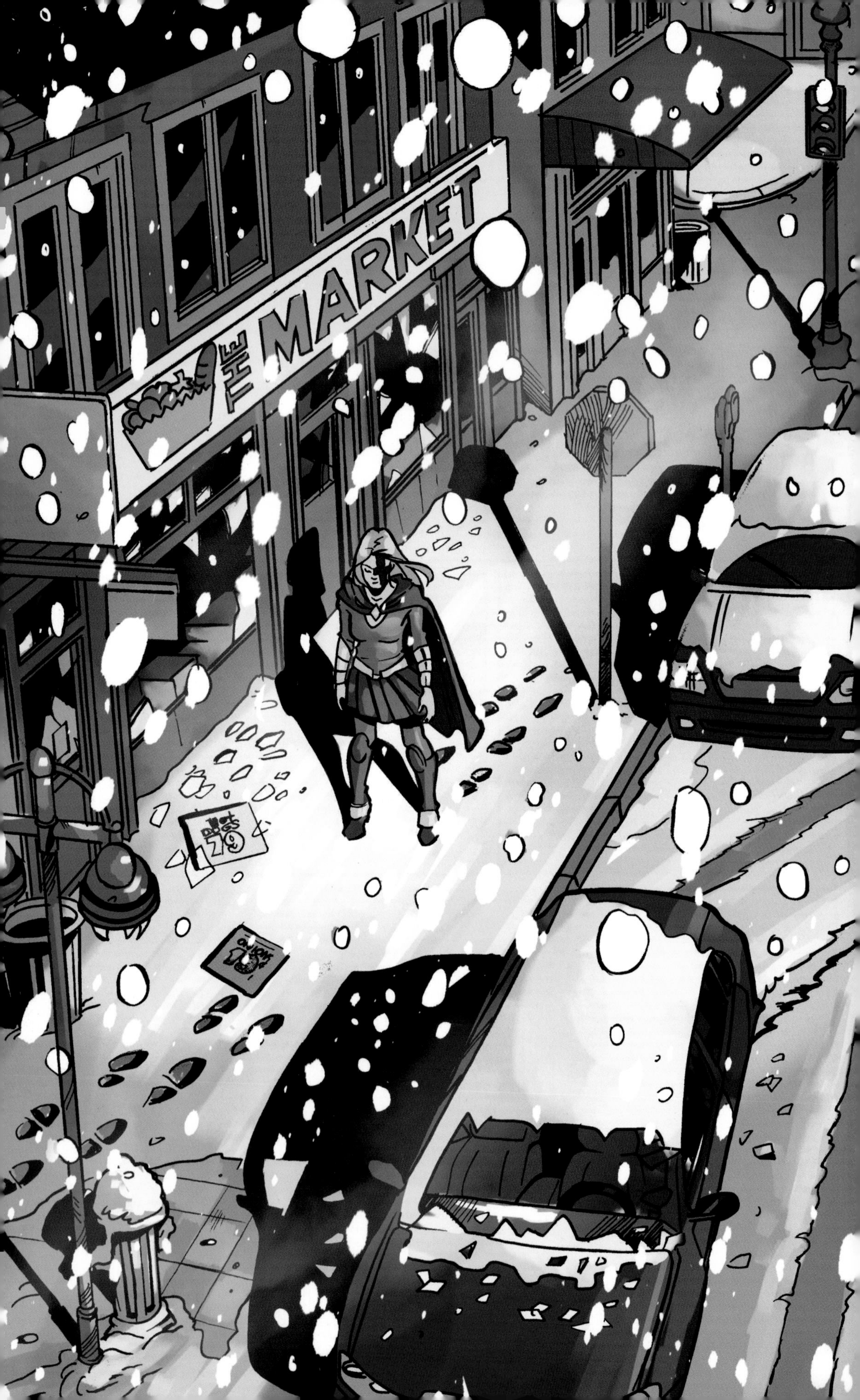
THE MARKET

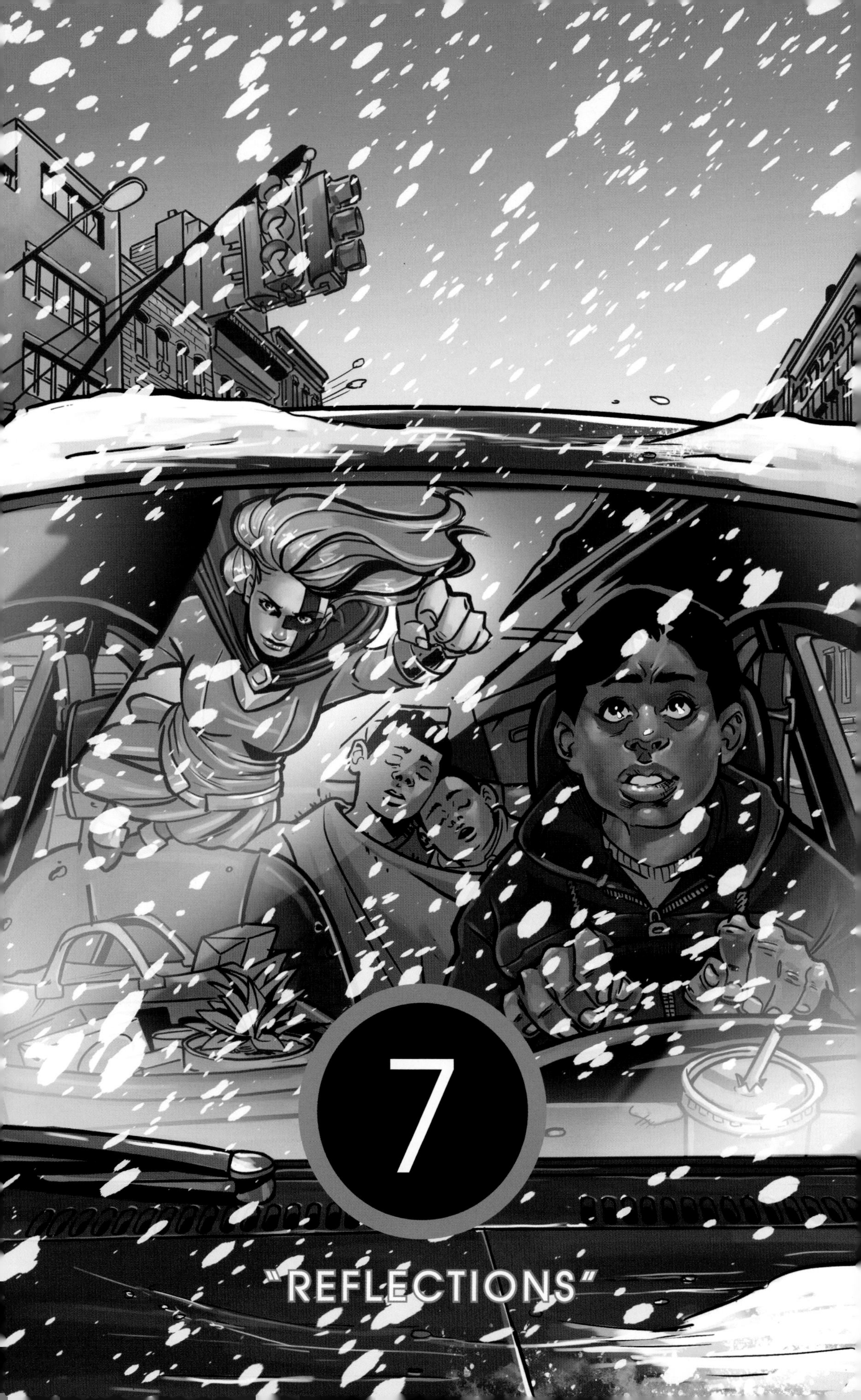
7
"REFLECTIONS"

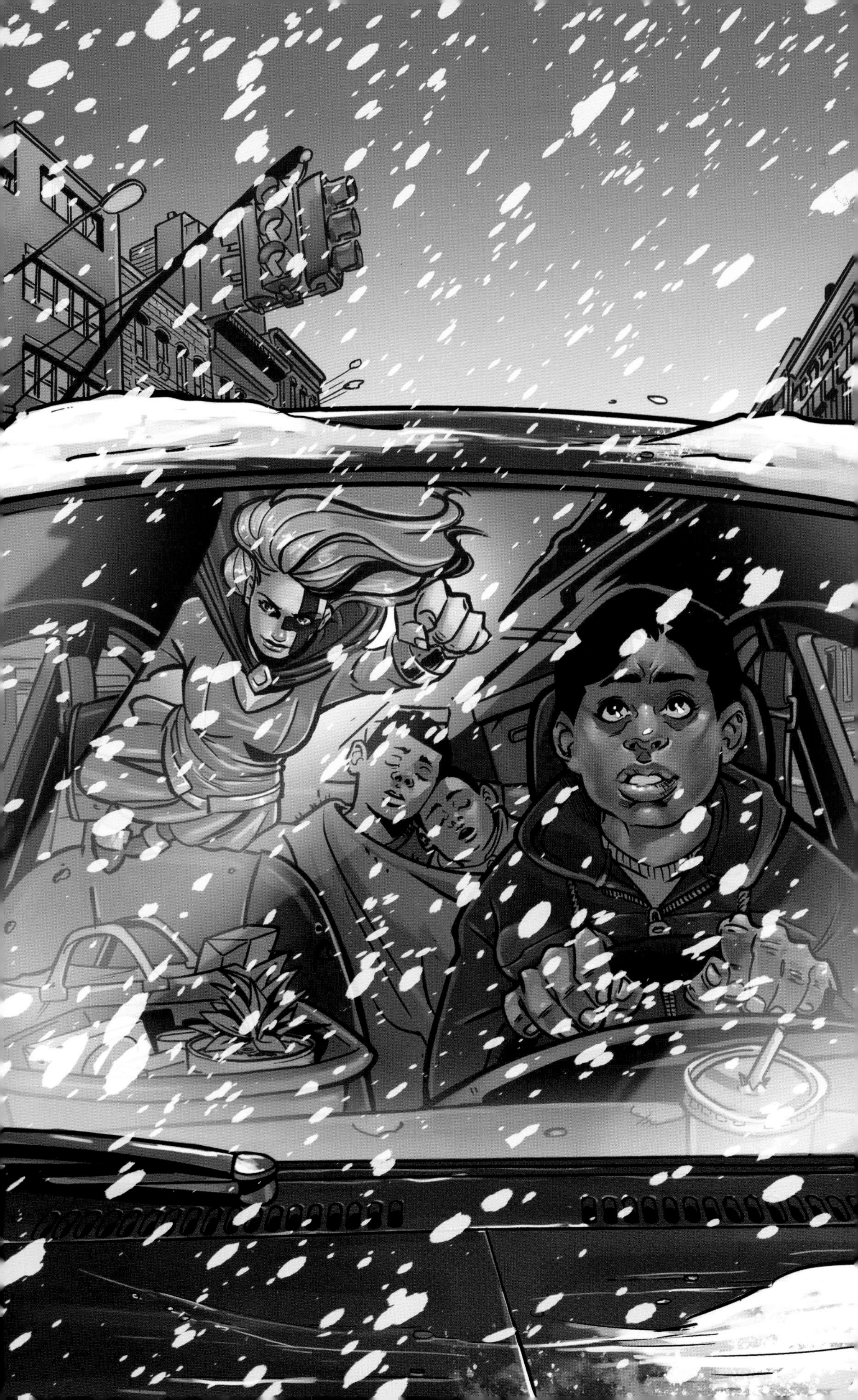

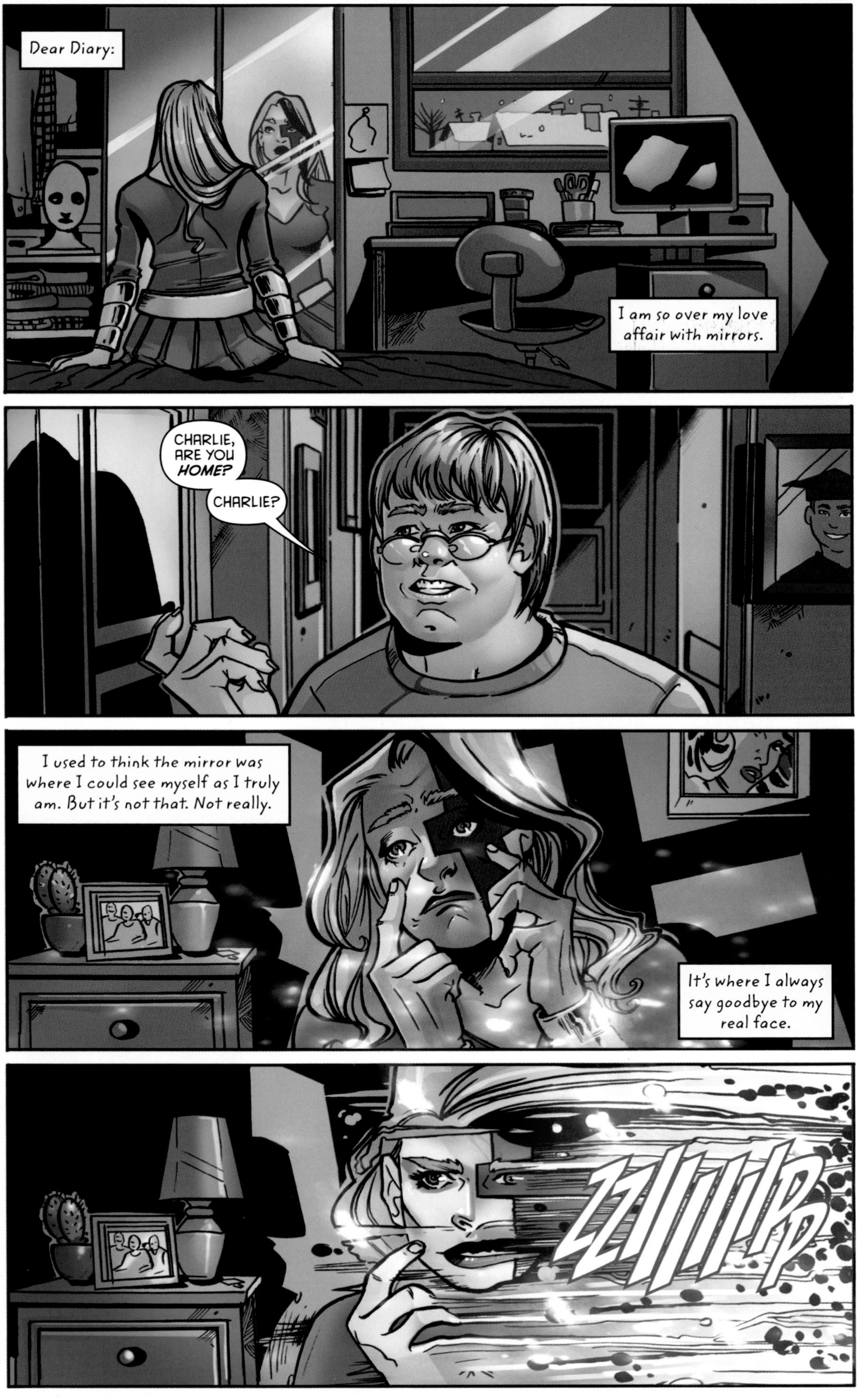

Dear Diary:
I am so over my love affair with mirrors.
CHARLIE, ARE YOU HOME?
CHARLIE?
I used to think the mirror was where I could see myself as I truly am. But it's not that. Not really.
It's where I always say goodbye to my real face.
ZZIIIIIP

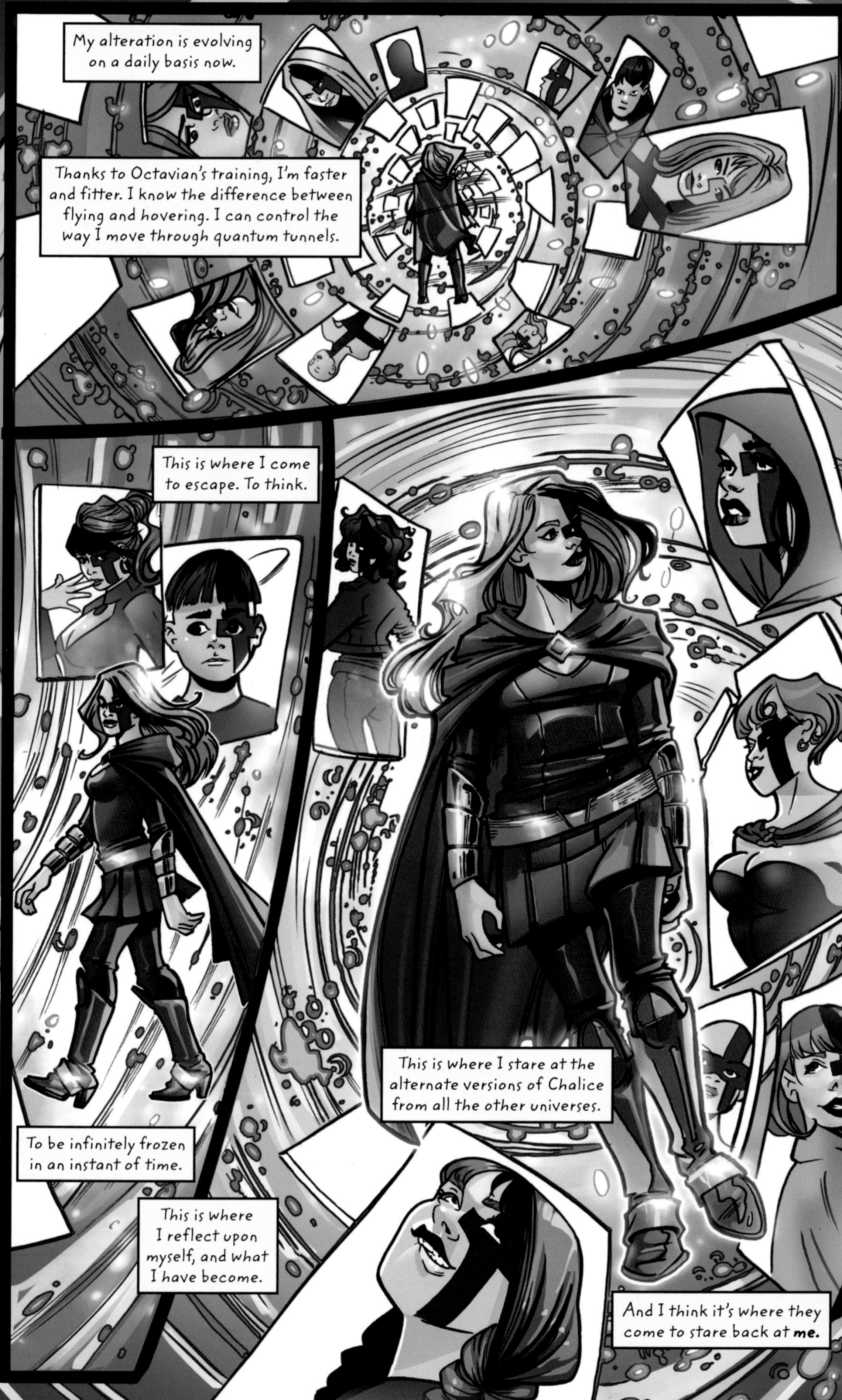
My alteration is evolving on a daily basis now.
Thanks to Octavian's training, I'm faster and fitter. I know the difference between flying and hovering. I can control the way I move through quantum tunnels.
This is where I come to escape. To think.
To be infinitely frozen in an instant of time.
This is where I reflect upon myself, and what I have become.
This is where I stare at the alternate versions of Chalice from all the other universes.
And I think it's where they come to stare back at **me.**

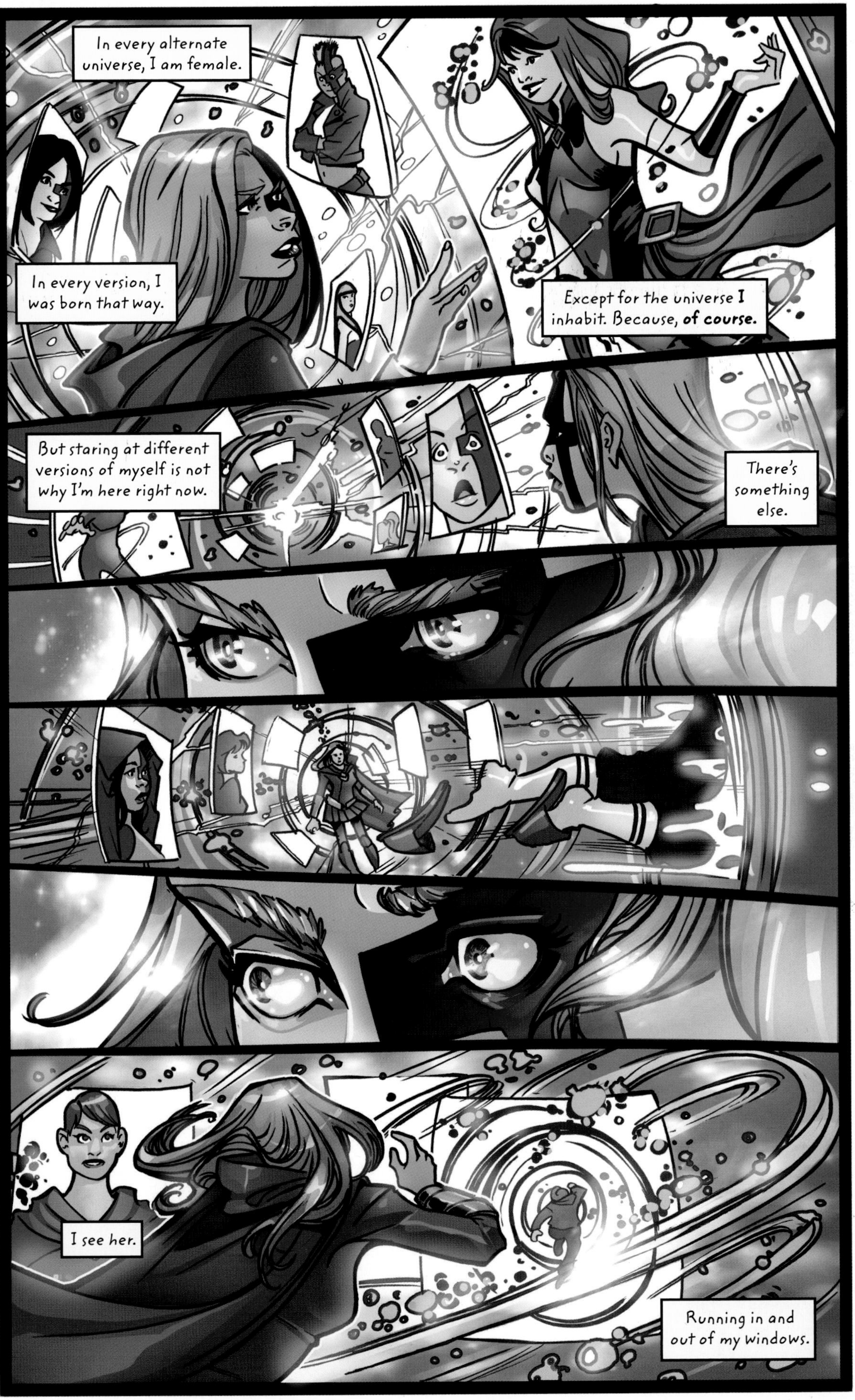
In every alternate universe, I am female.
In every version, I was born that way.
Except for the universe I inhabit. Because, **of course.**
But staring at different versions of myself is not why I'm here right now.
There's something else.
I see her.
Running in and out of my windows.

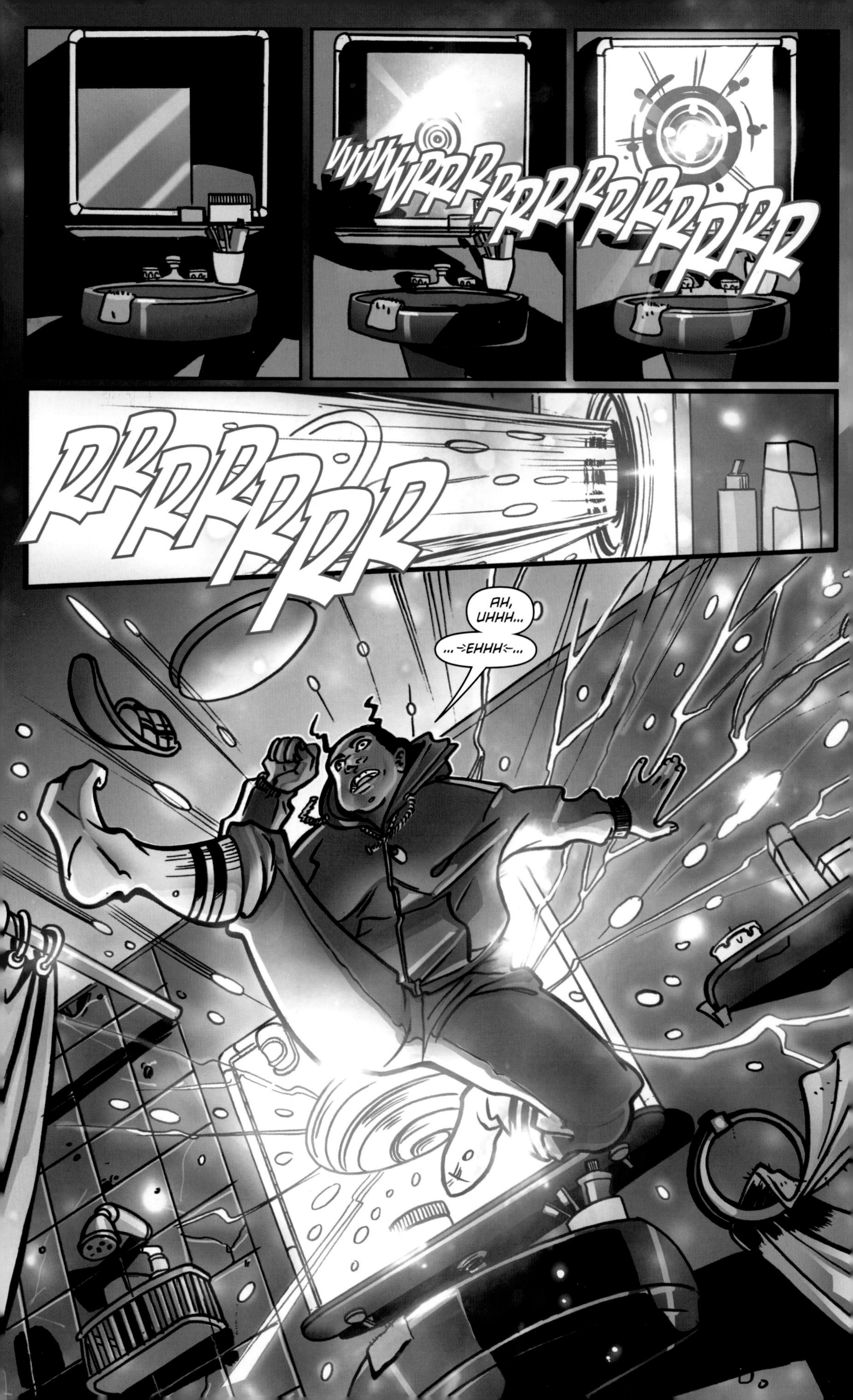
AH, UHHH...
...~EHHH~...

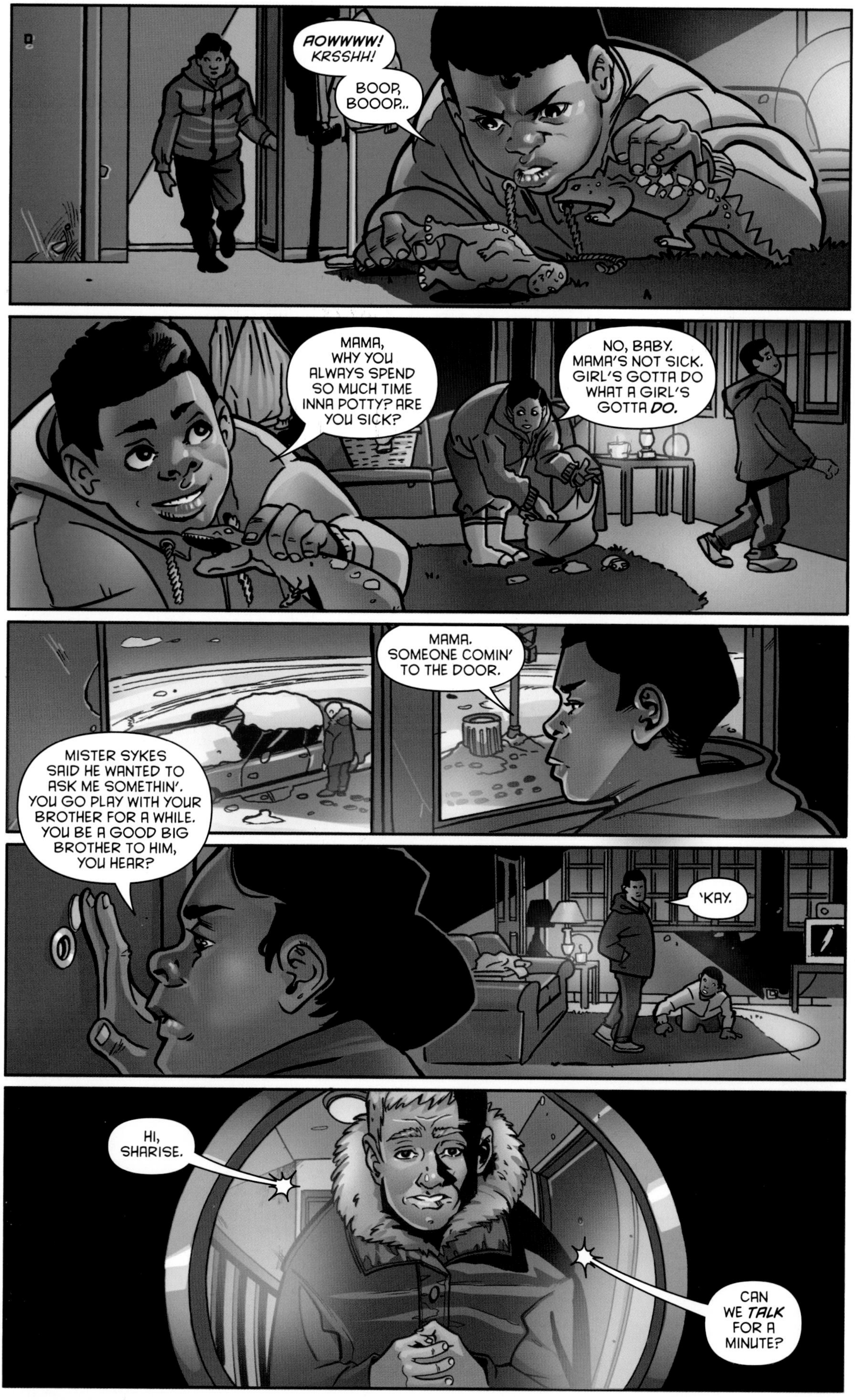
AOWWWW!
KRSSHH!
BOOP, BOOOP...
MAMA, WHY YOU ALWAYS SPEND SO MUCH TIME INNA POTTY? ARE YOU SICK?
NO, BABY. MAMA'S NOT SICK. GIRL'S GOTTA DO WHAT A GIRL'S GOTTA DO.
MAMA. SOMEONE COMIN' TO THE DOOR.
MISTER SYKES SAID HE WANTED TO ASK ME SOMETHIN'. YOU GO PLAY WITH YOUR BROTHER FOR A WHILE. YOU BE A GOOD BIG BROTHER TO HIM, YOU HEAR?
'KAY.
HI, SHARISE.
CAN WE TALK FOR A MINUTE?

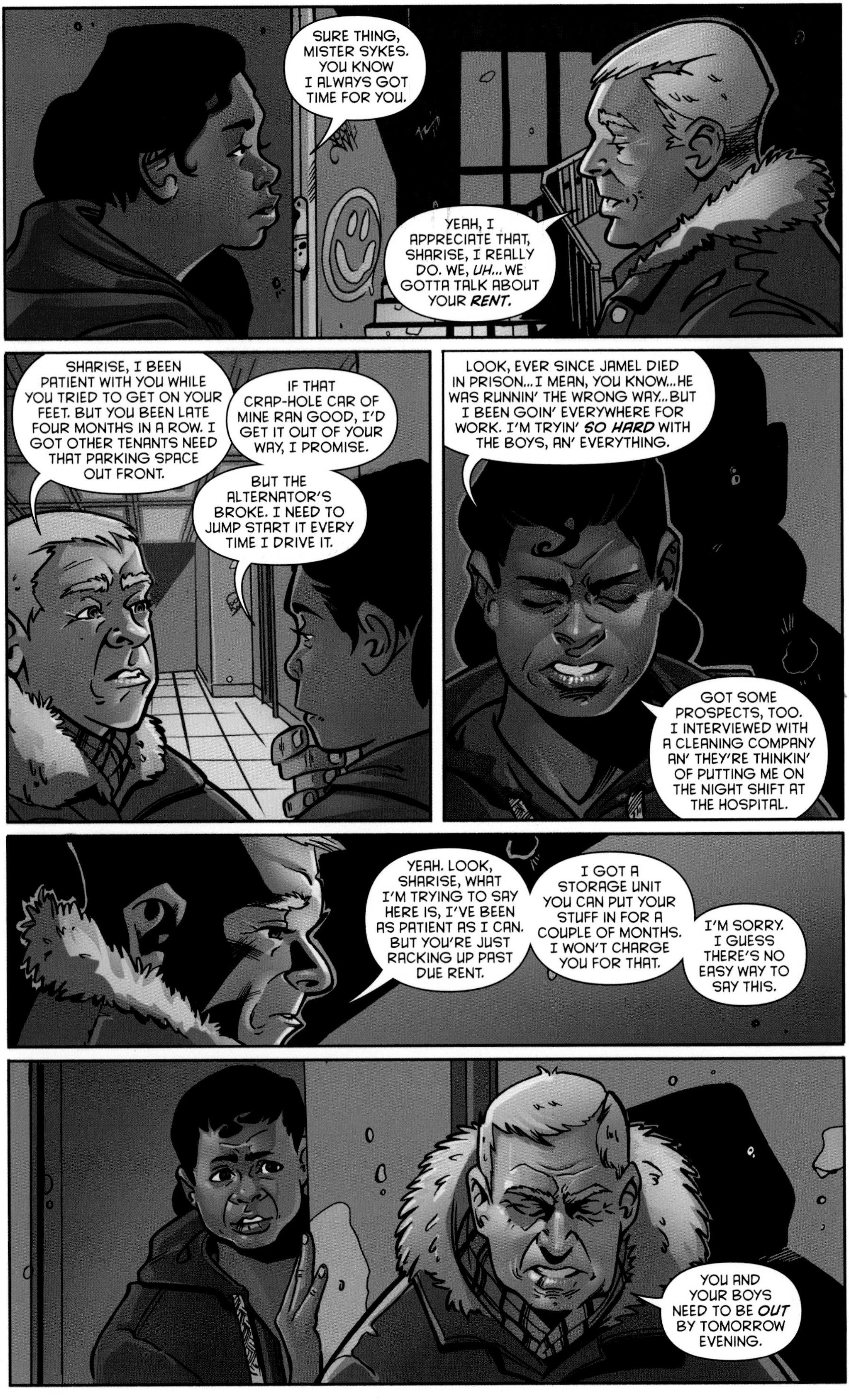
SURE THING, MISTER SYKES. YOU KNOW I ALWAYS GOT TIME FOR YOU.
YEAH, I APPRECIATE THAT, SHARISE, I REALLY DO. WE, *UH...* WE GOTTA TALK ABOUT YOUR ***RENT.***
SHARISE, I BEEN PATIENT WITH YOU WHILE YOU TRIED TO GET ON YOUR FEET. BUT YOU BEEN LATE FOUR MONTHS IN A ROW. I GOT OTHER TENANTS NEED THAT PARKING SPACE OUT FRONT.
IF THAT CRAP-HOLE CAR OF MINE RAN GOOD, I'D GET IT OUT OF YOUR WAY, I PROMISE.
BUT THE ALTERNATOR'S BROKE. I NEED TO JUMP START IT EVERY TIME I DRIVE IT.
LOOK, EVER SINCE JAMEL DIED IN PRISON... I MEAN, YOU KNOW... HE WAS RUNNIN' THE WRONG WAY... BUT I BEEN GOIN' EVERYWHERE FOR WORK. I'M TRYIN' ***SO HARD*** WITH THE BOYS, AN' EVERYTHING.
GOT SOME PROSPECTS, TOO. I INTERVIEWED WITH A CLEANING COMPANY AN' THEY'RE THINKIN' OF PUTTING ME ON THE NIGHT SHIFT AT THE HOSPITAL.
YEAH. LOOK, SHARISE, WHAT I'M TRYING TO SAY HERE IS, I'VE BEEN AS PATIENT AS I CAN. BUT YOU'RE JUST RACKING UP PAST DUE RENT.
I GOT A STORAGE UNIT YOU CAN PUT YOUR STUFF IN FOR A COUPLE OF MONTHS. I WON'T CHARGE YOU FOR THAT.
I'M SORRY. I GUESS THERE'S NO EASY WAY TO SAY THIS.
YOU AND YOUR BOYS NEED TO BE ***OUT*** BY TOMORROW EVENING.

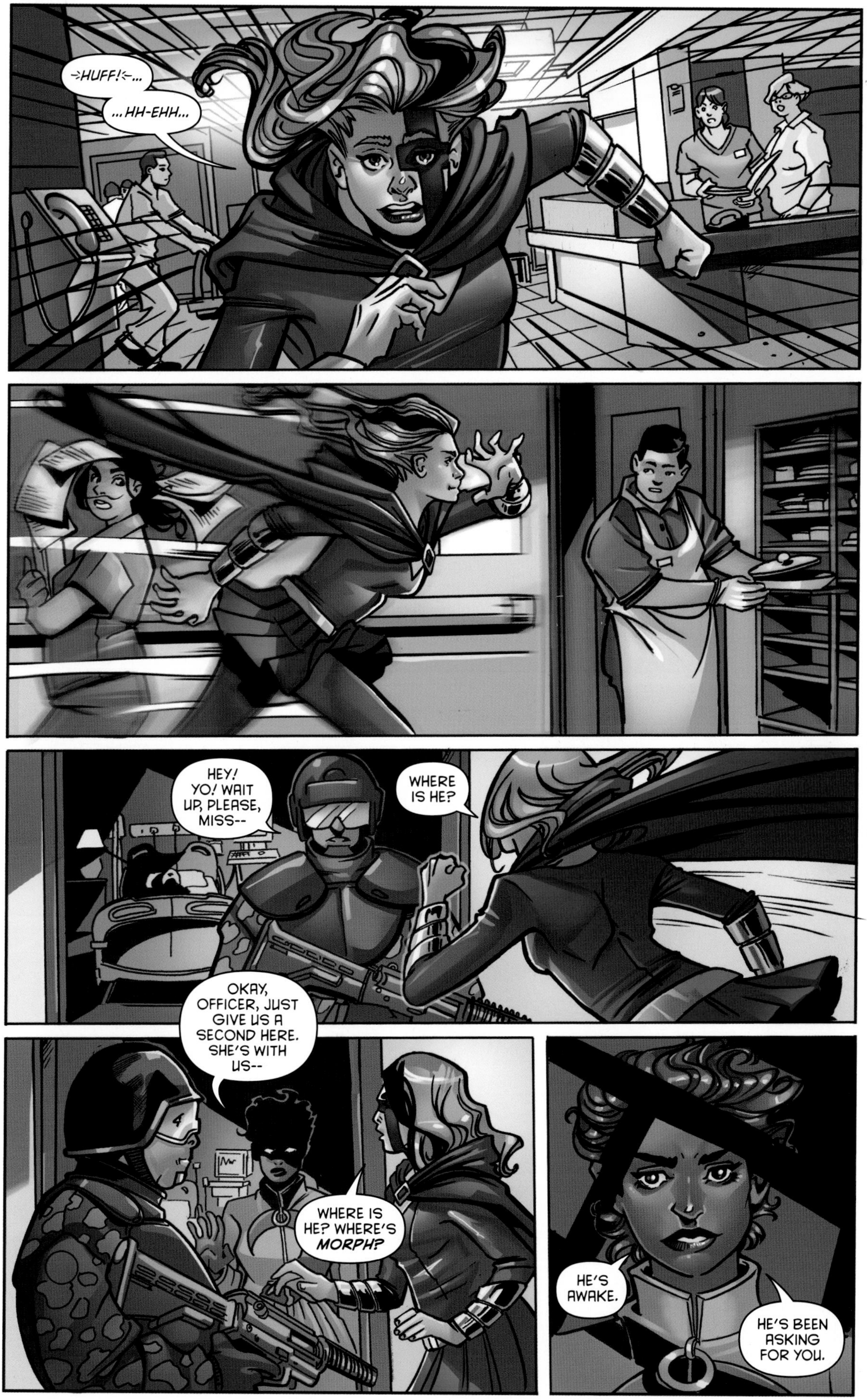

->HUFF!<-...
...HH-EHH...
HEY! YO! WAIT UP, PLEASE, MISS--
WHERE IS HE?
OKAY, OFFICER, JUST GIVE US A SECOND HERE. SHE'S WITH US--
WHERE IS HE? WHERE'S *MORPH?*
HE'S AWAKE.
HE'S BEEN ASKING FOR YOU.

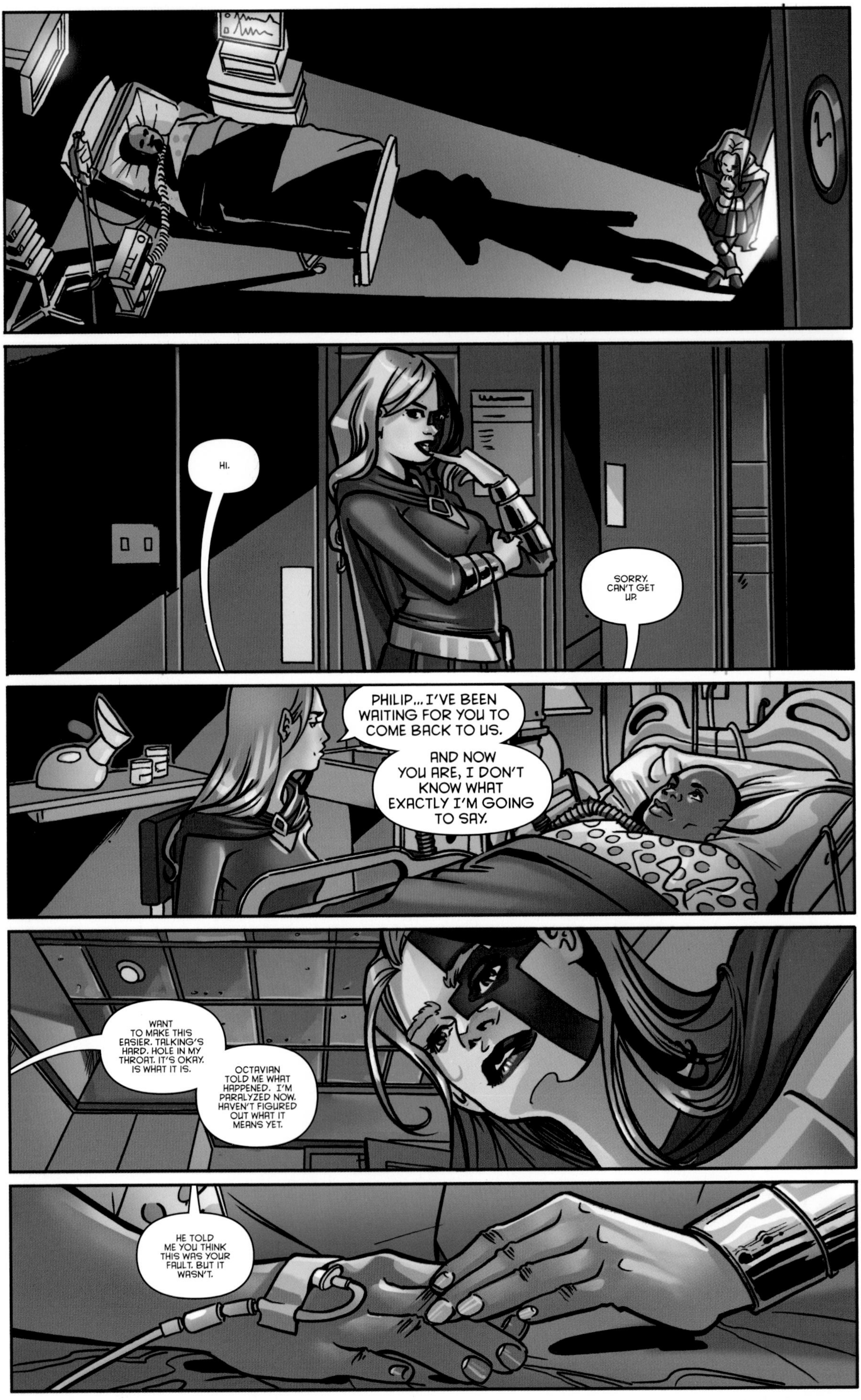
HI.
SORRY. CAN'T GET UP.
PHILIP... I'VE BEEN WAITING FOR YOU TO COME BACK TO US.
AND NOW YOU ARE, I DON'T KNOW WHAT EXACTLY I'M GOING TO SAY.
WANT TO MAKE THIS EASIER. TALKING'S HARD. HOLE IN MY THROAT. IT'S OKAY. IS WHAT IT IS.
OCTAVIAN TOLD ME WHAT HAPPENED. I'M PARALYZED NOW. HAVEN'T FIGURED OUT WHAT IT MEANS YET.
HE TOLD ME YOU THINK THIS WAS YOUR FAULT. BUT IT WASN'T.

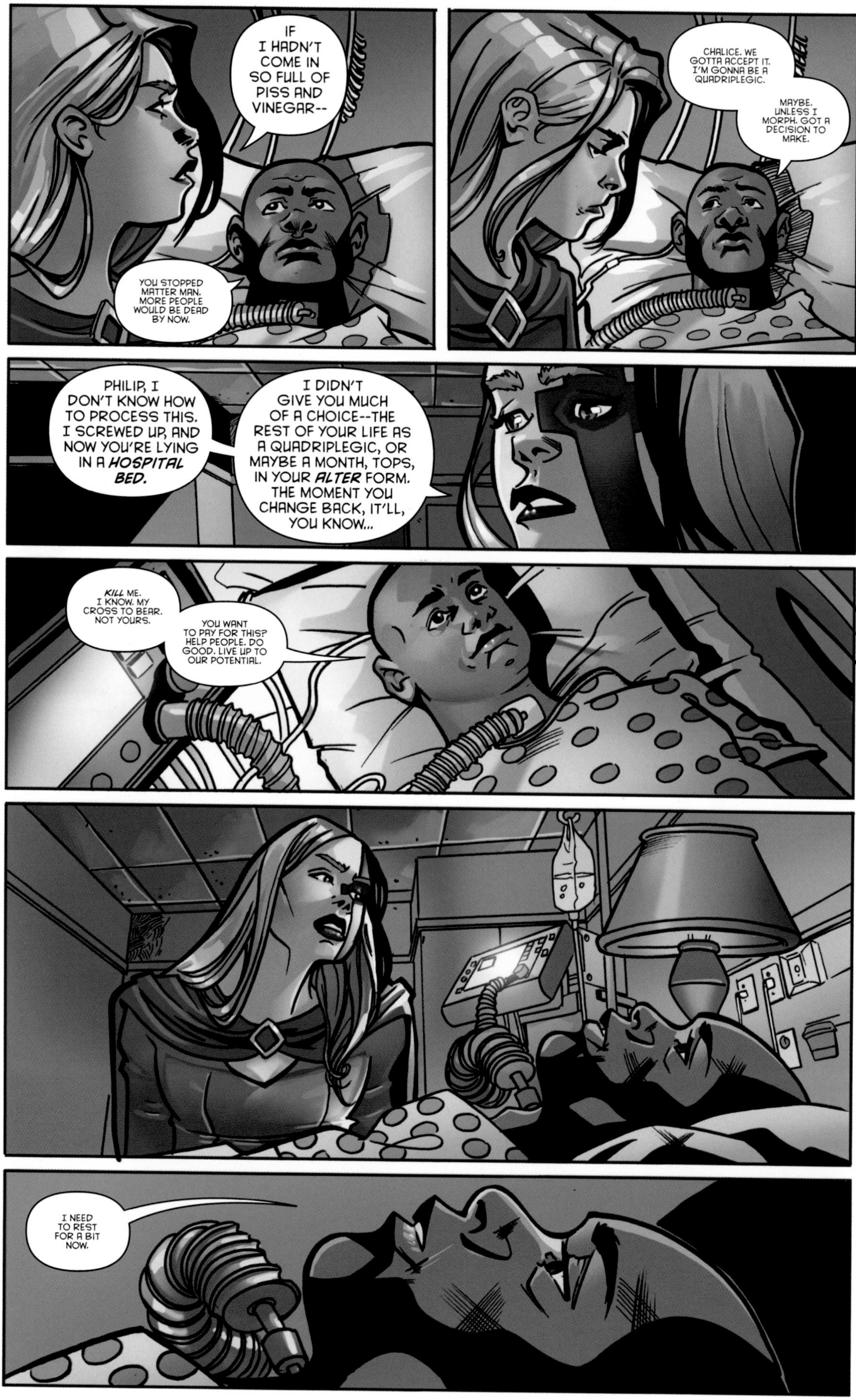
IF I HADN'T COME IN SO FULL OF PISS AND VINEGAR--
YOU STOPPED MATTER MAN. MORE PEOPLE WOULD BE DEAD BY NOW.
CHALICE. WE GOTTA ACCEPT IT. I'M GONNA BE A QUADRIPLEGIC.
MAYBE. UNLESS I MORPH. GOT A DECISION TO MAKE.
PHILIP, I DON'T KNOW HOW TO PROCESS THIS. I SCREWED UP, AND NOW YOU'RE LYING IN A HOSPITAL BED.
I DIDN'T GIVE YOU MUCH OF A CHOICE--THE REST OF YOUR LIFE AS A QUADRIPLEGIC, OR MAYBE A MONTH, TOPS, IN YOUR ALTER FORM. THE MOMENT YOU CHANGE BACK, IT'LL, YOU KNOW...
KILL ME. I KNOW. MY CROSS TO BEAR. NOT YOURS.
YOU WANT TO PAY FOR THIS? HELP PEOPLE. DO GOOD. LIVE UP TO OUR POTENTIAL.
I NEED TO REST FOR A BIT NOW.

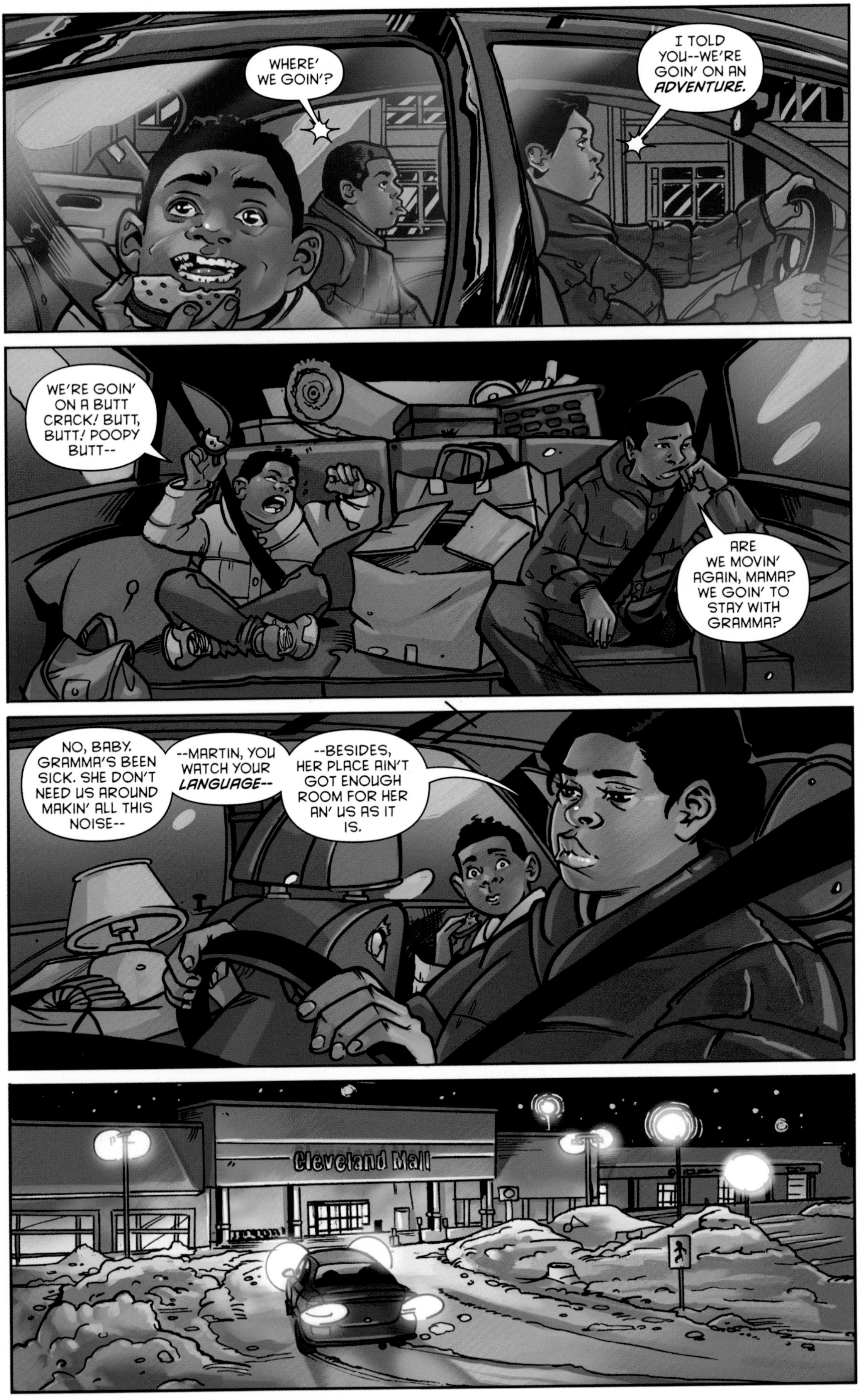

WHERE' WE GOIN'?
I TOLD YOU--WE'RE GOIN' ON AN ADVENTURE.
WE'RE GOIN' ON A BUTT CRACK! BUTT, BUTT! POOPY BUTT--
ARE WE MOVIN' AGAIN, MAMA? WE GOIN' TO STAY WITH GRAMMA?
NO, BABY. GRAMMA'S BEEN SICK. SHE DON'T NEED US AROUND MAKIN' ALL THIS NOISE--
--MARTIN, YOU WATCH YOUR LANGUAGE--
--BESIDES, HER PLACE AIN'T GOT ENOUGH ROOM FOR HER AN' US AS IT IS.
Cleveland Mall

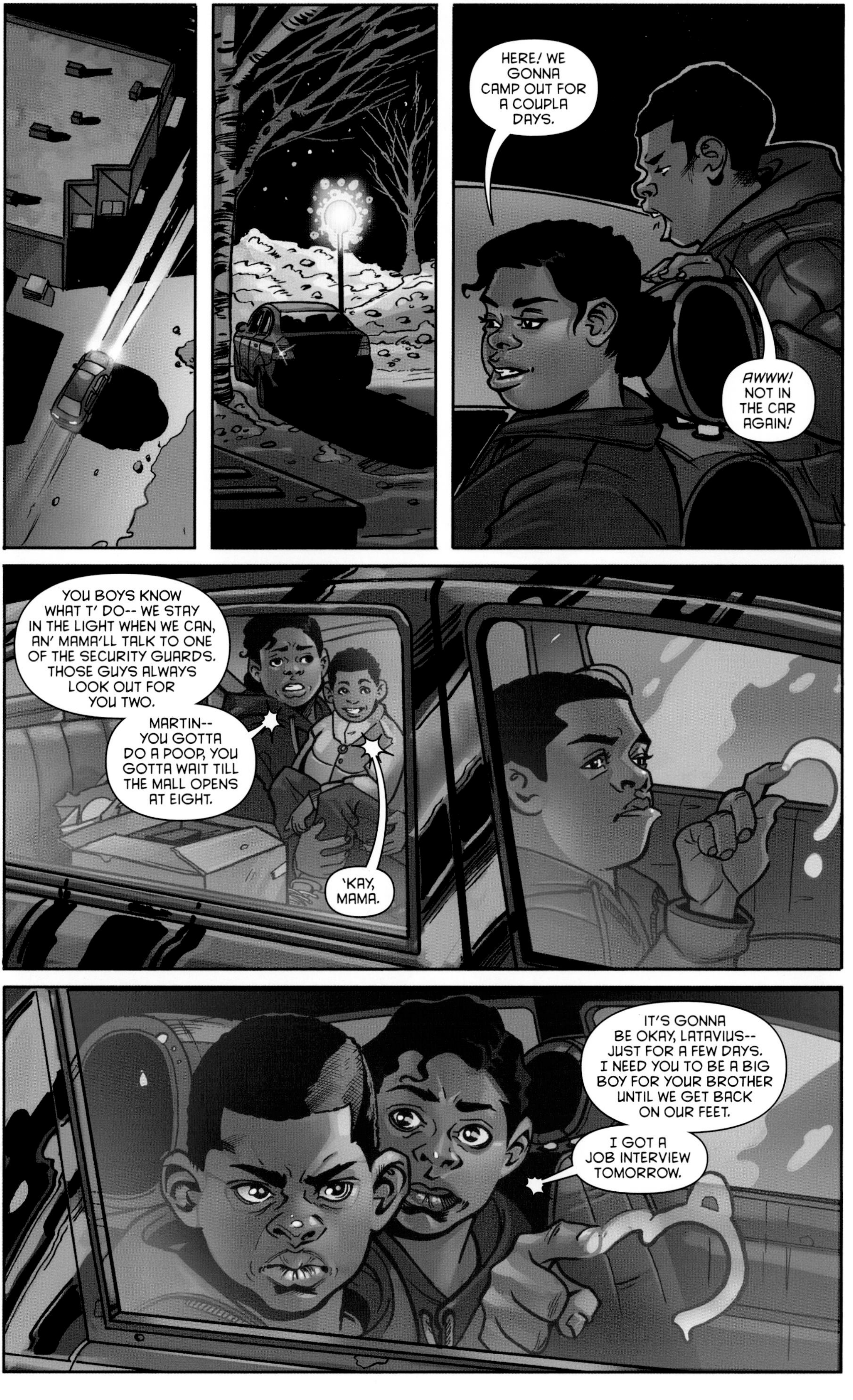
HERE! WE GONNA CAMP OUT FOR A COUPLA DAYS.
AWWW! NOT IN THE CAR AGAIN!
YOU BOYS KNOW WHAT T' DO-- WE STAY IN THE LIGHT WHEN WE CAN, AN' MAMA'LL TALK TO ONE OF THE SECURITY GUARDS. THOSE GUYS ALWAYS LOOK OUT FOR YOU TWO.
MARTIN-- YOU GOTTA DO A POOP, YOU GOTTA WAIT TILL THE MALL OPENS AT EIGHT.
'KAY, MAMA.
IT'S GONNA BE OKAY, LATAVIUS-- JUST FOR A FEW DAYS. I NEED YOU TO BE A BIG BOY FOR YOUR BROTHER UNTIL WE GET BACK ON OUR FEET.
I GOT A JOB INTERVIEW TOMORROW.

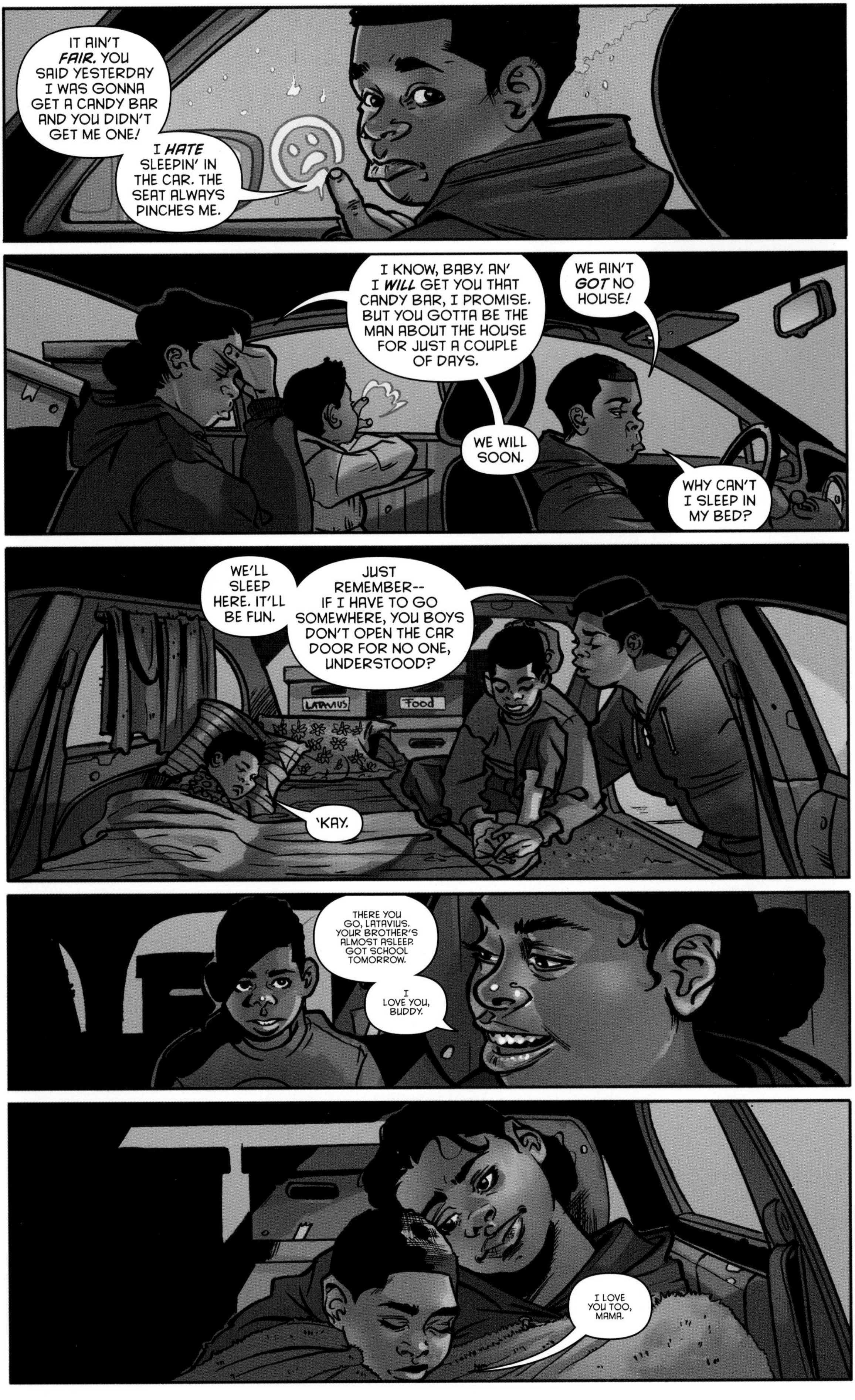
IT AIN'T *FAIR.* YOU SAID YESTERDAY I WAS GONNA GET A CANDY BAR AND YOU DIDN'T GET ME ONE!
I *HATE* SLEEPIN' IN THE CAR. THE SEAT ALWAYS PINCHES ME.
I KNOW, BABY. AN' I *WILL* GET YOU THAT CANDY BAR, I PROMISE. BUT YOU GOTTA BE THE MAN ABOUT THE HOUSE FOR JUST A COUPLE OF DAYS.
WE AIN'T *GOT* NO HOUSE!
WE WILL SOON.
WHY CAN'T I SLEEP IN MY BED?
WE'LL SLEEP HERE. IT'LL BE FUN.
JUST REMEMBER-- IF I HAVE TO GO SOMEWHERE, YOU BOYS DON'T OPEN THE CAR DOOR FOR NO ONE, UNDERSTOOD?
LATAVIUS
Food
'KAY.
THERE YOU GO, LATAVIUS. YOUR BROTHER'S ALMOST ASLEEP. GOT SCHOOL TOMORROW.
I LOVE YOU, BUDDY.
I LOVE YOU TOO, MAMA.

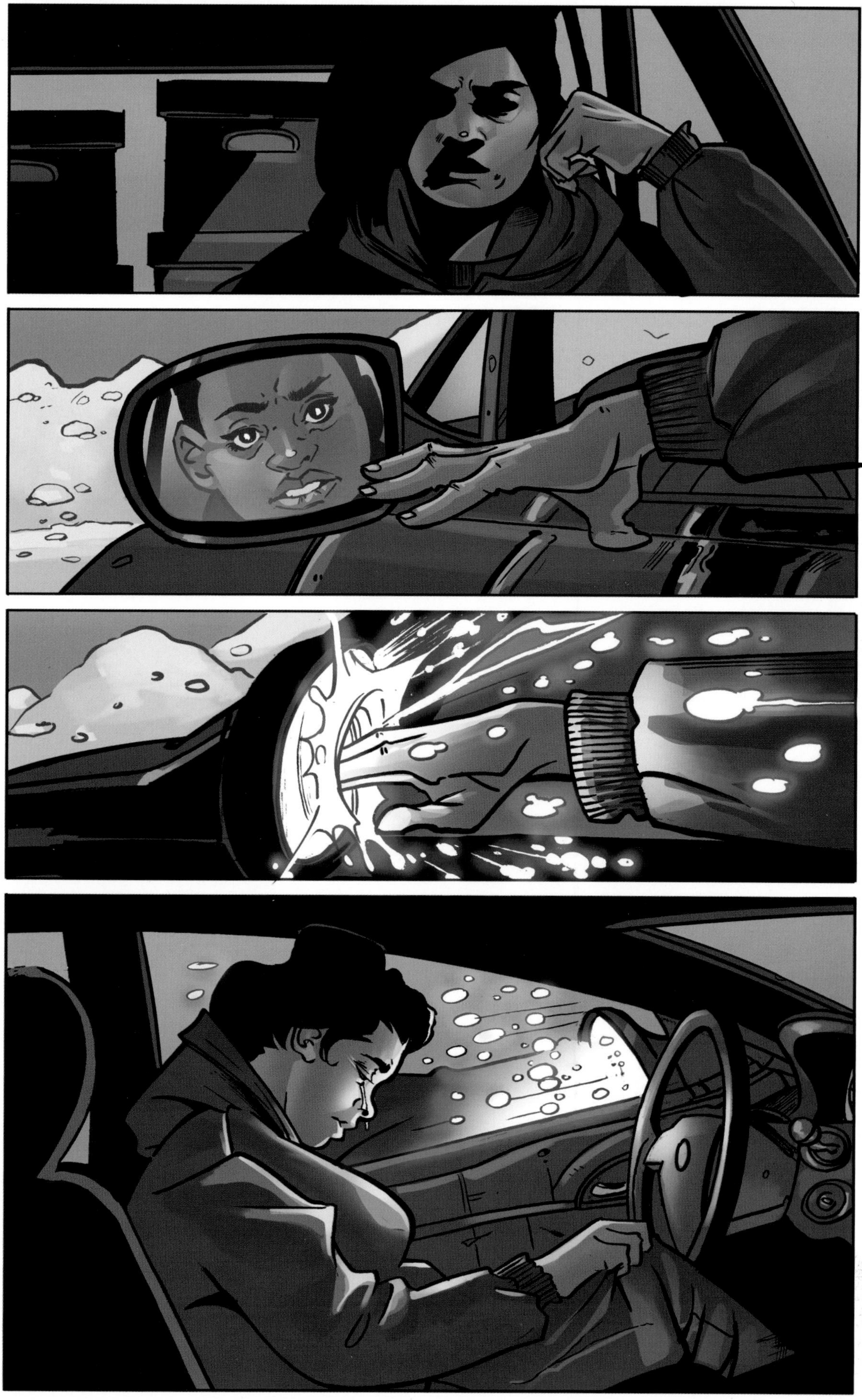

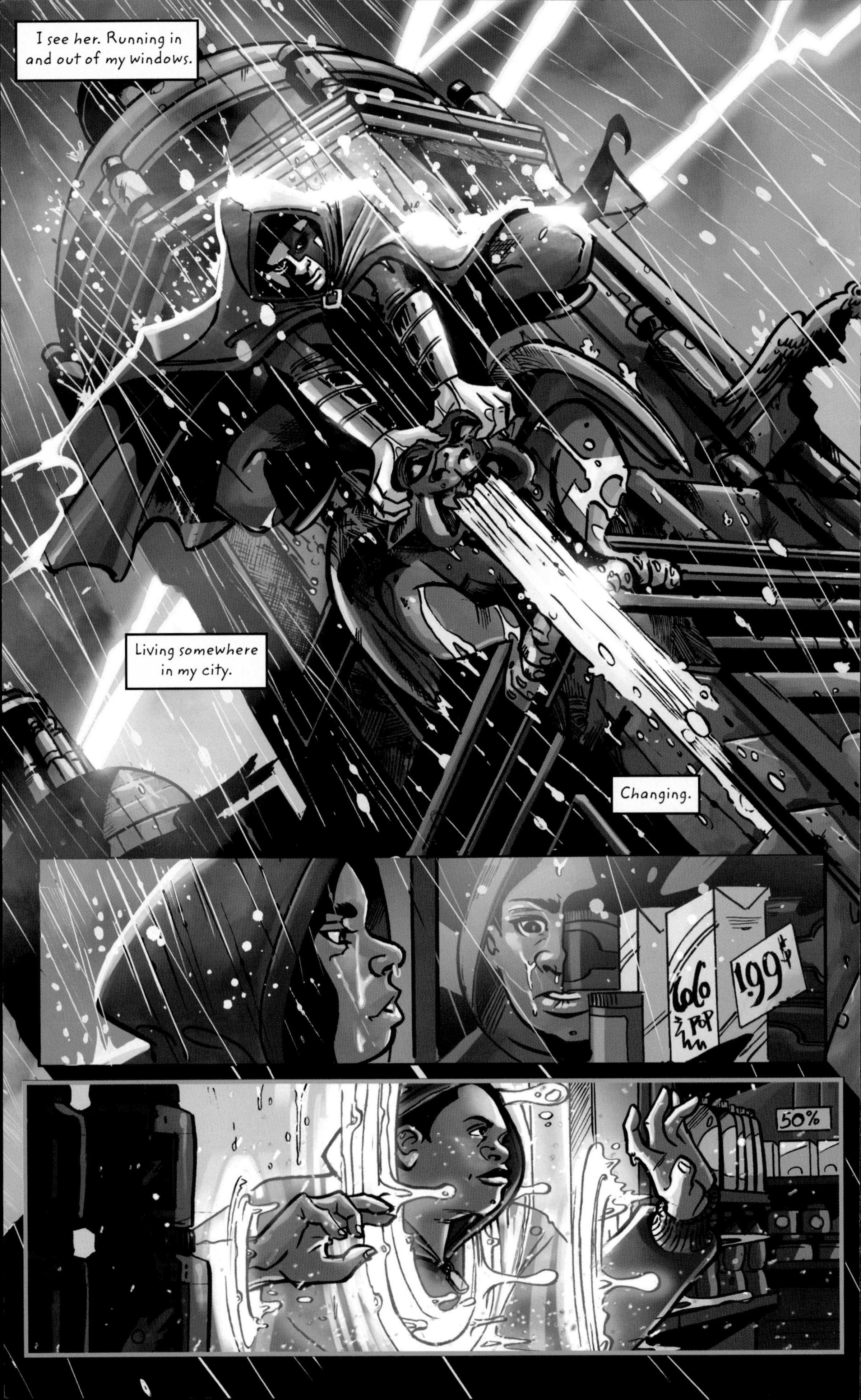
I see her. Running in and out of my windows.
Living somewhere in my city.
Changing.
POP
1.99¢
50%

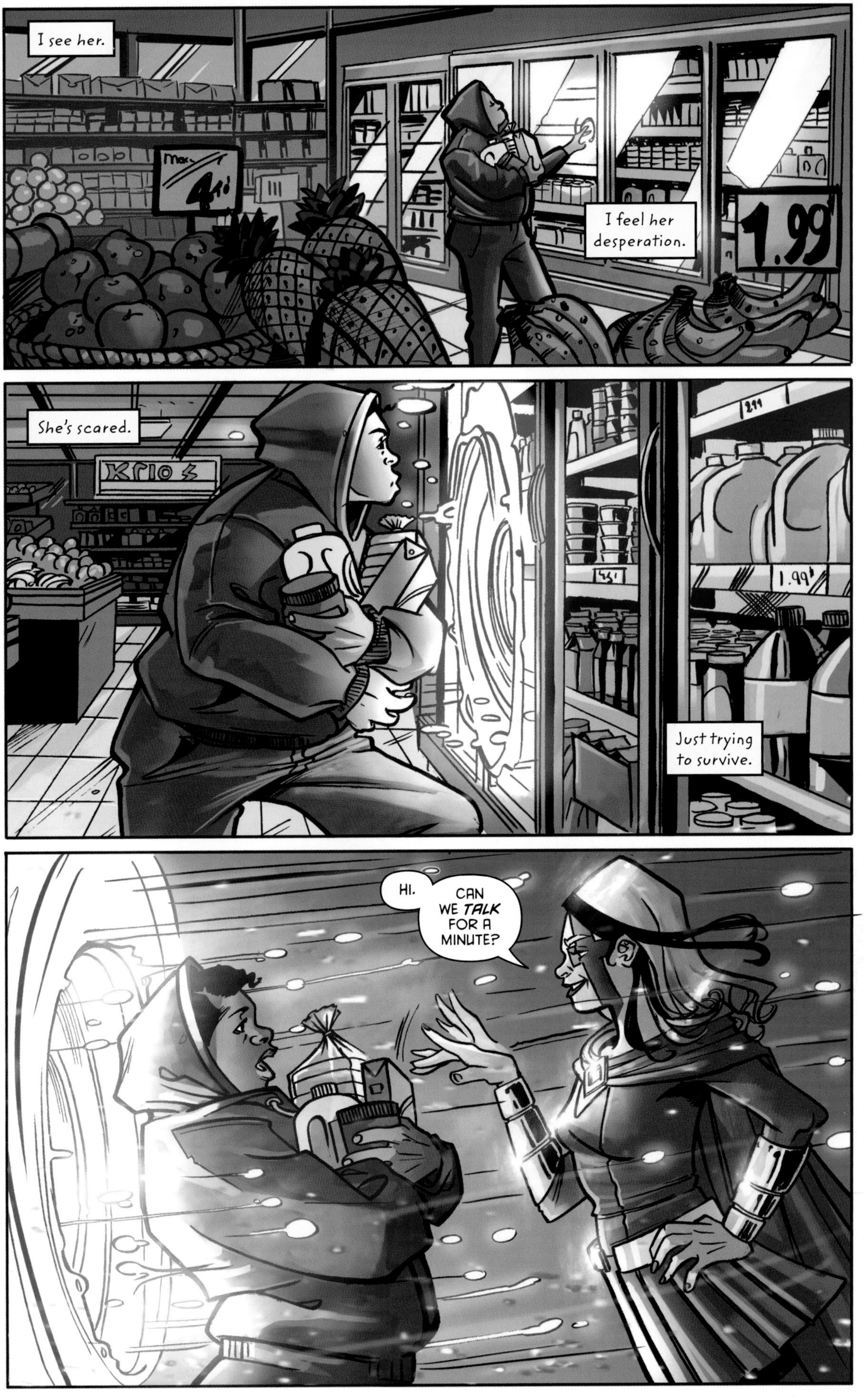
I see her.
I feel her desperation.
She's scared.
Just trying to survive.
HI.
CAN WE TALK FOR A MINUTE?

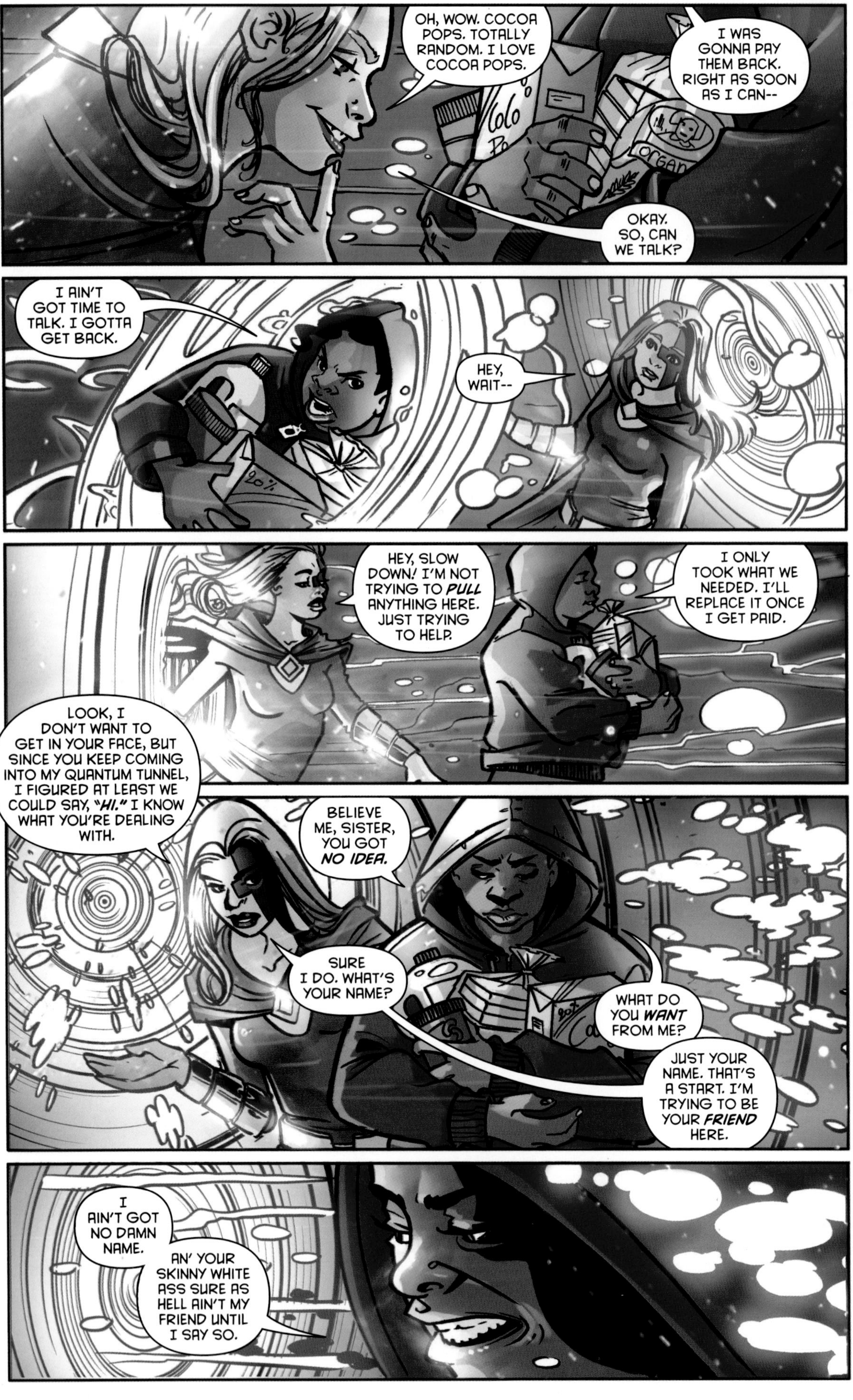

OH, WOW. COCOA POPS. TOTALLY RANDOM. I LOVE COCOA POPS.
I WAS GONNA PAY THEM BACK. RIGHT AS SOON AS I CAN--
OKAY. SO, CAN WE TALK?
I AIN'T GOT TIME TO TALK. I GOTTA GET BACK.
HEY, WAIT--
HEY, SLOW DOWN! I'M NOT TRYING TO PULL ANYTHING HERE. JUST TRYING TO HELP.
I ONLY TOOK WHAT WE NEEDED. I'LL REPLACE IT ONCE I GET PAID.
LOOK, I DON'T WANT TO GET IN YOUR FACE, BUT SINCE YOU KEEP COMING INTO MY QUANTUM TUNNEL, I FIGURED AT LEAST WE COULD SAY, "HI." I KNOW WHAT YOU'RE DEALING WITH.
BELIEVE ME, SISTER, YOU GOT NO IDEA.
SURE I DO. WHAT'S YOUR NAME?
WHAT DO YOU WANT FROM ME?
JUST YOUR NAME. THAT'S A START. I'M TRYING TO BE YOUR FRIEND HERE.
I AIN'T GOT NO DAMN NAME.
AN' YOUR SKINNY WHITE ASS SURE AS HELL AIN'T MY FRIEND UNTIL I SAY SO.

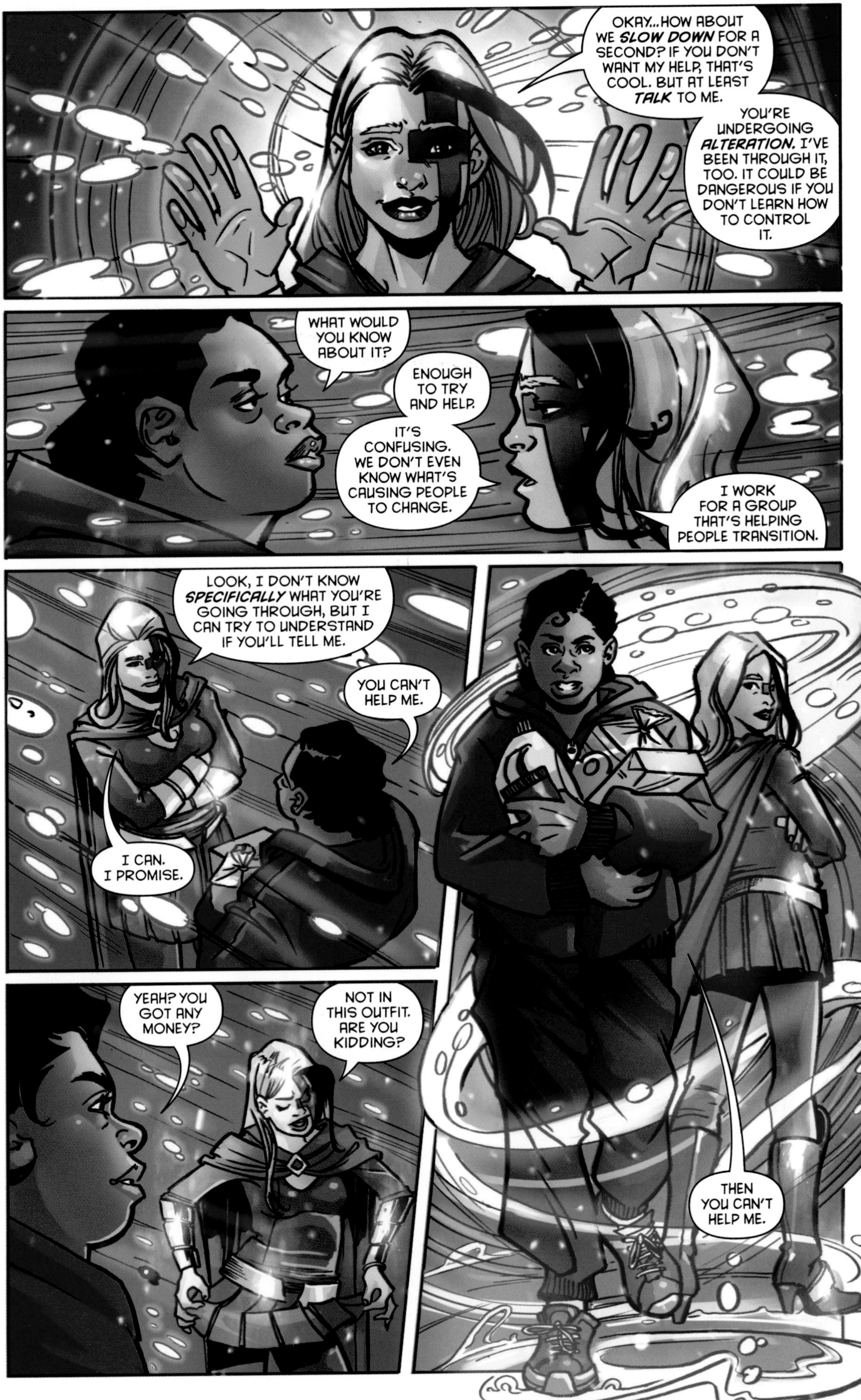
OKAY...HOW ABOUT WE SLOW DOWN FOR A SECOND? IF YOU DON'T WANT MY HELP, THAT'S COOL. BUT AT LEAST TALK TO ME.
YOU'RE UNDERGOING ALTERATION. I'VE BEEN THROUGH IT, TOO. IT COULD BE DANGEROUS IF YOU DON'T LEARN HOW TO CONTROL IT.
WHAT WOULD YOU KNOW ABOUT IT?
ENOUGH TO TRY AND HELP.
IT'S CONFUSING. WE DON'T EVEN KNOW WHAT'S CAUSING PEOPLE TO CHANGE.
I WORK FOR A GROUP THAT'S HELPING PEOPLE TRANSITION.
LOOK, I DON'T KNOW SPECIFICALLY WHAT YOU'RE GOING THROUGH, BUT I CAN TRY TO UNDERSTAND IF YOU'LL TELL ME.
YOU CAN'T HELP ME.
I CAN. I PROMISE.
YEAH? YOU GOT ANY MONEY?
NOT IN THIS OUTFIT. ARE YOU KIDDING?
THEN YOU CAN'T HELP ME.

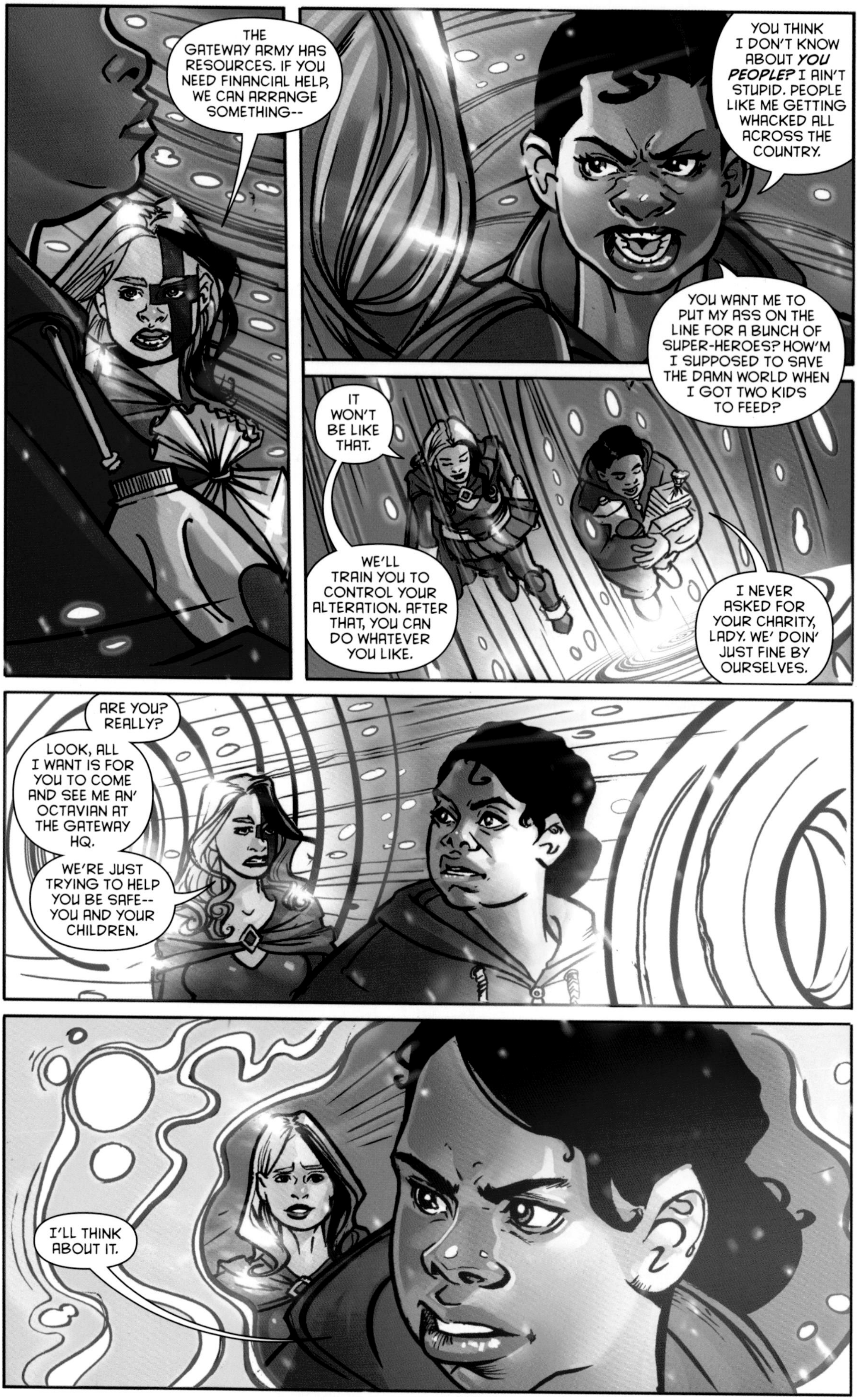
THE GATEWAY ARMY HAS RESOURCES. IF YOU NEED FINANCIAL HELP, WE CAN ARRANGE SOMETHING--
YOU THINK I DON'T KNOW ABOUT YOU PEOPLE? I AIN'T STUPID. PEOPLE LIKE ME GETTING WHACKED ALL ACROSS THE COUNTRY.
YOU WANT ME TO PUT MY ASS ON THE LINE FOR A BUNCH OF SUPER-HEROES? HOW'M I SUPPOSED TO SAVE THE DAMN WORLD WHEN I GOT TWO KIDS TO FEED?
IT WON'T BE LIKE THAT.
WE'LL TRAIN YOU TO CONTROL YOUR ALTERATION. AFTER THAT, YOU CAN DO WHATEVER YOU LIKE.
I NEVER ASKED FOR YOUR CHARITY, LADY. WE' DOIN' JUST FINE BY OURSELVES.
ARE YOU? REALLY?
LOOK, ALL I WANT IS FOR YOU TO COME AND SEE ME AN' OCTAVIAN AT THE GATEWAY HQ.
WE'RE JUST TRYING TO HELP YOU BE SAFE-- YOU AND YOUR CHILDREN.
I'LL THINK ABOUT IT.

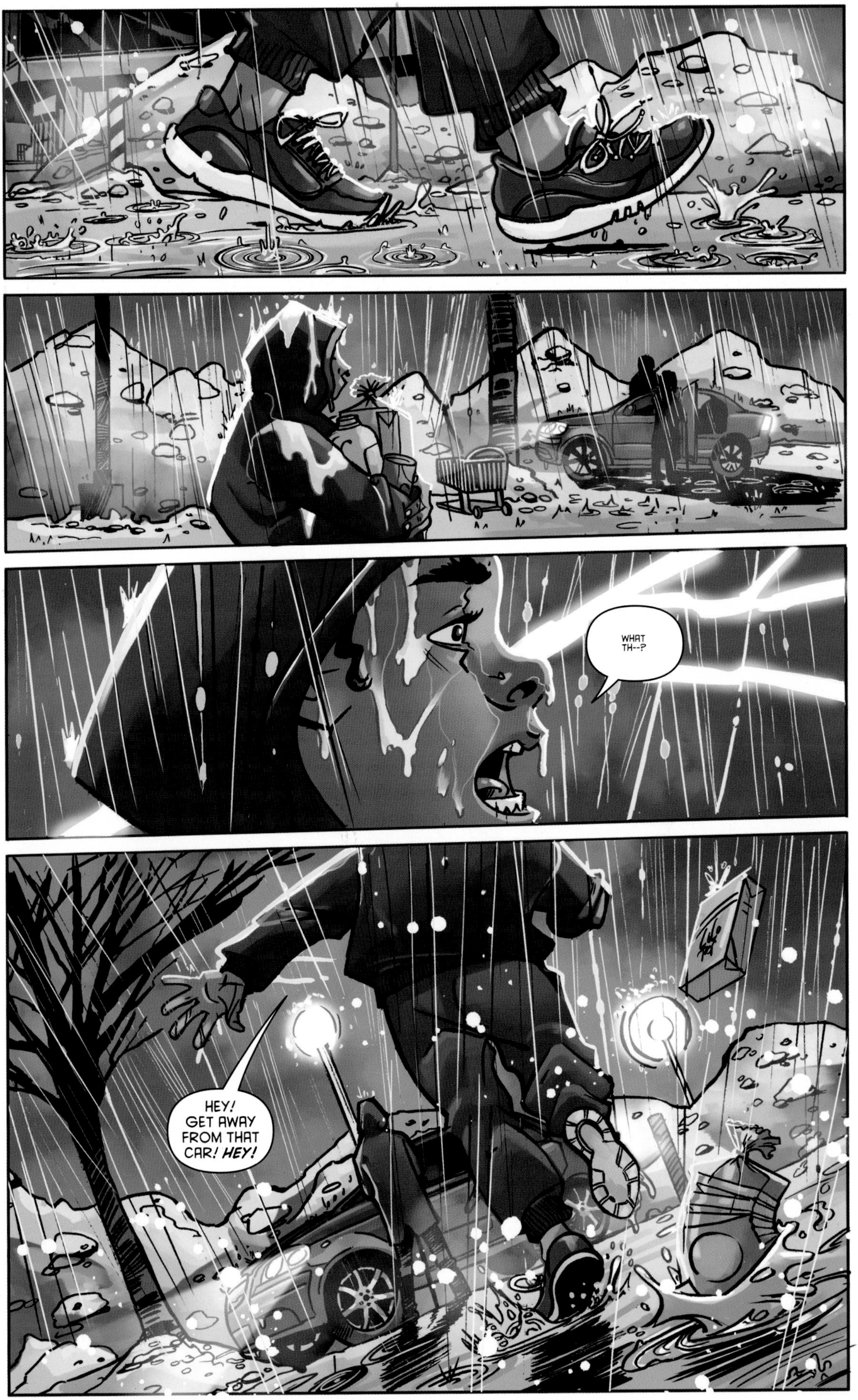
WHAT TH--?
HEY! GET AWAY FROM THAT CAR! HEY!

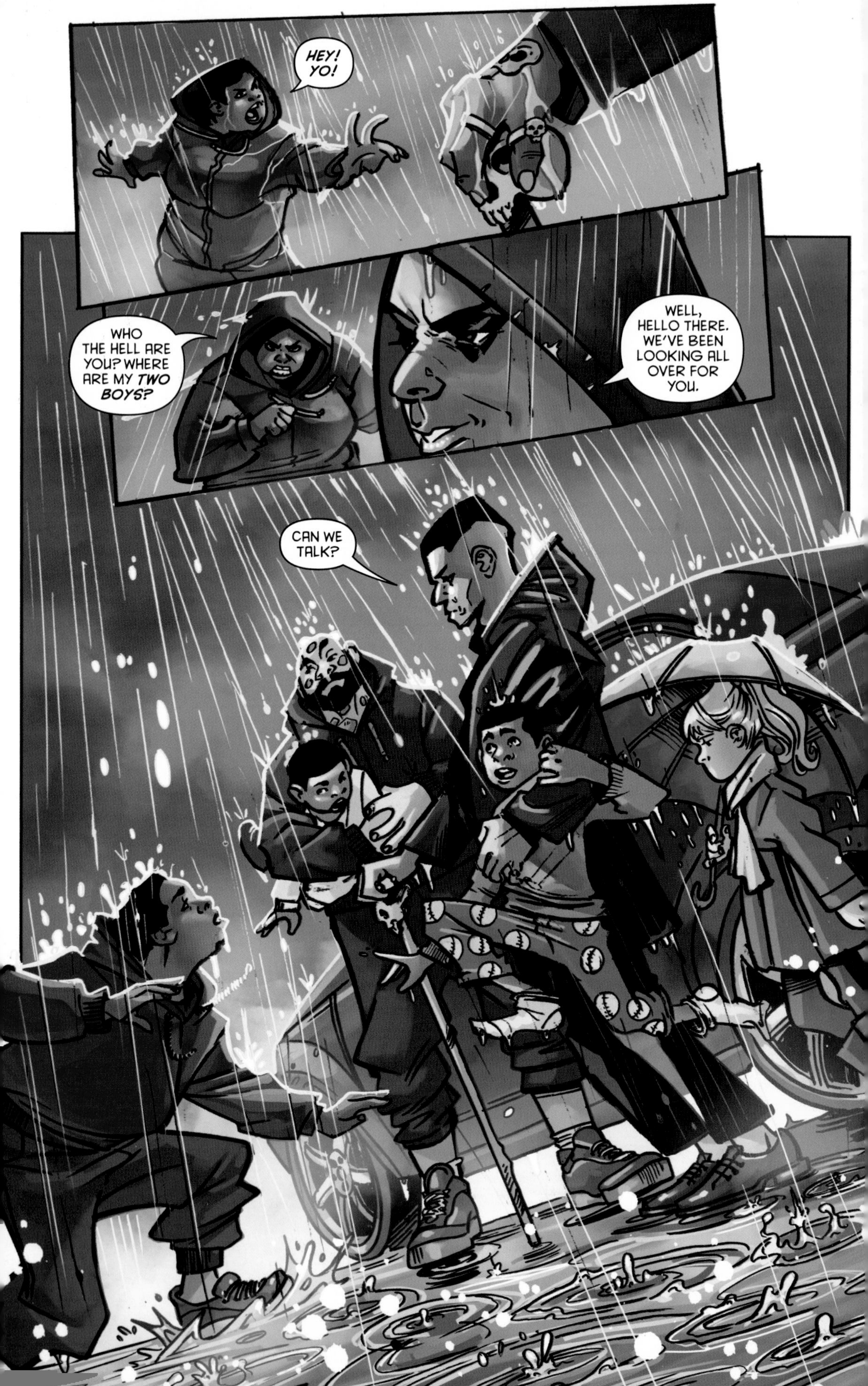
HEY! YO!
WHO THE HELL ARE YOU? WHERE ARE MY *TWO BOYS*?
WELL, HELLO THERE. WE'VE BEEN LOOKING ALL OVER FOR YOU.
CAN WE TALK?

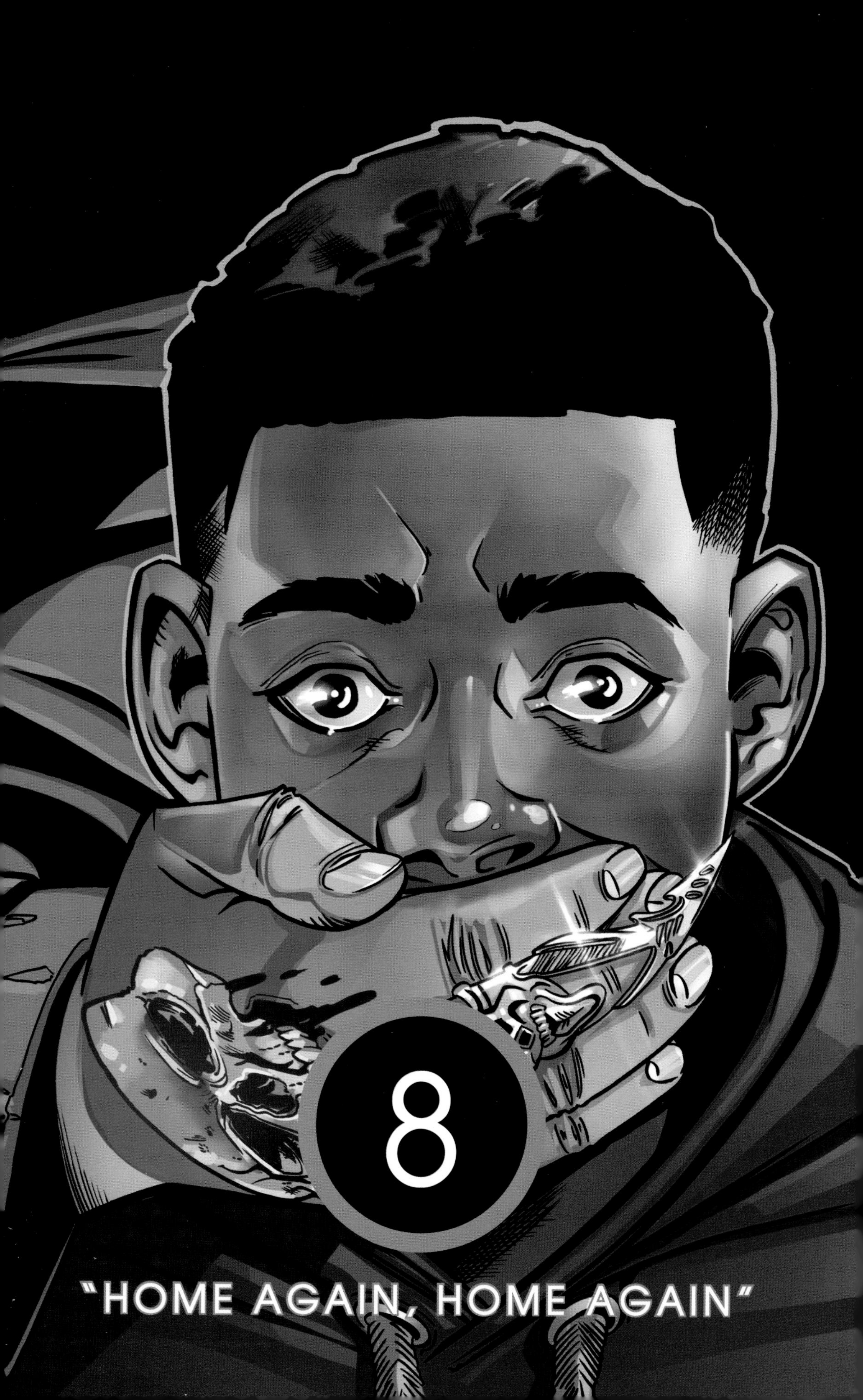

8

"HOME AGAIN, HOME AGAIN"

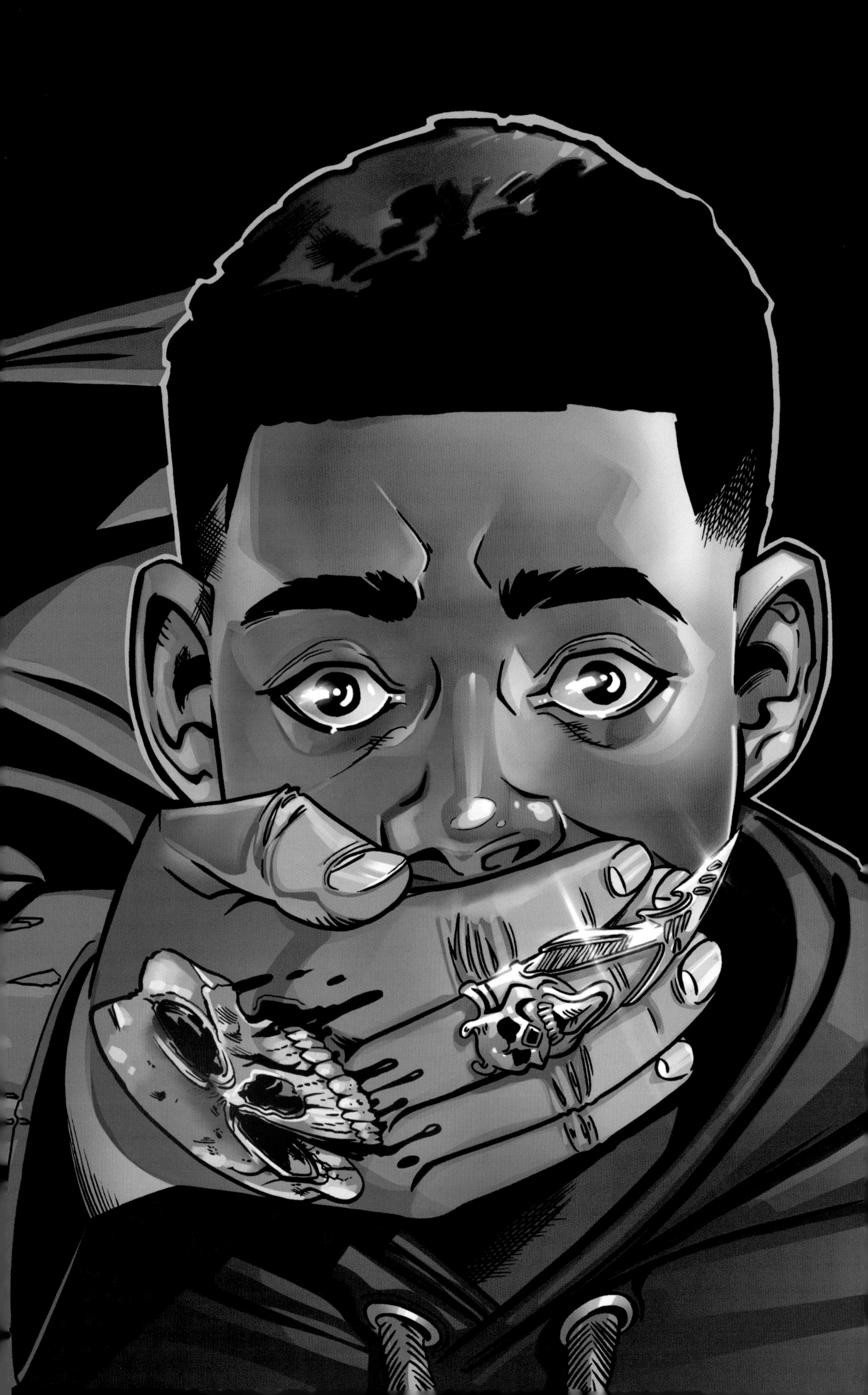

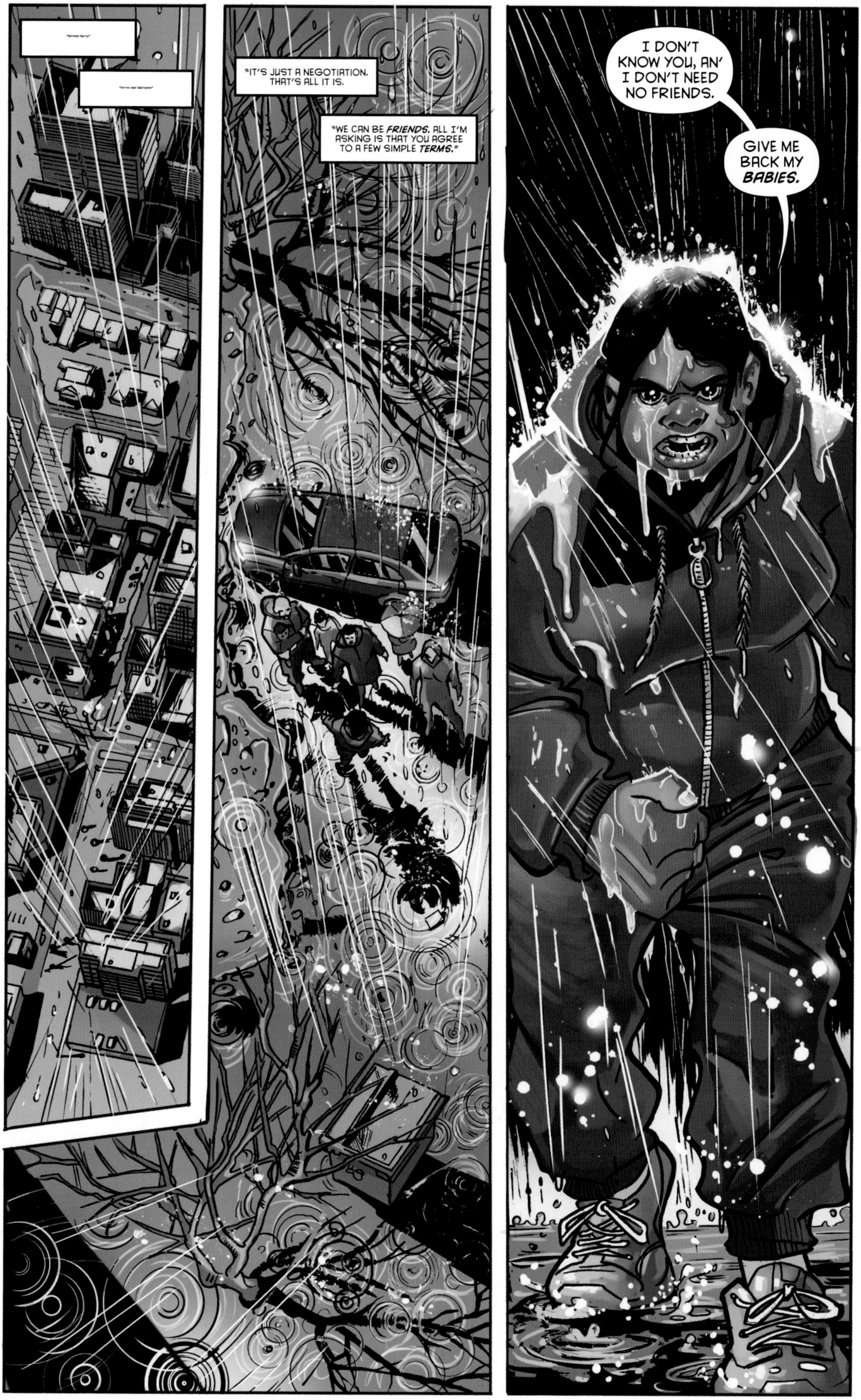
"IT'S JUST A NEGOTIATION. THAT'S ALL IT IS.
"WE CAN BE FRIENDS. ALL I'M ASKING IS THAT YOU AGREE TO A FEW SIMPLE TERMS."
I DON'T KNOW YOU, AN' I DON'T NEED NO FRIENDS.
GIVE ME BACK MY BABIES.

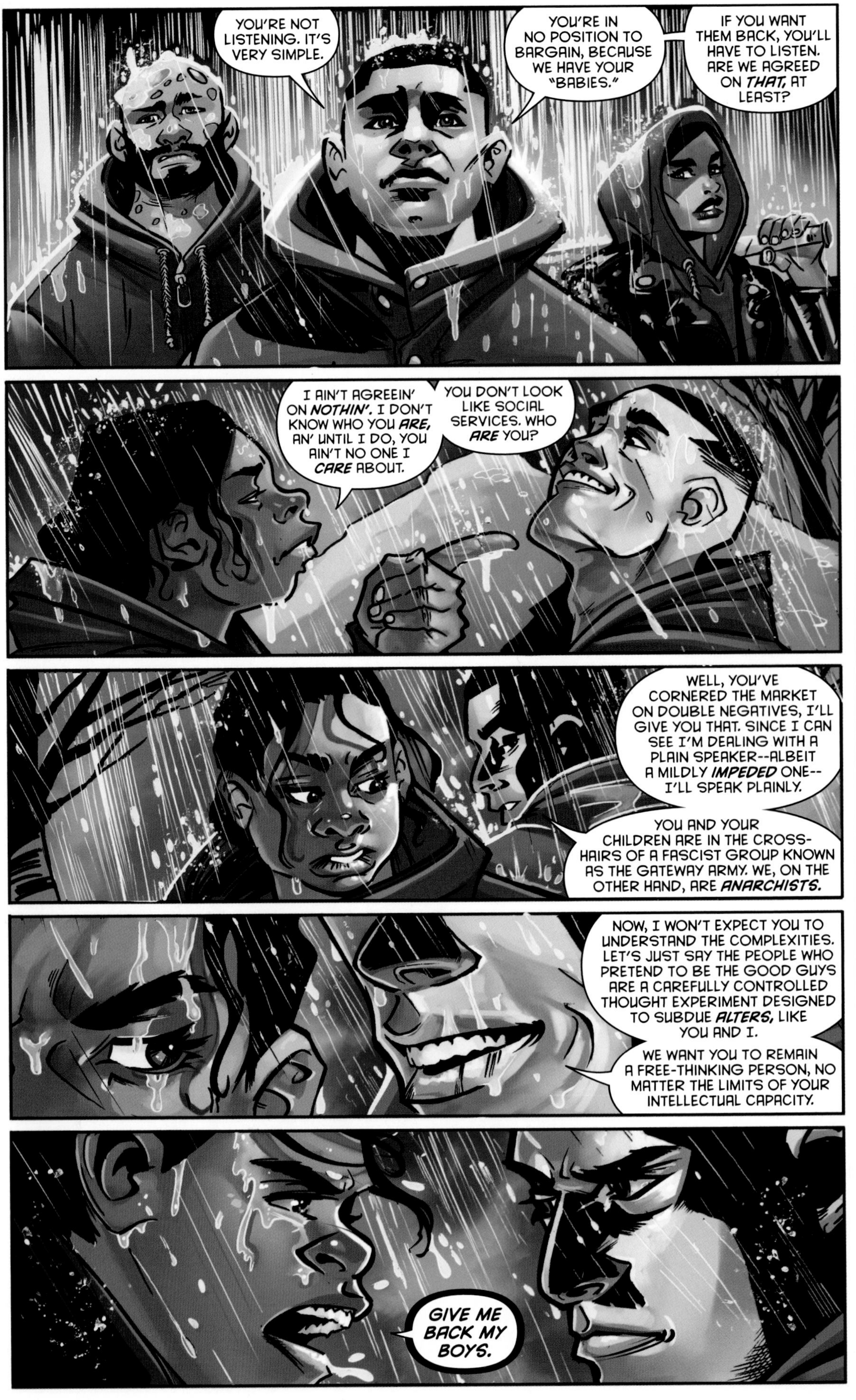
YOU'RE NOT LISTENING. IT'S VERY SIMPLE.
YOU'RE IN NO POSITION TO BARGAIN, BECAUSE WE HAVE YOUR "BABIES."
IF YOU WANT THEM BACK, YOU'LL HAVE TO LISTEN. ARE WE AGREED ON *THAT,* AT LEAST?
I AIN'T AGREEIN' ON *NOTHIN'.* I DON'T KNOW WHO YOU *ARE,* AN' UNTIL I DO, YOU AIN'T NO ONE I *CARE* ABOUT.
YOU DON'T LOOK LIKE SOCIAL SERVICES. WHO *ARE* YOU?
WELL, YOU'VE CORNERED THE MARKET ON DOUBLE NEGATIVES, I'LL GIVE YOU THAT. SINCE I CAN SEE I'M DEALING WITH A PLAIN SPEAKER--ALBEIT A MILDLY *IMPEDED* ONE--I'LL SPEAK PLAINLY.
YOU AND YOUR CHILDREN ARE IN THE CROSS-HAIRS OF A FASCIST GROUP KNOWN AS THE GATEWAY ARMY. WE, ON THE OTHER HAND, ARE *ANARCHISTS.*
NOW, I WON'T EXPECT YOU TO UNDERSTAND THE COMPLEXITIES. LET'S JUST SAY THE PEOPLE WHO PRETEND TO BE THE GOOD GUYS ARE A CAREFULLY CONTROLLED THOUGHT EXPERIMENT DESIGNED TO SUBDUE *ALTERS,* LIKE YOU AND I.
WE WANT YOU TO REMAIN A FREE-THINKING PERSON, NO MATTER THE LIMITS OF YOUR INTELLECTUAL CAPACITY.
GIVE ME BACK MY BOYS.

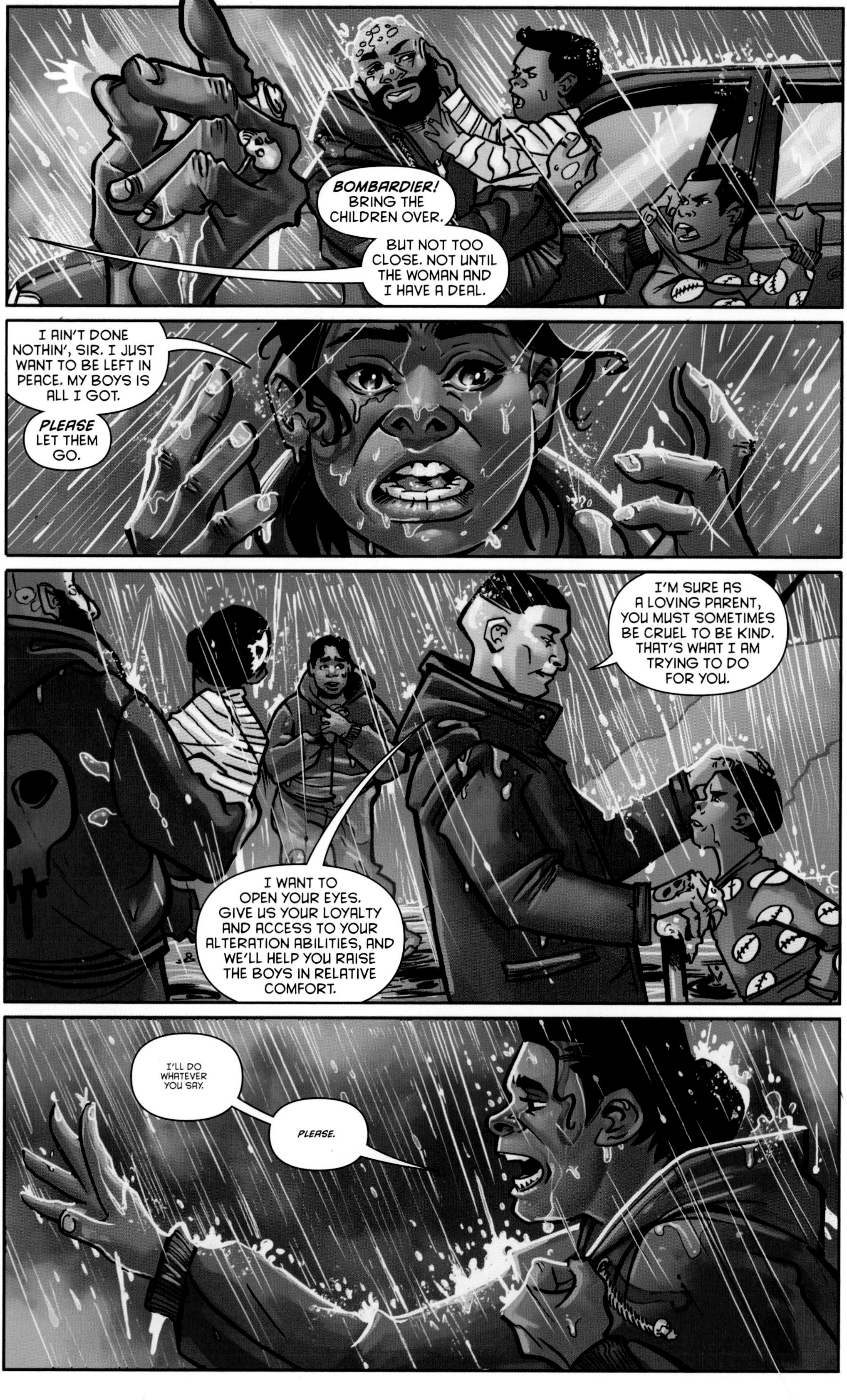
BOMBARDIER! BRING THE CHILDREN OVER.
BUT NOT TOO CLOSE. NOT UNTIL THE WOMAN AND I HAVE A DEAL.
I AIN'T DONE NOTHIN', SIR. I JUST WANT TO BE LEFT IN PEACE. MY BOYS IS ALL I GOT.
PLEASE LET THEM GO.
I'M SURE AS A LOVING PARENT, YOU MUST SOMETIMES BE CRUEL TO BE KIND. THAT'S WHAT I AM TRYING TO DO FOR YOU.
I WANT TO OPEN YOUR EYES. GIVE US YOUR LOYALTY AND ACCESS TO YOUR ALTERATION ABILITIES, AND WE'LL HELP YOU RAISE THE BOYS IN RELATIVE COMFORT.
I'LL DO WHATEVER YOU SAY.
PLEASE.

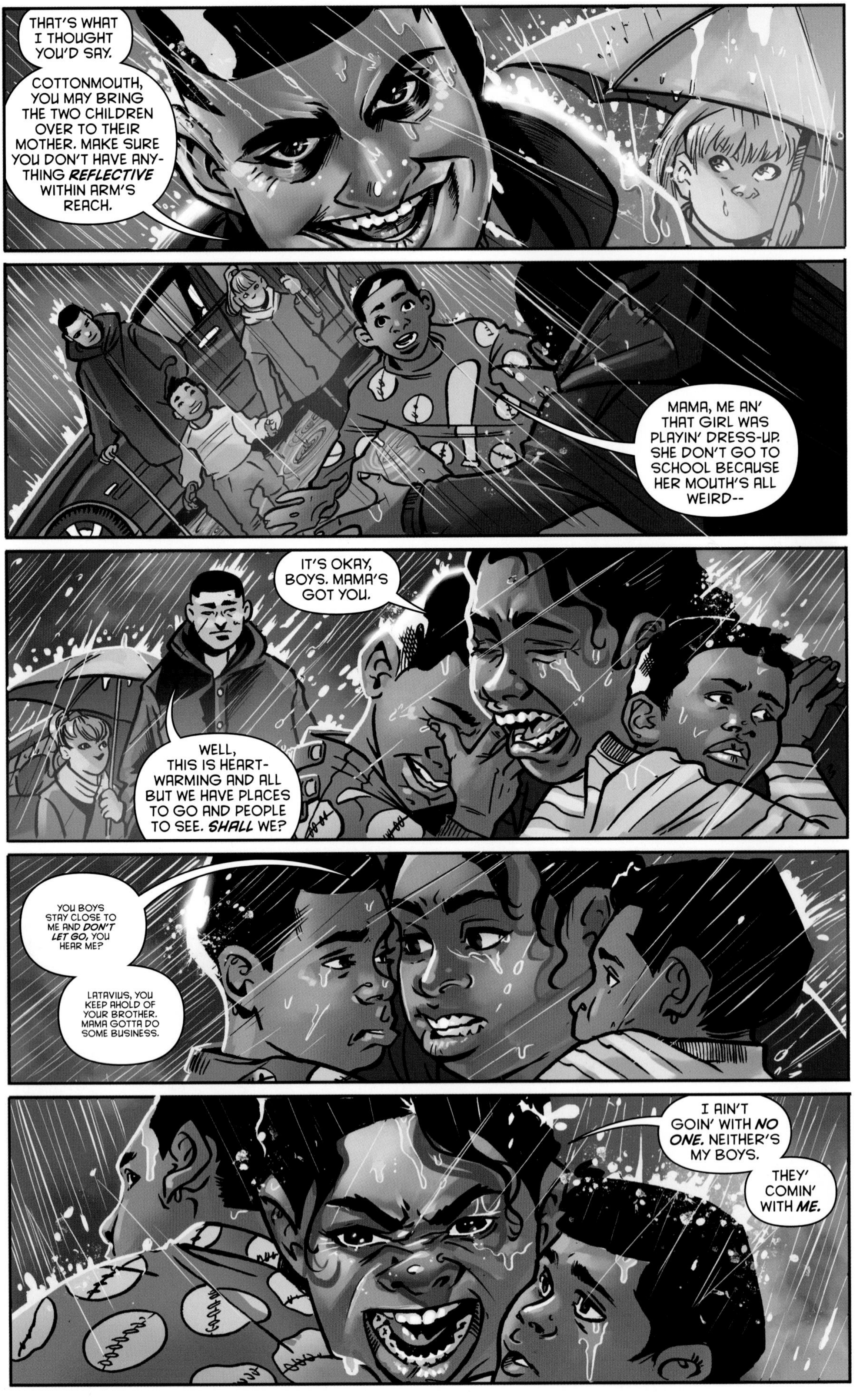
THAT'S WHAT I THOUGHT YOU'D SAY.
COTTONMOUTH, YOU MAY BRING THE TWO CHILDREN OVER TO THEIR MOTHER. MAKE SURE YOU DON'T HAVE ANY-THING *REFLECTIVE* WITHIN ARM'S REACH.
MAMA, ME AN' THAT GIRL WAS PLAYIN' DRESS-UP. SHE DON'T GO TO SCHOOL BECAUSE HER MOUTH'S ALL WEIRD--
IT'S OKAY, BOYS. MAMA'S GOT YOU.
WELL, THIS IS HEART-WARMING AND ALL BUT WE HAVE PLACES TO GO AND PEOPLE TO SEE. *SHALL* WE?
YOU BOYS STAY CLOSE TO ME AND *DON'T LET GO*, YOU HEAR ME?
LATAVIUS, YOU KEEP AHOLD OF YOUR BROTHER. MAMA GOTTA DO SOME BUSINESS.
I AIN'T GOIN' WITH *NO ONE.* NEITHER'S MY BOYS.
THEY' COMIN' WITH *ME.*

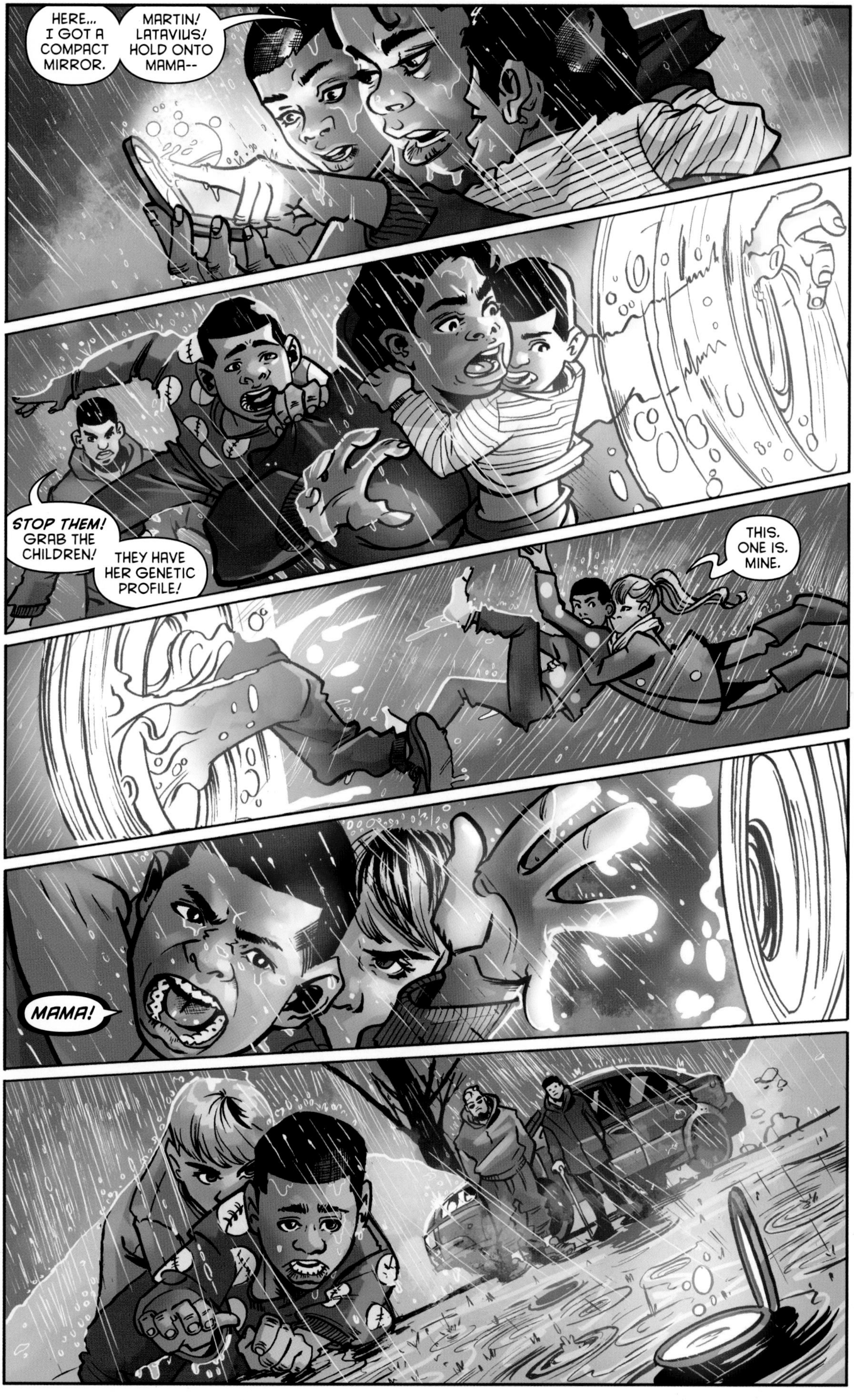
HERE... I GOT A COMPACT MIRROR.
MARTIN! LATAVIUS! HOLD ONTO MAMA--
STOP THEM! GRAB THE CHILDREN!
THEY HAVE HER GENETIC PROFILE!
THIS. ONE IS. MINE.
MAMA!

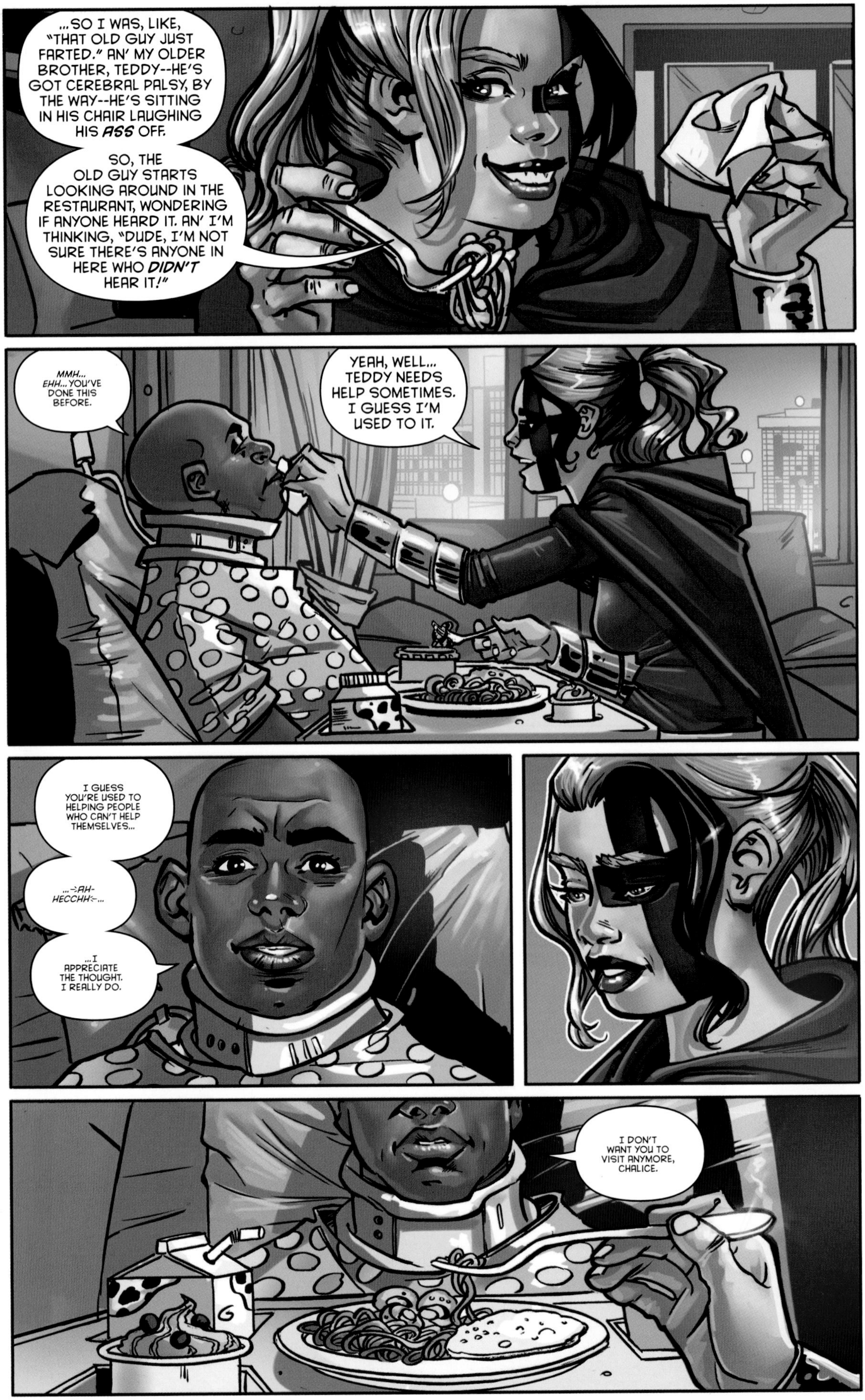
...SO I WAS, LIKE, "THAT OLD GUY JUST FARTED." AN' MY OLDER BROTHER, TEDDY--HE'S GOT CEREBRAL PALSY, BY THE WAY--HE'S SITTING IN HIS CHAIR LAUGHING HIS *ASS* OFF.
SO, THE OLD GUY STARTS LOOKING AROUND IN THE RESTAURANT, WONDERING IF ANYONE HEARD IT. AN' I'M THINKING, "DUDE, I'M NOT SURE THERE'S ANYONE IN HERE WHO *DIDN'T* HEAR IT!"
MMH... EHH... YOU'VE DONE THIS BEFORE.
YEAH, WELL... TEDDY NEEDS HELP SOMETIMES. I GUESS I'M USED TO IT.
I GUESS YOU'RE USED TO HELPING PEOPLE WHO CAN'T HELP THEMSELVES...
...→AH-HECCHH←...
...I APPRECIATE THE THOUGHT. I REALLY DO.
I DON'T WANT YOU TO VISIT ANYMORE, CHALICE.

LOOK, I LIKE SEEING YOU. I PROMISE. BUT YOU BRING ALL THIS *GUILT* IN WITH YOU. IT'S STARTING TO DRAG THE TWO OF US DOWN.

I'LL TRY TO BE MORE CHEER-FUL, PHILIP. BUT YOU'RE NOT GET-TING RID OF ME THAT EASILY.

I KNOW WHAT YOU'RE TRYING TO DO, BUT I *WANT* TO COME HERE. I DIDN'T GET A CHANCE TO KNOW YOU BEFORE... YOU KNOW...

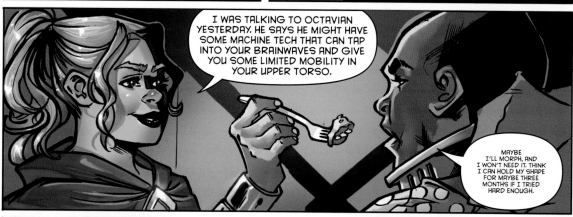
I WAS TALKING TO OCTAVIAN YESTERDAY. HE SAYS HE MIGHT HAVE SOME MACHINE TECH THAT CAN TAP INTO YOUR BRAINWAVES AND GIVE YOU SOME LIMITED MOBILITY IN YOUR UPPER TORSO.

MAYBE I'LL MORPH, AND I WON'T NEED IT. THINK I CAN HOLD MY SHAPE FOR MAYBE THREE MONTHS IF I TRIED HARD ENOUGH.

BUT IF YOU CHANGE, IT'LL *KILL* YOU--

MY CHOICE. I'LL LIVE WITH IT. BETTER THAN WATCHING YOU MOPE AROUND MY HOSPITAL ROOM EVERY NIGHT.

ONLY THING KEEPING YOU HERE IS *YOU*, CHALICE. I DON'T WANT YOU TO BE STUCK HERE JUST BECAUSE YOU FEEL GUILTY THAT *I* AM.

WE HAVE SOME CHOICES TO MAKE. THINK WE NEED TO STOP PUTTING THEM *OFF*.

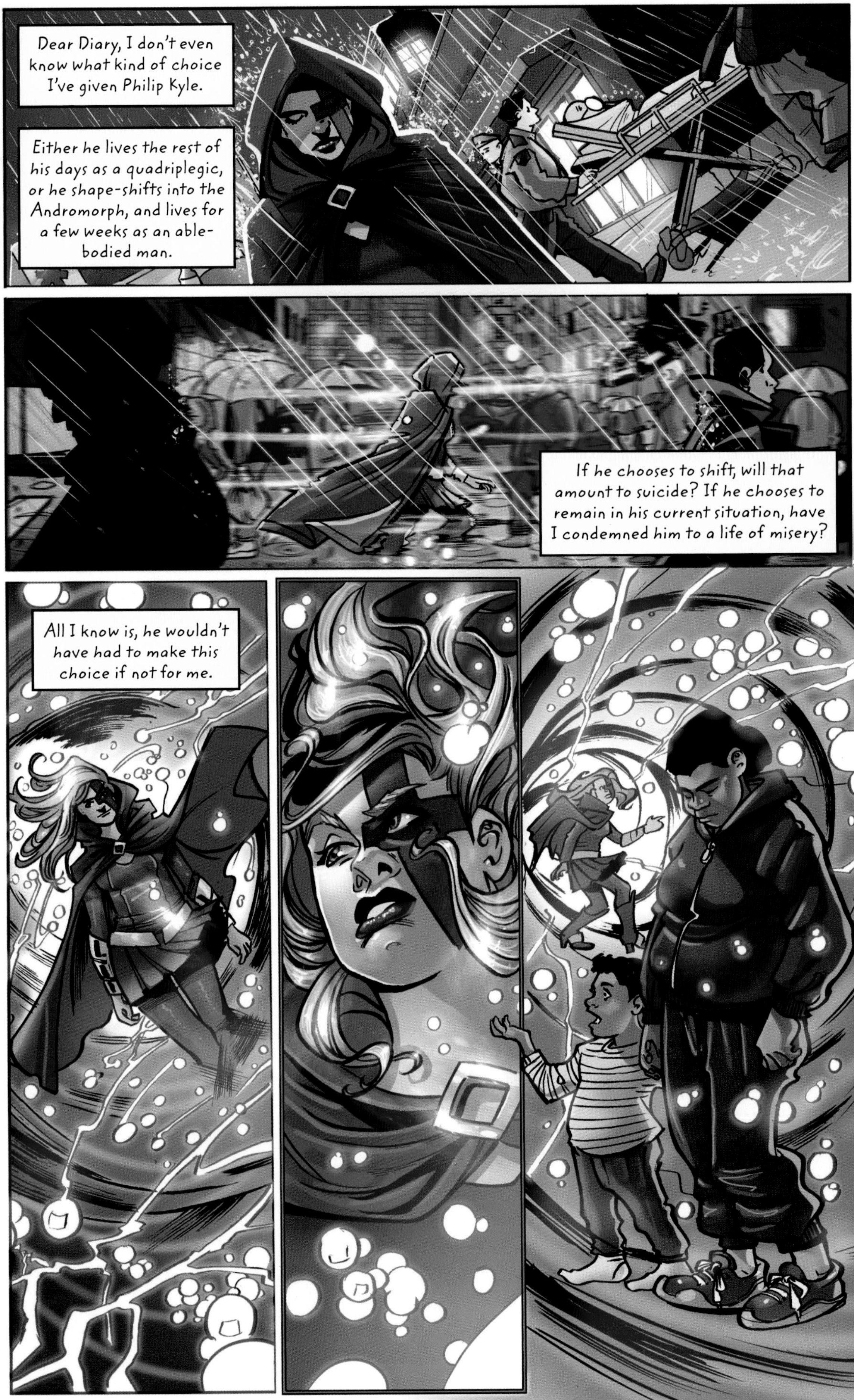
Dear Diary, I don't even know what kind of choice I've given Philip Kyle.
Either he lives the rest of his days as a quadriplegic, or he shape-shifts into the Andromorph, and lives for a few weeks as an able-bodied man.
If he chooses to shift, will that amount to suicide? If he chooses to remain in his current situation, have I condemned him to a life of misery?
All I know is, he wouldn't have had to make this choice if not for me.

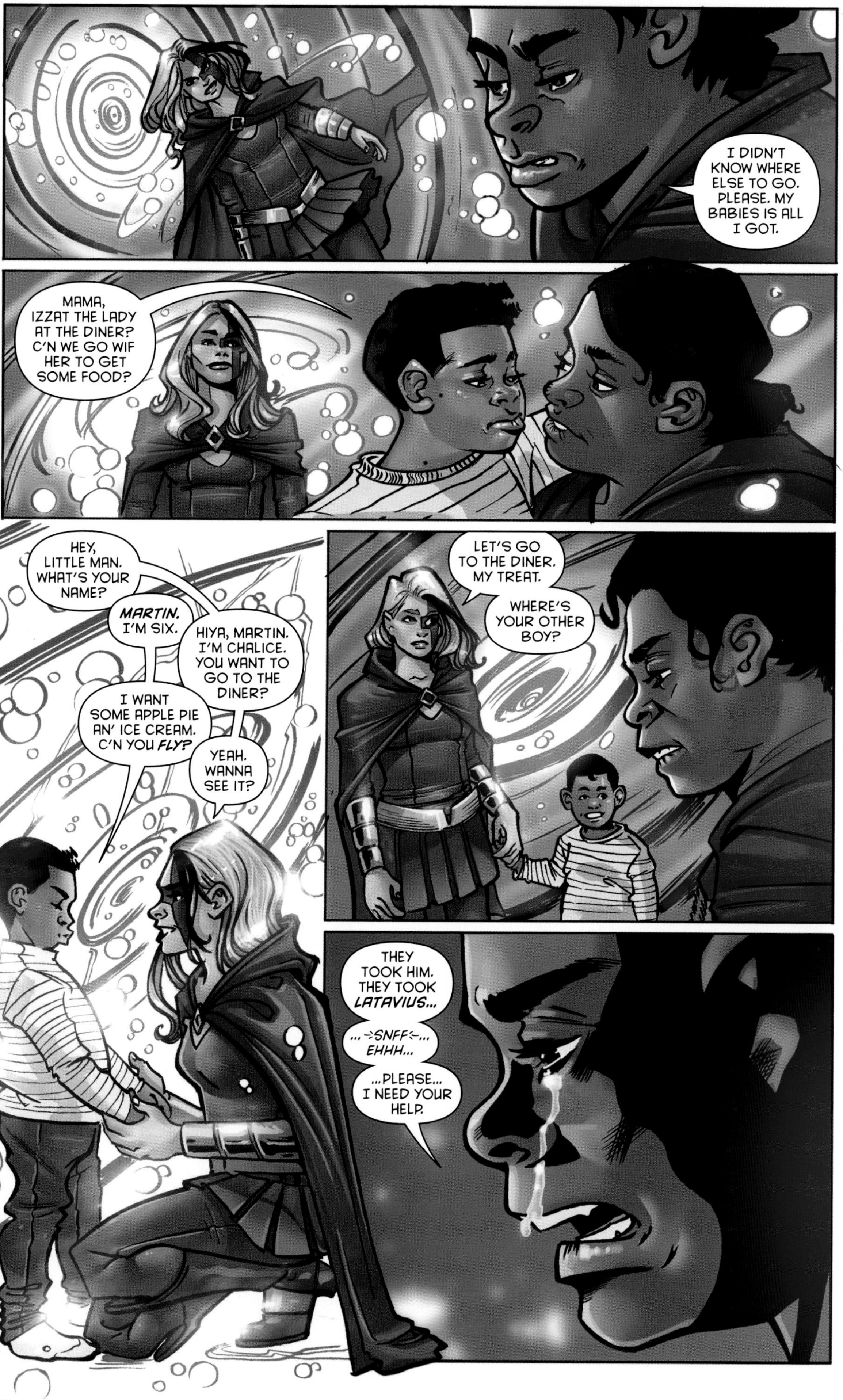

I DIDN'T KNOW WHERE ELSE TO GO. PLEASE. MY BABIES IS ALL I GOT.
MAMA, IZZAT THE LADY AT THE DINER? C'N WE GO WIF HER TO GET SOME FOOD?
HEY, LITTLE MAN. WHAT'S YOUR NAME?
MARTIN. I'M SIX.
HIYA, MARTIN. I'M CHALICE. YOU WANT TO GO TO THE DINER?
I WANT SOME APPLE PIE AN' ICE CREAM. C'N YOU *FLY?*
YEAH. WANNA SEE IT?
LET'S GO TO THE DINER. MY TREAT.
WHERE'S YOUR OTHER BOY?
THEY TOOK HIM. THEY TOOK *LATAVIUS...*
...⇒*SNFF*⇐... EHHH...
...PLEASE... I NEED YOUR HELP.

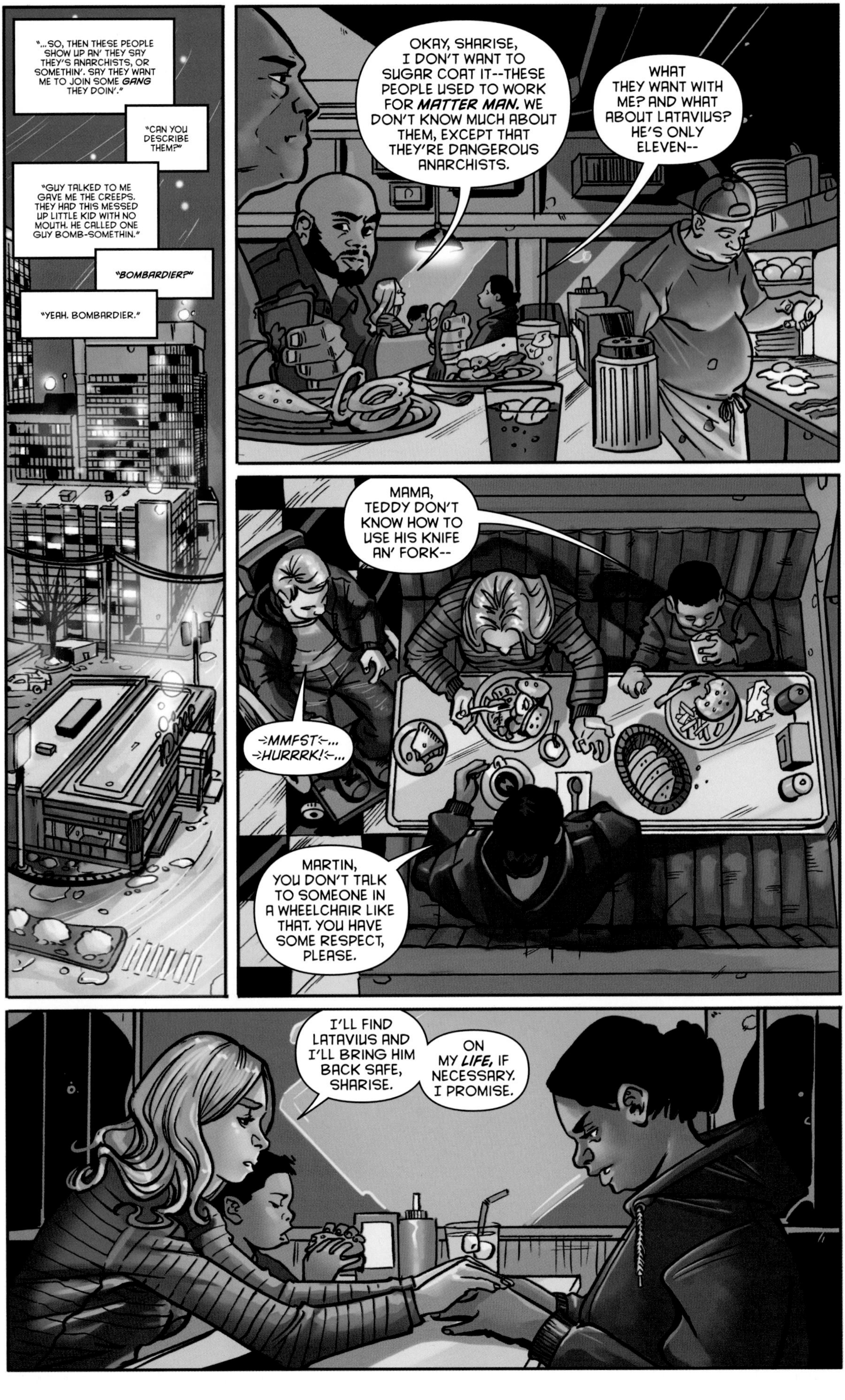
"...SO, THEN THESE PEOPLE SHOW UP AN' THEY SAY THEY'S ANARCHISTS, OR SOMETHIN'. SAY THEY WANT ME TO JOIN SOME *GANG* THEY DOIN'."
"CAN YOU DESCRIBE THEM?"
"GUY TALKED TO ME GAVE ME THE CREEPS. THEY HAD THIS MESSED UP LITTLE KID WITH NO MOUTH. HE CALLED ONE GUY BOMB-SOMETHIN."
"BOMBARDIER?"
"YEAH. BOMBARDIER."
OKAY, SHARISE, I DON'T WANT TO SUGAR COAT IT--THESE PEOPLE USED TO WORK FOR *MATTER MAN.* WE DON'T KNOW MUCH ABOUT THEM, EXCEPT THAT THEY'RE DANGEROUS ANARCHISTS.
WHAT THEY WANT WITH ME? AND WHAT ABOUT LATAVIUS? HE'S ONLY ELEVEN--
MAMA, TEDDY DON'T KNOW HOW TO USE HIS KNIFE AN' FORK--
MMFST... *HURRRK!*...
MARTIN, YOU DON'T TALK TO SOMEONE IN A WHEELCHAIR LIKE THAT. YOU HAVE SOME RESPECT, PLEASE.
I'LL FIND LATAVIUS AND I'LL BRING HIM BACK SAFE, SHARISE.
ON MY *LIFE*, IF NECESSARY. I PROMISE.

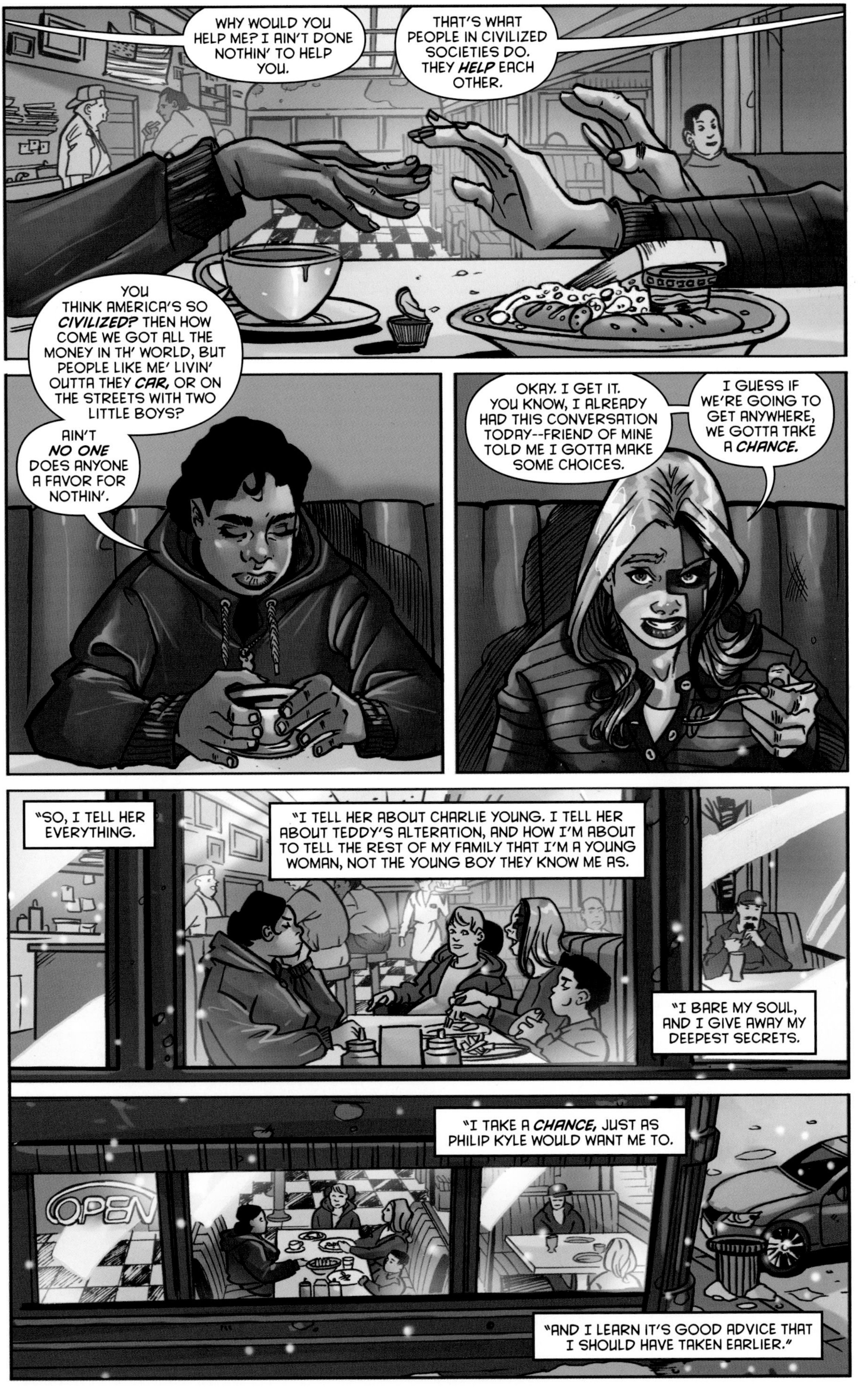

WHY WOULD YOU HELP ME? I AIN'T DONE NOTHIN' TO HELP YOU.
THAT'S WHAT PEOPLE IN CIVILIZED SOCIETIES DO. THEY *HELP* EACH OTHER.
YOU THINK AMERICA'S SO *CIVILIZED?* THEN HOW COME WE GOT ALL THE MONEY IN TH' WORLD, BUT PEOPLE LIKE ME' LIVIN' OUTTA THEY *CAR,* OR ON THE STREETS WITH TWO LITTLE BOYS?
AIN'T ***NO ONE*** DOES ANYONE A FAVOR FOR NOTHIN'.
OKAY. I GET IT. YOU KNOW, I ALREADY HAD THIS CONVERSATION TODAY--FRIEND OF MINE TOLD ME I GOTTA MAKE SOME CHOICES.
I GUESS IF WE'RE GOING TO GET ANYWHERE, WE GOTTA TAKE A ***CHANCE.***
"SO, I TELL HER EVERYTHING.
"I TELL HER ABOUT CHARLIE YOUNG. I TELL HER ABOUT TEDDY'S ALTERATION, AND HOW I'M ABOUT TO TELL THE REST OF MY FAMILY THAT I'M A YOUNG WOMAN, NOT THE YOUNG BOY THEY KNOW ME AS.
"I BARE MY SOUL, AND I GIVE AWAY MY DEEPEST SECRETS.
"I TAKE A ***CHANCE,*** JUST AS PHILIP KYLE WOULD WANT ME TO.
OPEN
"AND I LEARN IT'S GOOD ADVICE THAT I SHOULD HAVE TAKEN EARLIER."

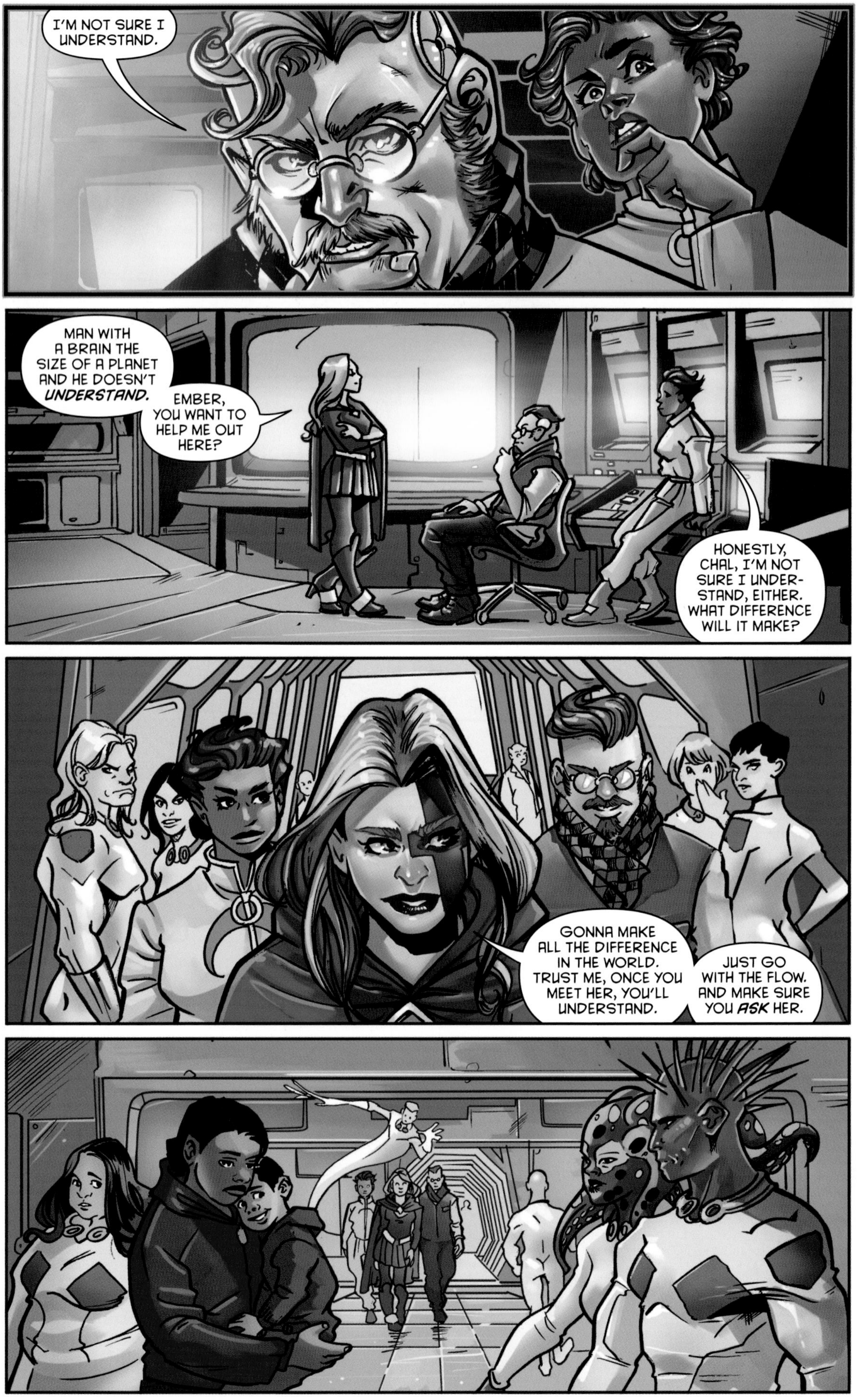
I'M NOT SURE I UNDERSTAND.
MAN WITH A BRAIN THE SIZE OF A PLANET AND HE DOESN'T *UNDERSTAND.*
EMBER, YOU WANT TO HELP ME OUT HERE?
HONESTLY, CHAL, I'M NOT SURE I UNDER-STAND, EITHER. WHAT DIFFERENCE WILL IT MAKE?
GONNA MAKE ALL THE DIFFERENCE IN THE WORLD. TRUST ME, ONCE YOU MEET HER, YOU'LL UNDERSTAND.
JUST GO WITH THE FLOW. AND MAKE SURE YOU *ASK* HER.

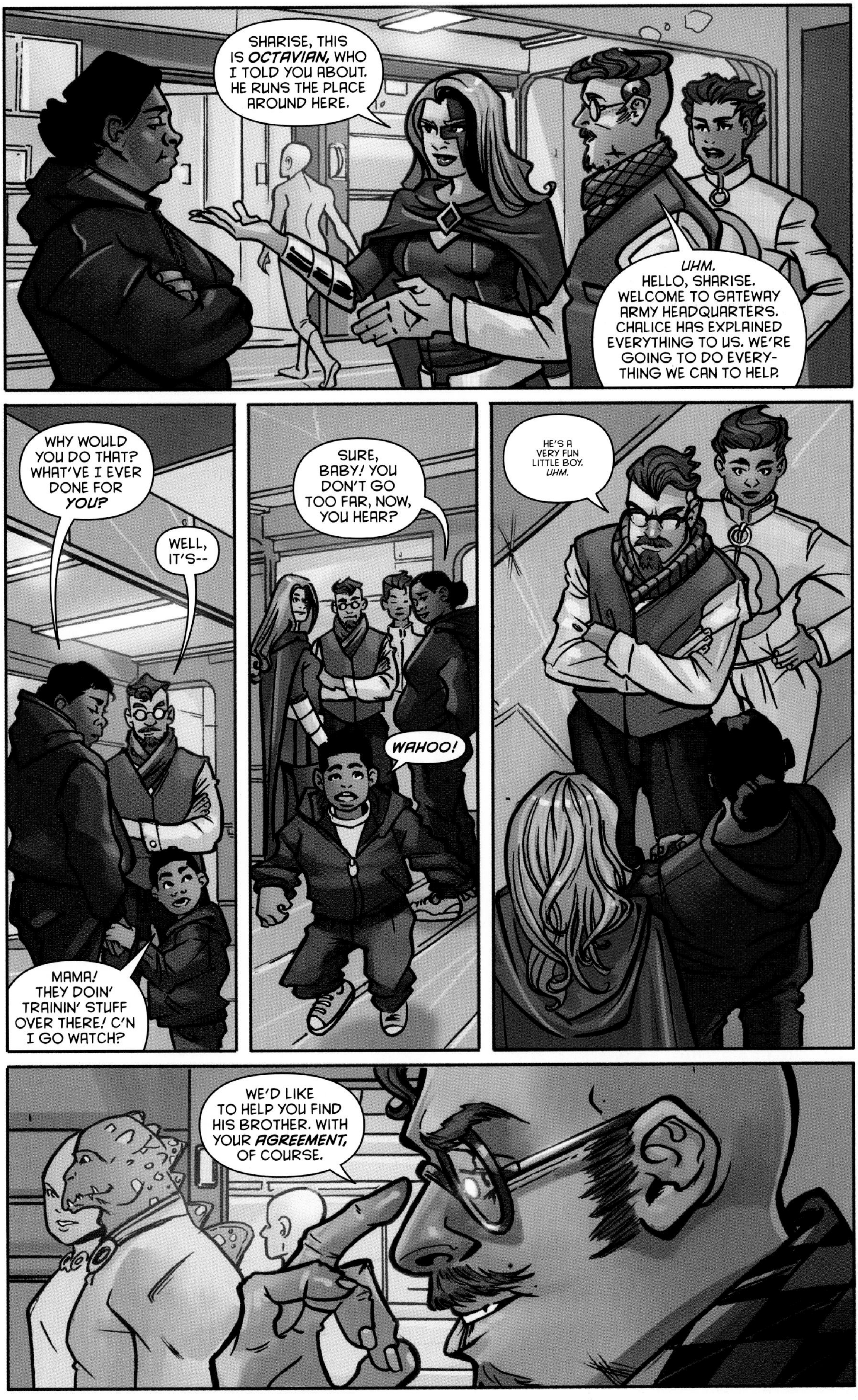
SHARISE, THIS IS *OCTAVIAN,* WHO I TOLD YOU ABOUT. HE RUNS THE PLACE AROUND HERE.
UHM. HELLO, SHARISE. WELCOME TO GATEWAY ARMY HEADQUARTERS. CHALICE HAS EXPLAINED EVERYTHING TO US. WE'RE GOING TO DO EVERY-THING WE CAN TO HELP.
WHY WOULD YOU DO THAT? WHAT'VE I EVER DONE FOR *YOU?*
WELL, IT'S--
MAMA! THEY DOIN' TRAININ' STUFF OVER THERE! C'N I GO WATCH?
SURE, BABY! YOU DON'T GO TOO FAR, NOW, YOU HEAR?
WAHOO!
HE'S A VERY FUN LITTLE BOY. *UHM.*
WE'D LIKE TO HELP YOU FIND HIS BROTHER. WITH YOUR *AGREEMENT,* OF COURSE.

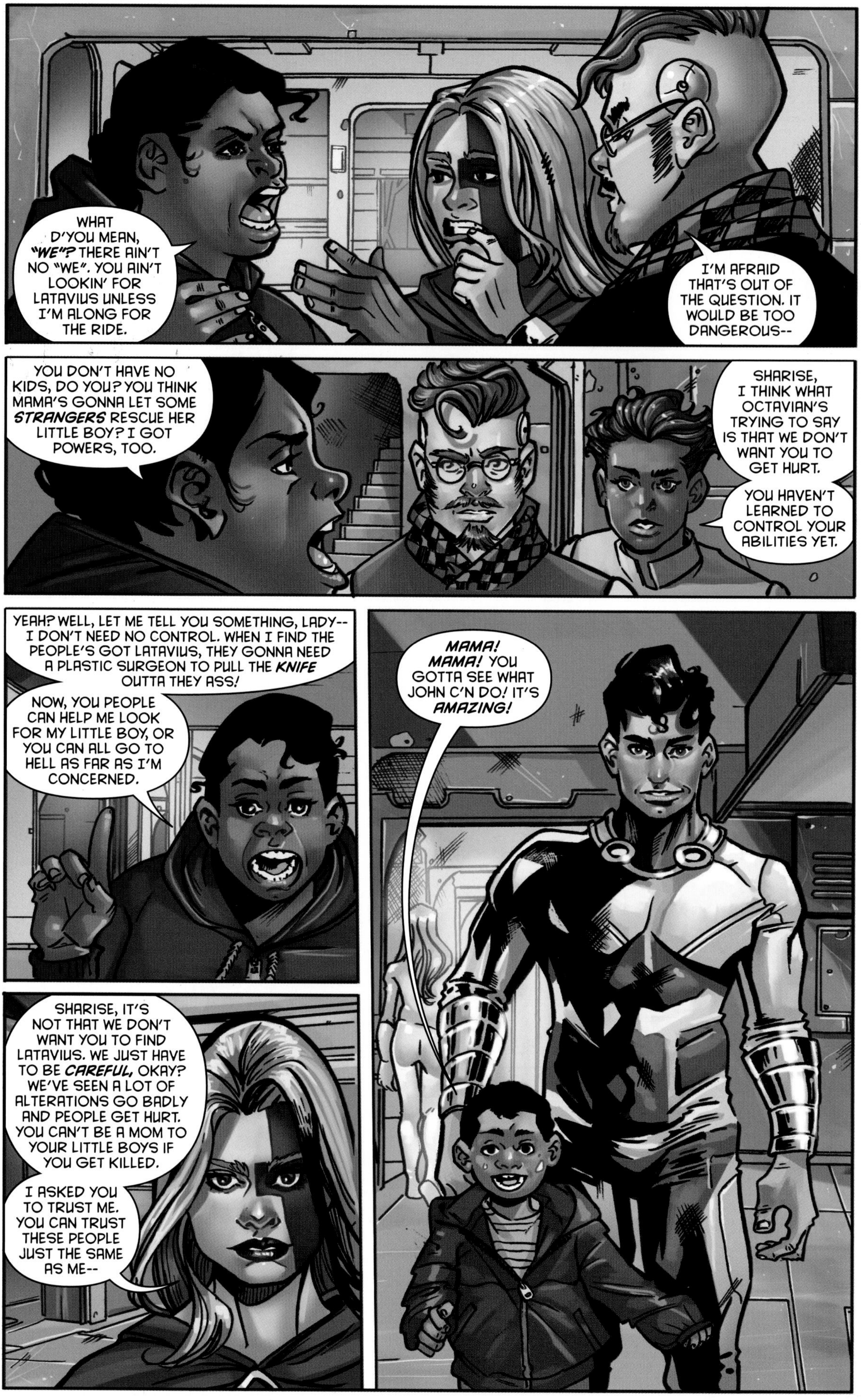
WHAT D'YOU MEAN, "WE"? THERE AIN'T NO "WE". YOU AIN'T LOOKIN' FOR LATAVIUS UNLESS I'M ALONG FOR THE RIDE.
I'M AFRAID THAT'S OUT OF THE QUESTION. IT WOULD BE TOO DANGEROUS--
YOU DON'T HAVE NO KIDS, DO YOU? YOU THINK MAMA'S GONNA LET SOME STRANGERS RESCUE HER LITTLE BOY? I GOT POWERS, TOO.
SHARISE, I THINK WHAT OCTAVIAN'S TRYING TO SAY IS THAT WE DON'T WANT YOU TO GET HURT.
YOU HAVEN'T LEARNED TO CONTROL YOUR ABILITIES YET.
YEAH? WELL, LET ME TELL YOU SOMETHING, LADY-- I DON'T NEED NO CONTROL. WHEN I FIND THE PEOPLE'S GOT LATAVIUS, THEY GONNA NEED A PLASTIC SURGEON TO PULL THE KNIFE OUTTA THEY ASS!
NOW, YOU PEOPLE CAN HELP ME LOOK FOR MY LITTLE BOY, OR YOU CAN ALL GO TO HELL AS FAR AS I'M CONCERNED.
SHARISE, IT'S NOT THAT WE DON'T WANT YOU TO FIND LATAVIUS. WE JUST HAVE TO BE CAREFUL, OKAY? WE'VE SEEN A LOT OF ALTERATIONS GO BADLY AND PEOPLE GET HURT. YOU CAN'T BE A MOM TO YOUR LITTLE BOYS IF YOU GET KILLED.
I ASKED YOU TO TRUST ME. YOU CAN TRUST THESE PEOPLE JUST THE SAME AS ME--
MAMA! MAMA! YOU GOTTA SEE WHAT JOHN C'N DO! IT'S AMAZING!

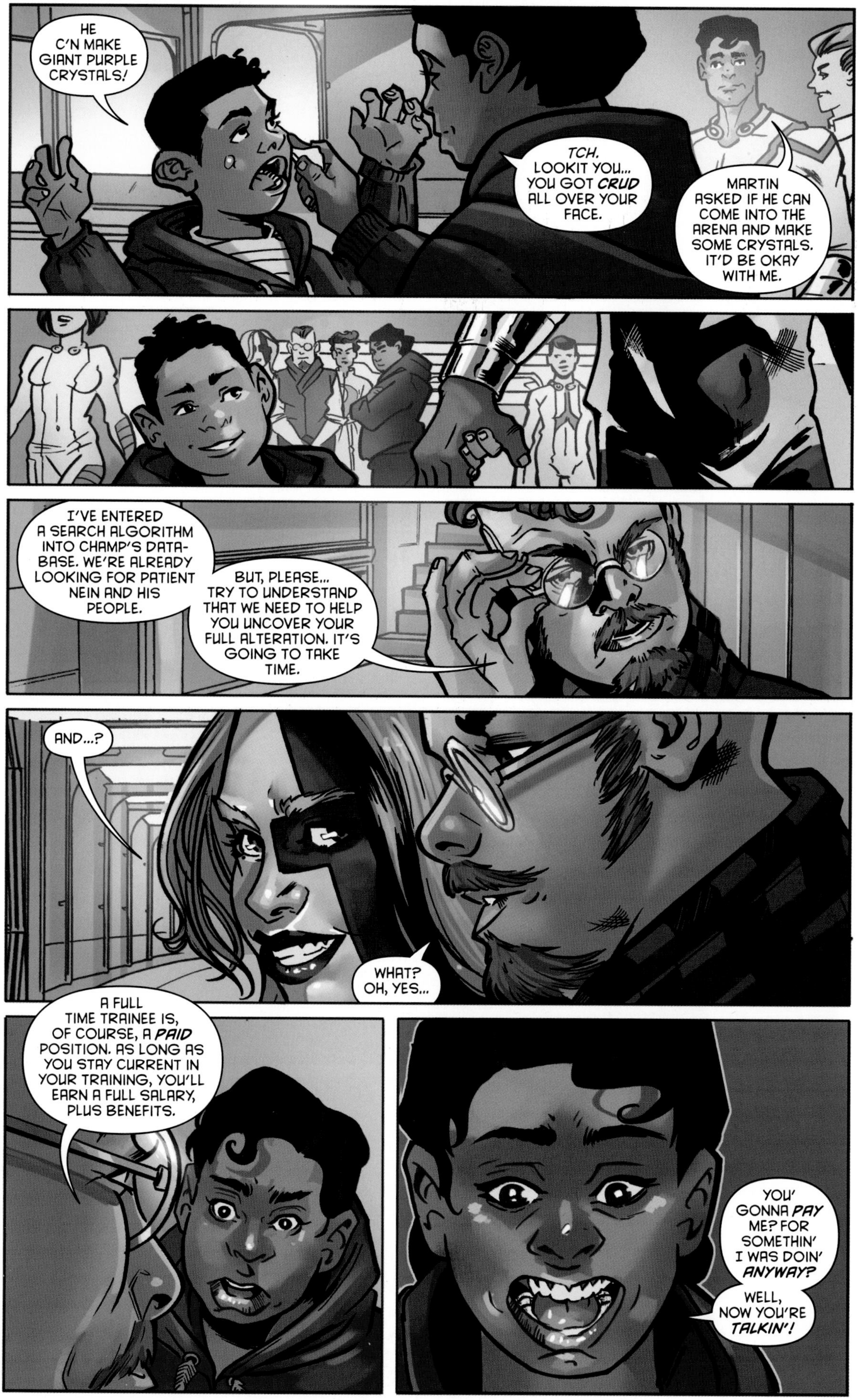
HE C'N MAKE GIANT PURPLE CRYSTALS!
TCH. LOOKIT YOU... YOU GOT CRUD ALL OVER YOUR FACE.
MARTIN ASKED IF HE CAN COME INTO THE ARENA AND MAKE SOME CRYSTALS. IT'D BE OKAY WITH ME.
I'VE ENTERED A SEARCH ALGORITHM INTO CHAMP'S DATA-BASE. WE'RE ALREADY LOOKING FOR PATIENT NEIN AND HIS PEOPLE.
BUT, PLEASE... TRY TO UNDERSTAND THAT WE NEED TO HELP YOU UNCOVER YOUR FULL ALTERATION. IT'S GOING TO TAKE TIME.
AND...?
WHAT? OH, YES...
A FULL TIME TRAINEE IS, OF COURSE, A PAID POSITION. AS LONG AS YOU STAY CURRENT IN YOUR TRAINING, YOU'LL EARN A FULL SALARY, PLUS BENEFITS.
YOU' GONNA PAY ME? FOR SOMETHIN' I WAS DOIN' ANYWAY?
WELL, NOW YOU'RE TALKIN'!

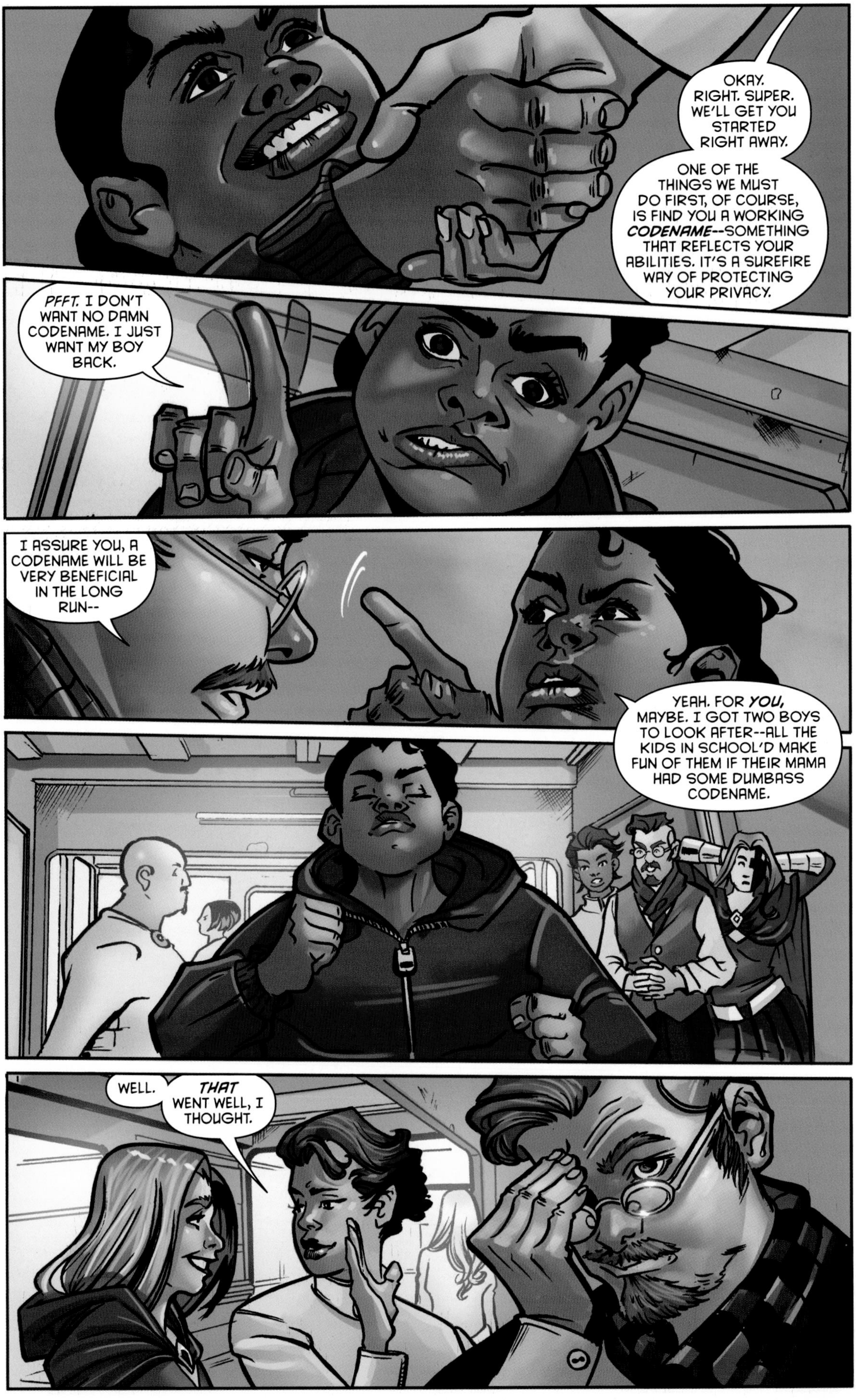
OKAY. RIGHT. SUPER. WE'LL GET YOU STARTED RIGHT AWAY.
ONE OF THE THINGS WE MUST DO FIRST, OF COURSE, IS FIND YOU A WORKING CODENAME--SOMETHING THAT REFLECTS YOUR ABILITIES. IT'S A SUREFIRE WAY OF PROTECTING YOUR PRIVACY.
PFFT. I DON'T WANT NO DAMN CODENAME. I JUST WANT MY BOY BACK.
I ASSURE YOU, A CODENAME WILL BE VERY BENEFICIAL IN THE LONG RUN--
YEAH. FOR YOU, MAYBE. I GOT TWO BOYS TO LOOK AFTER--ALL THE KIDS IN SCHOOL'D MAKE FUN OF THEM IF THEIR MAMA HAD SOME DUMBASS CODENAME.
WELL.
THAT WENT WELL, I THOUGHT.

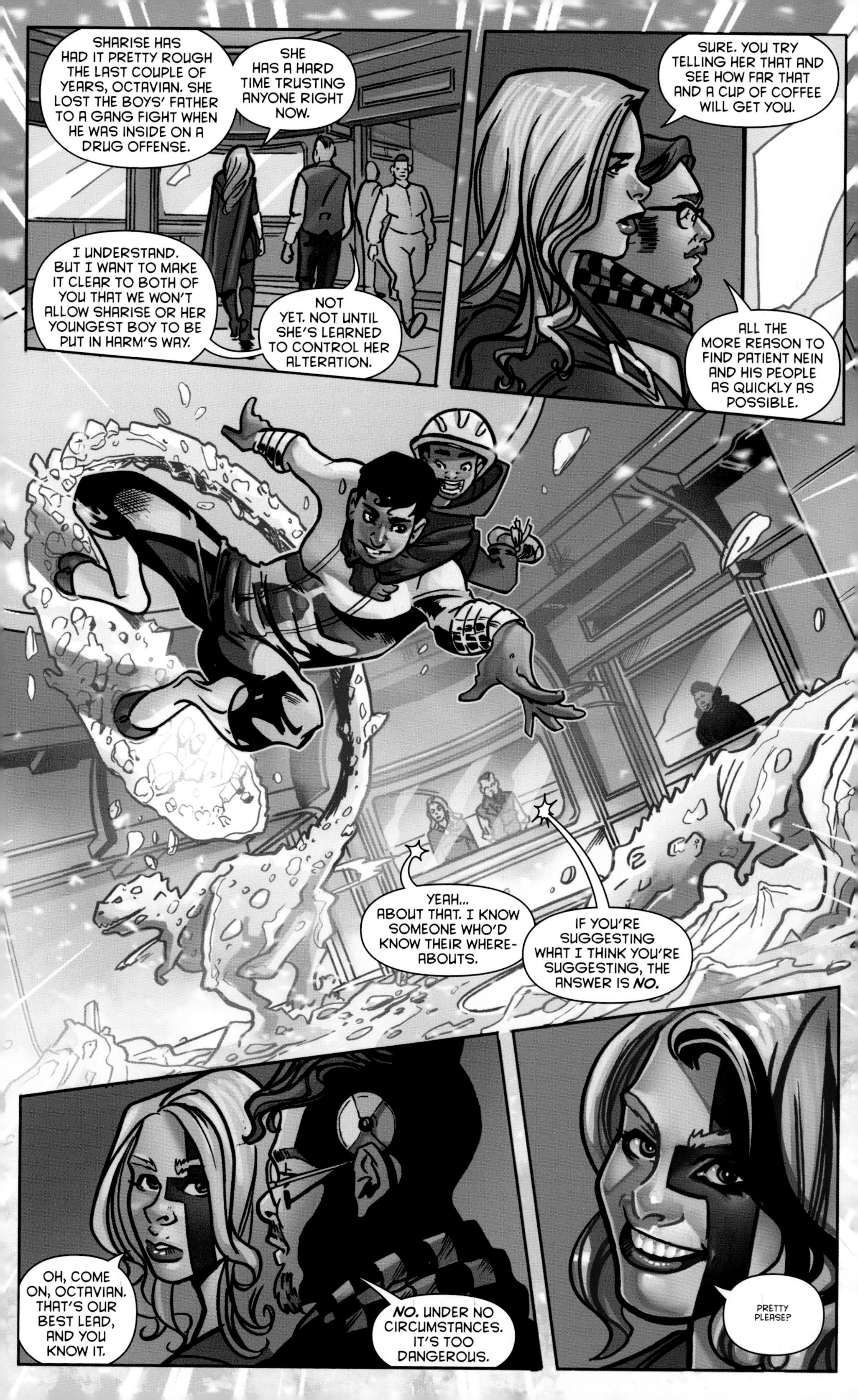
SHARISE HAS HAD IT PRETTY ROUGH THE LAST COUPLE OF YEARS, OCTAVIAN. SHE LOST THE BOYS' FATHER TO A GANG FIGHT WHEN HE WAS INSIDE ON A DRUG OFFENSE.
SHE HAS A HARD TIME TRUSTING ANYONE RIGHT NOW.
I UNDERSTAND. BUT I WANT TO MAKE IT CLEAR TO BOTH OF YOU THAT WE WON'T ALLOW SHARISE OR HER YOUNGEST BOY TO BE PUT IN HARM'S WAY.
NOT YET. NOT UNTIL SHE'S LEARNED TO CONTROL HER ALTERATION.
SURE. YOU TRY TELLING HER THAT AND SEE HOW FAR THAT AND A CUP OF COFFEE WILL GET YOU.
ALL THE MORE REASON TO FIND PATIENT NEIN AND HIS PEOPLE AS QUICKLY AS POSSIBLE.
YEAH... ABOUT THAT. I KNOW SOMEONE WHO'D KNOW THEIR WHERE-ABOUTS.
IF YOU'RE SUGGESTING WHAT I THINK YOU'RE SUGGESTING, THE ANSWER IS ***NO.***
OH, COME ON, OCTAVIAN. THAT'S OUR BEST LEAD, AND YOU KNOW IT.
NO. UNDER NO CIRCUMSTANCES. IT'S TOO DANGEROUS.
PRETTY PLEASE?

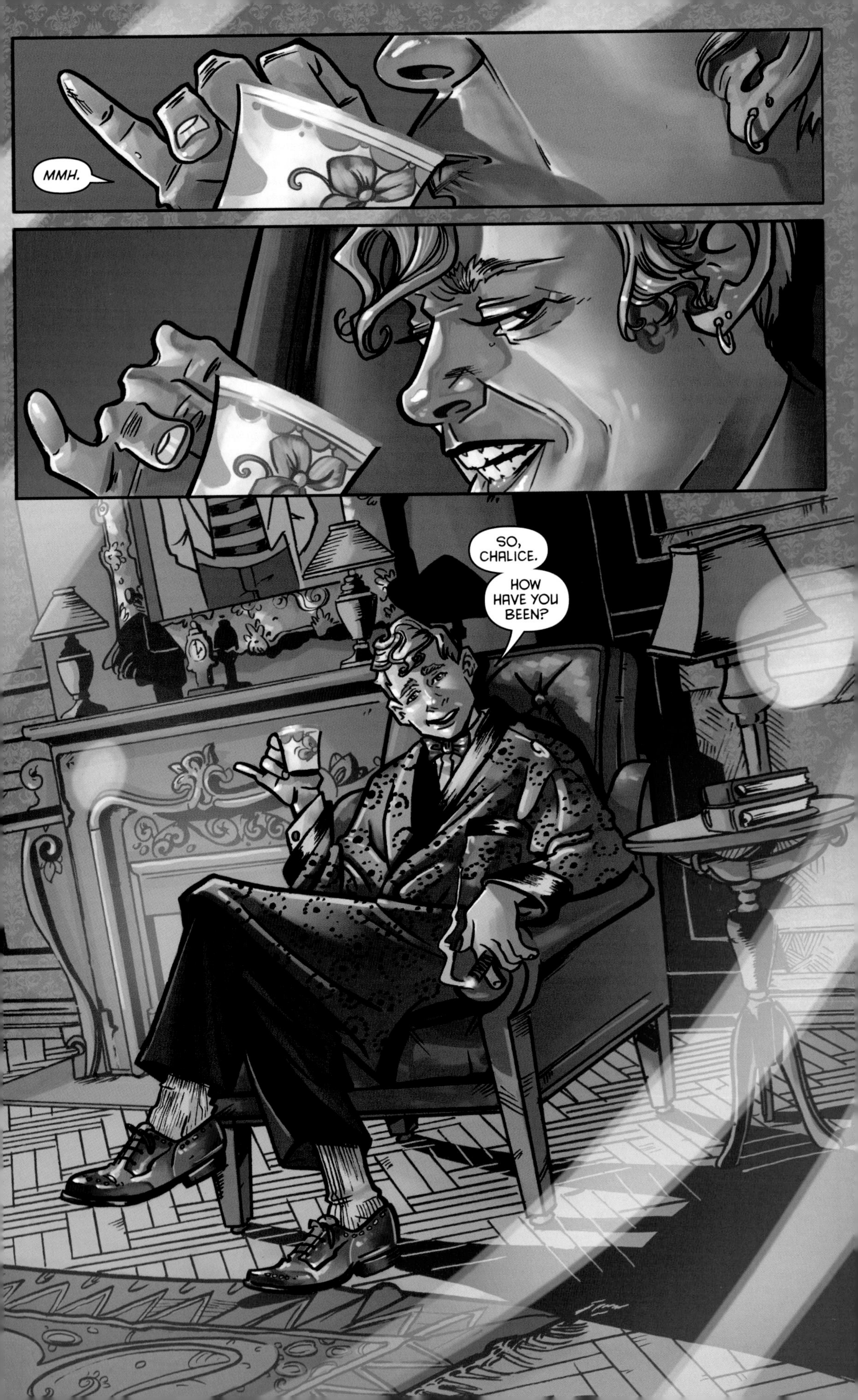
MMH.
SO, CHALICE.
HOW HAVE YOU BEEN?

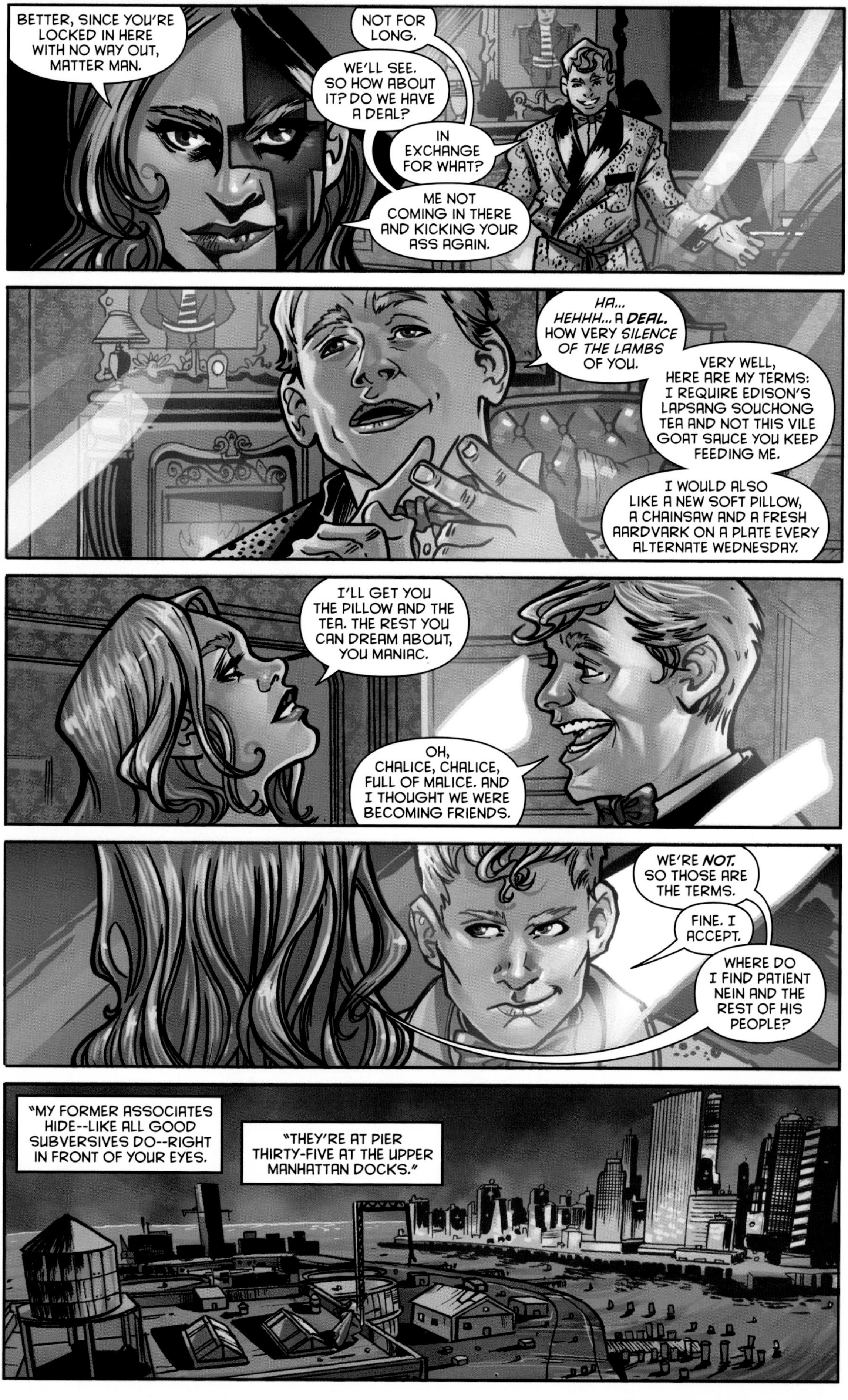
BETTER, SINCE YOU'RE LOCKED IN HERE WITH NO WAY OUT, MATTER MAN.
NOT FOR LONG.
WE'LL SEE. SO HOW ABOUT IT? DO WE HAVE A DEAL?
IN EXCHANGE FOR WHAT?
ME NOT COMING IN THERE AND KICKING YOUR ASS AGAIN.
HA... HEHHH... A DEAL. HOW VERY SILENCE OF THE LAMBS OF YOU.
VERY WELL, HERE ARE MY TERMS: I REQUIRE EDISON'S LAPSANG SOUCHONG TEA AND NOT THIS VILE GOAT SAUCE YOU KEEP FEEDING ME.
I WOULD ALSO LIKE A NEW SOFT PILLOW, A CHAINSAW AND A FRESH AARDVARK ON A PLATE EVERY ALTERNATE WEDNESDAY.
I'LL GET YOU THE PILLOW AND THE TEA. THE REST YOU CAN DREAM ABOUT, YOU MANIAC.
OH, CHALICE, CHALICE, FULL OF MALICE. AND I THOUGHT WE WERE BECOMING FRIENDS.
WE'RE NOT. SO THOSE ARE THE TERMS.
FINE. I ACCEPT.
WHERE DO I FIND PATIENT NEIN AND THE REST OF HIS PEOPLE?
"MY FORMER ASSOCIATES HIDE--LIKE ALL GOOD SUBVERSIVES DO--RIGHT IN FRONT OF YOUR EYES.
"THEY'RE AT PIER THIRTY-FIVE AT THE UPPER MANHATTAN DOCKS."

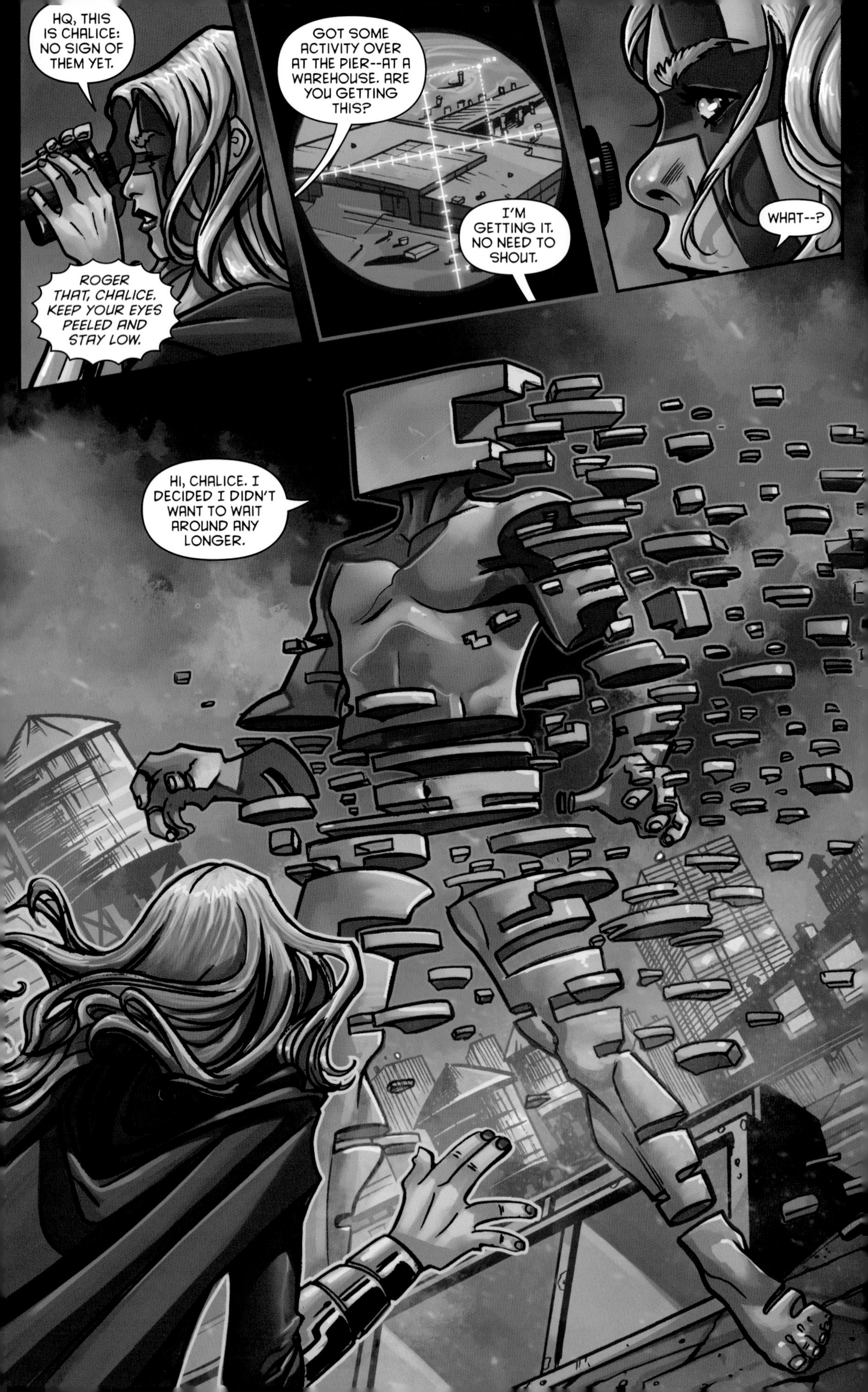
HQ, THIS IS CHALICE: NO SIGN OF THEM YET.
ROGER THAT, CHALICE. KEEP YOUR EYES PEELED AND STAY LOW.
GOT SOME ACTIVITY OVER AT THE PIER--AT A WAREHOUSE. ARE YOU GETTING THIS?
I'M GETTING IT. NO NEED TO SHOUT.
WHAT--?
HI, CHALICE. I DECIDED I DIDN'T WANT TO WAIT AROUND ANY LONGER.

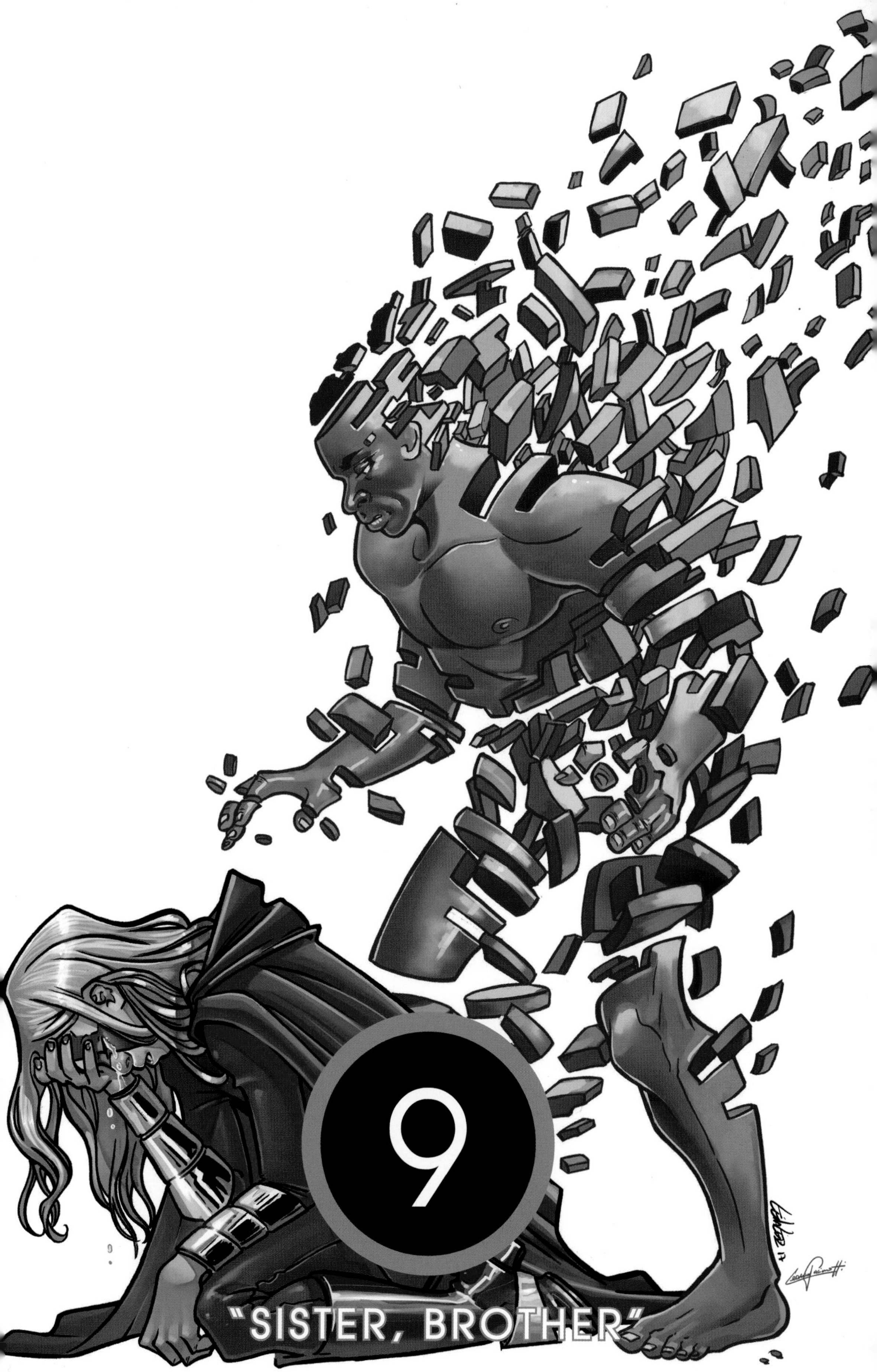

9

"SISTER, BROTHER"

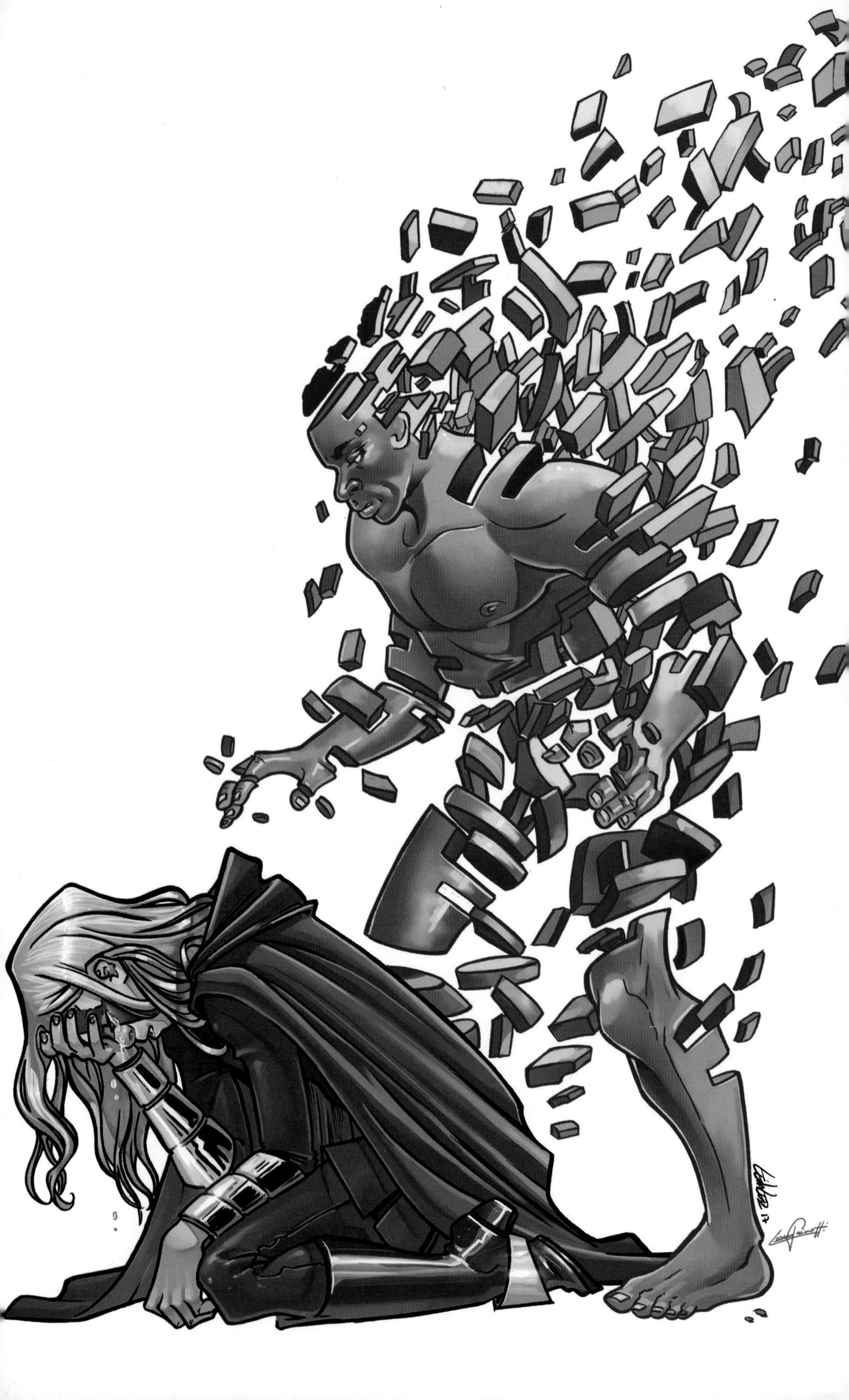

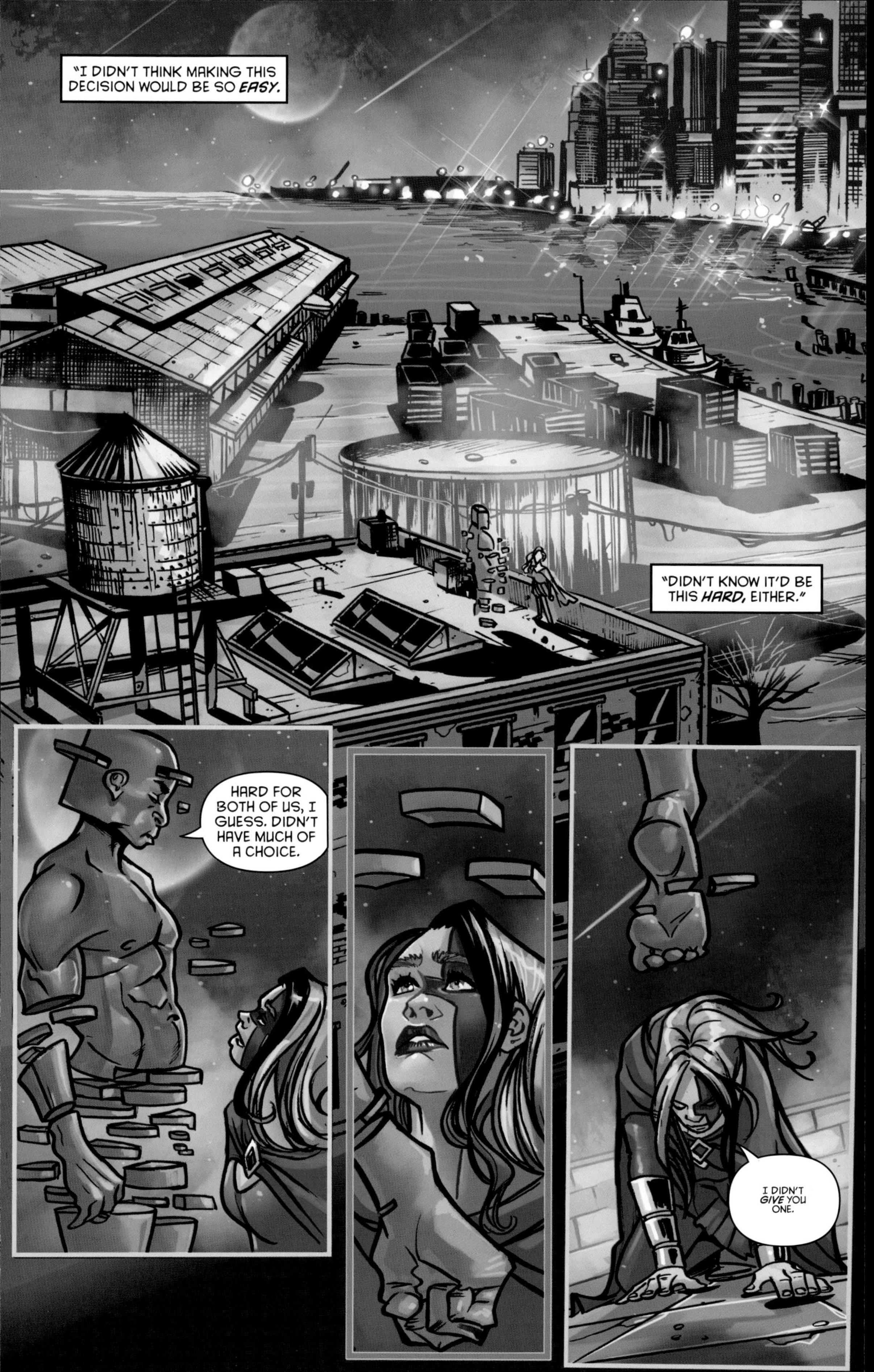
"I DIDN'T THINK MAKING THIS DECISION WOULD BE SO EASY.
"DIDN'T KNOW IT'D BE THIS HARD, EITHER."
HARD FOR BOTH OF US, I GUESS. DIDN'T HAVE MUCH OF A CHOICE.
I DIDN'T GIVE YOU ONE.

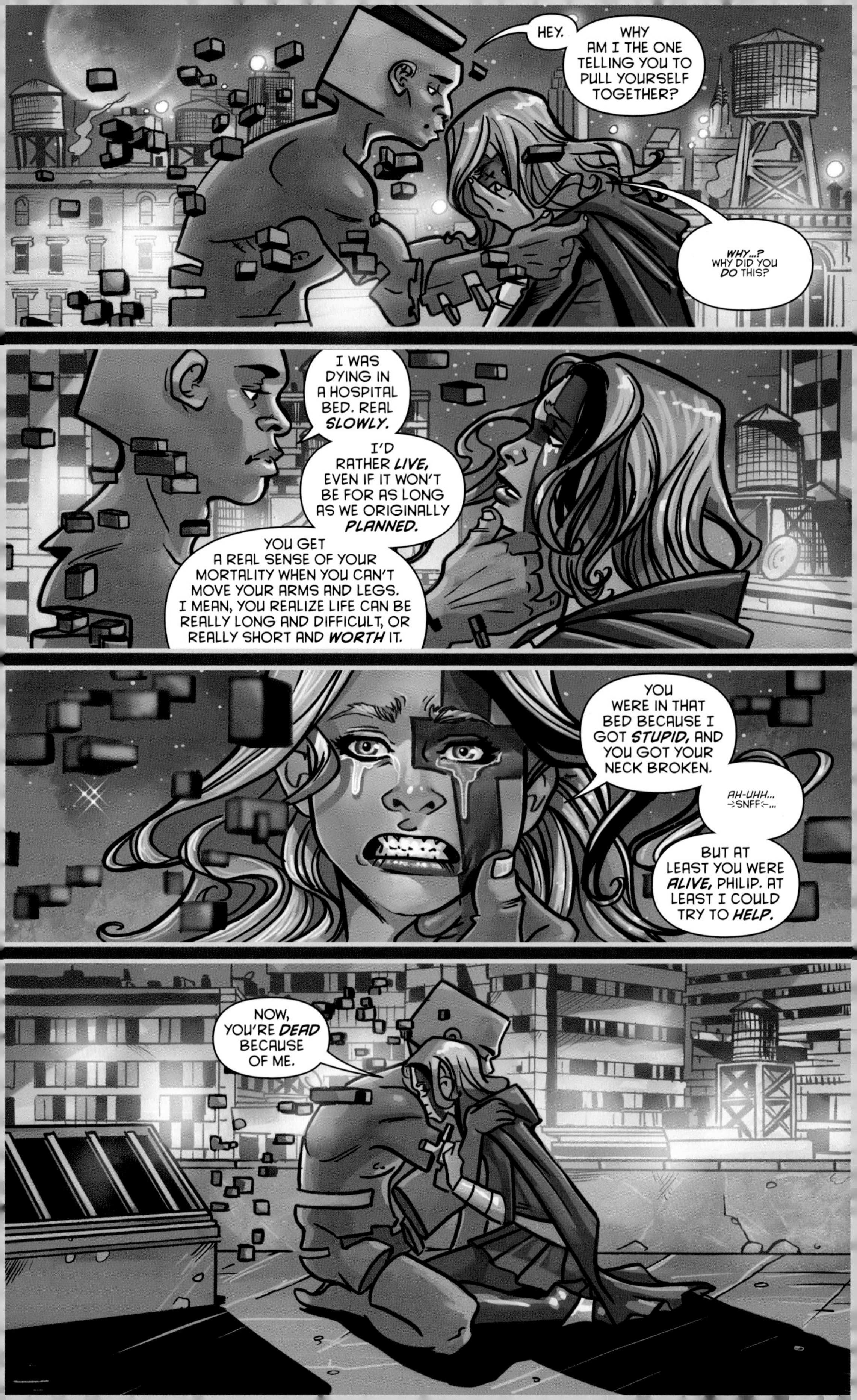
HEY.
WHY AM I THE ONE TELLING YOU TO PULL YOURSELF TOGETHER?
WHY...? WHY DID YOU DO THIS?
I WAS DYING IN A HOSPITAL BED. REAL SLOWLY.
I'D RATHER LIVE, EVEN IF IT WON'T BE FOR AS LONG AS WE ORIGINALLY PLANNED.
YOU GET A REAL SENSE OF YOUR MORTALITY WHEN YOU CAN'T MOVE YOUR ARMS AND LEGS. I MEAN, YOU REALIZE LIFE CAN BE REALLY LONG AND DIFFICULT, OR REALLY SHORT AND WORTH IT.
YOU WERE IN THAT BED BECAUSE I GOT STUPID, AND YOU GOT YOUR NECK BROKEN.
AH-UHH... SNFF...
BUT AT LEAST YOU WERE ALIVE, PHILIP. AT LEAST I COULD TRY TO HELP.
NOW, YOU'RE DEAD BECAUSE OF ME.

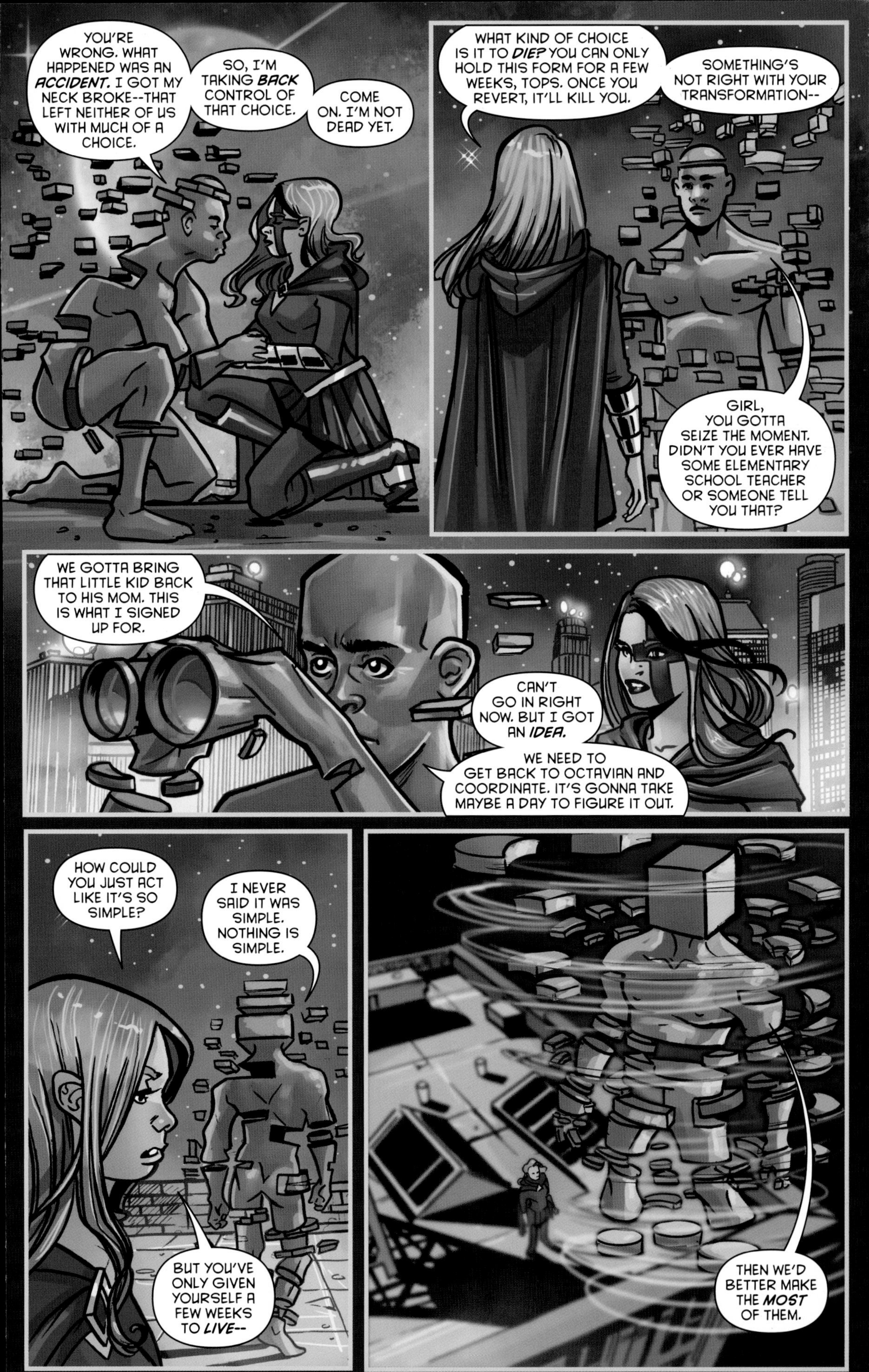

YOU'RE WRONG. WHAT HAPPENED WAS AN ACCIDENT. I GOT MY NECK BROKE--THAT LEFT NEITHER OF US WITH MUCH OF A CHOICE.
SO, I'M TAKING BACK CONTROL OF THAT CHOICE.
COME ON. I'M NOT DEAD YET.
WHAT KIND OF CHOICE IS IT TO DIE? YOU CAN ONLY HOLD THIS FORM FOR A FEW WEEKS, TOPS. ONCE YOU REVERT, IT'LL KILL YOU.
SOMETHING'S NOT RIGHT WITH YOUR TRANSFORMATION--
GIRL, YOU GOTTA SEIZE THE MOMENT. DIDN'T YOU EVER HAVE SOME ELEMENTARY SCHOOL TEACHER OR SOMEONE TELL YOU THAT?
WE GOTTA BRING THAT LITTLE KID BACK TO HIS MOM. THIS IS WHAT I SIGNED UP FOR.
CAN'T GO IN RIGHT NOW. BUT I GOT AN IDEA.
WE NEED TO GET BACK TO OCTAVIAN AND COORDINATE. IT'S GONNA TAKE MAYBE A DAY TO FIGURE IT OUT.
HOW COULD YOU JUST ACT LIKE IT'S SO SIMPLE?
I NEVER SAID IT WAS SIMPLE. NOTHING IS SIMPLE.
BUT YOU'VE ONLY GIVEN YOURSELF A FEW WEEKS TO LIVE--
THEN WE'D BETTER MAKE THE MOST OF THEM.

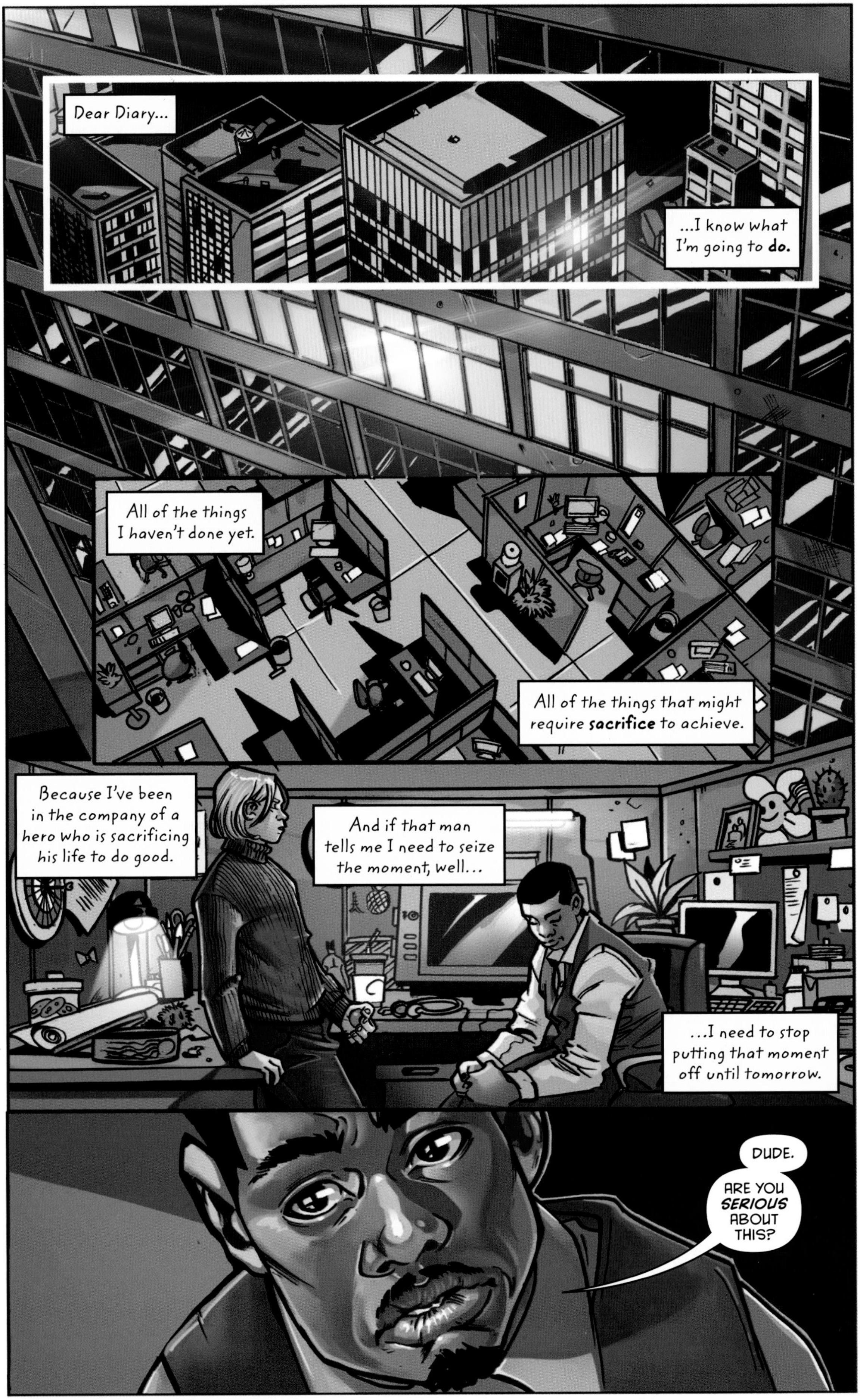
Dear Diary...
...I know what I'm going to **do.**
All of the things I haven't done yet.
All of the things that might require **sacrifice** to achieve.
Because I've been in the company of a hero who is sacrificing his life to do good.
And if that man tells me I need to seize the moment, well...
...I need to stop putting that moment off until tomorrow.
DUDE.
ARE YOU *SERIOUS* ABOUT THIS?

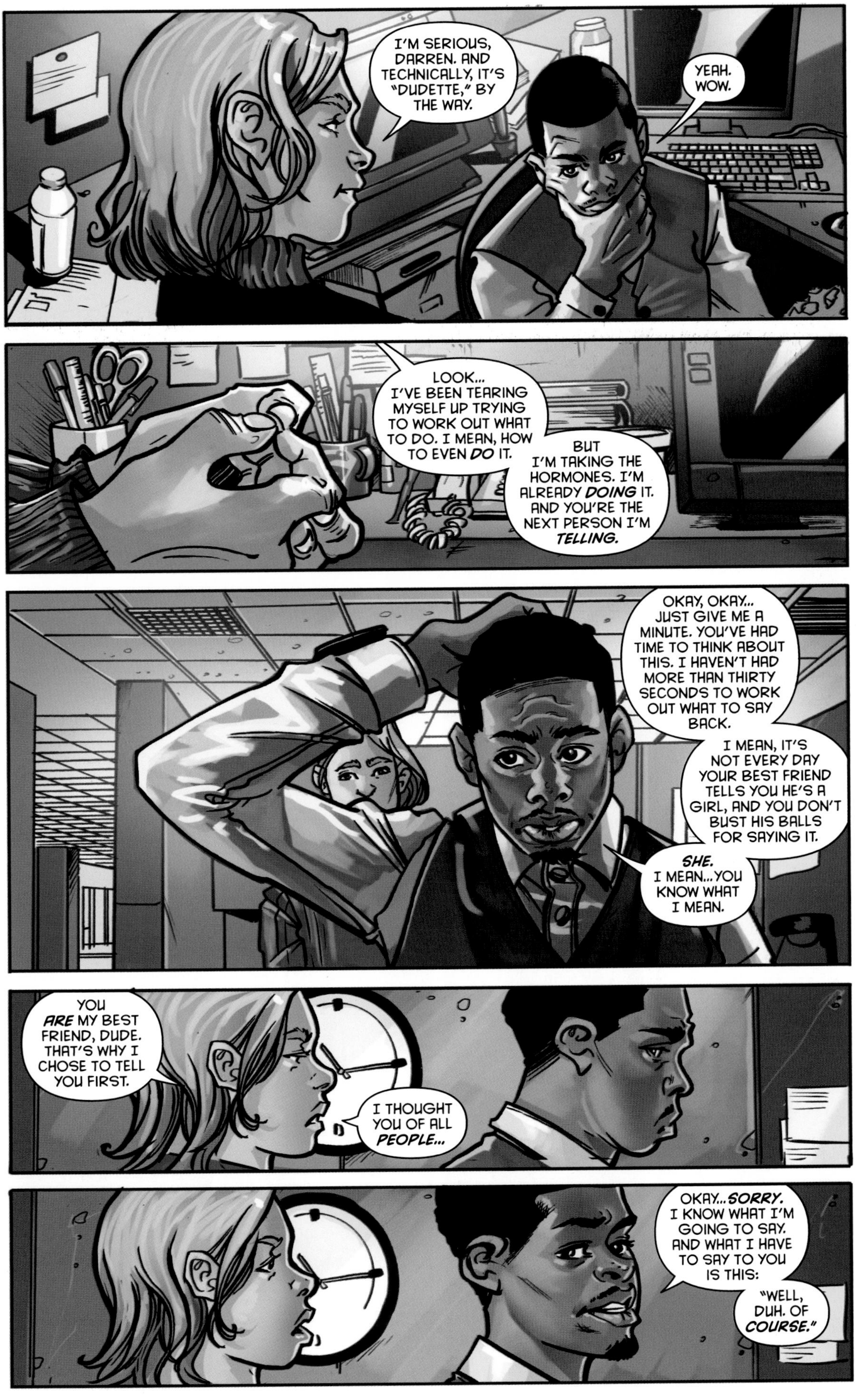
I'M SERIOUS, DARREN. AND TECHNICALLY, IT'S "DUDETTE," BY THE WAY.
YEAH. WOW.
LOOK... I'VE BEEN TEARING MYSELF UP TRYING TO WORK OUT WHAT TO DO. I MEAN, HOW TO EVEN *DO* IT.
BUT I'M TAKING THE HORMONES. I'M ALREADY *DOING* IT. AND YOU'RE THE NEXT PERSON I'M *TELLING.*
OKAY, OKAY... JUST GIVE ME A MINUTE. YOU'VE HAD TIME TO THINK ABOUT THIS. I HAVEN'T HAD MORE THAN THIRTY SECONDS TO WORK OUT WHAT TO SAY BACK.
I MEAN, IT'S NOT EVERY DAY YOUR BEST FRIEND TELLS YOU HE'S A GIRL, AND YOU DON'T BUST HIS BALLS FOR SAYING IT.
SHE. I MEAN... YOU KNOW WHAT I MEAN.
YOU *ARE* MY BEST FRIEND, DUDE. THAT'S WHY I CHOSE TO TELL YOU FIRST.
I THOUGHT YOU OF ALL *PEOPLE...*
OKAY... *SORRY.* I KNOW WHAT I'M GOING TO SAY. AND WHAT I HAVE TO SAY TO YOU IS THIS:
"WELL, DUH. OF *COURSE.*"

WHATEVER IT IS, YOU'RE MY BROTHER--

SISTER.

RIGHT. SISTER.

AND I'VE KNOWN YOU SINCE WE WERE IN DAYCARE. *BEFORE*, EVEN. SINCE WE WERE *BABIES*.

IT'S LIKE, I CAN'T EVEN IMAGINE HOW *HARD* THIS IS FOR YOU, CHARLIE. I KNOW YOU MUST BE SCARED TO TELL EVERYONE.

BUT I'M, LIKE, "OKAY. THAT EXPLAINS A FEW THINGS."

MEANING WHAT?

MEANING, I GUESS I ALREADY *KNEW*. CAN I ASK YOU A FEW QUESTIONS?

YOU GONNA BE PISSED AT ME IF I SCREW UP AND CALL YOU "BRO" OR "DUDE"?

NOT AS LONG AS I CAN CALL YOU "ASSWIPE" IN RETURN.

COOL. SO, I ALWAYS THOUGHT YOU WERE *GAY* OR SOMETHING. BUT YOU LIKE GIRLS. WHAT'S THE DEAL WITH THAT?

I *AM* GAY. I'M A GIRL WHO LIKES GIRLS.

MAKES SENSE. SO, IF YOU GO THROUGH WITH ALL OF THIS, WILL I STILL CALL YOU "CHARLIE"?

DON'T KNOW. HAVEN'T DECIDED YET.

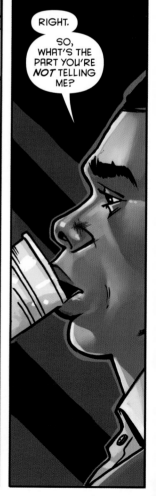

RIGHT.

SO, WHAT'S THE PART YOU'RE *NOT* TELLING ME?

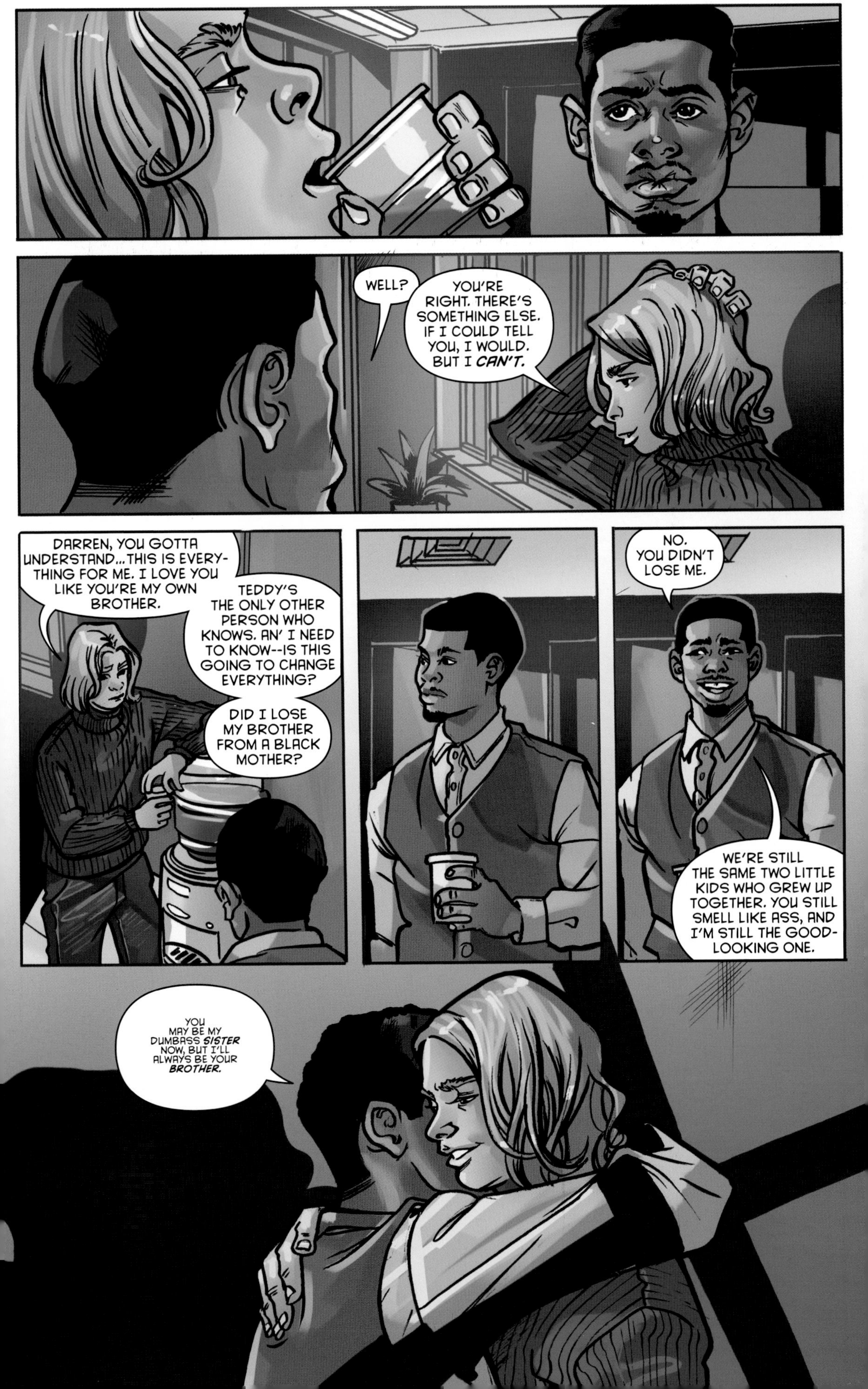
WELL?
YOU'RE RIGHT. THERE'S SOMETHING ELSE. IF I COULD TELL YOU, I WOULD. BUT I *CAN'T.*
DARREN, YOU GOTTA UNDERSTAND...THIS IS EVERYTHING FOR ME. I LOVE YOU LIKE YOU'RE MY OWN BROTHER.
TEDDY'S THE ONLY OTHER PERSON WHO KNOWS. AN' I NEED TO KNOW--IS THIS GOING TO CHANGE EVERYTHING?
DID I LOSE MY BROTHER FROM A BLACK MOTHER?
NO. YOU DIDN'T LOSE ME.
WE'RE STILL THE SAME TWO LITTLE KIDS WHO GREW UP TOGETHER. YOU STILL SMELL LIKE ASS, AND I'M STILL THE GOOD-LOOKING ONE.
YOU MAY BE MY DUMBASS *SISTER* NOW, BUT I'LL ALWAYS BE YOUR *BROTHER.*

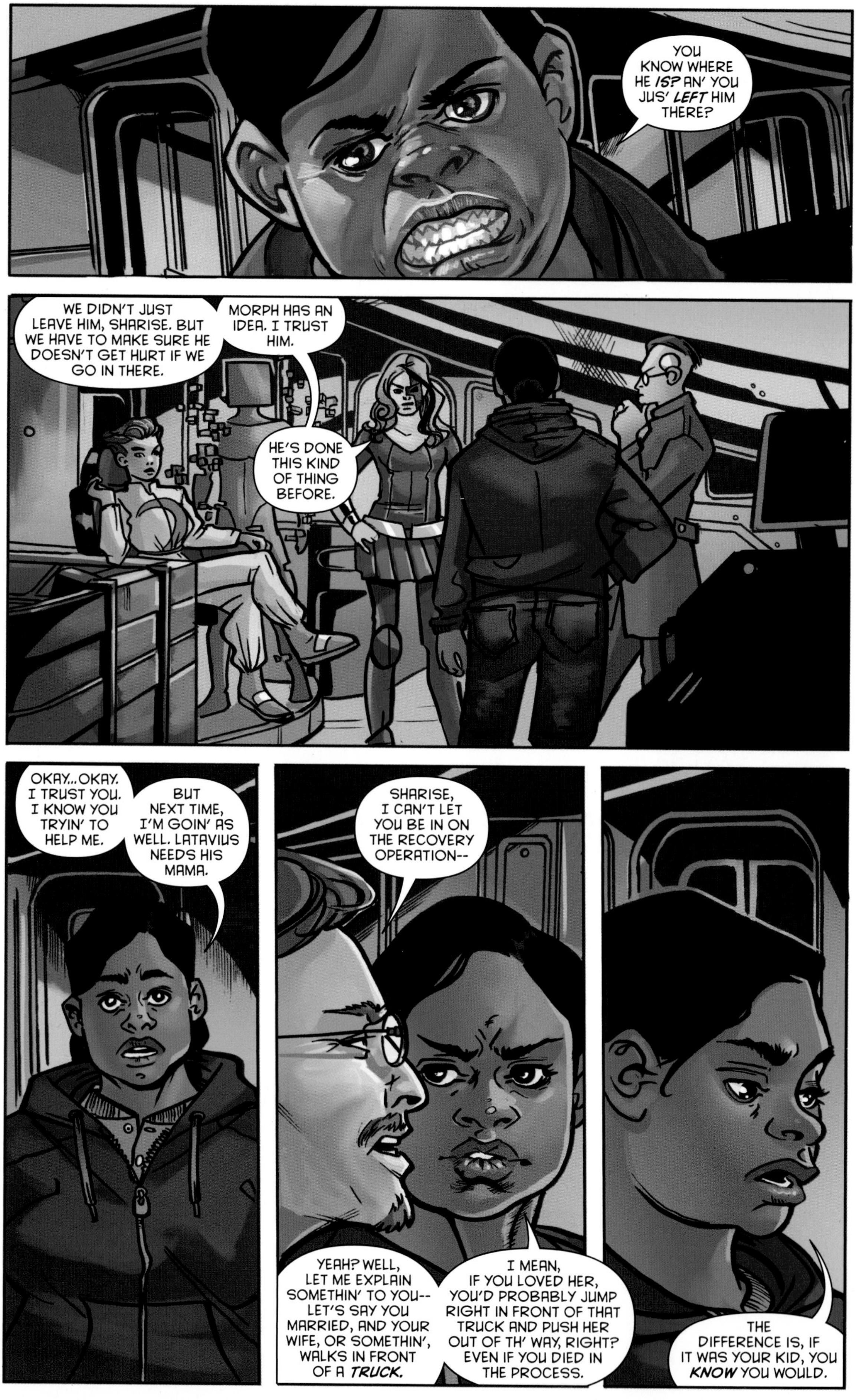
YOU KNOW WHERE HE *IS?* AN' YOU JUS' *LEFT* HIM THERE?
WE DIDN'T JUST LEAVE HIM, SHARISE. BUT WE HAVE TO MAKE SURE HE DOESN'T GET HURT IF WE GO IN THERE.
MORPH HAS AN IDEA. I TRUST HIM.
HE'S DONE THIS KIND OF THING BEFORE.
OKAY...OKAY. I TRUST YOU. I KNOW YOU TRYIN' TO HELP ME.
BUT NEXT TIME, I'M GOIN' AS WELL. LATAVIUS NEEDS HIS MAMA.
SHARISE, I CAN'T LET YOU BE IN ON THE RECOVERY OPERATION--
YEAH? WELL, LET ME EXPLAIN SOMETHIN' TO YOU-- LET'S SAY YOU MARRIED, AND YOUR WIFE, OR SOMETHIN', WALKS IN FRONT OF A *TRUCK.*
I MEAN, IF YOU LOVED HER, YOU'D PROBABLY JUMP RIGHT IN FRONT OF THAT TRUCK AND PUSH HER OUT OF TH' WAY, RIGHT? EVEN IF YOU DIED IN THE PROCESS.
THE DIFFERENCE IS, IF IT WAS YOUR KID, YOU *KNOW* YOU WOULD.

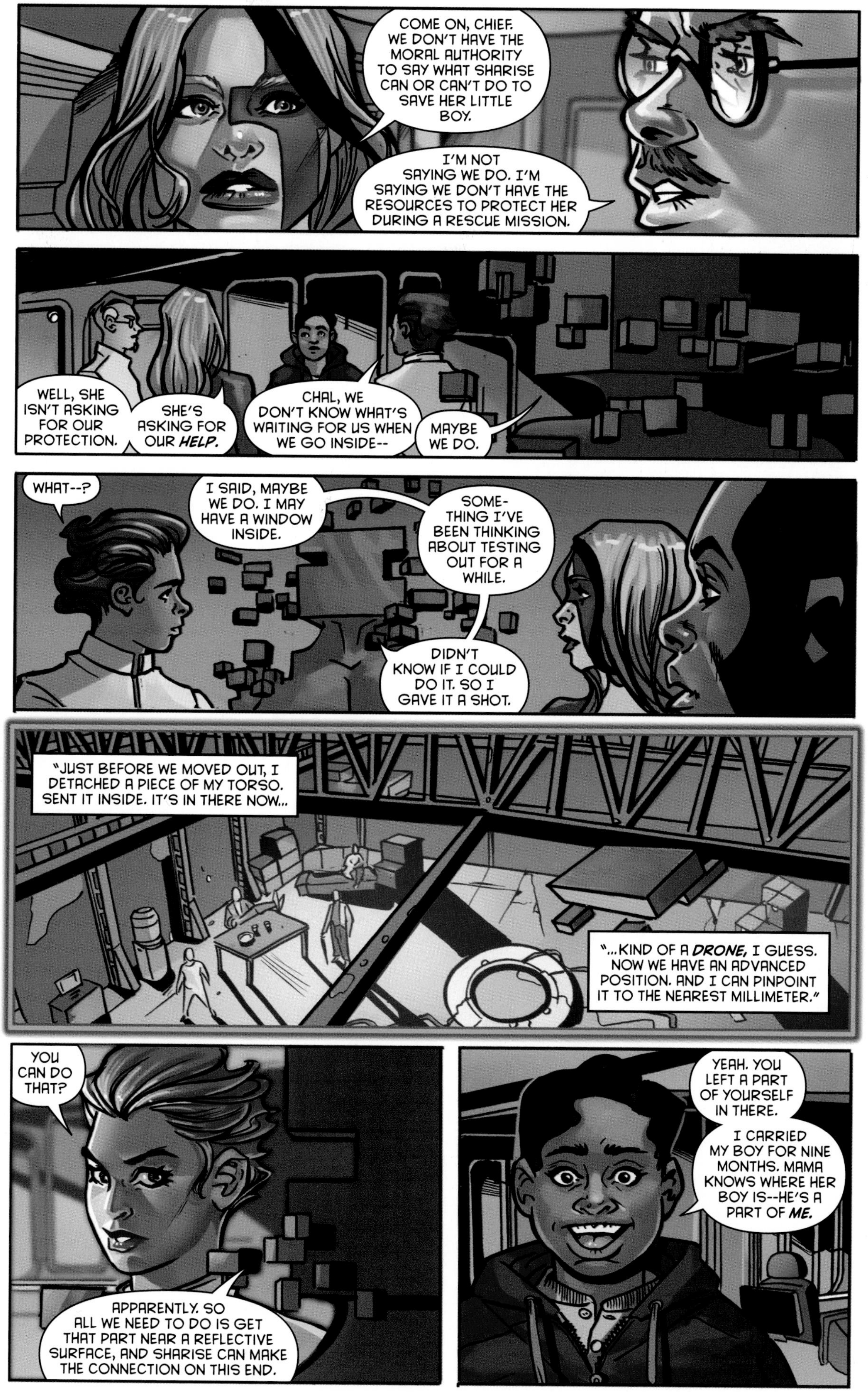
COME ON, CHIEF. WE DON'T HAVE THE MORAL AUTHORITY TO SAY WHAT SHARISE CAN OR CAN'T DO TO SAVE HER LITTLE BOY.
I'M NOT SAYING WE DO. I'M SAYING WE DON'T HAVE THE RESOURCES TO PROTECT HER DURING A RESCUE MISSION.
WELL, SHE ISN'T ASKING FOR OUR PROTECTION.
SHE'S ASKING FOR OUR **HELP.**
CHAL, WE DON'T KNOW WHAT'S WAITING FOR US WHEN WE GO INSIDE--
MAYBE WE DO.
WHAT--?
I SAID, MAYBE WE DO. I MAY HAVE A WINDOW INSIDE.
SOME-THING I'VE BEEN THINKING ABOUT TESTING OUT FOR A WHILE.
DIDN'T KNOW IF I COULD DO IT. SO I GAVE IT A SHOT.
"JUST BEFORE WE MOVED OUT, I DETACHED A PIECE OF MY TORSO. SENT IT INSIDE. IT'S IN THERE NOW...
"...KIND OF A **DRONE,** I GUESS. NOW WE HAVE AN ADVANCED POSITION. AND I CAN PINPOINT IT TO THE NEAREST MILLIMETER."
YOU CAN DO THAT?
APPARENTLY. SO ALL WE NEED TO DO IS GET THAT PART NEAR A REFLECTIVE SURFACE, AND SHARISE CAN MAKE THE CONNECTION ON THIS END.
YEAH. YOU LEFT A PART OF YOURSELF IN THERE.
I CARRIED MY BOY FOR NINE MONTHS. MAMA KNOWS WHERE HER BOY IS--HE'S A PART OF **ME.**

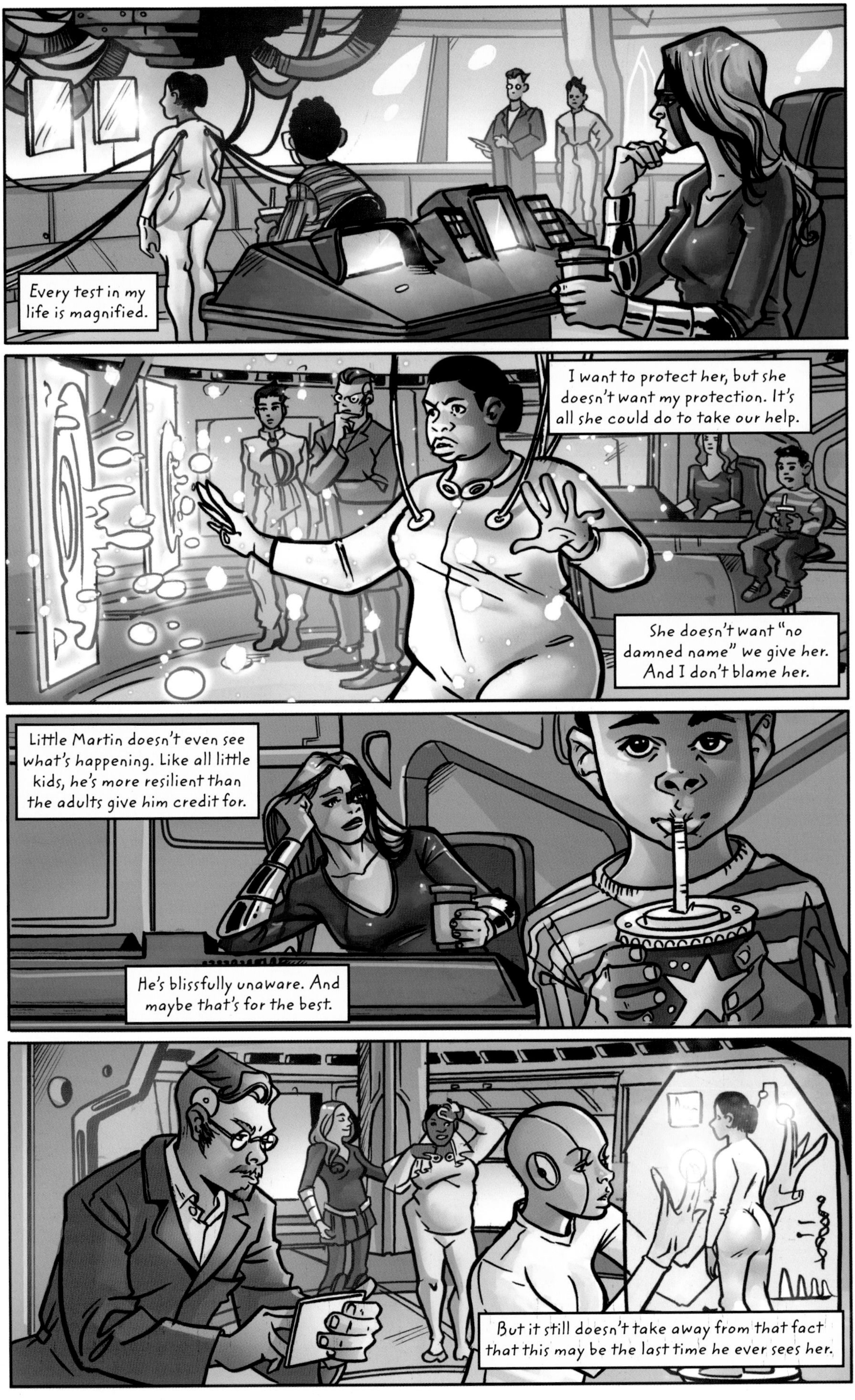
Every test in my life is magnified.
I want to protect her, but she doesn't want my protection. It's all she could do to take our help.
She doesn't want "no damned name" we give her. And I don't blame her.
Little Martin doesn't even see what's happening. Like all little kids, he's more resilient than the adults give him credit for.
He's blissfully unaware. And maybe that's for the best.
But it still doesn't take away from that fact that this may be the last time he ever sees her.

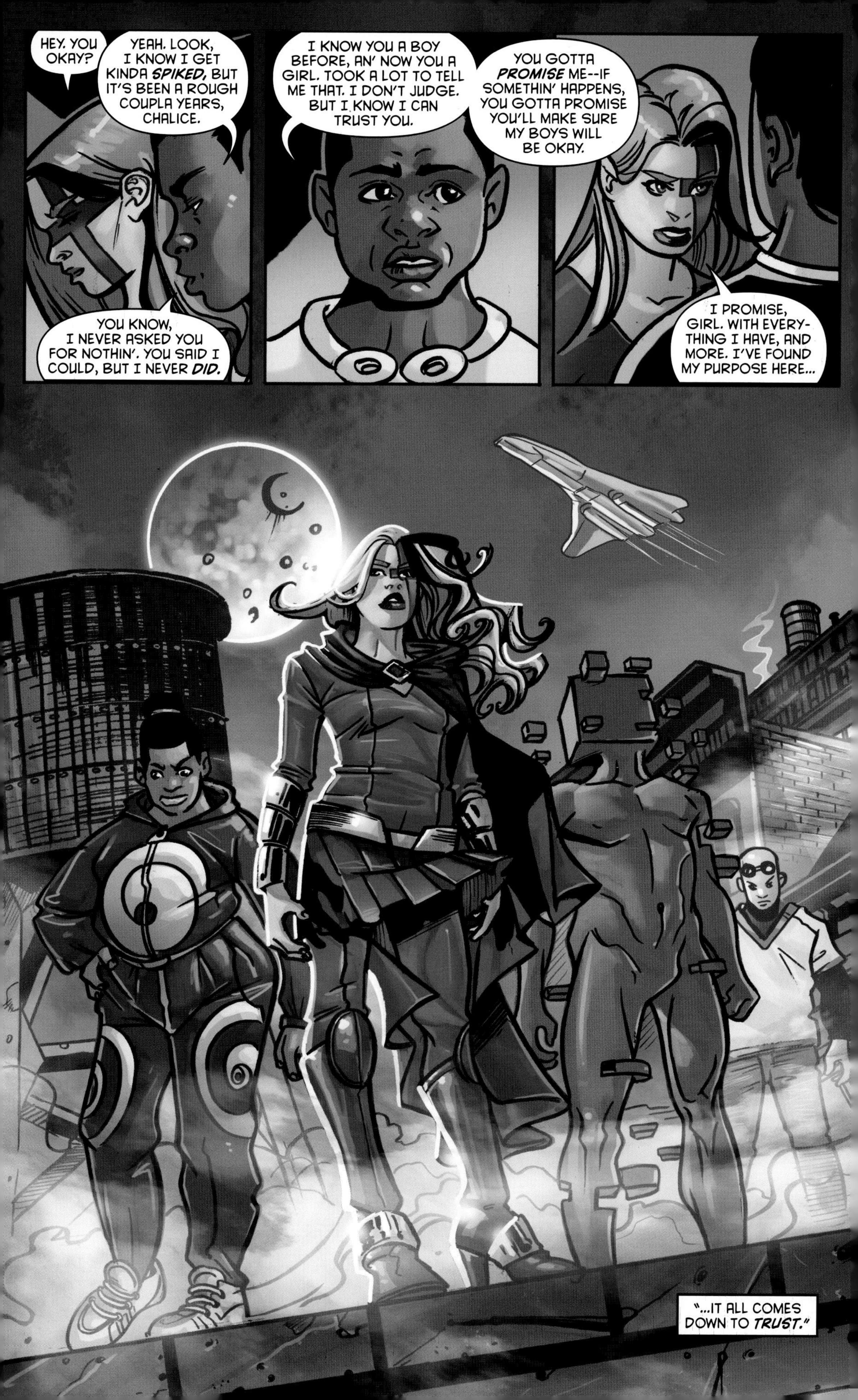
HEY. YOU OKAY?
YEAH. LOOK, I KNOW I GET KINDA SPIKED, BUT IT'S BEEN A ROUGH COUPLA YEARS, CHALICE.
YOU KNOW, I NEVER ASKED YOU FOR NOTHIN'. YOU SAID I COULD, BUT I NEVER DID.
I KNOW YOU A BOY BEFORE, AN' NOW YOU A GIRL. TOOK A LOT TO TELL ME THAT. I DON'T JUDGE. BUT I KNOW I CAN TRUST YOU.
YOU GOTTA PROMISE ME--IF SOMETHIN' HAPPENS, YOU GOTTA PROMISE YOU'LL MAKE SURE MY BOYS WILL BE OKAY.
I PROMISE, GIRL. WITH EVERYTHING I HAVE, AND MORE. I'VE FOUND MY PURPOSE HERE...
"...IT ALL COMES DOWN TO TRUST."

OKAY, TEAM. WE DON'T KNOW EXACTLY HOW THIS IS GOING TO WORK. IT NEEDS TO RELY ON SHARISE MAKING A CONNECTION.

I WANT YOU PEOPLE IN AND OUT. NO ONE GETS HURT.

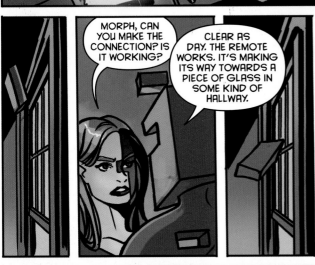

MORPH, CAN YOU MAKE THE CONNECTION? IS IT WORKING?

CLEAR AS DAY. THE REMOTE WORKS. IT'S MAKING ITS WAY TOWARDS A PIECE OF GLASS IN SOME KIND OF HALLWAY.

SHARISE...CAN YOU SEE IT?

I DON'T KNOW...I DON'T KNOW...

....I SEE IT!

GO! NOW!

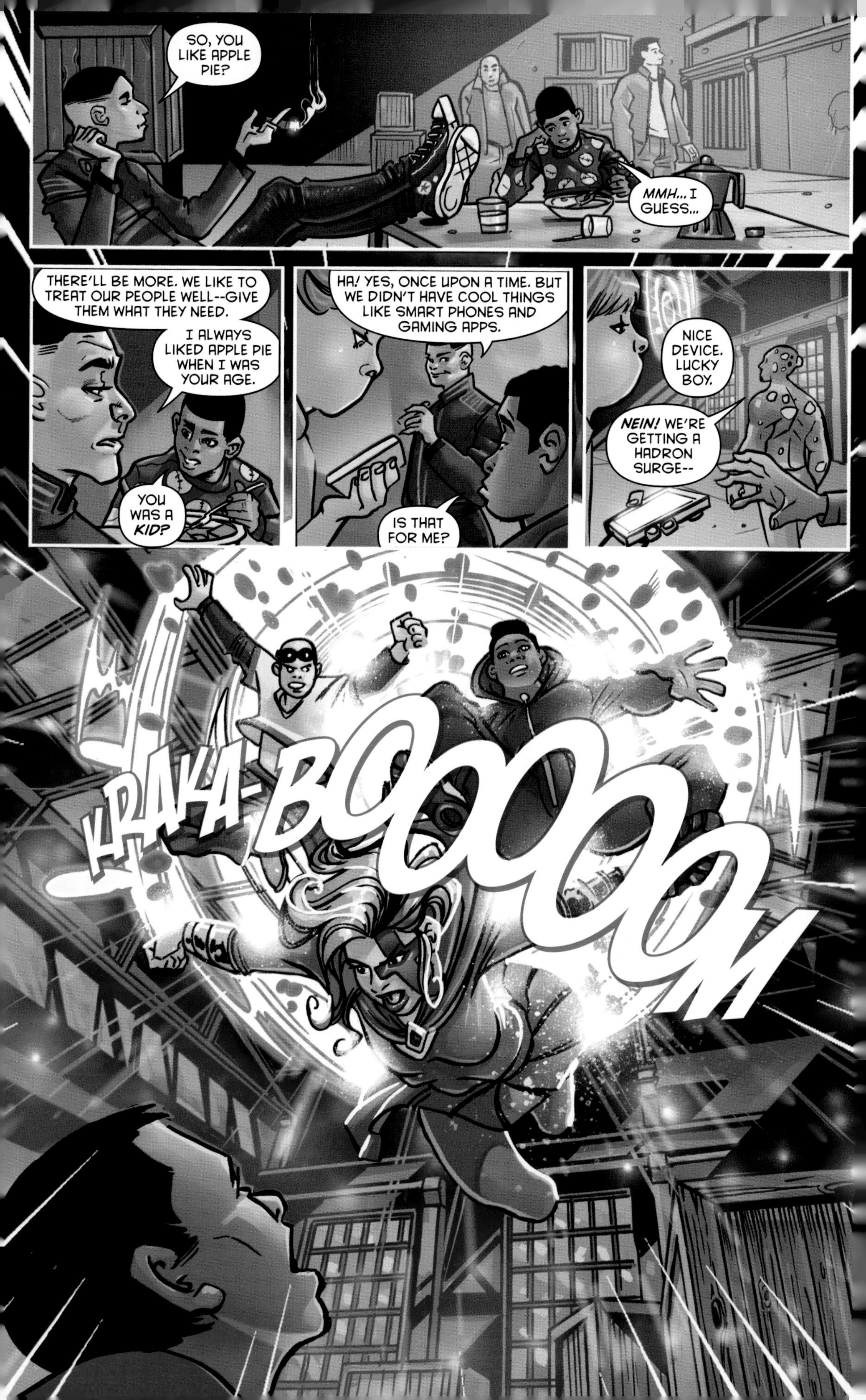
SO, YOU LIKE APPLE PIE?
MMH... I GUESS...
THERE'LL BE MORE. WE LIKE TO TREAT OUR PEOPLE WELL--GIVE THEM WHAT THEY NEED.
I ALWAYS LIKED APPLE PIE WHEN I WAS YOUR AGE.
YOU WAS A *KID*?
HA! YES, ONCE UPON A TIME. BUT WE DIDN'T HAVE COOL THINGS LIKE SMART PHONES AND GAMING APPS.
IS THAT FOR ME?
NICE DEVICE. LUCKY BOY.
NEIN! WE'RE GETTING A HADRON SURGE--
KRAKA-BOOOOOM

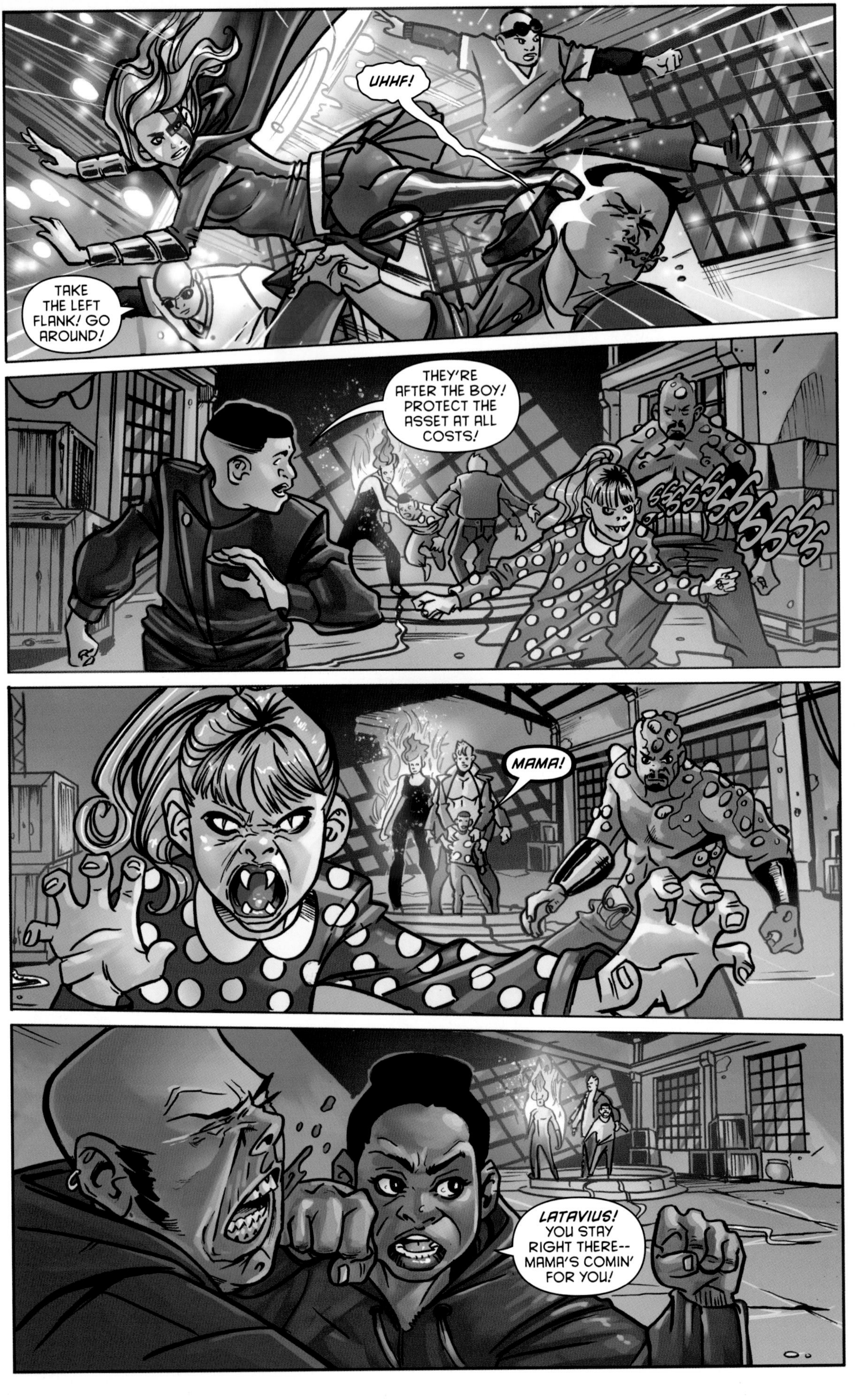
UHHF!
TAKE THE LEFT FLANK! GO AROUND!
THEY'RE AFTER THE BOY! PROTECT THE ASSET AT ALL COSTS!
MAMA!
LATAVIUS! YOU STAY RIGHT THERE-- MAMA'S COMIN' FOR YOU!

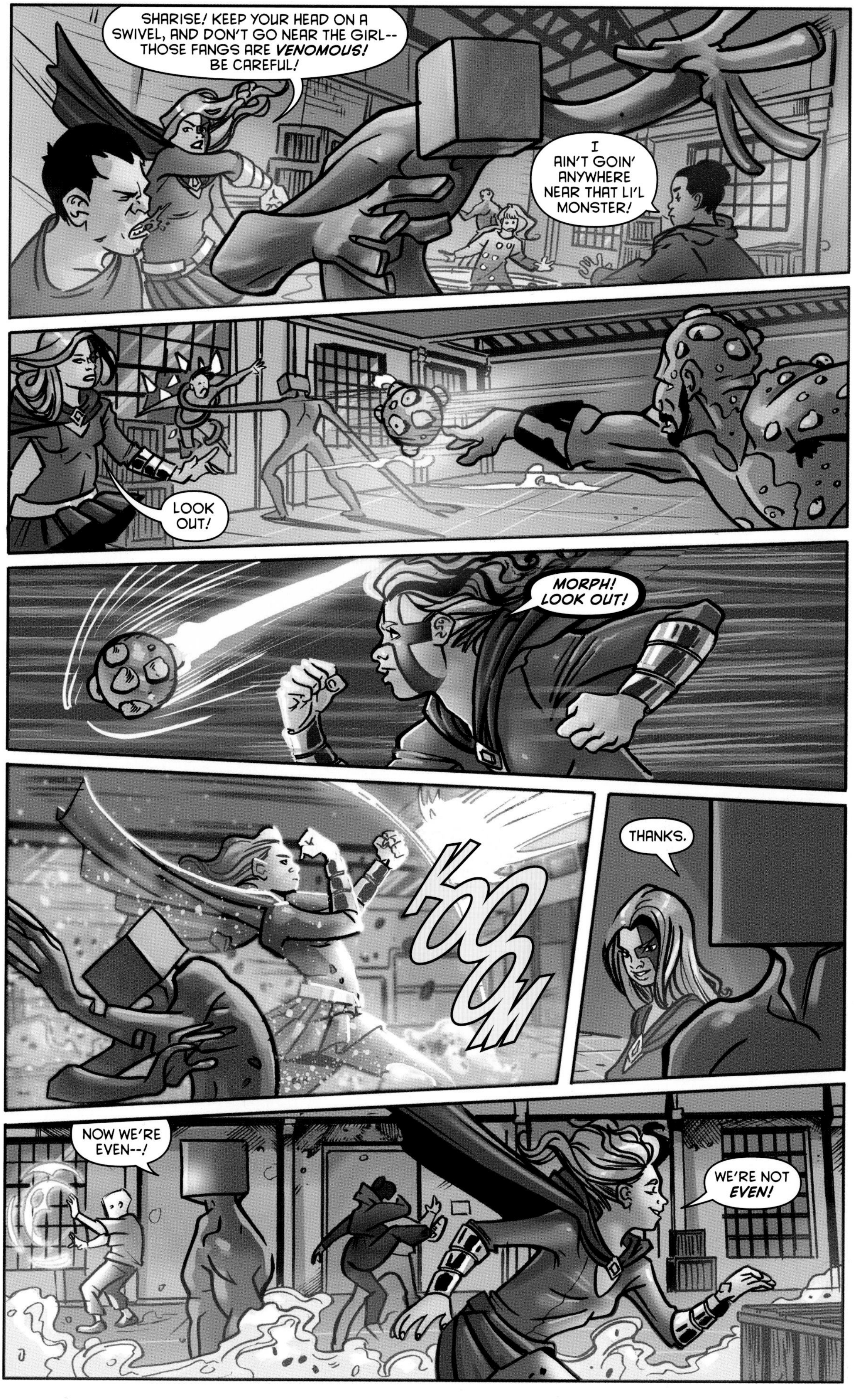
SHARISE! KEEP YOUR HEAD ON A SWIVEL, AND DON'T GO NEAR THE GIRL-- THOSE FANGS ARE VENOMOUS! BE CAREFUL!
I AIN'T GOIN' ANYWHERE NEAR THAT LI'L MONSTER!
LOOK OUT!
MORPH! LOOK OUT!
KOOOM
THANKS.
NOW WE'RE EVEN--!
WE'RE NOT EVEN!

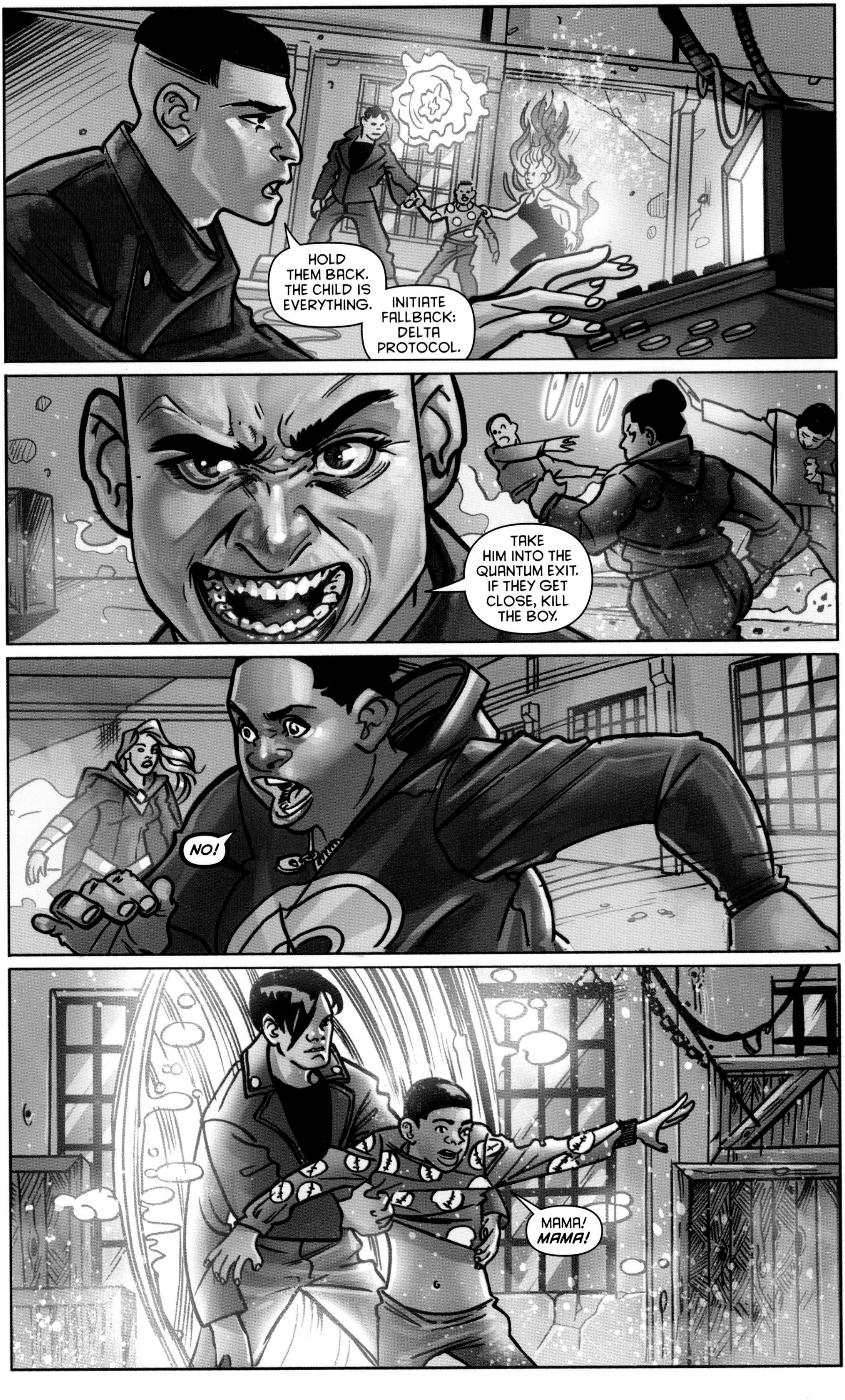
HOLD THEM BACK. THE CHILD IS EVERYTHING.
INITIATE FALLBACK: DELTA PROTOCOL.
TAKE HIM INTO THE QUANTUM EXIT. IF THEY GET CLOSE, KILL THE BOY.
NO!
MAMA! *MAMA!*

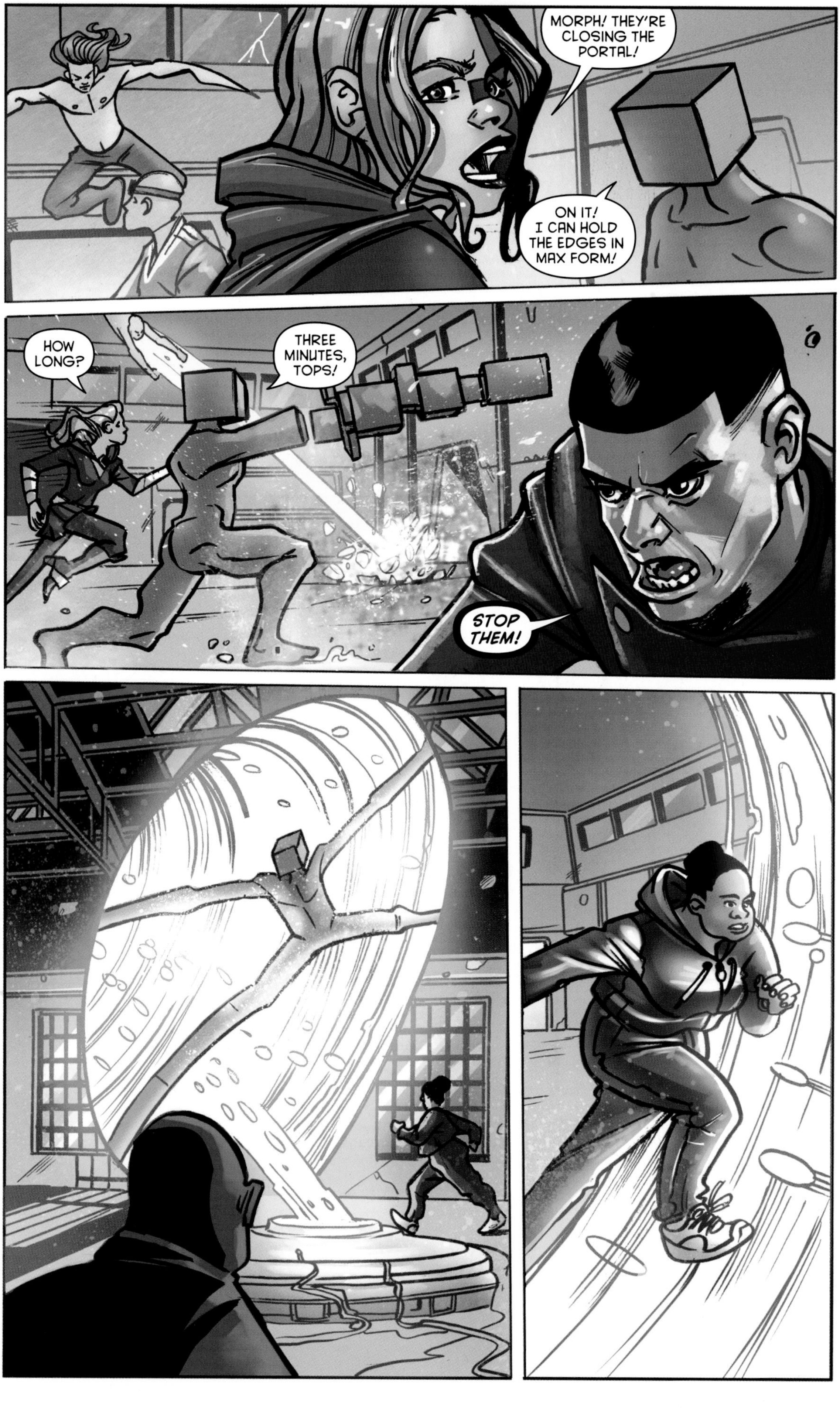
MORPH! THEY'RE CLOSING THE PORTAL!
ON IT! I CAN HOLD THE EDGES IN MAX FORM!
HOW LONG?
THREE MINUTES, TOPS!
STOP THEM!

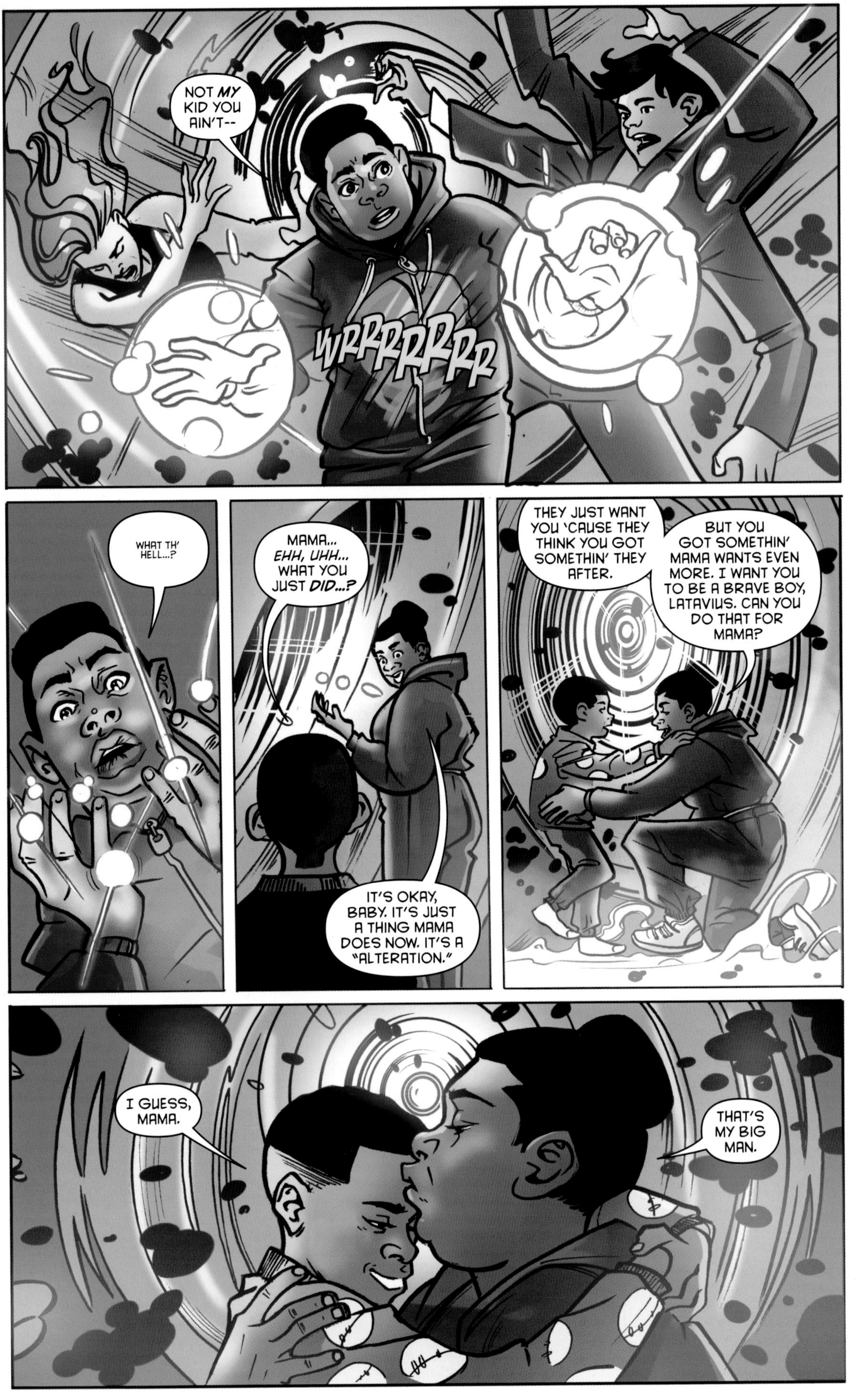
NOT *MY* KID YOU AIN'T--
WRRRRRRRR
WHAT TH' HELL...?
MAMA... *EHH, UHH...* WHAT YOU JUST *DID...?*
IT'S OKAY, BABY. IT'S JUST A THING MAMA DOES NOW. IT'S A "ALTERATION."
THEY JUST WANT YOU 'CAUSE THEY THINK YOU GOT SOMETHIN' THEY AFTER.
BUT YOU GOT SOMETHIN' MAMA WANTS EVEN MORE. I WANT YOU TO BE A BRAVE BOY, LATAVIUS. CAN YOU DO THAT FOR MAMA?
I GUESS, MAMA.
THAT'S MY BIG MAN.

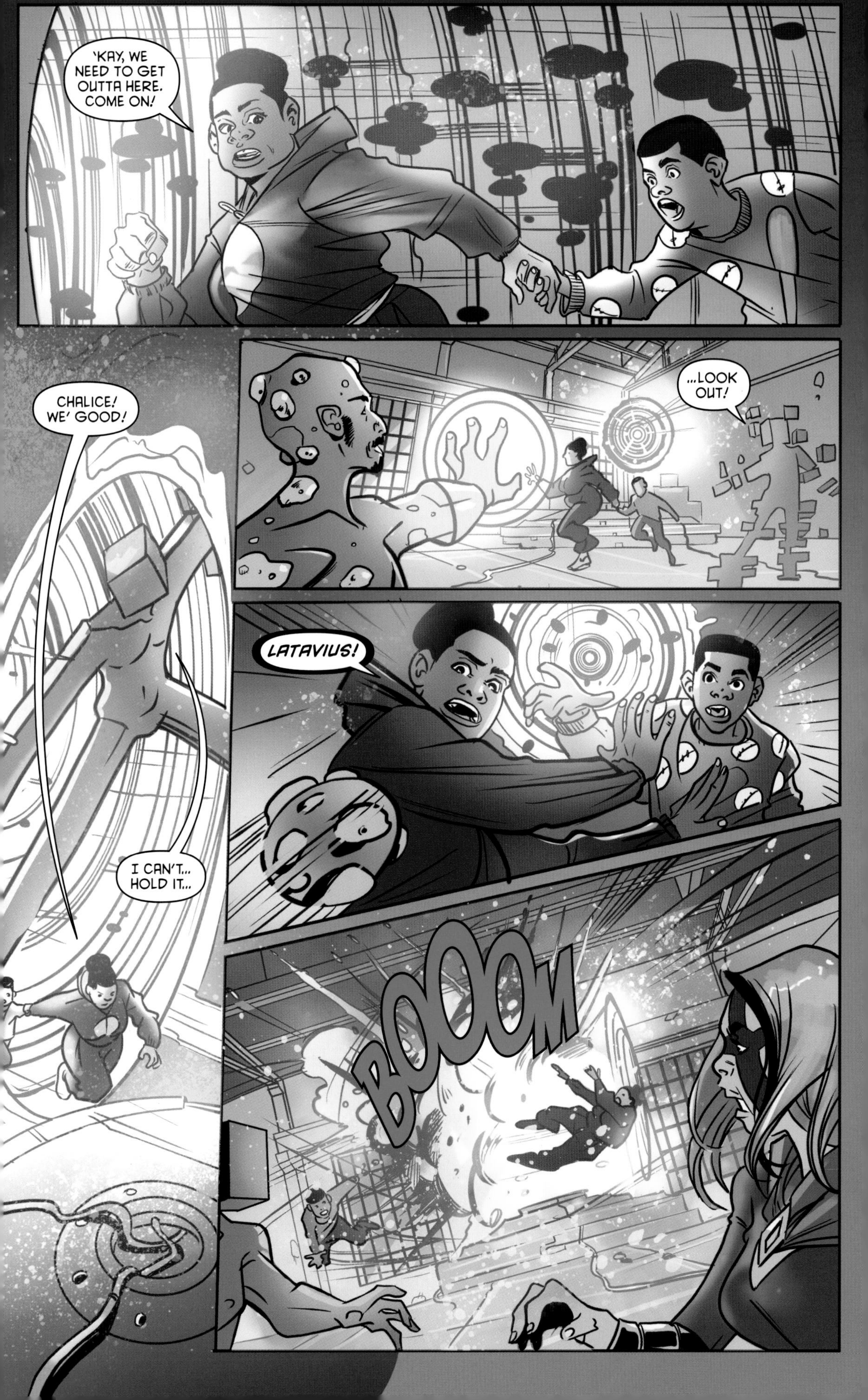
'KAY, WE NEED TO GET OUTTA HERE. COME ON!
CHALICE! WE' GOOD!
...LOOK OUT!
LATAVIUS!
I CAN'T... HOLD IT...
BOOOM

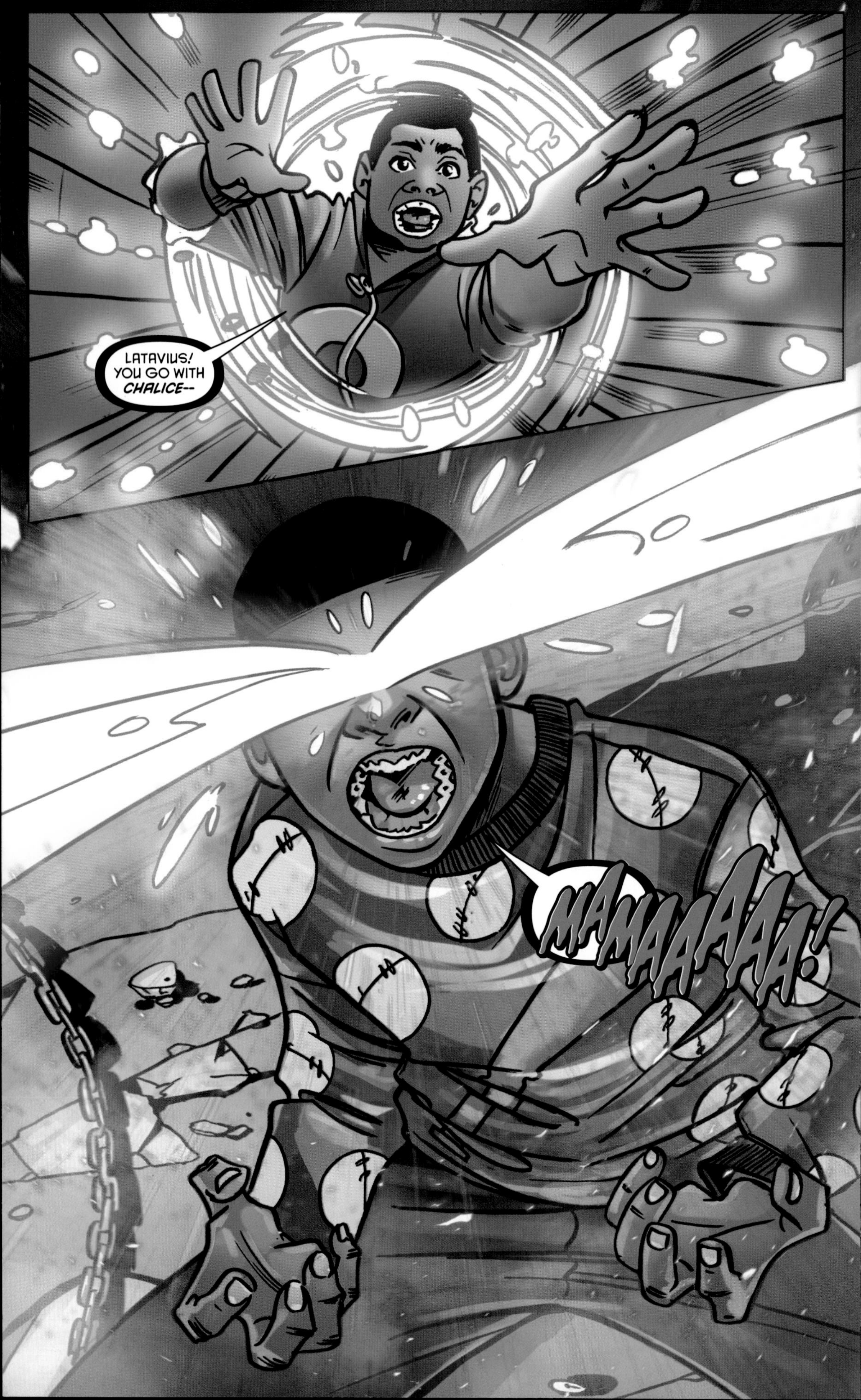
LATAVIUS! YOU GO WITH CHALICE--
MAMAAAAAA!

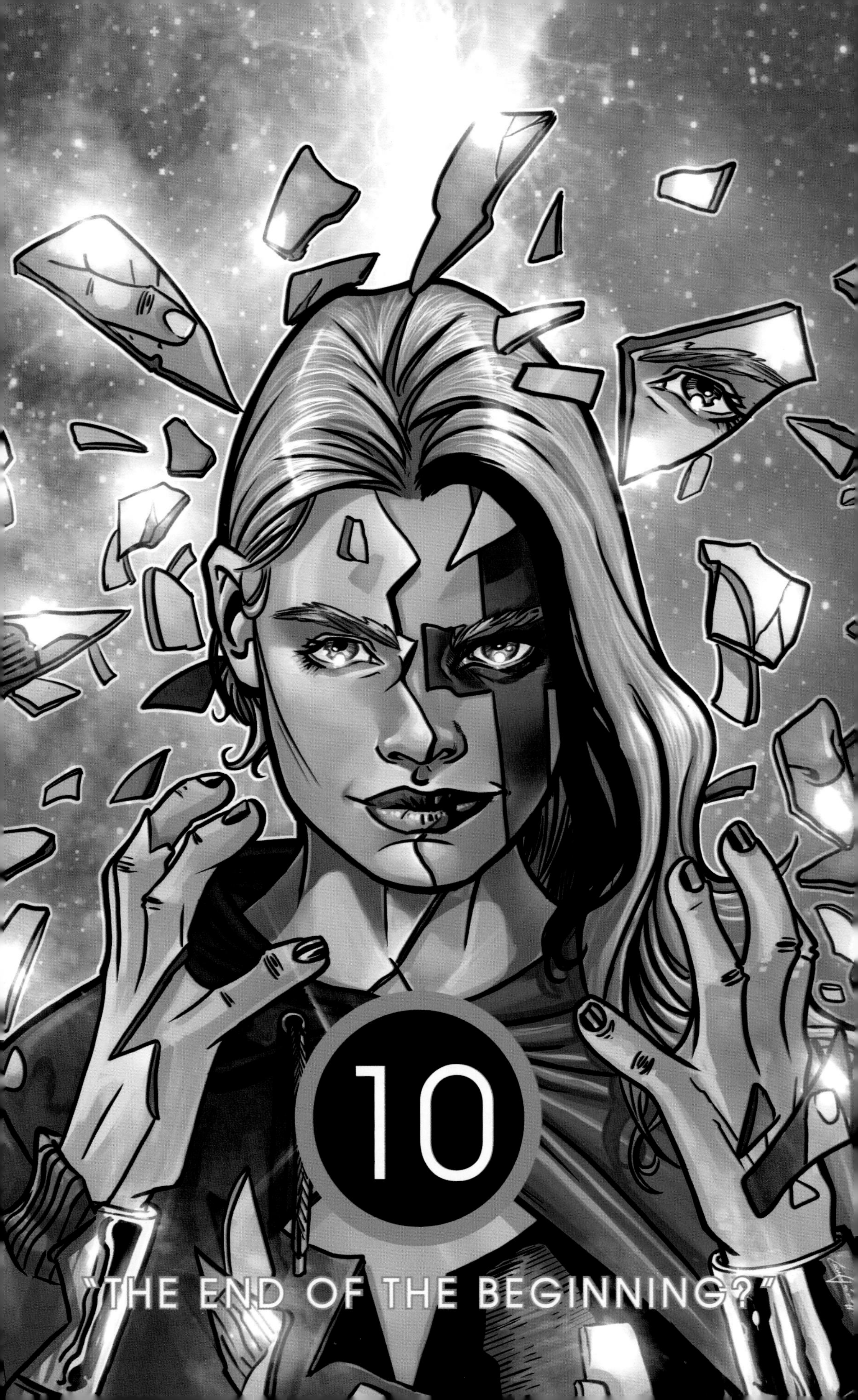
10
"THE END OF THE BEGINNING?"

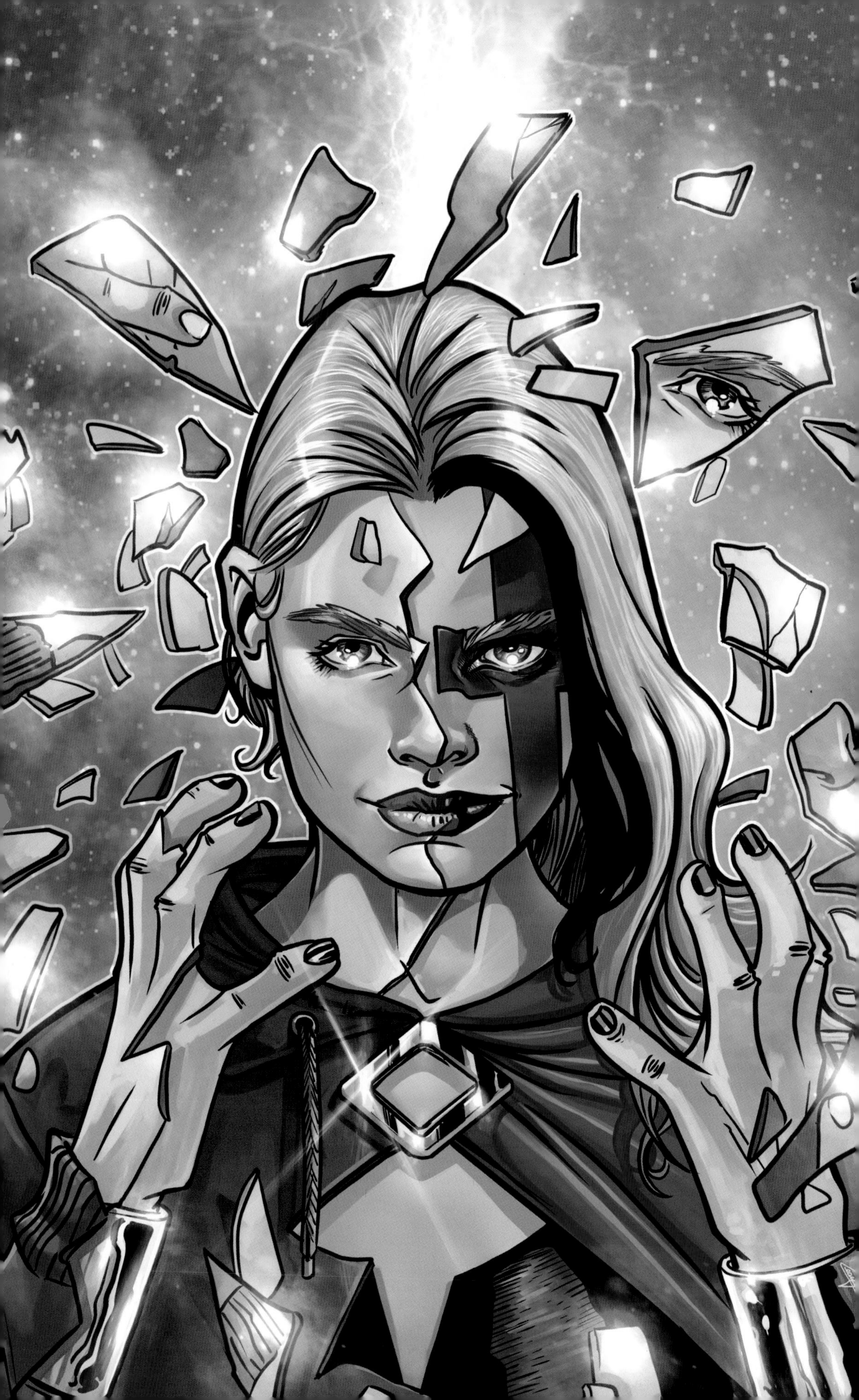

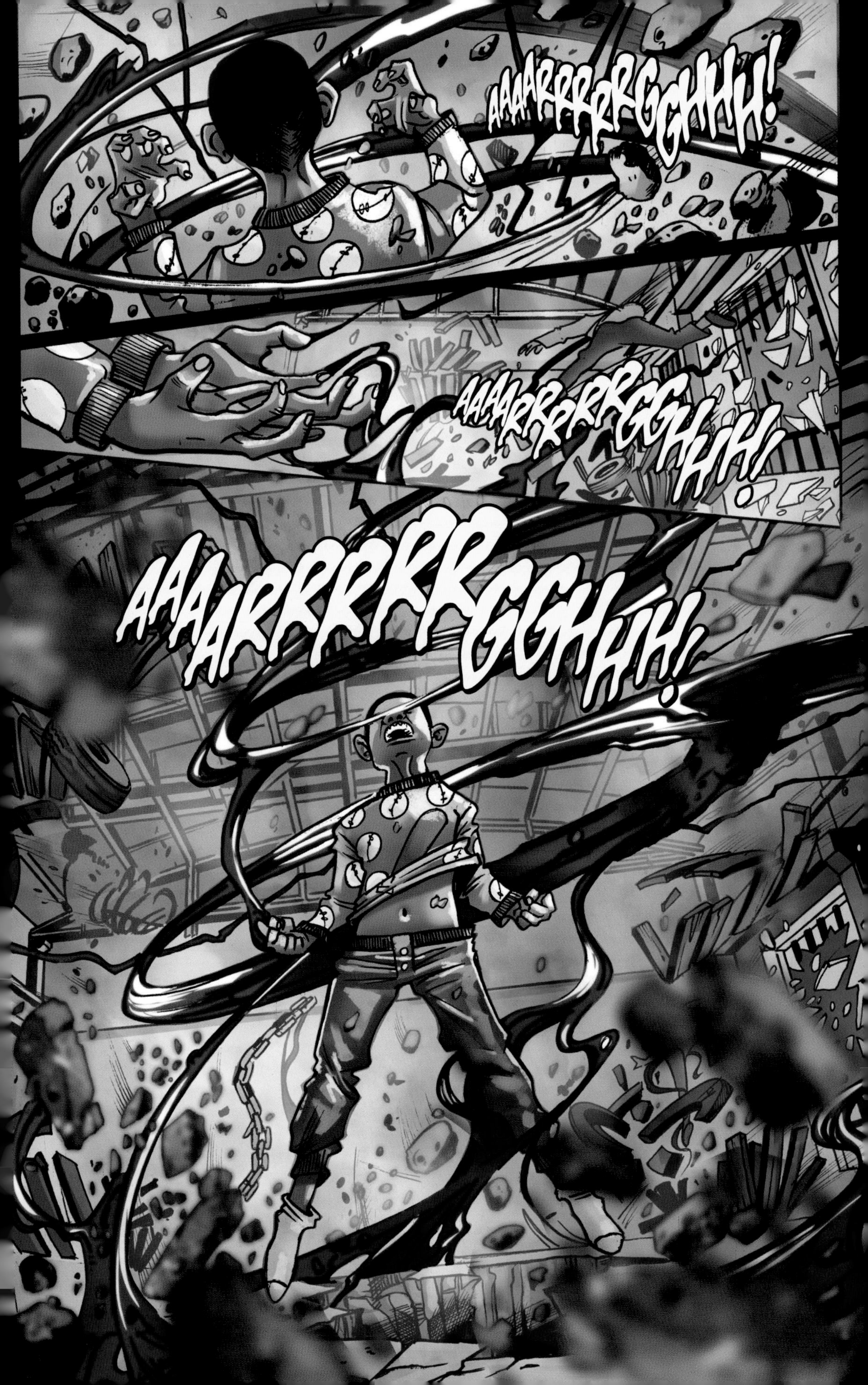
AAAARRRRRGGHHH!
AAAARRRRRRGGHHH!
AAAARRRRRGGHHH!

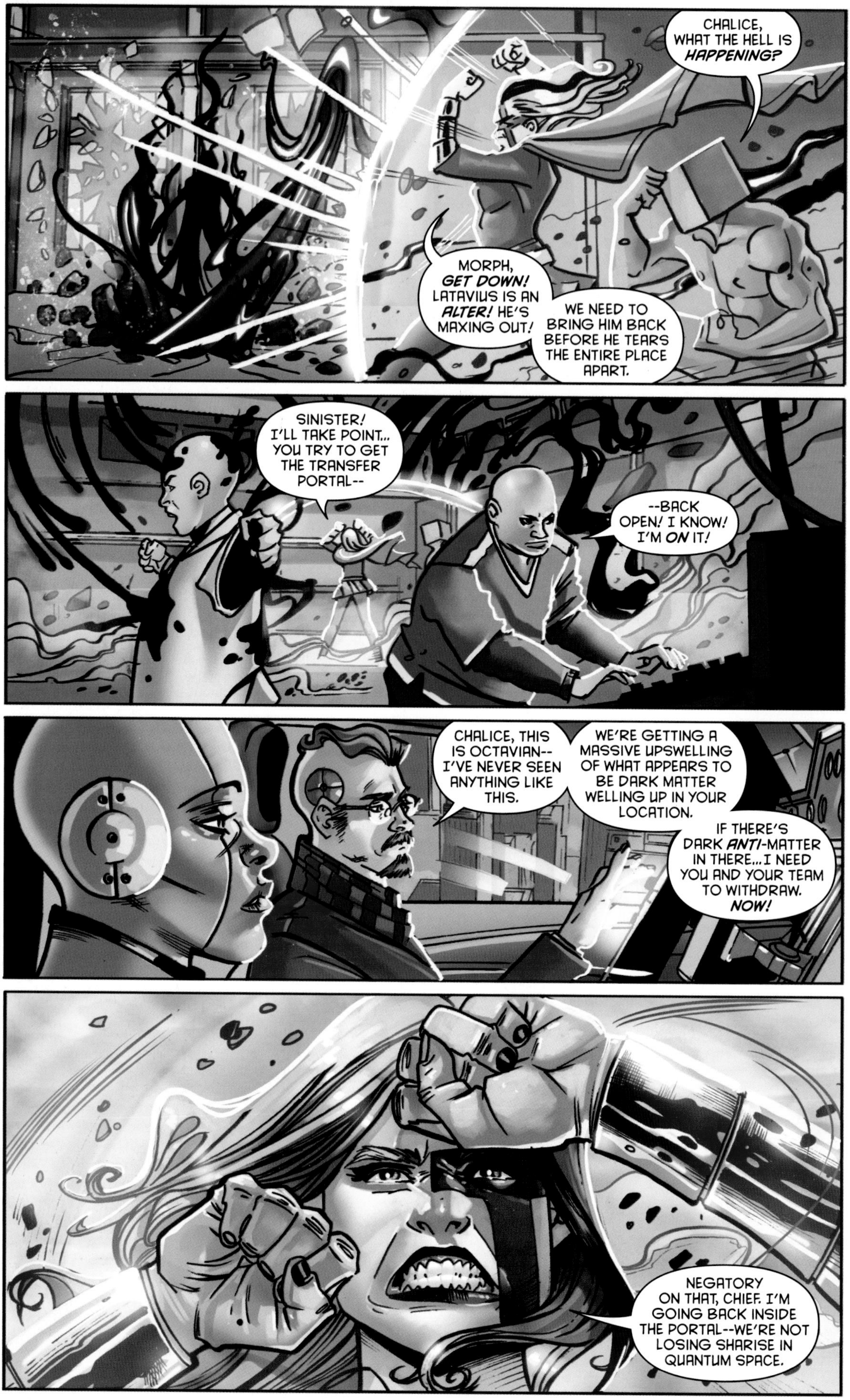
CHALICE, WHAT THE HELL IS HAPPENING?
MORPH, GET DOWN! LATAVIUS IS AN ALTER! HE'S MAXING OUT!
WE NEED TO BRING HIM BACK BEFORE HE TEARS THE ENTIRE PLACE APART.
SINISTER! I'LL TAKE POINT... YOU TRY TO GET THE TRANSFER PORTAL--
--BACK OPEN! I KNOW! I'M ON IT!
CHALICE, THIS IS OCTAVIAN-- I'VE NEVER SEEN ANYTHING LIKE THIS.
WE'RE GETTING A MASSIVE UPSWELLING OF WHAT APPEARS TO BE DARK MATTER WELLING UP IN YOUR LOCATION.
IF THERE'S DARK ANTI-MATTER IN THERE... I NEED YOU AND YOUR TEAM TO WITHDRAW. NOW!
NEGATORY ON THAT, CHIEF. I'M GOING BACK INSIDE THE PORTAL--WE'RE NOT LOSING SHARISE IN QUANTUM SPACE.

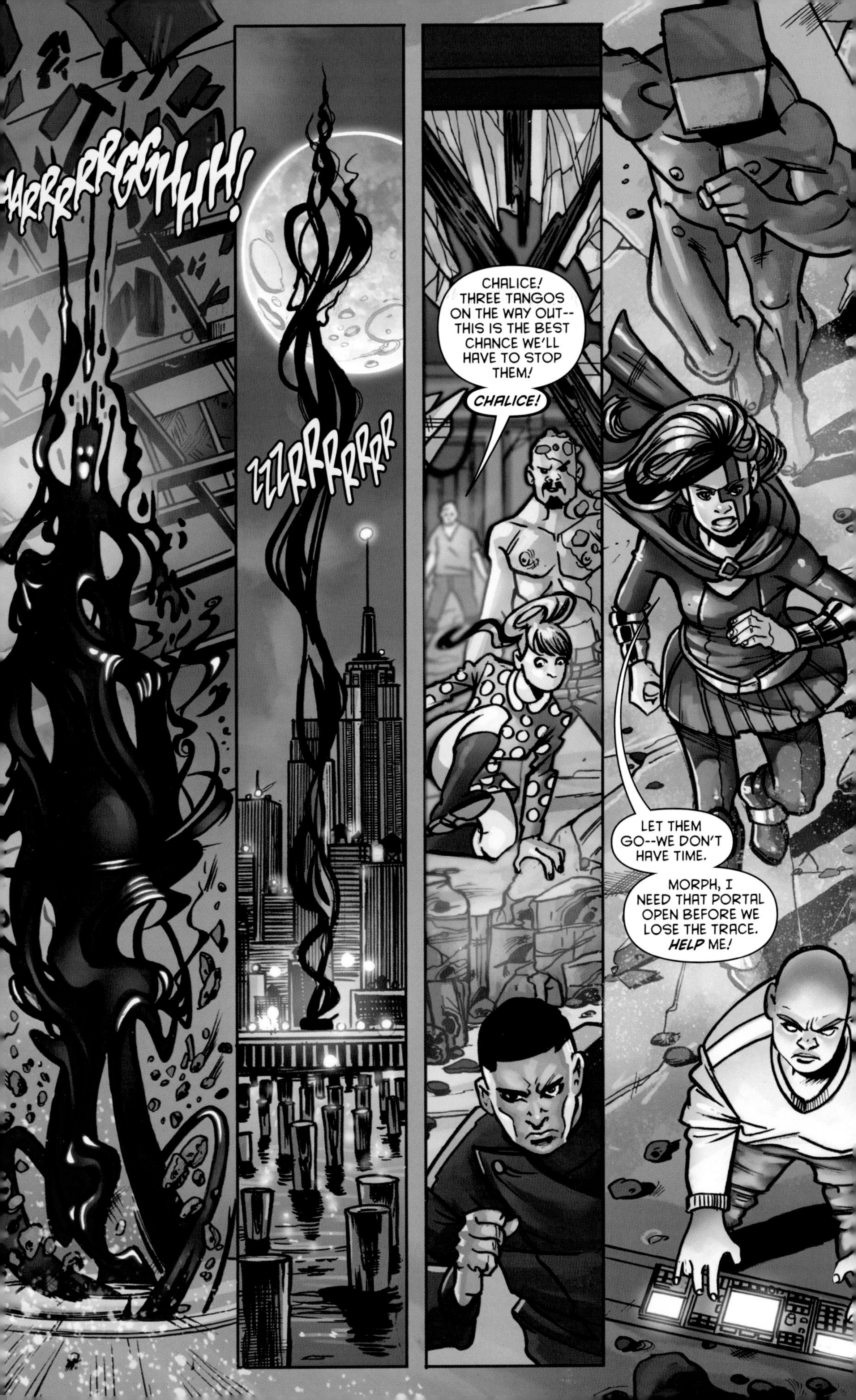
HARRRRRGGHHH!
ZZZRRRRRRR
CHALICE! THREE TANGOS ON THE WAY OUT-- THIS IS THE BEST CHANCE WE'LL HAVE TO STOP THEM!
CHALICE!
LET THEM GO--WE DON'T HAVE TIME.
MORPH, I NEED THAT PORTAL OPEN BEFORE WE LOSE THE TRACE. HELP ME!

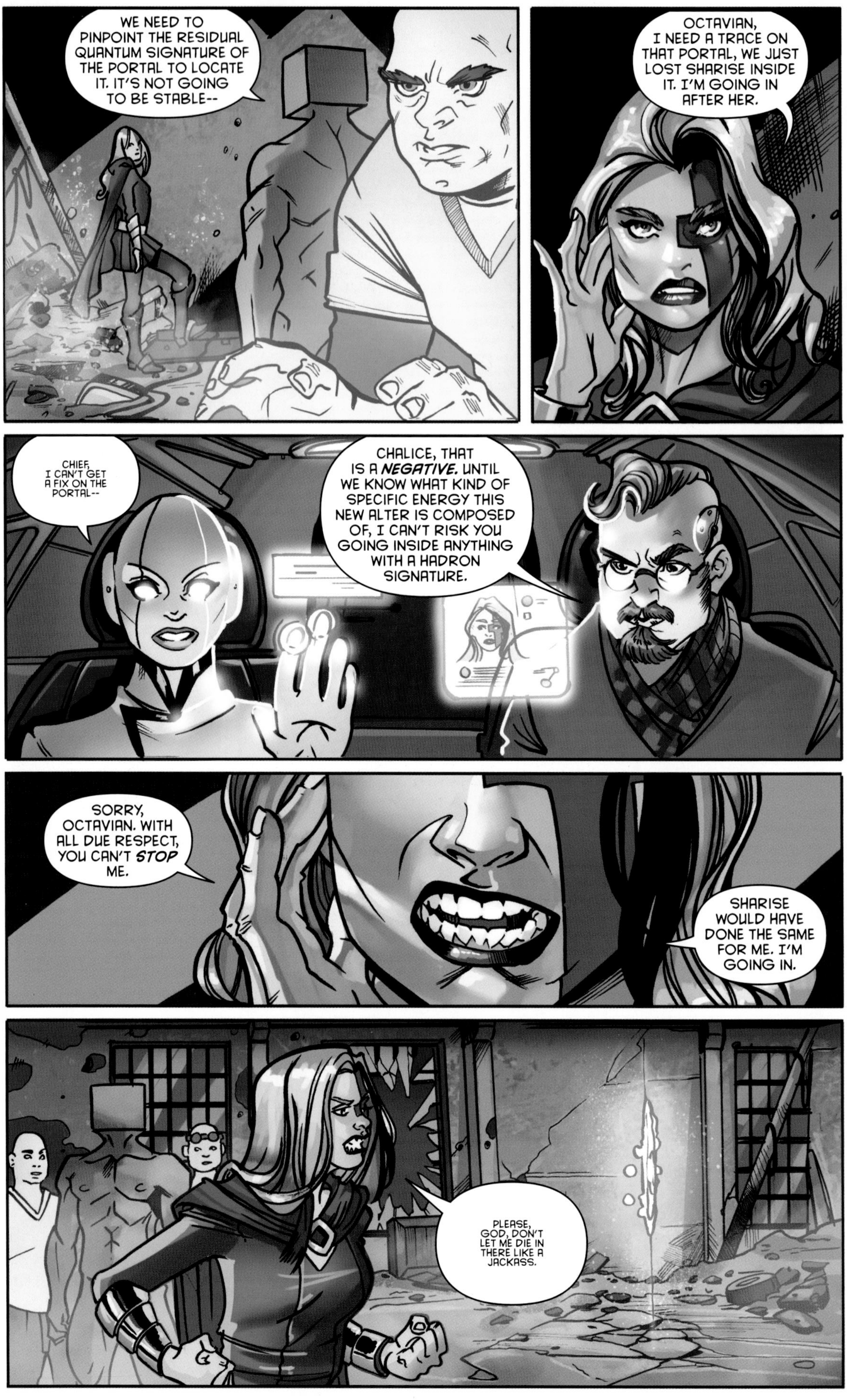

WE NEED TO PINPOINT THE RESIDUAL QUANTUM SIGNATURE OF THE PORTAL TO LOCATE IT. IT'S NOT GOING TO BE STABLE--
OCTAVIAN, I NEED A TRACE ON THAT PORTAL, WE JUST LOST SHARISE INSIDE IT. I'M GOING IN AFTER HER.
CHIEF, I CAN'T GET A FIX ON THE PORTAL--
CHALICE, THAT IS A *NEGATIVE.* UNTIL WE KNOW WHAT KIND OF SPECIFIC ENERGY THIS NEW ALTER IS COMPOSED OF, I CAN'T RISK YOU GOING INSIDE ANYTHING WITH A HADRON SIGNATURE.
SORRY, OCTAVIAN. WITH ALL DUE RESPECT, YOU CAN'T *STOP* ME.
SHARISE WOULD HAVE DONE THE SAME FOR ME. I'M GOING IN.
PLEASE, GOD, DON'T LET ME DIE IN THERE LIKE A JACKASS.

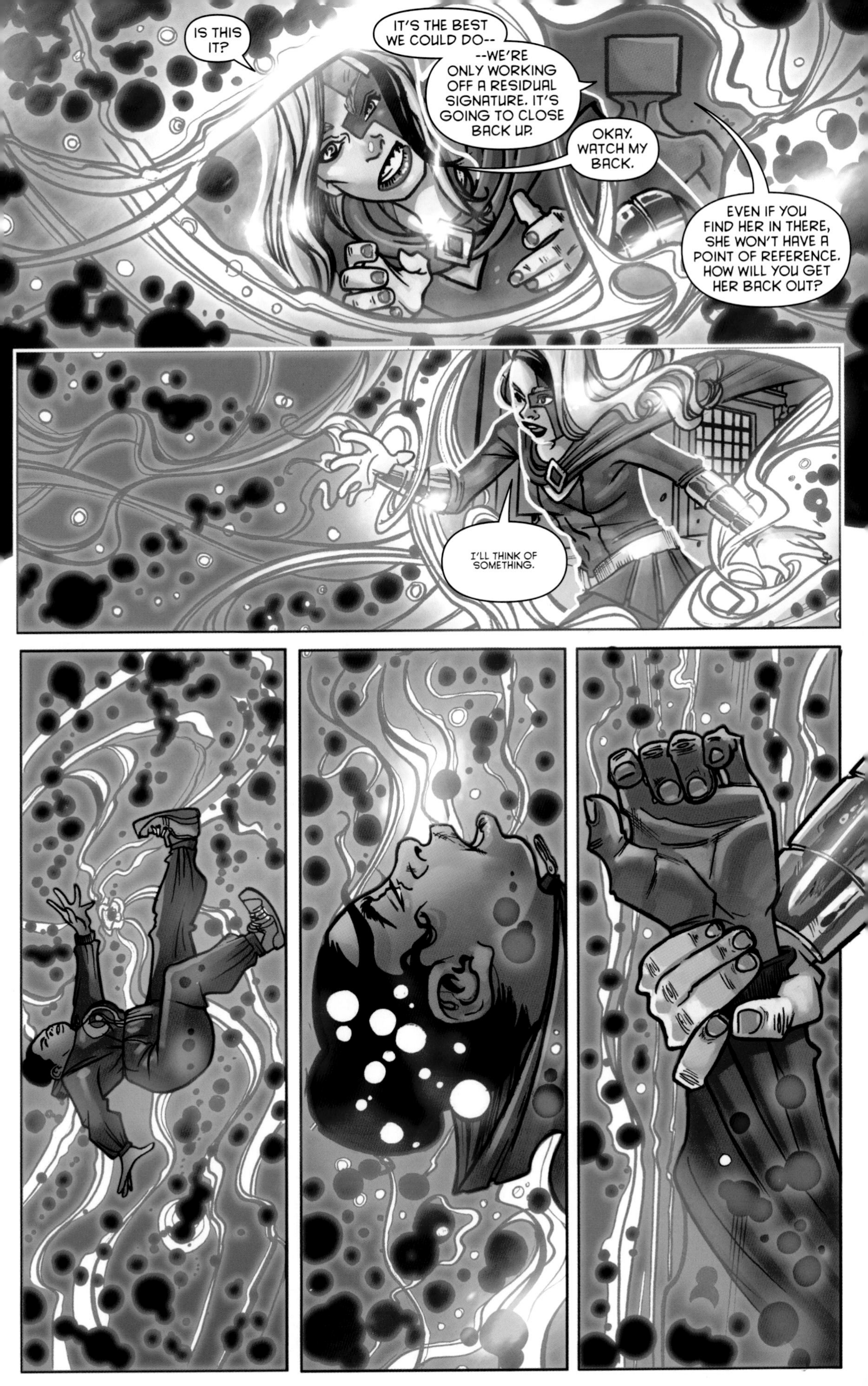
IS THIS IT?
IT'S THE BEST WE COULD DO--
--WE'RE ONLY WORKING OFF A RESIDUAL SIGNATURE. IT'S GOING TO CLOSE BACK UP.
OKAY. WATCH MY BACK.
EVEN IF YOU FIND HER IN THERE, SHE WON'T HAVE A POINT OF REFERENCE. HOW WILL YOU GET HER BACK OUT?
I'LL THINK OF SOMETHING.

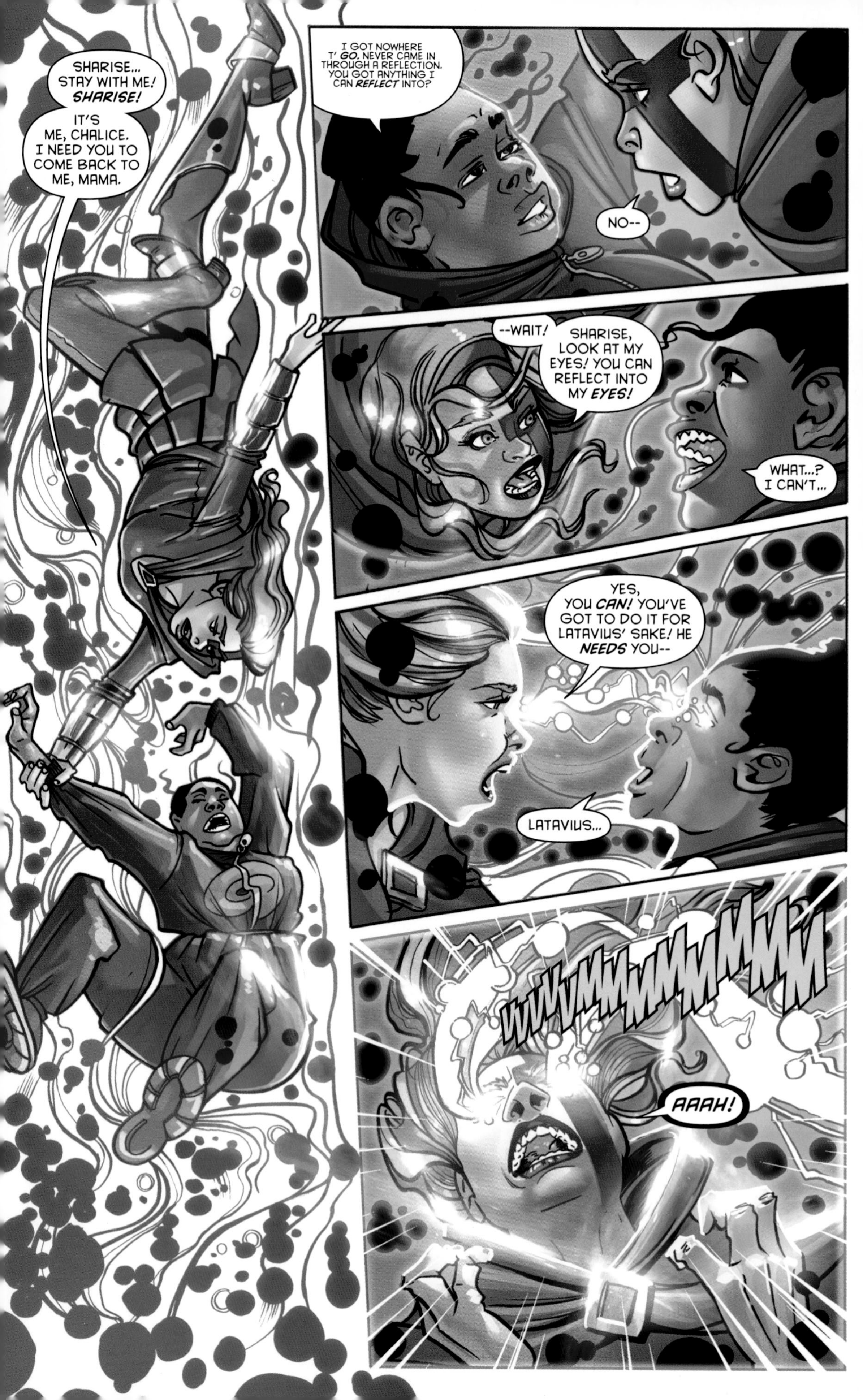
SHARISE... STAY WITH ME! SHARISE!
IT'S ME, CHALICE. I NEED YOU TO COME BACK TO ME, MAMA.
I GOT NOWHERE T' GO. NEVER CAME IN THROUGH A REFLECTION. YOU GOT ANYTHING I CAN REFLECT INTO?
NO--
--WAIT!
SHARISE, LOOK AT MY EYES! YOU CAN REFLECT INTO MY EYES!
WHAT...? I CAN'T...
YES, YOU CAN! YOU'VE GOT TO DO IT FOR LATAVIUS' SAKE! HE NEEDS YOU--
LATAVIUS...
VVVVVMMMMMMMMMMMM
AAAH!

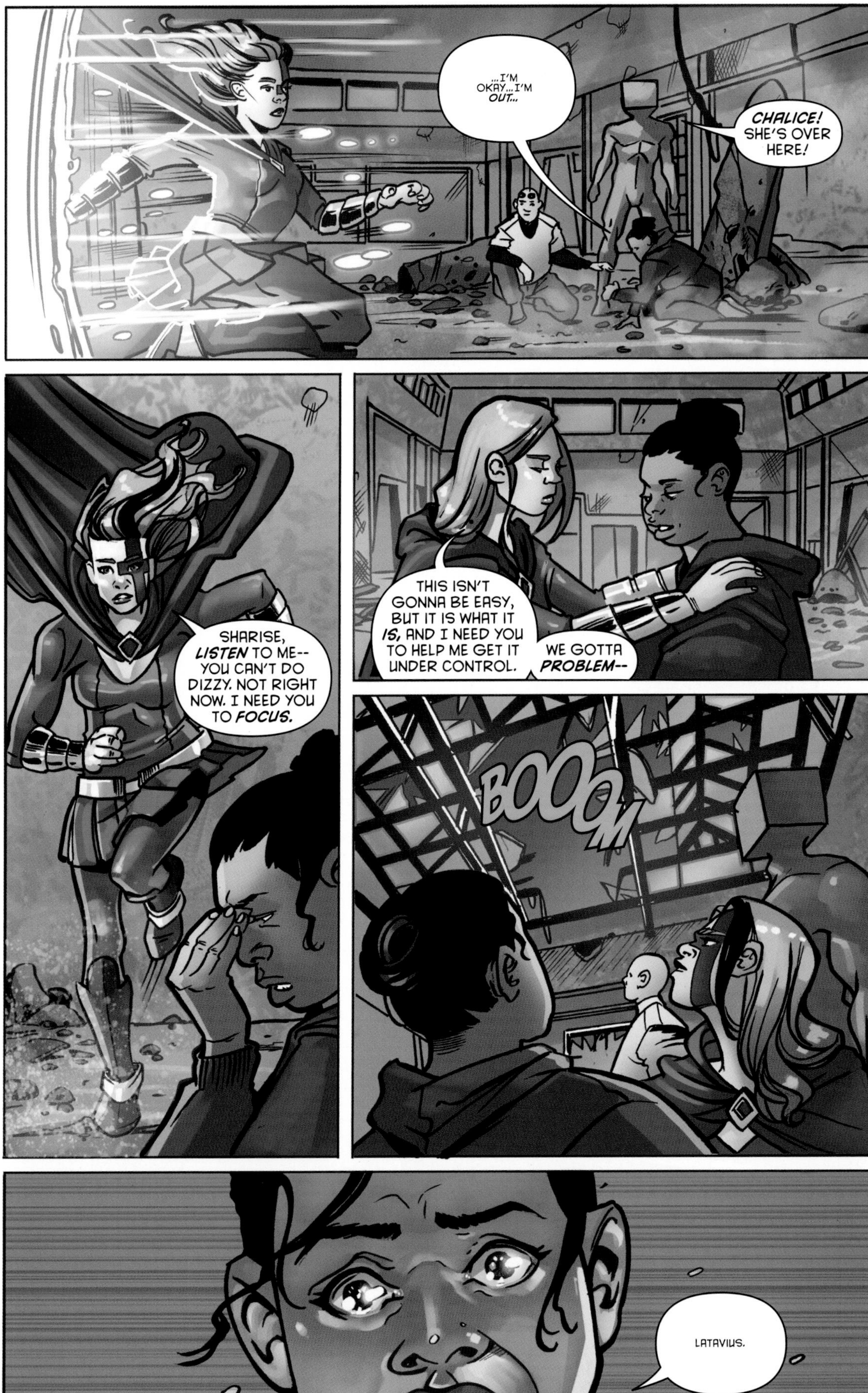
...I'M OKAY...I'M OUT...
CHALICE! SHE'S OVER HERE!
SHARISE, LISTEN TO ME-- YOU CAN'T DO DIZZY. NOT RIGHT NOW. I NEED YOU TO FOCUS.
THIS ISN'T GONNA BE EASY, BUT IT IS WHAT IT IS, AND I NEED YOU TO HELP ME GET IT UNDER CONTROL.
WE GOTTA PROBLEM--
BOOOM
LATAVIUS.

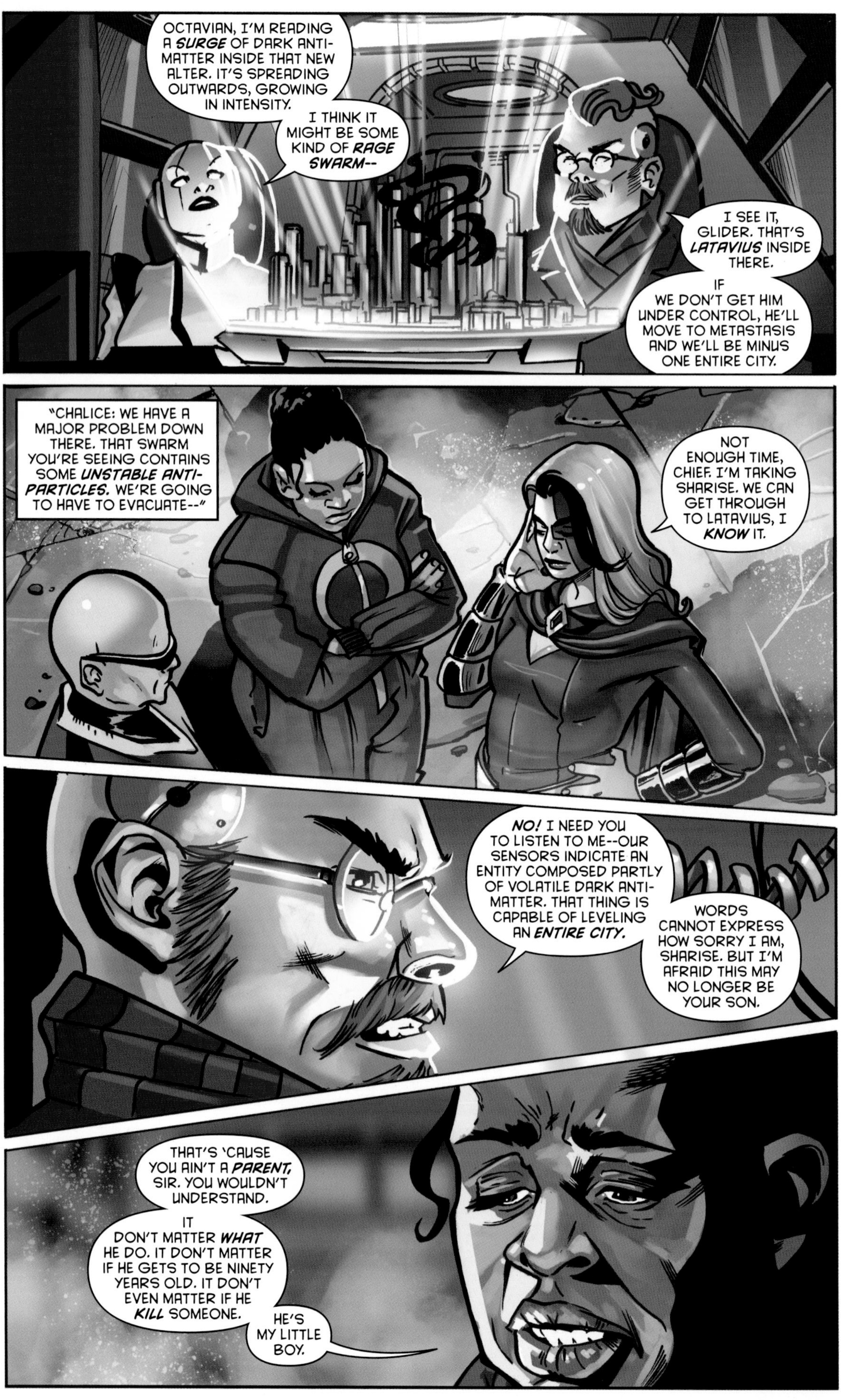
OCTAVIAN, I'M READING A *SURGE* OF DARK ANTI-MATTER INSIDE THAT NEW ALTER. IT'S SPREADING OUTWARDS, GROWING IN INTENSITY.
I THINK IT MIGHT BE SOME KIND OF *RAGE SWARM*--
I SEE IT, GLIDER. THAT'S *LATAVIUS* INSIDE THERE.
IF WE DON'T GET HIM UNDER CONTROL, HE'LL MOVE TO METASTASIS AND WE'LL BE MINUS ONE ENTIRE CITY.
"CHALICE: WE HAVE A MAJOR PROBLEM DOWN THERE. THAT SWARM YOU'RE SEEING CONTAINS SOME *UNSTABLE ANTI-PARTICLES.* WE'RE GOING TO HAVE TO EVACUATE--"
NOT ENOUGH TIME, CHIEF. I'M TAKING SHARISE. WE CAN GET THROUGH TO LATAVIUS, I *KNOW* IT.
NO! I NEED YOU TO LISTEN TO ME--OUR SENSORS INDICATE AN ENTITY COMPOSED PARTLY OF VOLATILE DARK ANTI-MATTER. THAT THING IS CAPABLE OF LEVELING AN *ENTIRE CITY.*
WORDS CANNOT EXPRESS HOW SORRY I AM, SHARISE. BUT I'M AFRAID THIS MAY NO LONGER BE YOUR SON.
THAT'S 'CAUSE YOU AIN'T A *PARENT,* SIR. YOU WOULDN'T UNDERSTAND.
IT DON'T MATTER *WHAT* HE DO. IT DON'T MATTER IF HE GETS TO BE NINETY YEARS OLD. IT DON'T EVEN MATTER IF HE *KILL* SOMEONE.
HE'S MY LITTLE BOY.

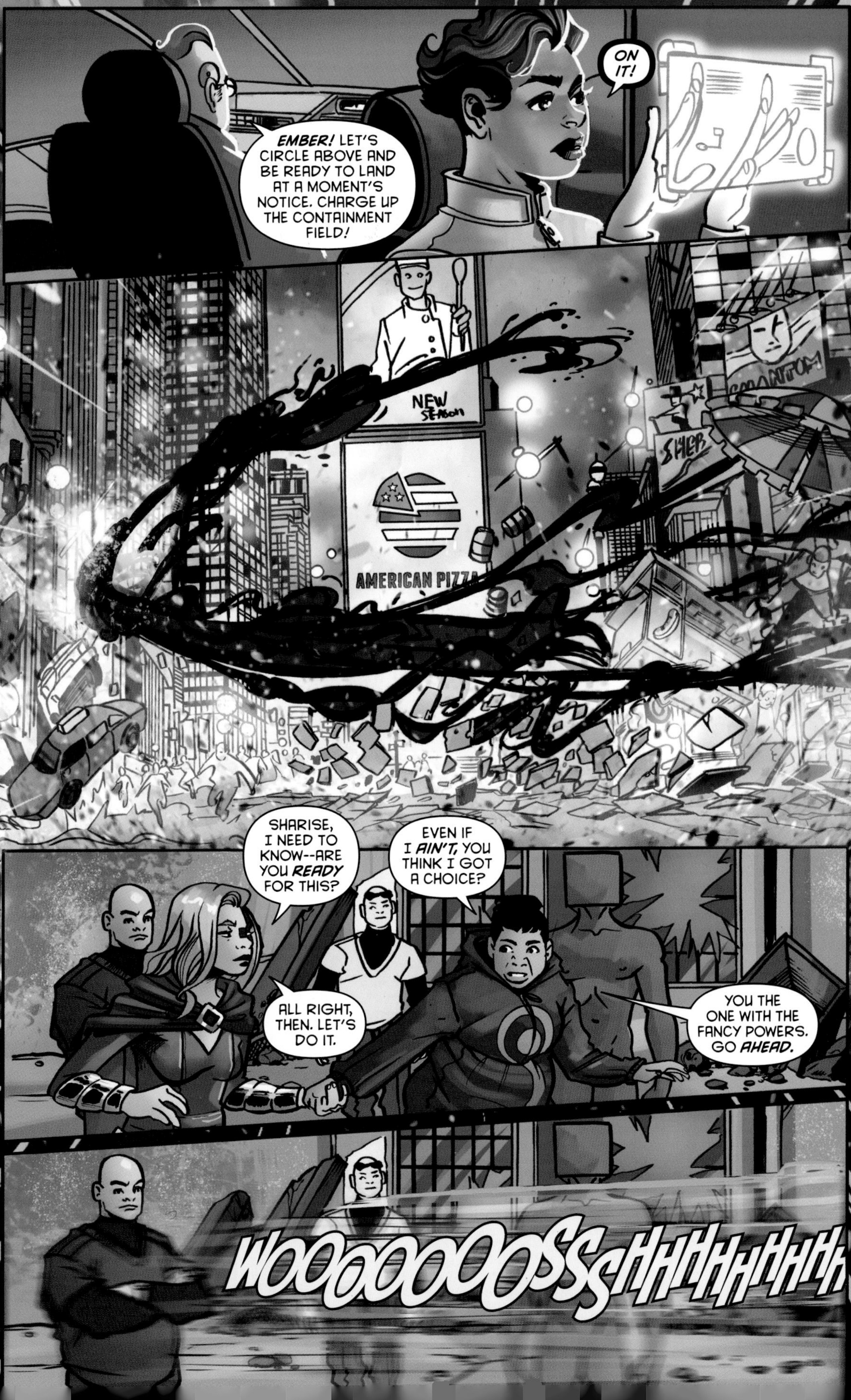
ON IT!
EMBER! LET'S CIRCLE ABOVE AND BE READY TO LAND AT A MOMENT'S NOTICE. CHARGE UP THE CONTAINMENT FIELD!
NEW SEASON
AMERICAN PIZZA
SHARISE, I NEED TO KNOW--ARE YOU READY FOR THIS?
EVEN IF I AIN'T, YOU THINK I GOT A CHOICE?
ALL RIGHT, THEN. LET'S DO IT.
YOU THE ONE WITH THE FANCY POWERS. GO AHEAD.
WOOOOOOOOSSSHHHHHHHHH

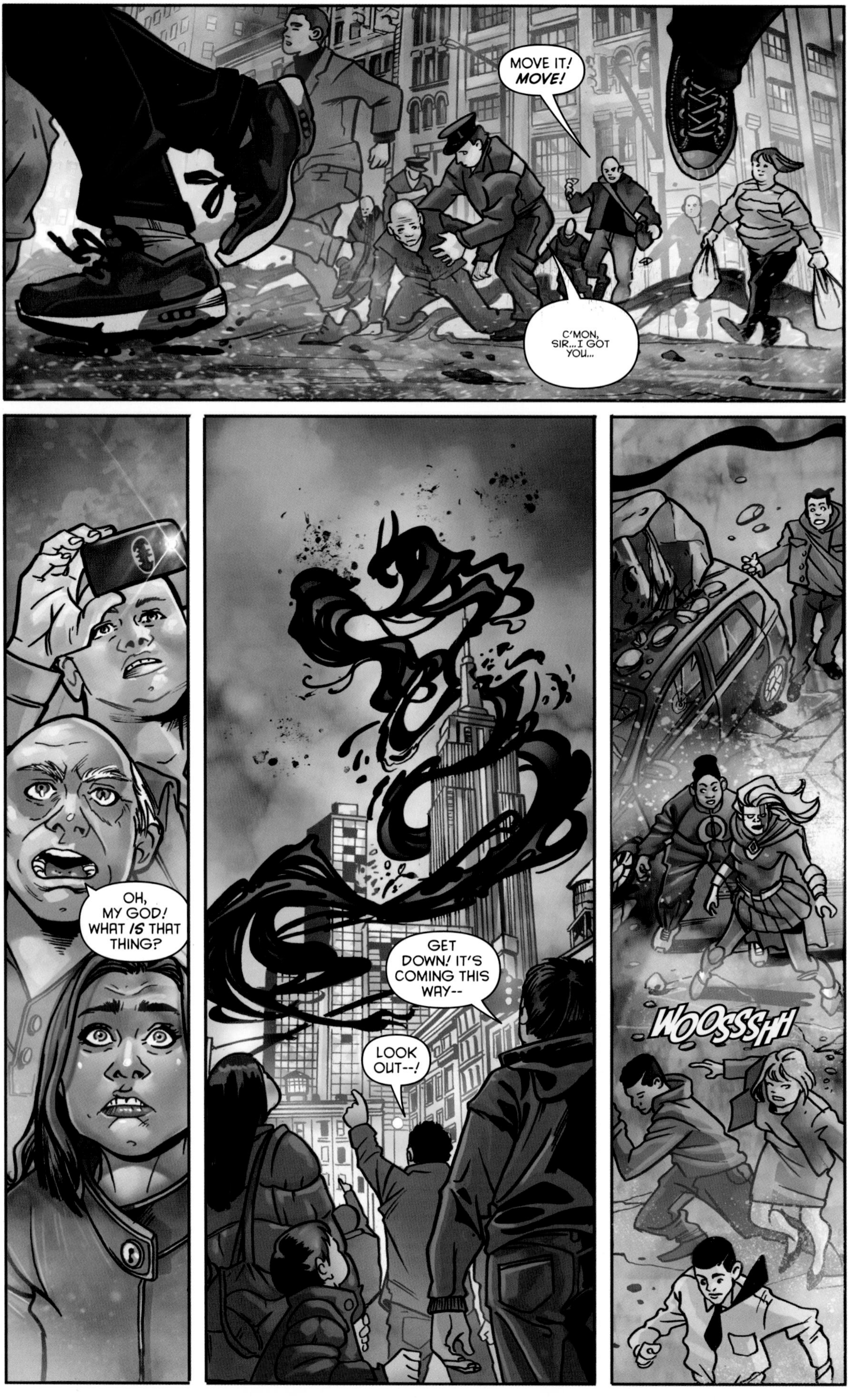
MOVE IT! *MOVE!*
C'MON, SIR... I GOT YOU...
OH, MY GOD! WHAT *IS* THAT THING?
GET DOWN! IT'S COMING THIS WAY--
LOOK OUT--!
WOOSSSHH

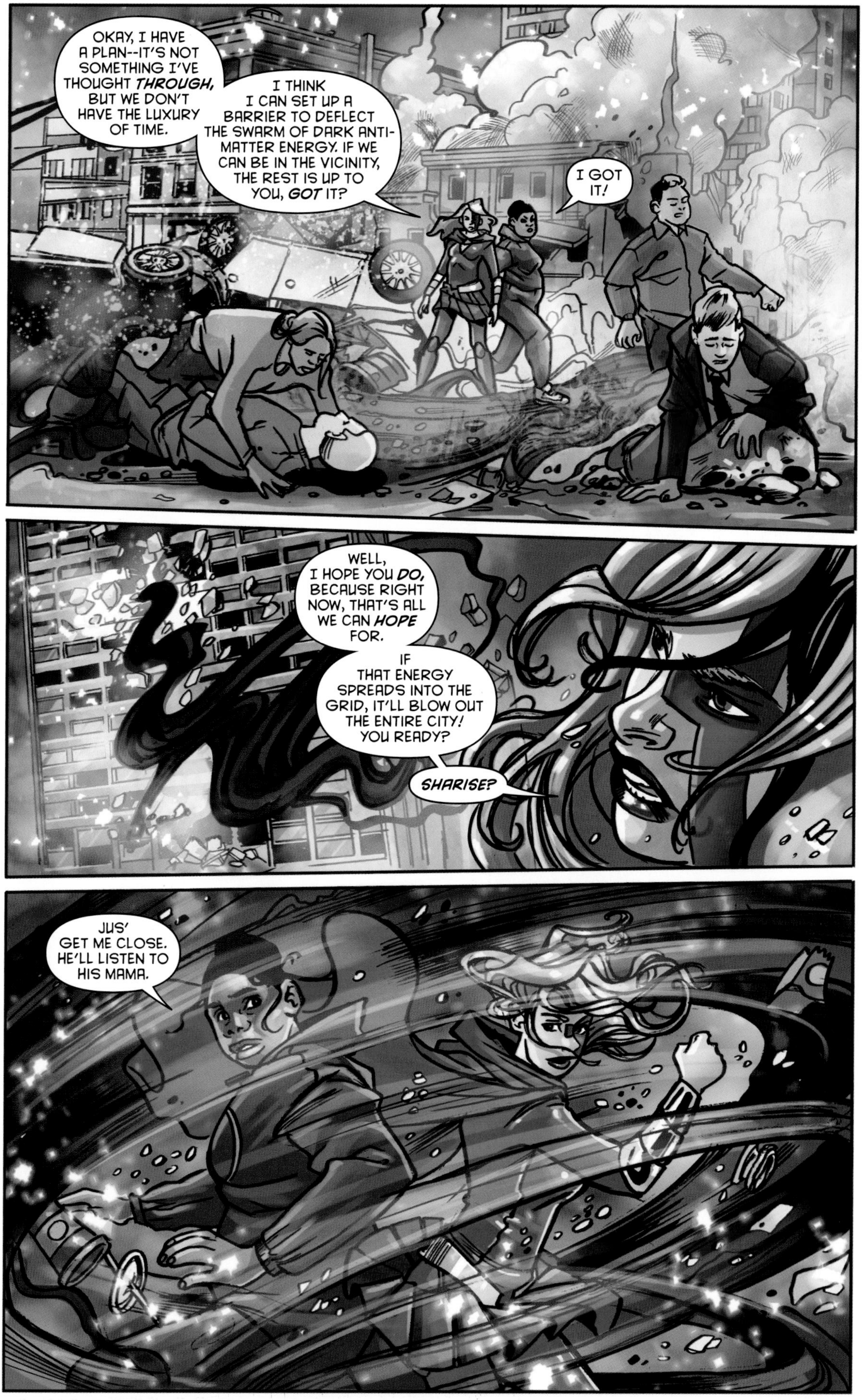
OKAY, I HAVE A PLAN--IT'S NOT SOMETHING I'VE THOUGHT *THROUGH,* BUT WE DON'T HAVE THE LUXURY OF TIME.
I THINK I CAN SET UP A BARRIER TO DEFLECT THE SWARM OF DARK ANTI-MATTER ENERGY. IF WE CAN BE IN THE VICINITY, THE REST IS UP TO YOU, *GOT* IT?
I GOT IT!
WELL, I HOPE YOU *DO,* BECAUSE RIGHT NOW, THAT'S ALL WE CAN *HOPE* FOR.
IF THAT ENERGY SPREADS INTO THE GRID, IT'LL BLOW OUT THE ENTIRE CITY! YOU READY?
SHARISE?
JUS' GET ME CLOSE. HE'LL LISTEN TO HIS MAMA.

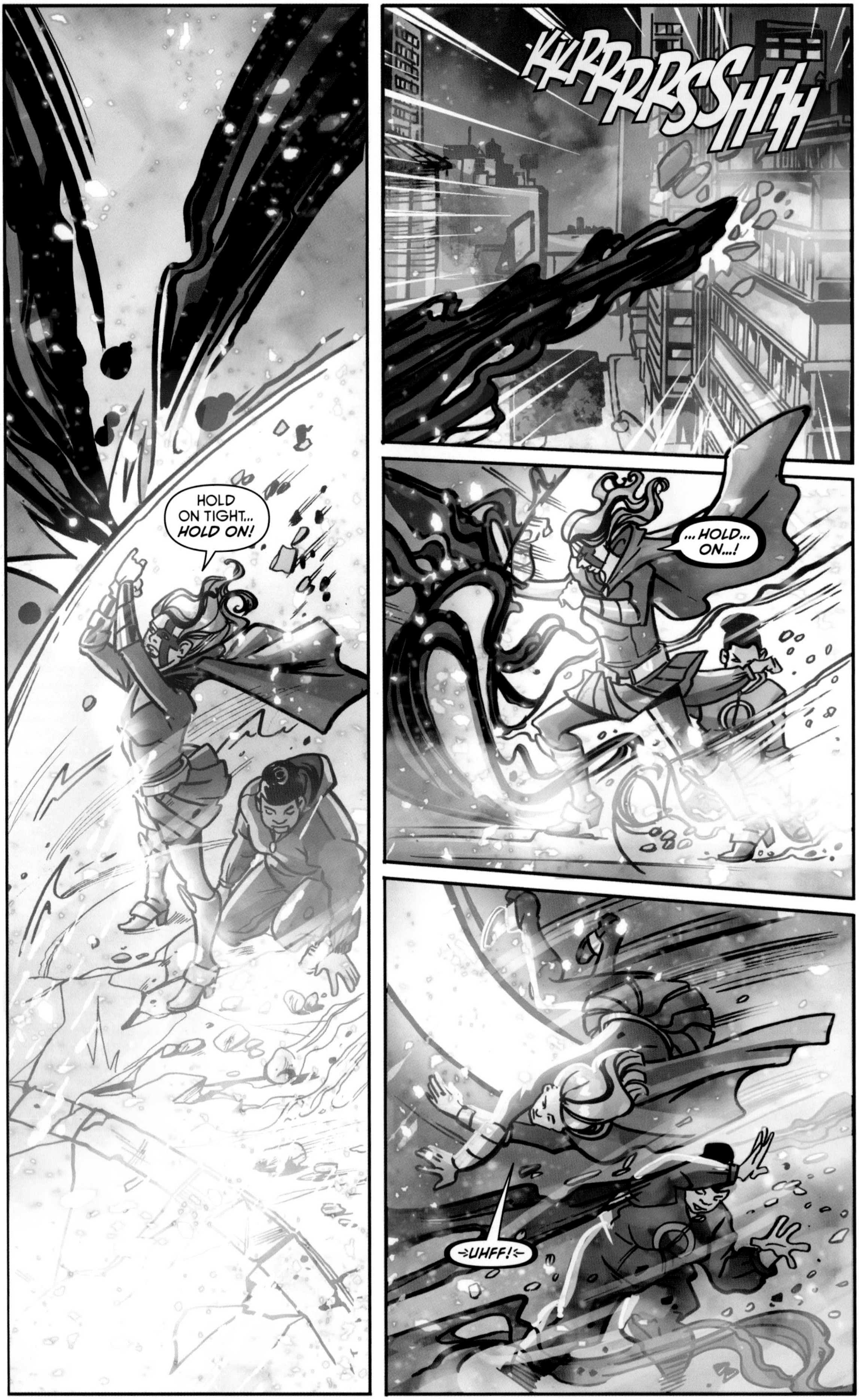
HOLD ON TIGHT... HOLD ON!
KRRRRRSHHH
...HOLD... ON...!
UHFF!

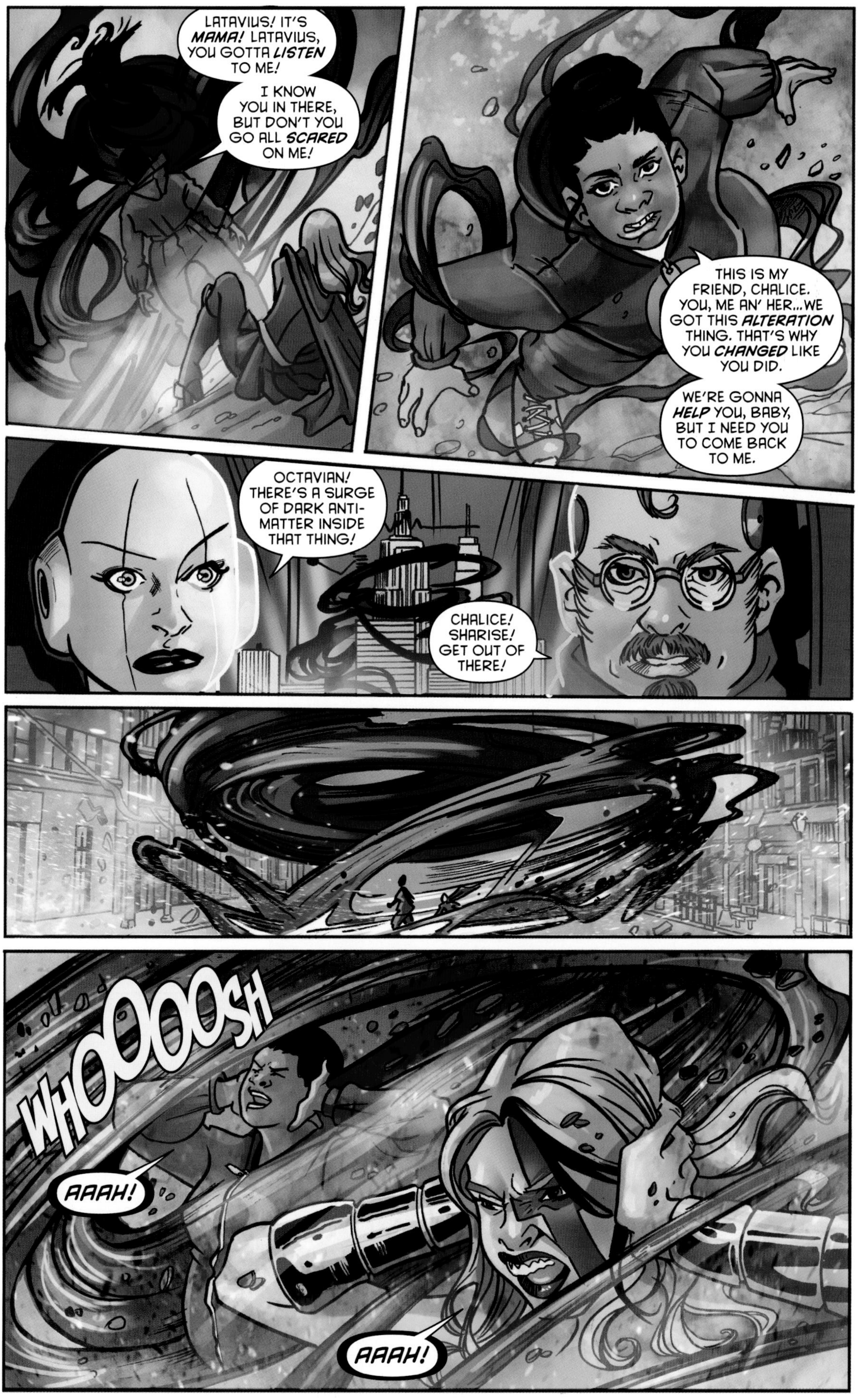
LATAVIUS! IT'S MAMA! LATAVIUS, YOU GOTTA LISTEN TO ME!
I KNOW YOU IN THERE, BUT DON'T YOU GO ALL SCARED ON ME!
THIS IS MY FRIEND, CHALICE. YOU, ME AN' HER...WE GOT THIS ALTERATION THING. THAT'S WHY YOU CHANGED LIKE YOU DID.
WE'RE GONNA HELP YOU, BABY, BUT I NEED YOU TO COME BACK TO ME.
OCTAVIAN! THERE'S A SURGE OF DARK ANTI-MATTER INSIDE THAT THING!
CHALICE! SHARISE! GET OUT OF THERE!
WHOOOOSH
AAAH!
AAAH!

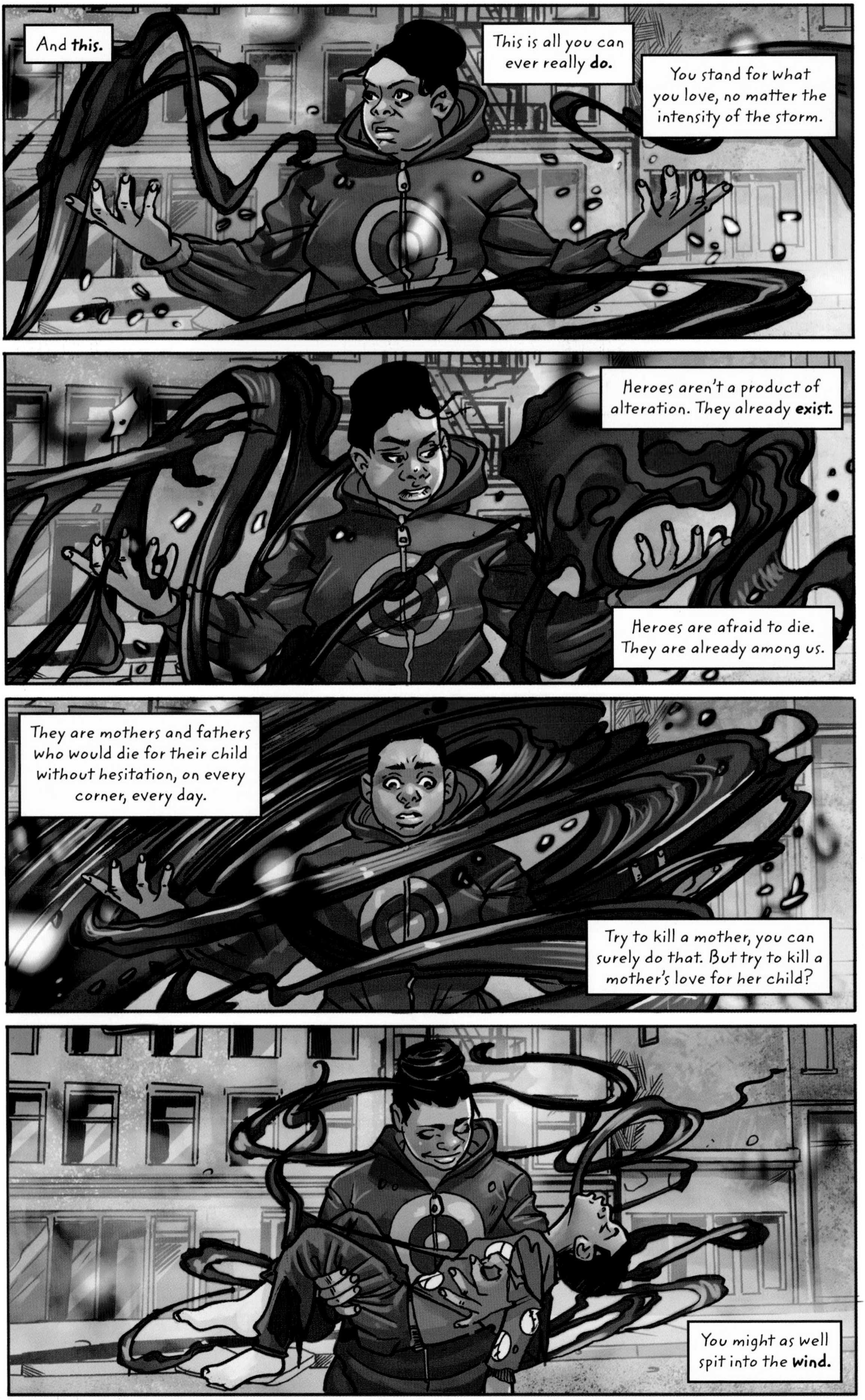
And **this.**
This is all you can ever really **do.**
You stand for what you love, no matter the intensity of the storm.
Heroes aren't a product of alteration. They already **exist.**
Heroes are afraid to die. They are already among us.
They are mothers and fathers who would die for their child without hesitation, on every corner, every day.
Try to kill a mother, you can surely do that. But try to kill a mother's love for her child?
You might as well spit into the **wind.**

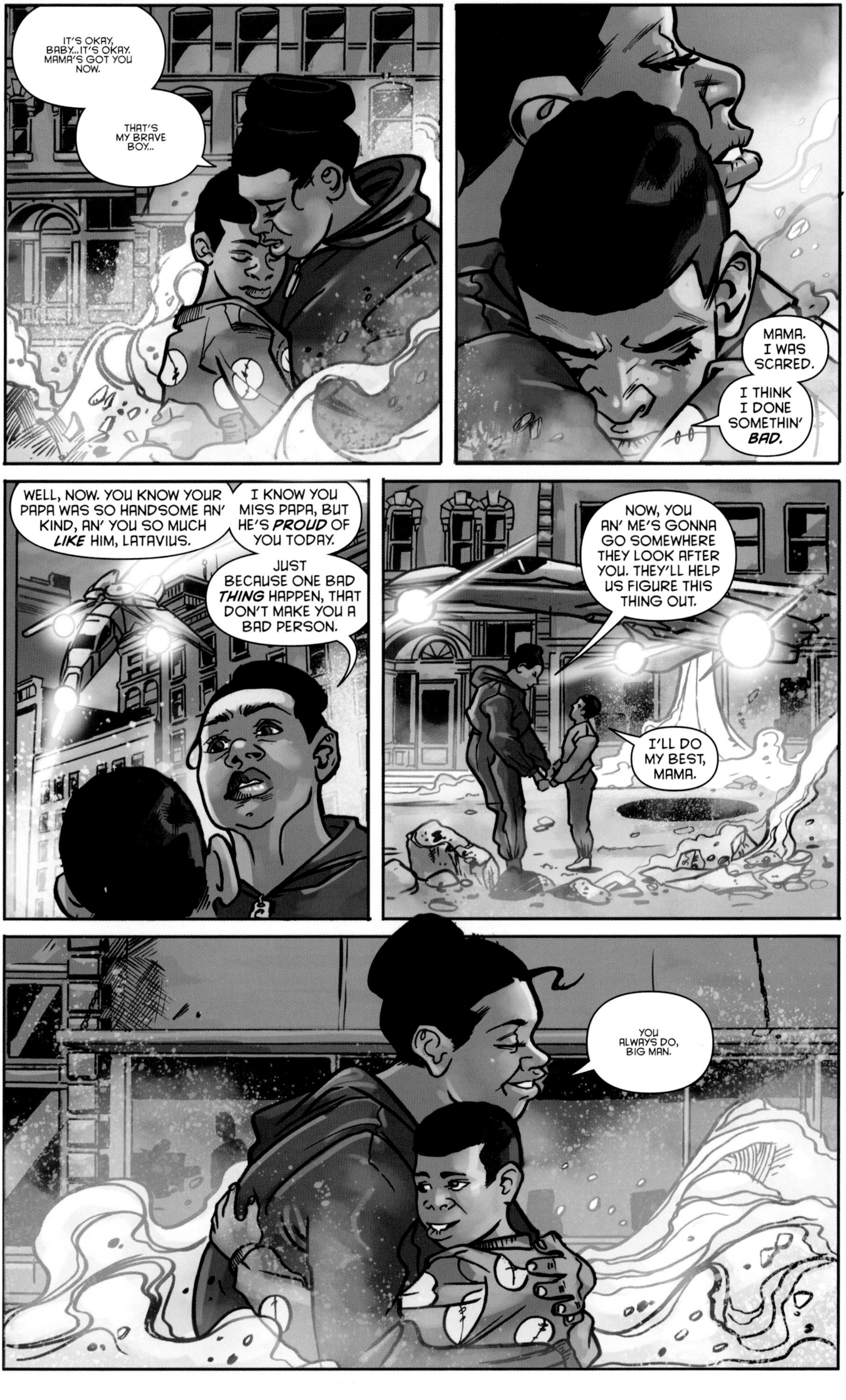
IT'S OKAY, BABY...IT'S OKAY. MAMA'S GOT YOU NOW.
THAT'S MY BRAVE BOY...
MAMA. I WAS SCARED.
I THINK I DONE SOMETHIN' *BAD.*
WELL, NOW. YOU KNOW YOUR PAPA WAS SO HANDSOME AN' KIND, AN' YOU SO MUCH *LIKE* HIM, LATAVIUS.
I KNOW YOU MISS PAPA, BUT HE'S *PROUD* OF YOU TODAY.
JUST BECAUSE ONE BAD *THING* HAPPEN, THAT DON'T MAKE YOU A BAD PERSON.
NOW, YOU AN' ME'S GONNA GO SOMEWHERE THEY LOOK AFTER YOU. THEY'LL HELP US FIGURE THIS THING OUT.
I'LL DO MY BEST, MAMA.
YOU ALWAYS DO, BIG MAN.

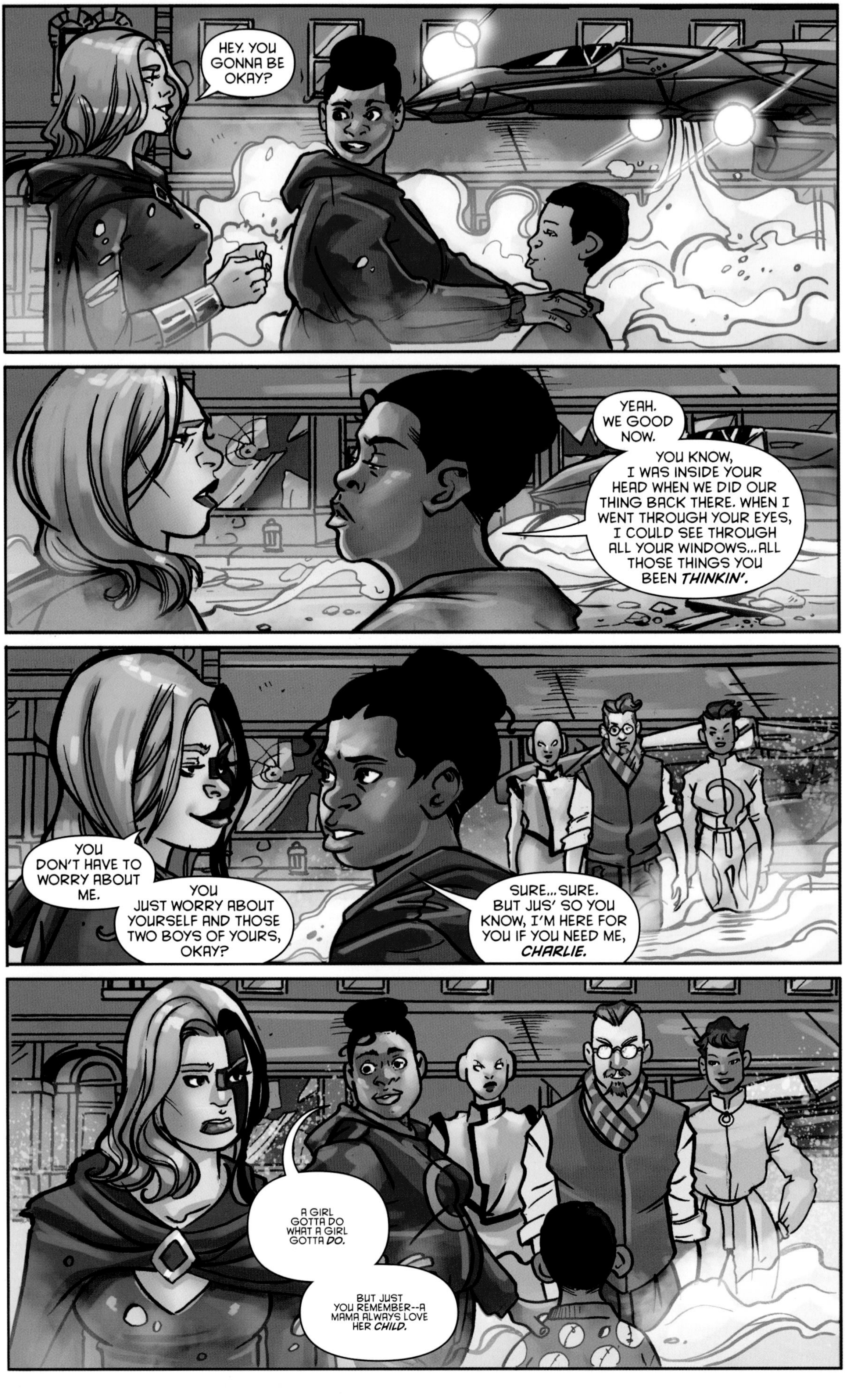
HEY. YOU GONNA BE OKAY?
YEAH. WE GOOD NOW.
YOU KNOW, I WAS INSIDE YOUR HEAD WHEN WE DID OUR THING BACK THERE. WHEN I WENT THROUGH YOUR EYES, I COULD SEE THROUGH ALL YOUR WINDOWS...ALL THOSE THINGS YOU BEEN *THINKIN'.*
YOU DON'T HAVE TO WORRY ABOUT ME.
YOU JUST WORRY ABOUT YOURSELF AND THOSE TWO BOYS OF YOURS, OKAY?
SURE... SURE. BUT JUS' SO YOU KNOW, I'M HERE FOR YOU IF YOU NEED ME, *CHARLIE.*
A GIRL GOTTA DO WHAT A GIRL GOTTA *DO.*
BUT JUST YOU REMEMBER--A MAMA ALWAYS LOVE HER *CHILD.*

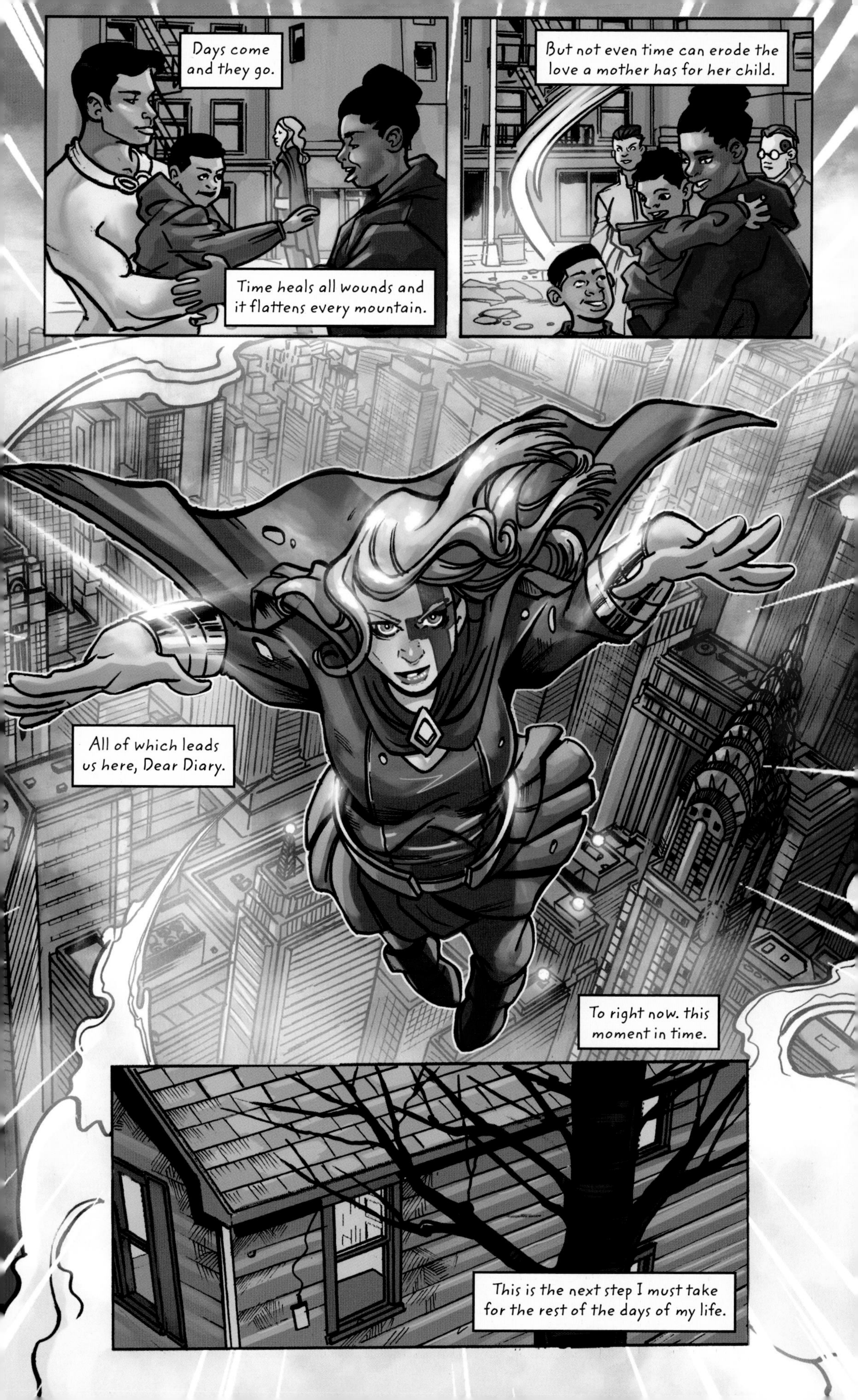
Days come and they go.
Time heals all wounds and it flattens every mountain.
But not even time can erode the love a mother has for her child.
All of which leads us here, Dear Diary.
To right now. this moment in time.
This is the next step I must take for the rest of the days of my life.

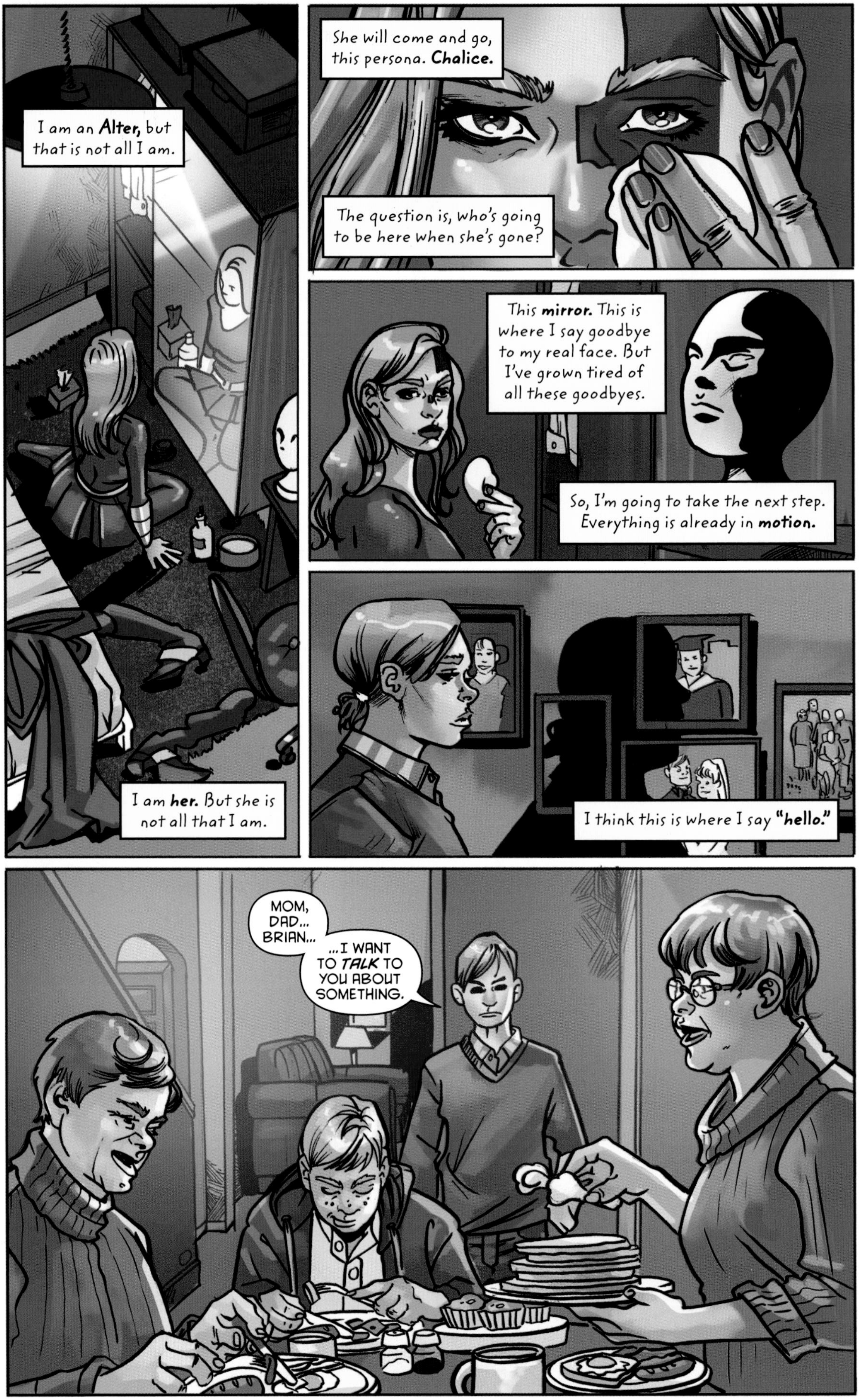

I am an Alter, but that is not all I am.
I am her. But she is not all that I am.
She will come and go, this persona. Chalice.
The question is, who's going to be here when she's gone?
This mirror. This is where I say goodbye to my real face. But I've grown tired of all these goodbyes.
So, I'm going to take the next step. Everything is already in motion.
I think this is where I say "hello."
MOM, DAD... BRIAN...
...I WANT TO TALK TO YOU ABOUT SOMETHING.

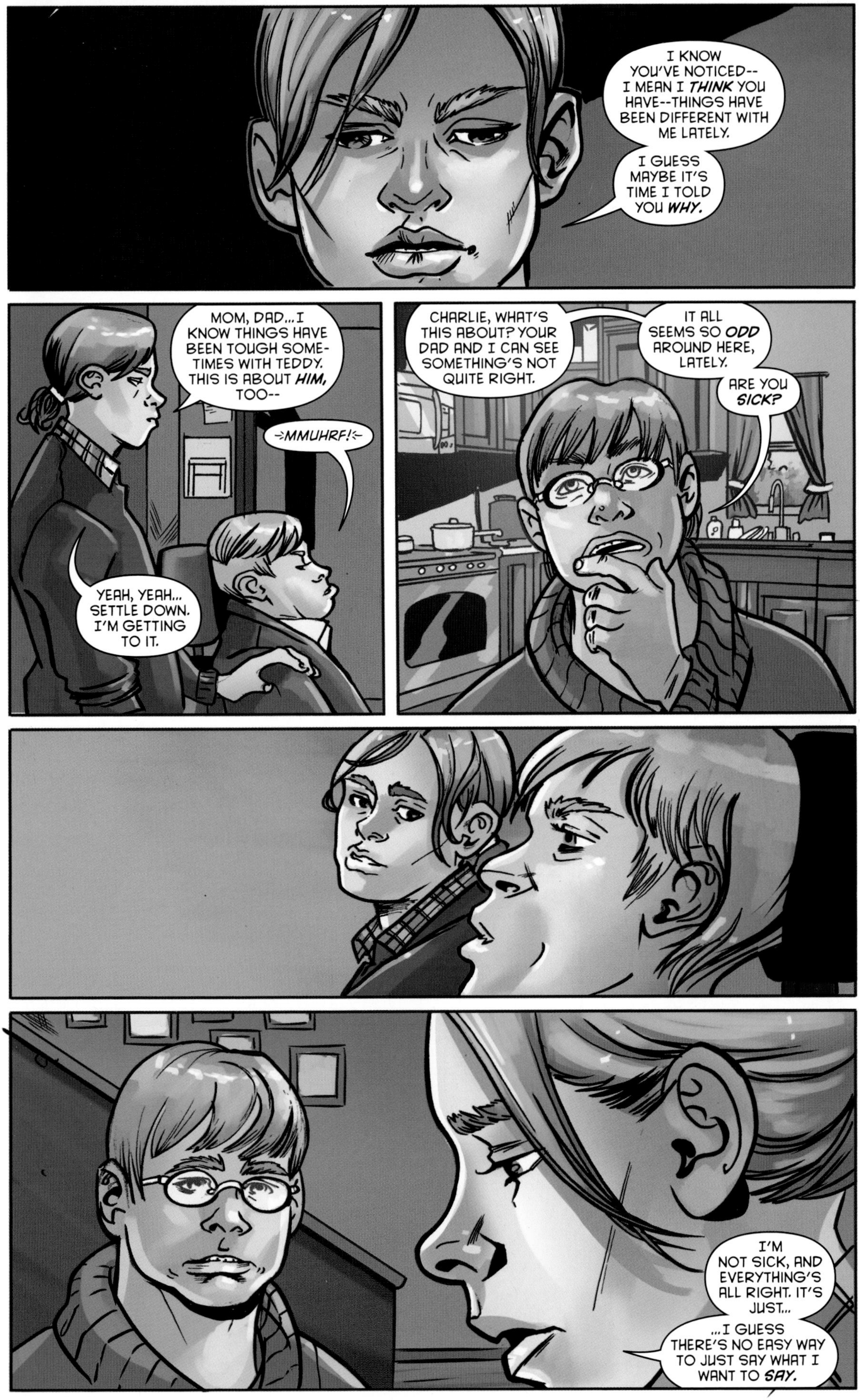
I KNOW YOU'VE NOTICED-- I MEAN I *THINK* YOU HAVE--THINGS HAVE BEEN DIFFERENT WITH ME LATELY.
I GUESS MAYBE IT'S TIME I TOLD YOU *WHY.*
MOM, DAD...I KNOW THINGS HAVE BEEN TOUGH SOMETIMES WITH TEDDY. THIS IS ABOUT *HIM,* TOO--
-MMUHRF!-
YEAH, YEAH... SETTLE DOWN. I'M GETTING TO IT.
CHARLIE, WHAT'S THIS ABOUT? YOUR DAD AND I CAN SEE SOMETHING'S NOT QUITE RIGHT.
IT ALL SEEMS SO *ODD* AROUND HERE, LATELY.
ARE YOU *SICK?*
I'M NOT SICK, AND EVERYTHING'S ALL RIGHT. IT'S JUST...
...I GUESS THERE'S NO EASY WAY TO JUST SAY WHAT I WANT TO *SAY.*

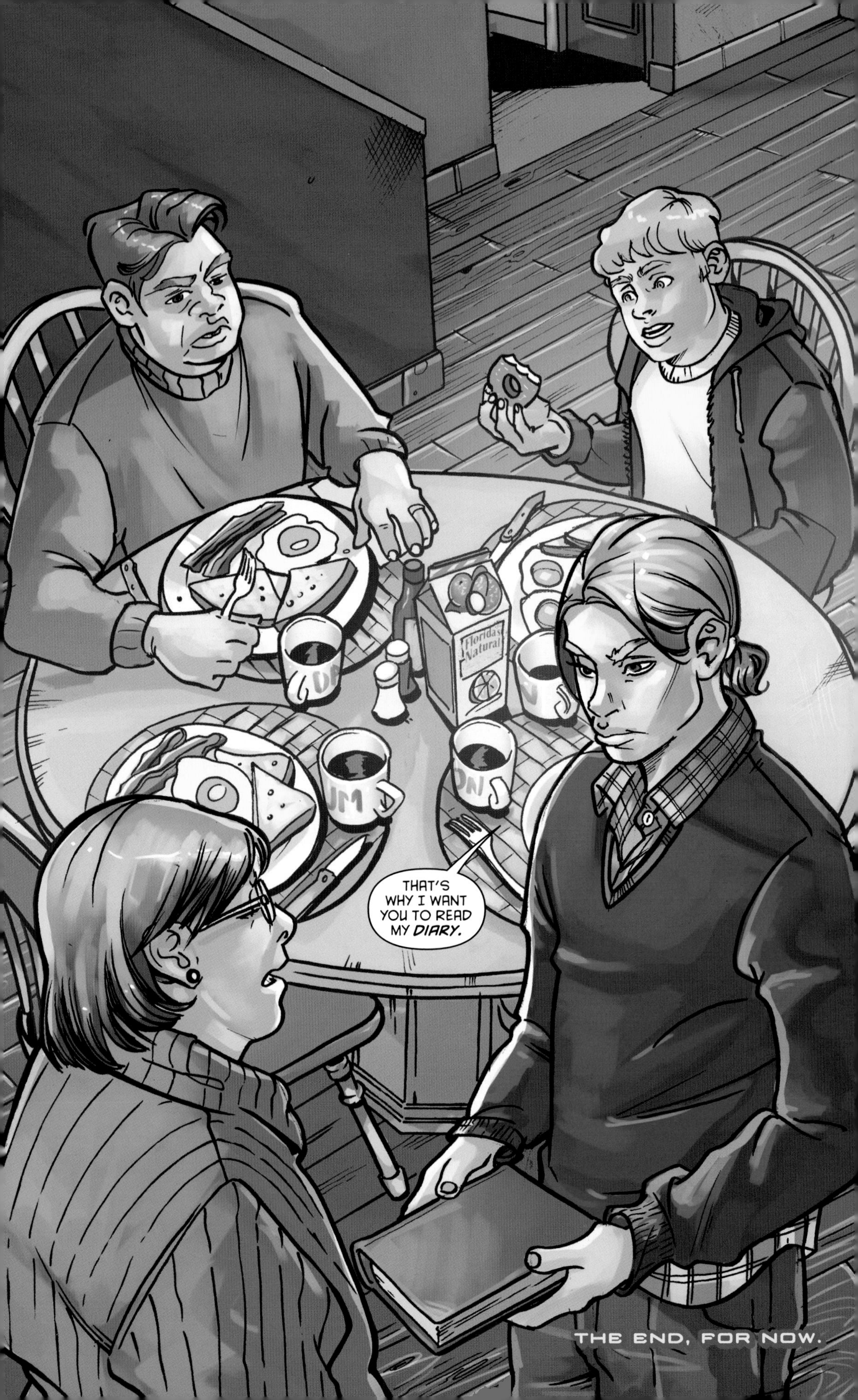
Florida's Natural
THAT'S WHY I WANT YOU TO READ MY *DIARY.*
THE END, FOR NOW.

E D I T O R I A L

by PAUL JENKINS (from ALTERS #6)

Welcome, everyone, to the second arc of ALTERS. For those of you who are new to the series, ALTERS details the story of certain characters who are dealing with some kind of disadvantage in society, and who are given a hyper-advantage in the form of a mutant superpower.

In this second arc, we are going to meet a new character, Sharise, who is dealing with issues of poverty and homelessness. And so, these new editorials will deal with that subject. I have a couple of simple guiding principles: These interviews or discussions are not intended to exploit, but merely to enlighten. Neither are they intended to intrude unnecessarily on a person's privacy. I ask interview subjects only to share what they are comfortable sharing. There's not enough space here to share the complexity of a person's life. We can only scratch the surface.

A lot of homeless people stand on the exit ramp near where I live in Atlanta. One day, I met Todd, carrying this sign with him as he walked along the line of cars waiting for the traffic light. This is what he had to say.

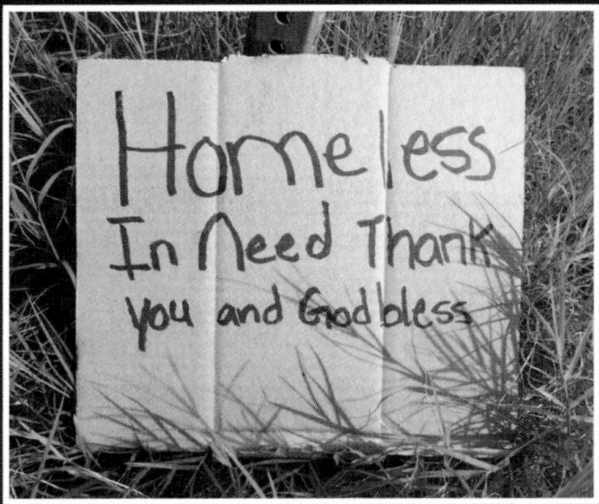
Homeless
In Need Thank
you and God bless

Paul: Todd, I'll go to the end of my interview first. When people see you by the side of the road, they see your sign, and they see a guy begging for money... what is it that they don't know about you that you'd like them to know?

Todd: I'd say that it hasn't always been like this, you know? I've been a productive member of society. I was in floor covering from around 1985, and I took a turn for the worse when my knees gave out on me. In floor covering, once you lose your knees or your back, that's it. But I have been a blessing to people throughout my life and not just somebody who looked for a handout.

Paul: So, you've lived in two different worlds, right? I mean, you've made decent money and been okay, and you've also found yourself falling on harder times where you've had to turn to others to help you out a bit. Do you feel other people are judgmental about your situation?

Todd: No, for the most part I feel people are quite polite and understanding. They're generous. They have a good heart, and it's only upon occasion that I run across the negative. Some people are mean, but I think that's just in some people's nature. That's life. It's just out of ignorance. I understand that.

Paul: That's cool, man. And generous of you to put it like that. Do you think you got to a point where you sort of thought to yourself, "Man, I can't seem to get out of this?" And so,

it became a spiral that you contributed to? Or do you think no matter what you did, things may have gone badly for you?

Todd: Look, I made some bad decisions and had some bad luck. I had some bad decision making...uh, a lack of anticipating certain things that I should have seen coming, that I could have avoided. After my knees gave out in 2000, I innocently enough went to a local physician and he prescribed me 5mg of Lortab. That's where you're talking about a downward spiral—from 5mg to 10mg. Then, Hydrocodone. Then, I'm stuck. Eventually that became heroin. Could I have avoided it? Sure. If I knew then what I know now. It wasn't such an epidemic in them days.

Paul: So, do you think you're getting a handle on it? I mean, you call it an epidemic—I think this is something so many people now have to deal with. How are you managing with it, mate? Are you doing okay?

Todd: I finally have a handle on it after seventeen years. I mean, it goes from "just enough Lortab" to heroin, and then the problem becomes, "How am I gonna pay for this?" It completely consumes you. But for the most part, I am out of the bad weather. I still think about it, but I don't...I enjoy the fact I don't have to be dependent now. And I draw a lot of strength from that—

Just at this point of the interview, two officers from the Forsythe County Sheriff's Department pulled up. Todd wasn't supposed to be panhandling—he was breaking the law. And obviously, the two officers wanted to know what the hell some British guy was doing out there in the sweltering heat talking to this homeless guy. However, they were incredibly respectful to Todd. They understood his position and gave him some info on a couple of options he might have for shelter that evening. It's a sad fact that there is not a single homeless shelter in the county, and they suggested that Todd go to a neighboring county for somewhere to stay. Imagine knowing the closest possibility for a bed was miles away. And why? Because the county is affluent now—so they have moved all the homeless shelters out. With more money and more potential resources came less generosity from my county, not more.

So, what have I learned this month? Well, I've had a chance to talk to a few people so far. And there is a recurring theme to each interview—one that I have not been able to shake from my mind. This is about luck. Every interview subject I have met so far is in their position because, hey...a couple of bad breaks and a few things they could not have predicted, and things can go to crap in a heartbeat. Sure, people make mistakes. All of us do. But not all of us find ourselves with medical bills that cannot be overcome, or a divorce that rips the heart out of a family. There's a "Todd" at virtually every off ramp. And as the saying goes, "There but for the grace of God (and a couple of unlucky breaks) go I."

I wish you all peace, love and happiness. Do well, and doubt not.

Paul

E D I T O R I A L

by PAUL JENKINS (from ALTERS #7)

This month I am going to take a break from the one-on-one interviews so that I can spend a little more time to explain my connection to the challenges of homelessness and address some of the things I have learned over the years.

People who know me well, know that I can be a little quirky about certain things: I don't attend awards ceremonies, I take "It can't be done!" as a challenge, and I often stop to chat with homeless people. (This happens, invariably, when I am out with my wife, Nigh Perfect—even after 15 years of marriage I am not sure she is getting used to it). Much of the writing about our homeless character, Sharise, is based on interactions I have had over the years with people on the street begging for money. I usually ask for a small deal: I'm happy to fork over a few bucks in exchange for a brief chat. Yes, I am *that* guy.

Writers tend to be a curious bunch; our primary function, I believe, is to examine the human condition. At least, that is what I believe my function to be, even when I am writing speculative science fiction or horror. At its core, writing is about observing the world and doing your best to describe what you see, and what you feel. I see a lot of homeless people, doing what they can to simply exist. I feel a certain sense of helplessness at our collective inability to solve this problem, despite the efforts of so many good people. So, for this editorial I'd like to relay a couple of the "general" things I have learned over the years.

Many of the people I have spoken to deal with issues of substance abuse. Let's be clear: I am not saying that all homeless people are addicts, not even close. But I think there is a prevalence of substance abuse issues among homeless people and this speaks to certain mistakes that we have allowed to occur in our society, especially over the last thirty years. I played soccer for many years, and at one time I had a fairly bad hip injury that caused me a lot of pain. One doctor gave me an open prescription for a particular opiate. The good news was that I did not like painkillers, as they made me feel nauseated. How lucky was I? Ever since, I have always looked at opiate addiction in a different light: I can see how easy it must be to start down a path of pain relief, and find yourself off track and stumbling through the dark forest of addiction rather quickly.

This segues into a sort of universal truth that I have noted over time: there but for the grace of God (In other words, a few lucky breaks) go I. We never know what might be around the corner. Almost all of the people I've met—those who have been willing to share a little of their story—have found themselves a victim of circumstance. We cannot legislate for the death of a loved one, the pain of an unexpected divorce, or a car accident that leaves us in constant pain. When I lived briefly in Los Angeles while working on a film project, I interacted daily with the many homeless people who center around Hollywood and Vine. It was upsetting to realize how many of these people were veterans, whose important contribution to their country had been met with a sort of societal indifference. It's easy to spot the physically injured combat veterans, as my great friend Bryan Anderson will attest (Bryan is a triple amputee—look him up!). Although we tend to feel uncomfortable with vets who must endure unbearable symptoms as a result of PTSD, we embrace some, and we avoid eye contact with others. Having once fractured my neck (yes, soccer again) and dealt with post-concussion syndrome, I got just a small glimpse of the difficulties faced by those with this type of situation. I spent about six months with a specific type of depression, which could not be farther from my usual personality.

Look, I am not telling any of you what you don't already know. This is not some kind of inspired insight. It's something that I feel we are all aware of. I certainly won't urge you to go and do something about it. Instead, I feel we all could use a reminder to think for a moment, to simply have compassion for the plight of our fellow humans. In these fractious times, that might do us all some good.

Paul

E D I T O R I A L

by PAUL JENKINS (from ALTERS #10)

This is my last editorial for a while...because this is the last issue of ALTERS for a while. We will do more, I have no doubt of that—but we are taking a break as we pursue other projects.

I know this is where I thank people. I want to do that first. Of course, I want to thank Leila for her amazing work and her brilliance, and Leo and Tamra for their stellar color work over the course of the series, and Ryane for her dedication to her craft on the lettering. I want to thank AfterShock for taking a chance with this book, which I have long considered to be a special and unique project—so thank you to Lee and Jon and Mike and Joe, to Lisa and Mike Z. and Ashley and Stephan and everyone else involved. Special thanks to all the script consultants over the course of the series, and eternal gratitude to Liz Luu for her amazing idea for Chalice's story. My most special thanks of all are reserved for my Nigh Perfect wife, Melinda, simply for continuing to agree to be married to me. You are beautiful. That is all.

As you know, ALTERS is about taking people in society who are dealing with a disadvantage, and giving them a hyper-advantage in the form of their "alteration" power. Every single one of us—whether we care to admit it or not—deals with some form of difficulty. Perhaps one of our relatives is leaving this world with dementia. Perhaps we have money worries, or are dealing with diabetes. We are all in this together, and so for my last editorial, I want to talk about this "shared experience" that we all somehow believe we do not share. Oh yeah, there are lots of political disagreements these days, and those fractures in society seem to dominate the news. "How could I possibly find common ground in all of this?" you may ask yourself. "Where is this mythical shared experience?"

When I went into this project, I thought myself to be a fairly informed person when it came to LGBT issues. Yet, throughout the course of the series, I began to realize how little I actually knew about the specifics of trans people's experiences, and by extrapolation, how little I really knew of the human condition. I have interviewed homeless people and activists, and have been helped by the good people at GLAAD among many others. I have had some life-changing experiences meeting a few trans people at signings who have expressed their love and gratitude for the series. I have been targeted by the Westboro Baptist Church, which was, frankly, fucking awesome. A few people have been critical of the fact that this series was written by a middle-aged white dude, and if you are possibly reading this, I promise, I have always understood your concerns and have always been open to listening and learning as I went. Some people have wondered what qualifies me to write a trans character. Who am I to talk about homelessness? What the hell do I know?

Well. (Deep breath).

I have been homeless. Twice, as a matter of fact (or, one-and-a-half times, I guess). I have lived in poverty, in places where there was no electricity, and in a tiny caravan in someone's back yard as a child. I have eaten at friends' houses because there was nothing at home, and I have walked outside my door to pick my food. At the age of seven years old, I knew how to snare rabbits for meat. To this day, I prefer to sleep in a freezing cold room. I have taken baths with one kettle full of boiling water poured into a freezing bathtub in the middle of winter. And I have slept on the streets.

I was five when my Dad left. All I remember of my parents' marriage was anger and fighting. And then, he was gone. My mum—an amazing woman, to be sure—found herself a job cleaning the farmer's house. We lived in a little cottage at the bottom of the hill, and when there was no money for the electricity meter, we would look up at the blazing lights in the farmer's huge house,

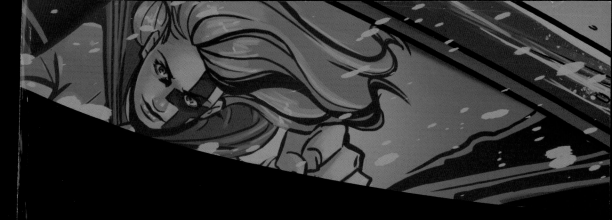

and wonder what it must be like. We played with the farmer's children, but were not allowed to attend their birthday parties. You know, that first issue of *Wolverine: Origin*—the one entitled, "The Hill?" Well, that was autobiographical. I was Dog at the bottom of the hill, dealing with the destitution and the uncertainty, and wondering how the hell I was going to ever get out of it all. I have stared out of a window at three in the morning as a seven-year-old child, and felt the hopelessness of poverty. Mum did her best to feed and clothe us. She mostly succeeded. The caravan was my "half a time."

My mum doesn't know this (she's about to find out): when I went to drama school, the government delayed my grant and I had nowhere to stay. I didn't know anyone, and I wasn't sure how to solve the problem. So, I had to sleep out on the streets as the October nights in southern England turned into November, and the needle-like rain bit me on the face. I slept outside Tesco's when I could, because the lighting was better there. But I would have to stay awake pretty much all night, and so I became a student zombie at times. I endured this by myself, with no one to turn to, and I carried the embarrassment that I was unable to provide for myself every day in class. I was cold, and I was miserable, and it took me about three months to find a second and third job as a barman (in addition to my full-time status as a student) just so that I could find enough money to rent a room.

So, you see, your assumption (I don't blame you) that homelessness is probably just a bit of research for me, is incorrect. It's a part of who I have been in my life. And as I write this editorial, I am all too aware that some of the people who have known me are about to find this out for the first time. It's a step, I suppose, and I do not take it lightly, because I have never considered this to be anyone's business but my own. ALTERS, however, is about more than just superheroes—it is about all of us, and this experience we share. What do I know about homelessness? What do I know about transgender, or bipolar disorder, or adult diabetes, or vertigo, or cerebral palsy, or Alzheimer's disease? Honestly, does it really matter which of these have been personal experiences, and which are the ones I have tried so hard to research and understand? I cannot write only what I know—if I did, you'd get an awful lot of shitty stories about a happily married, middle-aged white guy who likes to play golf and watch *Crystal Palace* on Saturdays. Instead, I try to write from a position of understanding, and I try to make sure I never pander to the person whose assumption is that I "just don't know."

So, what have I learned from this amazing experience writing ALTERS? It's that we should never look at any person and make an assumption about them. Don't assume that a rich person is happy—it's all relative. What if that person has money issues? What if they deal with bipolar disorder? Don't assume that a gay or straight person is a certain way, or a homeless person, or a person of color. Or a successful gymnast. Or an actor. Or a wealthy middle-aged white guy. Don't assume.

Just listen, and learn.

I wish you all peace, love and happiness.

Paul

ABOUT THE CREATORS OF ALTERS™

PAUL JENKINS writer

@mypauljenkins

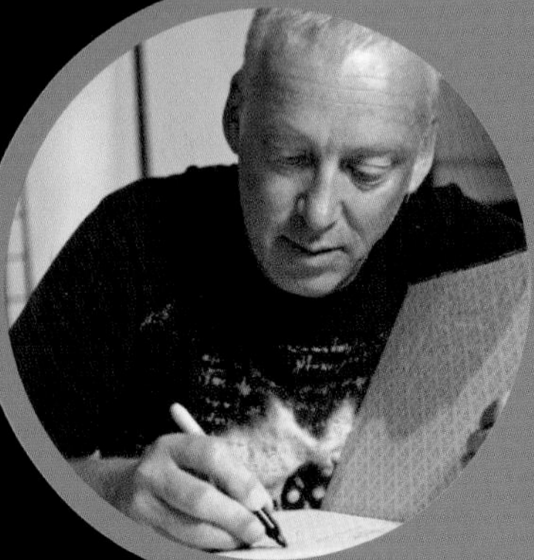

Paul Jenkins has been creating, writing and building franchises for over twenty years in the graphic novel, film and video game industries. Over the last two decades Paul has been instrumental in the creation and implementation of literally hundreds of world-renowned, recognizable entertainment icons.

From his employment with the creators of the *Teenage Mutant Ninja Turtles* at the age of 22 to his preeminent status as an IP creator, Paul has provided entertainment to the world through hundreds of print publications, films, video games and new media. With six Platinum-selling video games, a Number One MTV Music Video, an Eisner Award, Five Wizard Fan Awards and multiple Best Selling Graphic Novels, Paul Jenkins is synonymous with success. He has enjoyed recognition on *The New York Times* bestseller list, has been nominated for two BAFTA Awards, and has been the recipient of a government-sponsored Prism Award for his contributions in storytelling and characterization.

Paul's extensive list of comic book credits include *Batman* and *Hellblazer* for DC Comics; *Inhumans, Spider-Man, The Incredible Hulk, Wolverine: Origin, Civil War: Frontlines, Captain America: Theater of War* and *The Sentry* for Marvel Comics; and *Spawn* for Image Comics.

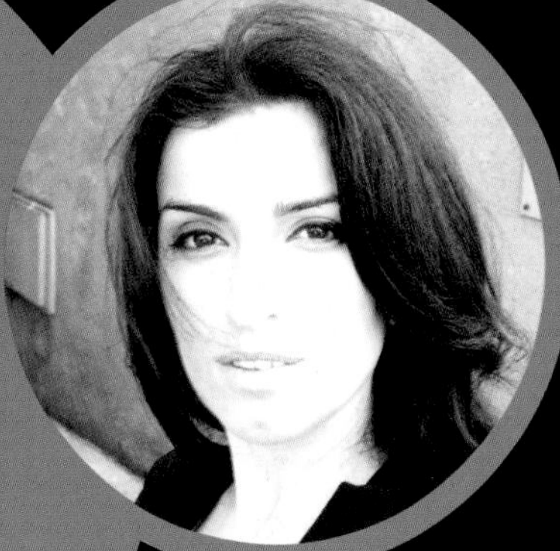

LEILA LEIZ artist

@LeilaLeiz

Born and raised in Italy, Leila is a self-taught artist who has seen her lifelong dream of working in American comics come true. After working for several years at European publishers like Soleil and Sergio Bonelli, Leila has made the exciting jump to AfterShock Comics, where she begins her new adventure on Paul Jenkins' series, ALTERS.

LEONARDO PACIAROTTI colorist

@LeoArts

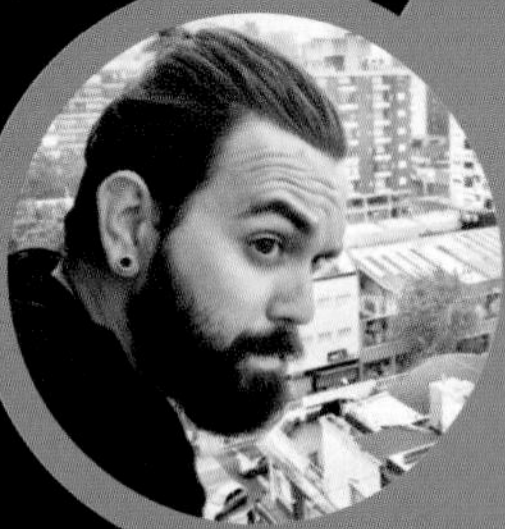

Though Leo has an Italian surname, he was born in Argentina where he learned to love super heroes at a young age...watching 1978's *Superman* and 1989's *Batman* countless times, until he finally earned his way into the world of professional comic books! Leo has colored for several publishers, including DC Comics, Zenescope and now, AfterShock Comics!

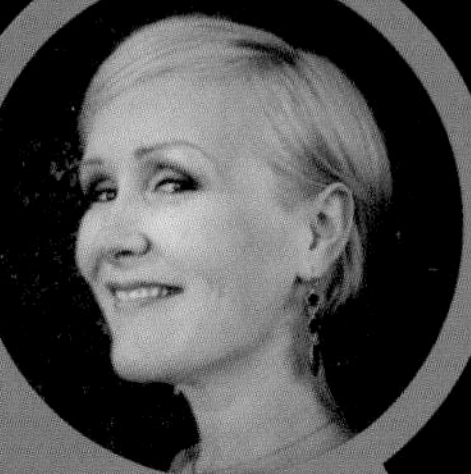

RYANE HILL letterer

@Ryane_Hill

Ryane Hill is a native Californian living with her husband and two French Bulldogs in the beautiful Pacific Northwest. After years of working in the background as a production assistant, and gaining experience with both lettering and design, she is extremely excited to have the opportunity to work with AfterShock Comics on ALTERS.